T0361664

CITY OF FICTION

ALSO BY

YU HUA

To Live
China in Ten Words

Yu Hua

CITY OF FICTION

*Translated from the Chinese
by Todd Foley*

Europa
editions

Europa Editions
27 Union Square West, Suite 302
New York NY 10003
www.europaeditions.com
info@europaeditions.com

Copyright © 2021 Yu Hua (余华)
Original Chinese edition published by Thinkingdom Media Group Ltd.
English language edition translated by Todd Foley,
and published by arrangement with Thinkingdom Media Group Ltd.
All rights reserved.
First publication 2025 by Europa Editions

Translated by Todd Foley
Original title: *Wencheng* 《文城》
Translation copyright © 2025 by Yu Hua

Library of Congress Cataloging in Publication Data is available
ISBN 979-8-88966-093-4

Yu, Hua
City of Fiction

Cover image © Zhang Xiaogang

Cover design by Ginevra Rapisardi

Prepress by Grafica Punto Print – Rome

Printed in Canada

C O N T E N T S

CITY OF FICTION

WENCHENG I

1.

There was a man in Xizhen who held property in the Wanmudang. He had over a thousand *mu* of fertile fields, crisscrossed by rivers and streams that stretched over the land like thickly tangled tree roots. Rice and wheat, corn and sweet potatoes, cotton and canola, wild reeds and grasses, stands of trees and bamboo—like the rising and setting sun, new crops sprang up to replace the old ones, flourishing throughout the four seasons. The woodworking business he established was known far and wide. It produced all manner of things—beds, tables, chairs, stools, wardrobes, chests, side tables, basins, toilet buckets—which could be found in homes everywhere within a hundred *li*. It also produced bridal sedans and burial coffins, which made striking appearances amidst the music of the *suona* horns.

There was not a person along any of the land or water routes between Xizhen and Shendian who didn't know this man named Lin Xiangfu. Everyone said he was a rich man, though when it came to his personal history and background, no one knew a thing. A thick northern accent was the only clue to his past, leading people to determine he had come to Xizhen from somewhere in the north. Many seemed to think he had arrived during the deepfreeze and blizzard seventeen years ago, when he had often been seen going door to door in the snow, clutching his infant daughter to his chest and begging for milk. He had looked like a clumsy bear, haltingly making his way over the snow and ice.

Back then, nearly every breastfeeding woman in Xizhen had encountered Lin Xiangfu, and they all have the same memory:

whenever their own baby was crying to be fed, they'd hear a knock at the door. These women, then still in their younger days, remember this knock—it sounded like the faint tapping of a fingernail, which would pause for a moment, and then lightly resume. They remember clearly how this exhausted-looking man would always walk through the door with his right hand stretched out in front of him, a few coppers in his open palm. With sorrowful yet tearless eyes, impossible to forget, he would say in a raspy voice:

"Please, take pity on my daughter—give her a few drinks of milk."

His lips were so dry and chapped they looked like the ruptured, puckered skin of a boiled potato, and his hands, split open from the cold, were covered in dark red cracks. He would stand motionless in their homes, a wooden expression on his face as though in a different world. If someone passed him a bowl of hot water, he would seem to wake, gratitude filling his eyes. But if someone asked where he was from, he immediately became hesitant, and a faint "Shendian" would escape his lips. That was the town 60 *li* to the north, a hub of water transport that was a bit livelier and more flourishing than Xizhen.

Everyone had a hard time believing that—his accent indicated he was from much farther north. He was unwilling to say where he'd come from, and unwilling to divulge his background. Unlike the men, the women of Xizhen were most interested in the baby's mother. But when they inquired about her, Lin Xiangfu's face would blanch, as blank as the snow covering the town, and his lips would close and remain shut.

This was their first impression of Lin Xiangfu—a man covered in snow, face obscured by his hair and beard, humble as a drooping willow bough and silent as the fields.

There was one person, though, who knew that Lin Xiangfu hadn't arrived in Xizhen during the blizzard, but actually right after the tornado that had struck the town earlier. This man's name was Chen Yongliang, and at the time he was the foreman of the goldmine in the western hills just outside of town.

The morning after the tornado, as he headed out toward the hills to assess the damage at the mine, he remembers seeing that stranger walking down the deserted streets. As Chen Yongliang left his house, which had lost its roof in the tornado, he saw that the whole of Xizhen was also roofless. Perhaps owing to the narrow streets and dense buildings, the trees had all luckily managed to stay put—although after the devastating winds they were now leaning this way and that, and had been stripped bare of their leaves, which had flown away along with the town's rooftiles. As if it had just gotten a clean shave, Xizhen was now completely bald.

It was right then that Lin Xiangfu arrived in Xizhen. Walking into the rays of the rising sun, squinting as he carried the baby, he crossed paths with Chen Yongliang. Lin Xiangfu left a deep impression on Chen Yongliang that morning—his face lacked the hopelessness that usually follows a disaster, and instead seemed to be filled with relief. As Chen Yongliang approached, Lin Xiangfu stopped and asked in his thick northern accent:

"Is this Wencheng?"

Chen Yongliang had never heard of such a place, so he shook his head and said,

"This is Xizhen."

Then Chen Yongliang noticed a pair of baby's eyes. The stranger appeared lost in thought, and his lips repeated the name "Xizhen." Chen Yongliang watched as the baby's shining, jet-black eyes excitedly darted around. Her lips were tightly closed, as if it required such effort to remain strapped to her father.

From behind, all Chen Yongliang could see of Lin Xiangfu was an enormous bundle. It was wrapped in a coarse white cloth woven on a rickety northern loom, not a fine southern cloth of blue calico. This had already begun to yellow and was covered with stains. Chen Yongliang had never seen a giant bundle like this, tottering on the back of this sturdy northern man, as if an entire home were stuffed inside.

2.

This roaming northerner had come from north of the Yellow River, over a thousand *li* away, where fields of sorghum, corn, and wheat covered the land, where in winter the yellow earth stretched as far as the eye could see. He had spent his childhood dashing in and out amongst the lush green crops, and the sky of his youth had been shaded over by sorghum leaves. By the time he was sitting in front of a kerosene lamp moving his fingers over an abacus to take stock of the year's harvest, he had already become an adult.

Lin Xiangfu had been born into a wealthy family. His father was the only one in their town to have passed the county-level imperial examinations, and his mother was the daughter of a man from the neighboring county who had passed the exams at the provincial level; although her family's fortunes were in decline at the time of her birth, she was still well-read in the Confucian classics, giving her an agile mind and nimble hands.

When Lin Xiangfu was five years old, his father suddenly passed away. He loved woodworking, and had been making a small desk for Lin Xiangfu, along with a little stool to go with it. When they were finished, he laid down his tools and called out for his son. The last few sounds he made, however, were not Lin Xiangfu's name, but rather cries of agony as he gripped his chest and fell to the floor. When the five-year-old Lin Xiangfu came to the door of the workshop, the sight of his father rolling around on the ground made him burst into giggles. He laughed until his mother came rushing in, knelt down beside his father, and began issuing a series of alarmed shrieks. Only then did the boy's laughter turn to terrified wails.

This was perhaps Lin Xiangfu's earliest memory. Several

days later he saw his father laid out on a door plank, perfectly still with a white cloth covering his body. The cloth was a little short, and his feet stuck out the end. The young Lin Xiangfu studied this pair of white, bloodless feet for a long time; on the sole of one, he noticed an open wound.

His mother donned clothing he had never seen before. Draped in a hempen mourning cloak, she carried a bowl of water past him and out to the front gate. She stepped over the threshold and set the water on the ground, then sat down on the threshold and stayed there until the sun set below the mountains and the sky was completely dark.

His father's death left Lin Xiangfu with over four hundred *mu* of land, a courtyard house with six rooms, and over a hundred books—bound volumes in their own cases, some with broken binding threads. His mother passed down to him both her familiarity with the Confucian classics and her deft management of the household, and as soon as he began to learn to read and write, his father's last piece of craftsmanship—the little desk and stool—was placed in front of his mother's loom. His mother would administer his lessons as she did her weaving. Amidst the creaking of the loom and his mother's gentle voice, his studies progressed from the *Three Character Classic* to the *Book of Han* and the *Records of the Grand Historian*.

When he was thirteen, he began accompanying Tian Da, the steward, down to the fields to examine the crops. Just like the tenant farmers who worked his family's land, he would walk along the edges of the fields, his legs covered in mud, sometimes crossing through paddy fields with Tian Da. When he returned home to continue his studies in front of his mother's loom, his legs would still be covered in mud. He inherited his father's love for woodworking, and at a young age he had already become familiar with axes, planes, and saws; when he set to work he would nearly forget to eat and sleep, and once he entered the workshop he would remain there for long stretches of time. When the fields were fallow, his mother would take him to neighboring towns and villages to learn from the master woodworkers there, and he would usually stay on as an apprentice for a month or two in the master's house. The woodworkers who taught him their skills all praised his ability and dexterity, as well as his capacity for hard work, which was nothing like one would expect from the young master of a wealthy family.

When he was nineteen, his mother fell ill. Although not yet forty, she had already reached the end of her life. Years of hard work and the burden of widowhood had turned her hair gray, and deep wrinkles covered her face. Now she examined her son with new eyes—she noticed that he had grown as tall and sturdy as his father had been, and a look of relief flooded over her face. Whenever he came in from his workshop or from surveying the fields, he would move his little desk and stool over by the kang where his mother lay, prepare his ink and paper, open his books, and continue receiving her tutelage. By that time his woodworking skills had begun to garner a reputation, and although there were plenty of buyers for the desks and stools he turned out, he still used the little set his father had made him.

Right before she passed away, a series of images floated in front of his mother's eyes—she saw her son grow bigger and bigger as he sat at the little desk and stool, while the writing brush in his hand grew smaller and smaller. A peaceful smile spread over her face, as if a lifetime of difficulty had finally achieved its just reward.

On the last day of the tenth lunar month, his mother, who for some time had been unable to move, gathered the last of her strength and turned to stare at the open door, waiting for her son to appear. But as she waited, the light in her expectant eyes gradually faded. Her parting words to her son were nothing more than two large tears hanging in the corners of her eyes, as if to show she still worried about her son walking the road of life alone.

The scene that Lin Xiangfu saw when he was five years old

repeated: now his mother lay on a door plank, her body covered with a white cloth she had woven before she died. Draped in filial mourning garb, Lin Xiangfu carried a bowl of water out to the gate, where he placed it on the ground. Just as his mother had done fourteen years earlier, he sat on the threshold. As evening approached, he looked out over the little path that stretched from their gate and wound its way to the main road. The main road continued on under the drifting chimney smoke and over the spacious land, stretching out toward the flaming sunset on the horizon.

Three days later, Lin Xiangfu buried his mother beside his father. Gripping the shovel with both hands, this young nineteen-year-old man stood there for a long time; behind him was the steward Tian Da and his four younger brothers. They stood there in total silence until night was about to fall, and only at Tian Da's prompting did Lin Xiangfu slowly trudge back home. Then he wiped the tears from his face and resumed his life, just as he had been living it before.

Just as before, he rose early each day and went out to the fields with Tian Da to survey the crops, chatting with the tenant farmers as they worked. Sometimes he would roll up his pantlegs and work alongside them—he was no less proficient at farm work than they were. When he had spare time, he would spend long stretches of it sitting on his threshold; without the sound of his mother weaving, he no longer went to read those volumes of thread-bound books. He lived by himself like this for five years, gradually becoming more and more reticent. The Tian brothers were the only ones who came to his home, and only when they discussed the fields and crops would Lin Xiangfu's voice be heard within those walls.

Every year in late autumn, Lin Xiangfu would gather together the silver he had accumulated from the year's harvest, lead his donkey into town, and go to a *qianzhuang*—a local private bank—to exchange the silver for a small gold bar. He would also buy one or two lengths of satin. The gold bar he would place in a box hidden in an interior wall, and the satin he would store in a wardrobe in one of the inner rooms.

When she was still alive, this was something his mother would do. Storing away the gold had begun with the Lin family ancestors, while the satin was to use when her son got married. In the last year of her life, on sunny mornings when the weather was nice, this severely ill woman continued to take a length of satin, put it in a satchel, and wearily climb up on a donkey. Then Tian Da would lead the donkey down the dusty road, rocking and swaying into the distance.

As Lin Xiangfu recalled, his mother must have done this around ten times. Each time she returned, there was no longer any satin in her satchel, so he knew that his mother must not have taken a liking to the young woman—the satin had been left to help her family get over the disappointment, as was the old custom. When his mother returned home and handed the donkey over to Lin Xiangfu, she would give an exhausted smile and say,

"I didn't stay for a meal."

Lin Xiangfu knew this was the answer to the potential match. If his mother had stayed for a meal, it would have meant she had taken a liking to the girl. After her death, Lin Xiangfu continued this custom—when he went to town, he would pick up a length or two of satin in preparation for when he got married.

Matchmakers had visited several times to introduce him to a future bride, and he dutifully followed them to the homes of these young women. Whenever he was in the home of a family of equal status and wealth, he appeared particularly hesitant.

Accustomed to his mother making these sorts of decisions for him, Lin Xiangfu was unsure how to handle all of this. The fact that she had come away empty-handed over ten times made Lin Xiangfu both hesitant and confused. Each time he met a new potential match, he wonder to himself: would his mother like this girl? In the end, it was always the same—he never stayed for a meal, and would leave behind the length of satin he'd brought.

One time there was a beautiful, charming young woman

who sparked his interest—this was in Liuzhuang, over thirty *li* away, and Lin Xiangfu was visibly impressed by the family's grand courtyard mansion. After he was seated in the main hall, the girl's father passed him some tobacco. Just as he was about to decline and say he didn't smoke, he caught a look from the matchmaker, so he accepted. A beautiful young woman entered the room and, head bowed, slowly approached Lin Xiangfu; after filling his pipe, she demurely retreated.

Lin Xiangfu knew this was the woman he had come to see. Her hands were shaking as she filled his pipe, and when the matchmaker asked her a few questions, she didn't respond. But when Lin Xiangfu and the young woman caught each other's glances, her eyes lit up, and Lin Xiangfu felt his blood begin to surge. In the formal conversation that followed, Lin Xiangfu's heart was racing and he had trouble expressing himself. When the young woman's father asked him to stay for a meal, he clearly wanted to, but the look the matchmaker gave him changed his mind. He wavered a bit, then removed the satin from his bag and placed it on the table. The shocked look on the father's face made him flush with shame, and he quickly stood up and took his leave.

On the way home, all Lin Xiangfu could see was the young woman's beauty and the stunned expression on her father's face, and a pain filled his heart. As they went, the matchmaker told him the reason she had indicated he should refuse the match was because she feared this Liu girl was deaf and mute: when she was filling Lin Xiangfu's pipe, the matchmaker had said a few playful words to her, but she didn't respond, and seemed not to have heard. Lin Xiangfu thought the matchmaker's reasoning made sense, and yet he couldn't seem to get this girl—Liu Fengmei from Liuzhuang—out of his mind. Only when they had nearly finished traveling the thirty *li* home and he could see his own house was he finally able to heave a long sigh and feel a bit more at ease.

3.

Just when twenty-four year-old Lin Xiangfu felt his marriage prospects slipping away, a young man and woman turned up at his door. The woman was wearing a floral qipao and a blue calico headscarf, and the man was in a bright blue *changshan*; both were carrying bundles on their backs. As they stood outside Lin Xiangfu's front gate, they spoke so rapidly their words seemed to be taking flight.

It was evening, and when Lin Xiangfu heard their voices outside, he couldn't understand a word. When he opened the door and went out, the man switched to an accent he could decipher. This bookish young man told Lin Xiangfu that they had been traveling on a horse-drawn cart when one of its wheels broke—the cart wouldn't budge, it was getting dark, and the nearest inn was over ten *li* away. He paused for a moment, and then ventured to ask Lin Xiangfu if he might be willing to put them up for the night.

The young woman stood behind the man and looked Lin Xiangfu over with a timid smile as she removed her blue and white headscarf. Lin Xiangfu noticed a ray of the setting sun illuminating her graceful, delicate face. As she removed her scarf, she tilted her face slightly to the right, and something about that brief movement sent a jolt through Lin Xiangfu.

That evening, as the three of them sat chatting around a kerosene lamp, Lin Xiangfu learned that they weren't husband and wife, but rather brother and sister. From the way they referred to each other, he learned that the sister was named Xiaomei, and her older brother was Aqiang. Lin Xiangfu studied them carefully and got the feeling they didn't really seem like brother and sister. Aqiang, the brother, saw what Lin Xiangfu was thinking, and said his sister took after their mother, while he looked like their father. He added that the reason they didn't look like brother and sister was because their parents looked so different from each other. Lin Xiangfu laughed when he heard this, and went on to learn that they came from a town called Wencheng, far away in the south—six hundred *li* on the other side of the Yangtze river, among the river and canal towns of the Jiangnan region. Aqiang said their hometown was right on the river, and as soon as you put a foot out your door you could step on a boat. Their parents had both passed away, so they were headed north to Beijing in search of their uncle. He had once worked in Prince Gong's mansion, so Aqiang believed this uncle would have enough power and influence to get them set up in Beijing.

As they were talking they heard some loud braying outside, and Lin Xiangfu noticed that the brother and sister looked alarmed. He told them it was just his donkey, and they both exclaimed upon discovering that that was what a donkey sounded like. From this, Lin Xiangfu gleaned that their life in their southern Jiangnan town did not involve donkeys.

Lin Xiangfu talked about himself at length that evening. He talked about his hazy memories of his father and the clear ones of his mother, his thread-bound books, his mother's loom, and the green curtain of crops that shaded his childhood. Finally, he told them that he was considered the wealthiest man within a hundred *li*. When he said this, he noticed that Aqiang's eyes lit up, but when he looked at Xiaomei, she was still wearing the same shy smile.

Lin Xiangfu felt this was a joyful evening. After his mother died, this room had fallen into silence, but now it was filled with the continuous sound of voices. He liked this young woman named Xiaomei—although she didn't say much, her eyes always suggested a smile. She sat across from him, fiddling nonstop with her calico headscarf, which Lin Xiangfu noticed featured a pattern of alternating phoenixes and peonies. Out of curiosity he leaned over for a better look and praised the elegance of the scarf, noting that the local scarves were all plain white. He heard her sweet voice say it was the "phoenix and peony" pattern, which signified wealth and prosperity. She looked over at Lin Xiangfu after she said this, her bright eyes piercing through the light of the kerosene lamp, and they made the normally reserved Lin Xiangfu become garrulous. He felt that Xiaomei possessed a delicate grace he had never encountered before—her face had the dewy glow of a woman who had grown up amongst the emerald mountains and abundant waters of the south, and even after such long and arduous travels, she remained tender and spirited.

The next day, this tender and spirited woman fell ill. She lay on Lin Xiangfu's kang with a wet handkerchief on her forehead, her long hair hanging over the side of the kang like southern willow branches along the water. Her brother, his brows knitted in concern, sat on the edge of the kang; after talking with her in that rapid accent, he went up to Lin Xiangfu and anxiously described his sister's condition, saying she'd had spells of dizziness after getting up that morning, and had fallen before she even made it to the door. He said he'd felt her forehead, and it was as hot as a roasted sweet potato. Sounding helpless, he said, as if to himself, that he would have to continue on alone. He cautiously asked Lin Xiangfu: might he be able to temporarily look after his sister? He said that once he located their uncle in Beijing, he would return for her. Lin Xiangfu nodded, and the brother walked back to the kang and said a few words to his sister in that accent Lin Xiangfu was unable to understand. Then he put his bundle on his back, lifted up the long *changshan* he was wearing, stepped over the threshold, and exited the house. He followed the small path to the main road and headed north under the rays of the morning sun.

Lin Xiangfu thought back to the restless night he had just passed: Xiaomei's smile kept drifting before his eyes, and as he slept her beautiful appearance rocked back and forth in front of him as if it were floating on water. Then a golden road glided over to him, and he saw her lovely form on it, moving further away from him.

He came suddenly to his senses, and an uneasy sense of loss welled up inside him and stayed with him for the rest of that long night. When the morning arrived and Xiaomei was still there, daylight also returned to his heart.

Lin Xiangfu walked over to Xiaomei and saw her open her eyes. She opened her turned-up lips and said,

"A bowl of water, please."

That afternoon while he was out, Xiaomei got down off the kang and took a pair of wooden clogs out of her bag. She put them on and started doing some housework. In the evening, she sat on the threshold in the red glow of the setting sun, smiling as she watched Lin Xiangfu return from looking over the crops.

Lin Xiangfu walked up to her, and she rose and followed him into the house. She handed him a bowl of water she had ready and waiting on the table, then turned and walked away. Lin Xiangfu heard a strange sound coming from inside the room, and when he went in to look he saw the wooden clogs on Xiaomei's feet—as she walked around the room, they made a crisp clacking sound. The surprised look on his face made her smile, and she told him they were called "wooden clogs." Lin Xiangfu said he had never seen them before. Xiaomei said the girls in her hometown all wore them, especially on summer evenings. After washing their feet at the riverside, they would put on their wooden clogs and walk down the flagstone streets of the town, the click-clack of their steps ringing out like a xylophone. Lin Xiangfu asked what a xylophone sounded like, but Xiaomei wasn't sure how to answer. She lowered her head in thought, and then got up and walked around in a circle.

"That's what a xylophone sounds like."

Lin Xiangfu noticed that the room had been tidied and food had already been set on the table. Xiaomei stood smiling to one side, as if she were waiting for something. Lin Xiangfu felt like he had come into someone else's house, and the scene before him made him a bit ill at ease. He sensed that Xiaomei was also feeling a little uneasy, so he sat down on a stool, and Xiaomei did the same; then he picked up his chopsticks, and so did

Xiaomei. She blushed, and Lin Xiangfu thought to himself that she must have already recovered from her illness that morning. This sudden recovery surprised him—it seemed as if the illness had left as quickly as it had come.

4.

After this, the days went by. Several times on his way home from the fields, Lin Xiangfu caught sight of Xiaomei sitting on the threshold with her head propped on her hands, deep in thought, staring off into the distance. Lin Xiangfu thought she must be waiting for her brother to return, watching for that man in his bright blue *changshan* to appear on that dusty road.

When they sat down together for meals, that brother of hers—Aqiang—became a frequent topic of conversation. In an effort to comfort her, Lin Xiangfu would always say that Aqiang must have made it to Beijing, and would soon be coming back for her. As he said this, a certain image would appear before his eyes: Xiaomei, in her floral qipao, slowly following her brother down the main road as the morning sun rose, her delicate feet in a pair of stockings and wooden clogs. After this, Lin Xiangfu would be filled with sadness. Once she left—this woman from the south he had spent so much time with, who had cooked for him and washed his clothes—he had no idea what his life afterwards would be like.

One day some time later, Xiaomei sat down at the loom left behind by Lin Xiangfu's mother. It creaked and squeaked as she tried it; it was her first time using a loom, but by evening she had it nearly figured out. When Lin Xiangfu returned from the fields and entered the courtyard, he heard the sound of the loom, which produced the momentary illusion that his mother was there in the room—then he realized it must be Xiaomei. He stepped over the threshold and saw her sitting in front of the loom, her face flushed with beads of sweat on her forehead.

Xiaomei saw him enter the room and immediately stood up to greet him, telling him all about it: this loom was much louder than the ones in her hometown, much like the cries of the donkey were much louder than her hometown goats; at first it scared her, thinking she had broken it, but then she figured out how to weave a cloth.

She wore a smile as she told him this, and her eyes sparkled—it was the first time Lin Xiangfu had seen her like this. This woman, whose clogs moving across the room were often her only sound, and whose smile played on her lips but never broke out into laughter, was now positively glowing.

Lin Xiangfu sensed that his mother's loom made Xiaomei feel at ease. From that point on, he never again saw her sitting on the threshold, but instead heard the continuous sound of her weaving at the loom. After sitting idle for five years after his mother's death, it came to life again under the hands of another woman. Lin Xiangfu never again brought up Aqiang, and this name seemed to recede into the distance. Xiaomei also seemed to have forgotten about her brother—when she wasn't cooking, washing clothes, or doing the other housework, she would become immersed in the creaking of the loom. Lin Xiangfu began taking books off the shelf, dusting off their cases with his sleeve, and reading them in his spare time. As he sat on his little stool at his little desk, he would look over and see Xiaomei with her hand over her mouth, suppressing a giggle—he knew it was the sight of his large body at that tiny desk, and he would also chuckle. Xiaomei had seen more appropriately sized stools and desks in his workshop, and she wasn't sure why he was using this child's set.

These peaceful, cozy days went by one after the other. From time to time Lin Xiangfu would worry. Staring at Xiaomei's figure sitting at the loom, he would wonder—why hadn't any matchmakers come by?

5.

One evening in the beginning of winter there was a hailstorm, which came to pummel the earth just as Lin Xiangfu was falling asleep. He was awoken by what sounded like firecrackers, and sat up to see that the window had been blown open by the wind. Hailstones as white as silkworm cocoons poured down like a giant billowing curtain, casting a shimmering light into the dark room.

Lin Xiangfu saw that Xiaomei was holding herself and standing in front of his kang, the light reflecting from the rain and hail revealing the scared look on her face. Just then a giant hailstone the size of a bowl came crashing through the roof and smashed on the floor beside her. Xiaomei shrieked, scrambled up on the kang, and burrowed under the covers. More bowl-sized hailstones came raining down through the hole in the roof. As they smashed on the floor and melted, they looked like flowers blooming, then fading.

Lin Xiangfu felt Xiaomei's body curled up and trembling against his chest. Like smoothing out a supple sheet of *xuan* calligraphy paper, his body gradually encouraged her huddled form to stretch out. He felt her relax, and their clothes pressed tightly up against one another. It was as if her body had been ignited, and her scorching heat passed through their clothing and transferred to him. From that point on, Lin Xiangfu no longer heard the rain and hail. Although the two of them were pressed up against each other, their bare skin was not touching; yet he was engulfed by her fiery warmth and rapid breathing. As if suddenly woken from a dream, he felt a violent tremor, as if the whole room were about to collapse; after a moment of shock, he immersed himself once more in Xiaomei's body heat and breathing. Only when he opened the door the next morning and saw a hailstone the size of a stone mortar lying in front of the house did he recall the earsplitting crash from the night before.

The hard, winter earth was covered by a layer of ice shards for as far as the eye could see, glistening under the sunlight like a frozen lake. Many of the thatched roofs in the village had collapsed in the storm, and the villagers, shocked and injured, stood outside in the cold wind like withered trees dotting a forbidding landscape.

As Lin Xiangfu walked around the village, tearful women and children wrapped in blankets looked at him pitifully, and random items plucked from the downed thatching were lying all around. Some men were in the process of trying to put one of the roofs back up, but the grass thatching broke apart and scattered in the winter wind, catching on the branches of trees and getting stuck in people's hair and clothing. Some livestock that had been beaten to death by the hail lay strewn on the ground—there was not a speck of blood on their bodies, but when they were pulled from their sheds, they were covered with grass thatching and chunks of ice. The deaths of these animals drove the women to bitter tears, and they shouted up to the sky:

"How are we supposed to survive now?"

The men, their faces cracked from the cold and their eyes full of tears, said in lower, more downcast tones:

"We have no way to survive now."

By a few graves at the south end of the village, an old man pummeled to death by the hailstones had been laid out on a door plank. The grieving here was nothing like the crying and shouting of those who had lost their livestock; those who had lost their family member appeared calm. A tattered white cloth lay across the face of the deceased.

No one was crying for him, but five men over to the side were wielding mattocks on his behalf, digging his grave. They were the five Tian brothers, their warm bodies steaming in the cold, their mattocks cutting through the hard winter ground, their hands marred by bloody cracks and splits. Lin Xiangfu walked over to them, and they held their mattocks and looked at him. Tian Da said,

"Young master, this dead man is our father, beaten to death by the hail. A hailstone the size of a wooden basin hit him in the face, and didn't even break."

An image of the man when he was still alive floated before Lin Xiangfu's eyes—thin, bony, squatting at the corner of his thatched cottage, his hands tucked into his sleeves, coughing.

Twenty-two years earlier, this man had brought his five sons before the main gate of Lin Xiangfu's home. He said his name was Tian Donggui, then gestured to his sons and, as if counting them, said their names: Tian Da, Tian Er, Tian San, Tian Si, and Tian Wu. They had come here fleeing famine, and were wondering if there were any fields they could rent. Back then Tian Da was sixteen and Tian Wu was only four, sleeping on his big brother's back.

Lin Xiangfu's father stood outside the gate and talked with Tian Donggui for a long time. Then Tian Donggui and his sons moved into two thatched rooms attached to the back of the Lin family compound. Later, as the five Tian brothers got married, one after the other, ten new thatched rooms were added. After Lin Xiangfu's father died, his mother felt that Tian Da was kind and honest, so she made him steward. As his four younger brothers grew up, they became responsible for collecting the rents and various other tasks. When Tian Donggui and his five sons first arrived, Lin Xiangfu was only two years old, and the villagers would often see Tian Da carrying him on his back through both the village and the fields.

Now, as Tian Da removed the tattered white cloth, Lin Xiangfu saw that battered face with bits of grass and ice still covering the body. He knelt down and pulled the tattered cloth back, then stood up and said,

"Take him home, wash him with well water, and put him in clean clothes. I'll go make a coffin for him. Then he can be buried."

Tian Da nodded and said, "Yes, young master."

Back in the house, Xiaomei could hear the wails of grief

floating over from the village, and she began to feel anxious. When she heard Lin Xiangfu's footsteps returning, she went out to ask him what was going on, but as soon as she saw the grave look on his face, she remained quiet. Lin Xiangfu asked her to go to the wardrobe and find a white cloth while he went to his workshop. Shortly afterwards, Xiaomei entered carrying a white cloth, while Lin Xiangfu was going through his lumber stock and selecting out long, wide pieces of fir. She put the cloth on a stool and watched him place the fir boards in a neat stack on the ground, then squat down to mark a line. Carefully, she ventured,

"Was someone beaten to death by the hail?"

"Yes, one person was," said Lin Xiangfu.

"With so many people crying, I was afraid it might be more," Xiaomei said.

"A good deal of livestock was lost," said Lin Xiangfu.

After a pause, he added, "For farmers, livestock is a major part of their property."

"Are you making a coffin?" Xiaomei asked.

Lin Xiangfu nodded and looked over earnestly at the astute Xiaomei. Xiaomei looked at Lin Xiangfu squatting on the ground and thought to herself that this was a good man. As Lin Xiangfu sawed up the fir boards, Xiaomei noticed how long they were and asked him if the man who died was exceptionally tall. Lin Xiangfu shook his head and said he wasn't that tall, but that the size of the coffin was predetermined. Then he told her an old saying:

"All coffins under heaven measure seven *chi*, three *cun*."

Once the Tian brothers had taken care of their father's corpse, they came over to help Lin Xiangfu with the coffin, and Xiaomei left the workshop to go prepare lunch. By this time he had already worked the wood to the proper dimensions and was drilling holes to fit the tenons, while the Tian brothers were helping him shape the tenons and assemble and adjust the coffin. The brothers insisted on doing the sanding and polishing themselves, and they pulled a chair over so Lin Xiangfu could take a rest and direct them from there.

As the brothers sanded and polished, they remarked on the young master's excellent craftsmanship—he had made a coffin in one day without using a single nail, and there was not another one like it within a hundred *li*.

Lin Xiangfu said that all the woodworkers within a hundred *li* knew how to make a coffin, and that his first master had told him: if you're a wife you can make shoes; if you're a woodworker you can make a coffin. The only reason he was able to make this in one day, he added, was because the five of them had all helped—for such a large, heavy coffin, even if he pushed himself as hard as he could, it would still take him at least three days, maybe even five.

As evening approached, the Tian brothers carried the coffin out the back door, and Lin Xiangfu followed behind with the white cloth that Xiaomei had woven. In one of the Tian family's rooms that still had a roof overhead, the brothers lifted their father's corpse, which they had cleaned and dressed, into the coffin. Placing the newly-made white cloth over his body and closed the top. The Tian brothers and their families all bowed to Lin Xiangfu. Tian Da uttered a "young master," but was too choked up to get anything else out. Eyes brimming with tears, Lin Xiangfu said to them:

"May he rest in peace."

On this dreary day, the villagers' sobs and moans rose and fell amidst gusts of winter wind. Lin Xiangfu and Xiaomei were enveloped by these miserable sounds. They were also in a daze from the events that had suddenly transpired the previous night, and they fell into silence; Xiaomei set to work at the loom, while Lin Xiangfu sat blankly. Then Lin Xiangfu got up, went his room, and lay down on the kang. The loom continued to sound, as if it were Xiaomei's continuous babbling. After a while it suddenly stopped, and he could hear her push the stool out and stand up. Her footsteps sounded like she was carefully treading on thin ice as she walked into another room.

Lin Xiangfu was on edge that evening. Moonlight streamed down through the hole in the roof like a sparkling column of water, and the mournful village had fallen silent under the dark night. The only sound was that of the wind brushing past the eaves as it flew out into the night sky, the distant sound of its swishing like soft words of encouragement. This led Lin Xiangfu to get up and walk over to Xiaomei's room. As he passed that glittering column of moonlight, he looked up through the hole in the roof and saw a boundless darkness as gusts of frigid wind assaulted him. He walked out of that room and into the other one, and stood before Xiaomei's kang. In the moonlight he could see her wrapped in her blanket and sleeping on her side, curled up and perfectly still. Lin Xiangfu hesitated for a moment and then quietly lay down beside her. He could hear her quiet, even breaths as he slowly pulled back her blanket and made room for himself underneath it.

Xiaomei flipped around and darted over to his body like a fish in water.

6.

After the hailstorm, people mended their roofs and fixed their doors and windows. They stuffed their necks down into their collars, pulled their hands up into their sleeves, straightened their frozen red noses, puffed out breaths of warm air, and began facing an unusually cold winter.

As far as Lin Xiangfu was concerned, getting through this sort of winter wasn't that difficult. Freezing days were followed by steamy nights. Sleeping next to Xiaomei, absorbing her endless warmth, made Lin Xiangfu feel as if spring had arrived.

The stability of her life allowed Xiaomei's thin face to fill out a bit, and Lin Xiangfu also began to put on some weight. He became infatuated with these strange new intimate pleasures, and as nighttime approached, unable to wait any longer, he would say to Xiaomei,

"Get on the kang."

Xiaomei would give a little smile and tidy up the loose ends at the loom, then proceed to follow the strapping Lin Xiangfu into the other room.

In the second month of the new year, that distant look once again appeared in Xiaomei's eyes. She was standing in the doorway, in front of that mortar-sized hailstone, looking off into the distance. Lin Xiangfu guessed she must be thinking of her brother, so he went over to comfort her, telling her not to worry—Aqiang had perhaps already left Beijing and was on his way there. Lin Xiangfu pointed at the hailstone and told Xiaomei that before it melted, her brother would appear at their door.

After Lin Xiangfu said this, Xiaomei lowered her head and said quietly, "If Aqiang came, I couldn't follow him to Beijing."

Xiaomei's words gave Lin Xiangfu a rush of excitement. He grabbed her sleeve and led her to the graveyard at the eastern edge of the village, where he had her kneel with him in front of a pair of light gray tombstones.

The afternoon was sunny and calm, and the fields glistened under the sunshine. Xiaomei looked out across the boundless expanse of white, dotted with barren elm trees stretching out their broken branches and a few thatched cottages scattered here and there—the scene was utterly different from her hometown in the south. Beside her, Lin Xiangfu was calling out to his parents. Xiaomei lowered her head. Lin Xiangfu's voice sounded like he was crying, but also like he was laughing, as words poured from his mouth:

"Father, Mother, I've brought Xiaomei here for you to have a look. I want to marry her, and I'd like your blessing. She has had a bitter fate—her parents are both dead, and she has only one older brother; he went to Beijing a long time ago and hasn't returned for her. She's my woman, and I want to marry her, so please give your blessing. Mother, Xiaomei knows how to weave, just like you, and the cloth she weaves is just as strong . . ."

7.

One morning three days later, the women of the village came to Lin Xiangfu's home with some red paper and a red quilted jacket. They had Xiaomei take off the floral-print jacket she was wearing and put on the red one, and then they began cutting "double happiness" 囍 characters out of the red paper. The village men brought a hog and a sheep, which they butchered at the doorway—their hot blood splattered on the mortar-sized hailstone, causing a few rivulets to melt on its surface. The color of the blood grew lighter as it ran down over the ice.

One villager turned up in a bright blue *changshan*. Wearing a thin garment meant for spring or autumn on such a cold winter day, his face had turned purple from the freezing cold. He was the only one who had worn a *changshan* to come offer his congratulations, and the other villagers surrounded him to admire his attire—complete with a few stains—asking where he had managed to find such dapper clothing. This villager proudly told them that he had taken two sacks of corn to sell in town, and that when he had just half a sack left, he'd seen a man in his fifties who looked like he was starving hobbling over to him. The man then held out the *changshan*, which he exchanged for the remaining half sack of corn. After the villager had told his story, he added that the man had a scar on his forehead, as if he'd been attacked with a knife.

That forenoon, the village women chattered inside like sparrows, while outside the village men brayed like livestock. As Xiaomei was quietly watching them all, Lin Xiangfu walked over and said: Don't do any work today—you're a new bride. Then he went into town with the five Tian brothers to buy some alcohol.

"Take the donkey with you," someone said, "it can help you carry things back."

Lin Xiangfu shook his head and said, "Driving a donkey in this kind of weather would harm it."

The six of them set off walking in a line down the small path, their necks and hands tucked into their clothing. When they came to a charred elm that had been burned by a lightning strike, they turned onto the main road into town.

The afternoon passed, the pork and mutton was set on the table, and the "double happiness" characters had been pasted on the windows and doors. The women kept chattering and the men were still braying. The men said that the drinking bowls were on the table, all lined up in rows, but those motherfuckers who went into town for the alcohol still weren't back. The town was just over ten *li* away, they said—even a turtle should have made it back by now, but not these motherfuckers. The women inside said who cares—the groom still wasn't back, and even so the bride wasn't worried.

"He'll be back," Xiaomei said with a smile.

It was nearly evening when Lin Xiangfu and the brothers appeared on the main road, the six of them staggering along in a group, looking like a goatskin raft floating in a sea of white. They turned at the old burned-out elm tree onto the small village road, shouting and laughing as they stumbled along.

The six drunks approached the gate, each carrying two empty bottles. Lin Xiangfu staggered forward, his breath reeking of alcohol. He raised his empty drinking bowl to the waiting crowd and announced:

"The alcohol's here, the alcohol's here!"

He stumbled up to the entrance and felt around at the doorframe to confirm it was the door; then with a giggle he went inside. He set the empty bottles on the table and said to everyone,

"Drink, drink—drink up!"

The men, whose mouths had been watering in anticipation for so long, looked at the empty bottles on the table and said to one another,

"Drink what, their farts? They drained everything on their way back!"

Lin Xiangfu's wedding continued amidst the sounds of

snoring from the six sleeping drunks and the ravenous feasting from that group of hungry ghosts and wild beasts. Xiaomei sat quietly off to the side staring at Lin Xiangfu as he lay on the kang, his hair like a tangled mess of weeds. The main hall was full of people, and there were also quite a few in the courtyard. Everyone who had been suffering from hunger throughout the afternoon now had their cheeks stuffed with food. The way they were all bent over eating made Xiaomei think back to her hometown far away in the south—how on any given summer evening someone would spread some rice fodder on the ground, and the chickens and geese would immediately come flapping over. The scene before her looked the same.

Lin Xiangfu passed his wedding in a deep slumber; when he woke up, it was the middle of the night, and all was quiet. His head ached and there was a dull ringing in his ears. By the dancing flame of the kerosene lamp, Lin Xiangfu looked over at the wall and saw Xiaomei's shadow, perfectly still and sitting up straight. He let out a groan, which prompted Xiaomei to turn around—only then did he realize she was sitting right beside him.

Xiaomei bent down and related all of his drunken activities to him. Her breath, invisible and odorless, swept over his face like a fresh morning breeze, with a certain softness that was impossible to describe.

Then Xiaomei got up and went to make him some ginger soup. His head must be hurting after drinking so much, she said as she walked away; a bowl of ginger soup would help. When she returned, she was also carrying a plate of meat, which she said she'd had to secretly set side—she'd never seen such a mess of hungry ghosts.

"A whole hog and two sheep," she said, a bit pained.

That night, Xiaomei opened up her satchel, removed her clothing, and took out three blue calico headscarves. She said she had nothing to her name but these three scarves, which were her prized possessions, and she spread them out on the kang. Lin Xiangfu recognized the "phoenix and peony" pattern, but the other two he had never seen. Xiaomei pointed to a print of magpies and plum blossoms and explained that it was meant to evoke the phrase, "a face glowing with joy"; the other print showed lions playing with satin pom-poms.

"This is all I have for my dowry," she said to Lin Xiangfu.

It was also that night that Lin Xiangfu removed a brick in the wall and took out a wooden box. He spread out two yellowed papers: one was the deed to the house, the other the deed to the land. He pointed to the latter and told Xiaomei that it was the deed to 476 *mu* of land. Then he took a heavy parcel out of the box wrapped in a red cloth. When he opened it up, Xiaomei saw seventeen large gold bars and three small ones. Lin Xiangfu said that the large ones were known as big croakers, after the fish, and the small ones were called little croakers. Ten little croakers could be exchanged for one big croaker.

As Lin Xiangfu set out the gold bars one by one, events of the past came rushing before his eyes. He told Xiaomei that his ancestors were the ones who had begun saving this gold. He still had a few scattered childhood memories of his father wearing straw sandals, returning wearily from a trip into town. After his father died, his mother made the trip every year after the harvest—she would ride on the back of a donkey, led by Tian Da, and head for the bank. Thinking back on these scenes made his heart ache. As a young boy he would see his mother sitting on the threshold, placing her cloth shoes inside straw ones, and then starting down the path with Tian Da; by the time they made it to the main road she would be riding on the back of the donkey. They would disappear off into the morning light, and return home later in the afternoon. Every time they came home, his mother would be carrying a stick of candied haw berries for him. Back then the family donkey had red tassels on its forehead and a little bell around its neck, and when it went down the road, the tassels would flutter and the bell would tinkle. After the harvest the year his mother fell ill, Lin

Xiangfu continued this tradition and went into town himself. When he returned home that afternoon, his mother was already gone—she had died with her eyes open.

Lin Xiangfu sighed and said that when a person dies, they should have their children and grandchildren there with them. To have no one was like a piece missing from the moon; the deceased couldn't close their eyes. Lin Xiangfu said his mother left the world with no one by her side, like dark clouds obscuring the moon.

On that long, dark winter night, events of the past kept flooding his memory one after the other. The headache from his drinking caused the memories to sprout in his mind like a profusion of unruly weeds. Only after he fell asleep was he able to find some peace.

8.

In that second month of the new year, Lin Xiangfu went with Tian Da every day to examine the wheat. One day on their way back from the fields, he saw Xiaomei standing out in front of the door, lost in a daze. She said it looked like spring would arrive soon, and still her brother had not come.

Lin Xiangfu stood in a stupor for a long while. He had already long forgotten about Xiaomei's brother, that man in the bright blue *changshan*. He had set off one morning last fall, and—like a clay figurine of an ox dropped into the sea, as the saying goes—he was never heard from again.

Xiaomei asked Lin Xiangfu: Is there a temple nearby? She wanted to go burn some incense and ask the bodhisattva Guanyin to protect her brother.

Lin Xiangfu turned around and pointed west, where the sky was ablaze with the setting sun, and said there was a temple to Guan Yu fifteen *li* in that direction.

That evening Xiaomei placed a small satchel on the kang,

then twisted down the wick of the kerosene lamp and crawled under the covers. She rested her head on Lin Xiangfu's arm as if it were a pillow, and said to him softly,

"The food is on the shelf by the stove, and the clothes are all in the wardrobe—to the left are the clothes with patches, so wear those when you go out to the fields; the clothes to the right don't have patches, so wear those when you go into town. There's also one new outfit and two new pairs of cloth shoes I've made for you over the past several days, which are in the wardrobe as well."

Upon hearing this, Lin Xiangfu said, "You're just going for a day, not a whole year."

Xiaomei said nothing more, and Lin Xiangfu soon began snoring. It was the last night of the second month; moonbeams shone into the room, sprinkling light over the kang and the floor, and a soft breeze was blowing in through the window, carrying the moist scent of melting snow.

When Lin Xiangfu awoke to the first rays of the morning sun, Xiaomei had already gone. Noises from the livestock drifted in from the fields, mixed with the sounds of tree branches being used as whips and the shouts of people. Lin Xiangfu went into the outer room and found an old cloth covering the loom. She is very conscientious, he thought to himself—she covers the loom even when she's away for just a day. He went into the kitchen and found the shelf by the stove piled high with food, enough for a few weeks. Xiaomei had cleaned and tidied everything before she left, which greatly satisfied Lin Xiangfu. After breakfast, he went out to have a look at the fields.

On his way out he ran into Tian Si, who told him that early that morning before sunrise, he had seen Xiaomei on the main road at the village entrance. She had a bundle on her back and a satchel in her hand, and looked like she was headed back to visit her parents.

Visit what parents, said Lin Xiangfu—she was going to burn some incense at the Guan Yu temple. With a look of surprise,

Tian Si asked why she was heading south, when the Guan Yu temple was to the west? When Lin Xiangfu heard this, he felt a pit in his stomach, worried that Xiaomei had taken the wrong road.

That evening, after the sun had set and night had fallen, Xiaomei hadn't come home. Two more days passed, and she still hadn't returned.

Xiaomei left and never came back.

Lin Xiangfu discovered her clothes were not in the wardrobe and her cloth shoes were not under the kang; her wooden clogs and her "phoenix and peony" headscarf were also gone. The clogs and headscarf were a sense of the south that arrived with Xiaomei, and now they had left with her, too.

She left two scarves behind—the one with magpies and plum blossoms, and the one with lions playing with satin pom-poms—which she placed in the wardrobe on top of Lin Xiangfu's clothes. Like the cry of an eagle that continues echoing after it leaves, these two headscarves were all that remained of her.

For the next few days, Lin Xiangfu was on edge. He slept so lightly it was as if he were floating. Chickens clucking, dogs barking, even the wind blowing over the grass would wake him; the occasional sound of footsteps in the distance would cause his heart to thump.

He knew that Xiaomei hadn't gone west to the Guan Yu temple, but had instead headed south. He had a feeling that Xiaomei had really left him, but he had no idea why. Lin Xiangfu was confused, and he felt as lonely and desolate as the wide open fields in winter. Sometimes in his daze he would imagine that Xiaomei would suddenly appear before him one evening, a satchel in her hand. These reveries came and went like the rising and setting sun, appearing and then disappearing, over and over.

Finally one day Lin Xiangfu became certain Xiaomei wasn't coming back.

That evening, he ate the last of the food Xiaomei had left by the stove, then put out the lamp and lay down on the kang. The moonlight streaming in the window prevented him from falling asleep. The food Xiaomei had prepared before she left had lasted about two weeks, and now it was all gone, so he thought that perhaps she would be coming back now—she had surely calculated the length of her trip, and had prepared this amount of food for him. The flame of hope in his heart now burned brighter, and he started to feel anxious and excited.

Then he suddenly thought of the wooden box hidden in the interior wall. He remembered that evening when he took out the box and opened it to show Xiaomei the bars of gold, along with the deeds to the property. He remembered her face had frozen, and it seemed like she hadn't been listening to anything he said; when he had reached out and nudged her, she'd trembled.

He leapt up from the kang, lit the lamp, and moved the brick in the wall to take out the wooden box. When he opened it and saw that the deeds and the parcel wrapped in red cloth were still there, he calmed down. But when he picked up the parcel, it was much lighter than usual. He opened it to discover that of the seventeen big croakers, there were now only ten, and that one of the little croakers was missing as well. He felt like an explosion went off in his head—he now knew why Xiaomei hadn't returned. Late that night, many of the villagers were awoken to a terrifying sound, sometimes shrill and piercing, sometimes low and deep, racing through the night air in frightful waves that made their hair stand on end. The next day, everyone said there had been ghosts in the village.

But the sounds had come from Lin Xiangfu. When he discovered Xiaomei had taken nearly half of the gold his family had been saving for generations, he began weeping and shaking. His cries were longer than those of a newborn baby, and began to resemble the cries of a bereft child looking for his parents. Under the cold and desolate light of the moon, he made his way to his parents' graves and knelt before them. Sometimes he sobbed so hard he couldn't get any words out, and sometimes he would shout,

"Father! Mother! I've wronged you, I've wronged our ancestors. Father! Mother! I'm your unfilial son, I'm the ruination of the Lin family. Father! Mother! I was blind, and I've been tricked! I'm a fool, and our money's been stolen. Father! Mother! Xiaomei's not a good woman . . . "

9.

From that point on, Lin Xiangfu rarely spoke, and any trace of a smile disappeared from his face. His heart felt heavy, and he would often stare at the main road at the village entrance. Sometimes he would think of Xiaomei, and Aqiang, that brother of hers, and suspect that they weren't actually siblings. The amount of time she occupied his thoughts gradually decreased—her sweet smile dropped from his memory like a fallen leaf in autumn, and her clear, bright voice blew away in the wind. As she became more distant in his mind, his anger toward her lessened.

He thought of something his mother had said to him before she died. He had been in his workshop, covered in perspiration, when she had appeared at the door—she felt deeply gratified that her son loved woodworking like his father, and with her voice full of praise she had said:

"Even if you have all the money in the world, it's still not as good as having a skill."

After suffering this financial loss, Lin Xiangfu often thought back to his mother's words. The more he thought about it, the more sense it made. No matter how much wealth he accumulated, there could always come a day when it was gone—there have been examples of that ever since ancient times. Whether a person met with wealth or misfortune in this life, one could never tell, but possessing a skill could always help reverse a decline, because a skill couldn't be lost like money. Lin Xiangfu felt that he should take his woodworking skills to the next level; he should continue learning from the masters.

Winter was over and spring had arrived, and the giant hailstone in front of the door had finally begun to melt. The trees were putting out green buds, the earth was waking up, and birds migrated back and chirped incessantly on Lin Xiangfu's roof. He led his donkey, its bell tinkling and its red tassels fluttering, to the main road at the village entrance.

Lin Xiangfu set out in search of master woodworkers, expertly skilled at their trades. The first one was a cabinetmaker named Cabinets Chen, who lived about ten *li* away. Not only could he make tables, chairs, and benches as well, but he was also the only woodworker within a hundred *li* who had been to Beijing—he had seen something of the world. He had even seen the emperor out making his rounds, which was the most precious experience of his life. The very first thing he said to Lin Xiangfu was,

"Have you ever seen the emperor making his rounds?"

The first time Lin Xiangfu saw Cabinets Chen, he was fixing up an old chest. He was smoking a pipe while he worked, and continued to do so as he described at length his sighting of the emperor. First to emerge, he told Lin Xiangfu, was not the emperor himself, but his sword, solemnly carried out by one of his officials. Only after the official shouts, "The sword has arrived!" does the emperor make his appearance.

Cabinets Chen had seen five decades of life, and all his hair had gone gray. As he recounted the scene of the emperor making his rounds, he had to continuously keep swallowing his saliva, as if he weren't talking about the emperor's rounds but the emperor's meal. His description of the emperor's commanding presence was more like describing the tasty delicacies of land and sea, and the formation of the emperor's attendants more like an inventory of dishes at the imperial banquet. The more thoughts came rushing to Cabinets Chen's mind, the more saliva came drooling forth.

Lin Xiangfu, who had never heard of anything like this before, was mesmerized by his verbose recounting. But what he found even more impressive was his craftsmanship. As he spoke, he transformed the old chest into what looked like a brand new one. When Lin Xiangfu expressed his admiration, he gave a slight smile and said,

"People in our line of work not only have to be able to make wardrobes, chests, tables, chairs, and benches, but they also have to learn a particular skill, like knowing how to refurbish old furniture."

Cabinets Chen told Lin Xiangfu he only worked with softwood, but that the really first-rate woodworkers built things from hardwood, although they could obviously work with softwood as well. He said that not only could hardwood craftsmen refurbish old furniture, but they could also build new furniture to make it look like it was old. At the bottom rung of the profession, he said, were those who did Western-style woodworking. He said that ever since foreigners started coming to Beijing, the city degenerated by the day, and Western-style furniture became more popular. Woodworkers with his types of skills, who had always been in high demand, eventually found themselves out of work and destitute. A bitter smile appeared on Cabinets Chen's face when he reached this point, sighing as he lamented the unpredictable changes of the world.

"You can't just randomly hammer nails in a piece of furniture; woodworkers specializing in hardwood hardly even use dowels. Western furniture has nails sticking out all over the place."

Then he raised his hand and pointed out the door, saying, "Head west for over twenty *li,* and you'll come to a village called Xuzhuang. There you'll find a man I really admire named Hardwood Xu. He's specialized in working with hardwood for over forty years. He's never once used a dowel peg, and nails— well, he wouldn't even look at one."

Hardwood Xu in Xuzhuang was the second master wood-worker Lin Xiangfu sought out. Unlike Cabinets Chen, this hardwood specialist who had seen six decades of life didn't look down on Western-style woodworkers as inferior. He said that the soft, padded parts of Western furniture really required some skill; for instance, covering a padded chair in sheepskin was incredibly tedious work. He went on at great length about coopers and sieve farmers and wainwrights and coffin makers, about every wood trade under the sun.

Hardwood Xu said that woodworking merely had different categories, and one was not necessarily better or worse than the other. For example, most people who work at sawmills don't do woodworking, but they're excellent at assessing amounts and costs for projects of all sizes, and they can work out everything that's required. They can also draw up plans and make samples. Carpenters, for example, work in building construction—the rafters, beams, pillars, purlins, doors, windows, and partitions are their main craft. Then take those who make wooden molds—if you're making a decorative mold for a small cake, for example, it has to be beautiful and intricate, and the size and depth has to undergo extremely careful consideration, because even if the patterns printed on the cakes are different, they all have to weigh the same. Take those who make moldings—not just any-one can carve those decorative edgings. Take those who make small furnishings and utensils—vase stands, basin stands, and trivets are their specialty, and they must all be made to fit the appropriate object; it's a craft that originally came from Suzhou and Hangzhou. Take those who use the lathe—they special-ize in cylindrical objects, and can handle anythe thickness, and length, constantly changesor new design. Take those who make rounded chairs—they have to use green willow and bend it while it's wet to make an armchair. This specialty depends on a large ax—saws and chisels are considered accessories, and not only is an ink-marking line not necessary, but you can even get by without a ruler. Take a cooper—barrels, toilet buckets, wash

basins, they make them all. Take sieve framers—in addition
to making tiered lunch boxes, hatboxes, steamers, and sieves,
they can also make rocking cradles. Take those who make shoe
soles for the Manchus—in Beijing, the Manchu women all wear
shoes with wooden soles, the thickest being six or seven *cun;*
this is something most woodworkers couldn't produce. Take
those who make carrying poles for barbers—most woodworkers could make the cabinet stool that hangs in back, while the
round bucket in the front should be the work of a sieve framer,
although they have to know how to make this, too. Take those
who make the carrying poles for handymen—at first glance the
boxes they carry look like they would be a job for cabinetmak-
ers, but only they can make the interior drawers for the piston
bellows. Take those who make clappers and wooden fish—these
percussion blocks used for reciting scriptures require their own
particular skill. Take those who make the props used in Peking
opera—these fake weapons used for stage fighting are also a
major area of specialization. Take a wainwright—they specialize in making wagons. Take those who make horse-drawn carriages—they have to work with finer details than wainwrights,
and spend most of their time on the wheels. Then there are
those who specialize in hand-drawn carts, those who specialize in Western-style horse-drawn carts, and those who specialize
in rickshaws. Take saddlemakers—they specialize in different
kinds of saddles for horses, as well as pack saddles for donkeys
and mules. Take those who make sedan chairs—these are different from carriages, because they're carried and don't have
wheels. Take those who make the objects carried by the imperial
honor guard—they are the only ones who can make the flags,
gongs, parasols, and fans that the guard carries. Take coffin
makers—their craft can't be done by just any old woodworker.
A large piece of lumber can be used for a number of different
things, and a coffin maker pays particular attention to making
the best use of all of it in order to save on labor and materials,
while at the same time producing a beautiful coffin.

Finally, Hardwood Xu said to Lin Xiangfu, "Even jobs that might appear simple and straightforward, like sawyers or pall-bearing pole makers, still require their own special skills. Take the sawyer—if he's a good one, when he's sawing up boards, he won't ruin the wood, and he'll make fine, careful cuts. Now take the guy who makes pallbearing poles—even though at a funeral it looks like they're only using a few sticks to lift the casket, if the poles weren't made by someone who knows what they're doing, the pallbearers' shoulders wouldn't be able to take it—so even making these poles requires its own tricks of the trade."

Lin Xiangfu studied diligently, and early in the mornings the villagers would often see him with a white scarf tied around his head, making his way toward the main road with his donkey, its red tassel fluttering in the breeze. Then, just as night was about to fall, they would hear the bell tinkling around the donkey's neck as Lin Xiangfu returned. The days continued to pass like this, as calmly as a dawn breeze under a lingering moon.

10.

As Lin Xiangfu traveled from village to village learning from the master woodworkers, rumors began circulating about Xiaomei's departure, following him as he went. Privately, people discussed this wife of woodworker Lin; although they didn't know any details, they simply remarked that Xiaomei had gone to the south to visit her family and never returned—while also offering a few of their own baseless speculations.

One afternoon, the rumors about Xiaomei led the long-absent matchmaker to turn up at Lin Xiangfu's house. She padded into the room on her little bound feet and sat cross-legged on the kang.

First, she asked Lin Xiangfu if he and Xiaomei had written out a horoscope card before getting married. What horoscope card, asked Lin Xiangfu. The matchmaker slapped her leg and exclaimed,

"So it's possible for such a thing to happen—a man and woman can go to bed as husband and wife without writing out a horoscope card!"

The matchmaker asked the time and date of Xiaomei's birth, but Lin Xiangfu could only shake his head; she then asked about Xiaomei's zodiac animal, but Lin Xiangfu didn't know that, either. Once again the matchmaker sighed and exclaimed,

"So it's possible for such a thing to happen—a man can not know a woman's birth date, horoscope, or even her zodiac animal, and still take her as his wife! No wonder Xiaomei left and never returned."

The matchmaker said that only by knowing their birthdates, horoscopes, and zodiac animals could she know if their matrimony would be mutually beneficial or mutually destructive—if it would lead to happiness or disaster, long life or early death. "Someone born in the year of the horse can't marry someone born in the year of the ox," she said, "and a person born in the year of the goat will never get along with someone born in the year of the rat—this is what's known as, 'White horse fears a strong young ox, goat and rat will hit the rocks; snake and tiger split by knife, rabbit and dragon cry in strife; rooster and dog in disaster are cast, pig and monkey will never last; a pair of dogs go separate ways, a pair of dragons never stays; goat falls into tiger's maw' . . . you were born in the year of the goat, so I'm afraid you're a marriage of goat and rat—either that or goat and tiger."

The matchmaker began counting on her fingers as she said, "If you didn't write out a horoscope card, and you don't know her birth date or zodiac animal, then you surely at least collected her with a bridal sedan on the day you got married?"

Lin Xiangfu once again shook his head. This time the matchmaker slapped her thighs with both hands and cried out, "So it's possible for such a thing to happen! There's an old saying, 'a broken fan can still make a breeze, a broken sedan chair still carries some prestige.' Never mind about the prestige—if you didn't even fetch her in a bridal sedan, then her feet don't belong to you—they're still her own, so she can walk away whenever she wants. This Xiaomei is certainly never coming back."

Lin Xiangfu sat on the stool and listened as the matchmaker sat on the kang, her tongue flapping and spittle flying, the opium pipe in her hand jerking up and down. Finally, she sighed and said okay, how about this—she'd go around making inquiries again and see if she could find a young woman from a suitable family. She told Lin Xiangfu that this time she was afraid she wouldn't be able to find a young woman from a well-to-do family. Even though Xiaomei was gone, she still remained his legal wife, so any woman he married now could only be considered a concubine—and no girl from a well-to-do family would be willing to become a concubine.

Feeling a bit discouraged, Lin Xiangfu nodded and said to the matchmaker, "A young woman from a respectable family will do."

Just as the matchmaker was about to leave, she suddenly thought of something and asked Lin Xiangfu if he still remembered the girl from Liuzhuang. The young woman's lovely appearance suddenly emerged from the depths of his memory—he thought of how, in the great hall of that expansive courtyard mansion, she had once touched his heart. He remembered how she had first walked slowly up to him and filled his pipe, her hands shaking uncontrollably. He also remembered her name—the matchmaker was referring to Liu Fengmei.

The matchmaker told Lin Xiangfu that this lovely young woman, Liu Fengmei, was actually neither deaf nor mute. She said she had already gotten married—into the Sun family, who had opened a *qianzhuang* bank in town. She sighed and said Liu Fengmei's home was stuffed full of people before the wedding—tailors, woodworkers, lacquerware makers, bamboo weavers, metalworkers, woodcarvers, artisans of all sorts. Before she got married, they made her a full wardrobe with clothes for every season, along with a whole array of useful items. They had worked day and night, so the courtyard had been hung full of lanterns, and people were constantly coming and going. When it came to the day of her wedding, the scene was even more impressive: her dowry required dozens of carrying poles and stretched out in a line so long it seemed nearly endless. Most wealthy families would provide the basic dowry for their daughters, but the dowry prepared by the Liu family included fields and other properties—something not seen in years. This daughter of the Liu family rode in a bridal sedan transported by eight carriers, and the sedan itself was decorated on all sides with red silk; on each of its four corners hung a glass-beaded lamp with a large red silk ball hanging underneath. Most striking, though, was the coffin, which followed at the end of the procession. It had been given at least ten coats of paint, and the color was so deep and lustrous it was difficult to tell if it was red or black.

To include a coffin in a dowry was an even greater rarity—such was the impressive extent of the Liu family's consideration, presenting a dowry that provided for all of their daughter's expenses for the rest of her life, right down to her coffin.

The matchmaker said that back when they had made their visit, this daughter of the Liu family needed only give a word of assent, and she would have become Lin Xiangfu's wife.

She looked at Lin Xiangfu and, not without some regret, said to him, "What a pity—it would have been a wonderful match."

The matchmaker went on to tell him she'd heard that the Liu girl had worn a phoenix tiara atop her head, and her face had been covered by a red veil. She wore a red silk top covered by a red overgarment with floral embroidery, and below that was a red skirt, red pants, and red silk embroidered shoes. This daughter of the Liu family was dressed in red from head to toe. When she arrived in town and alighted from the bridal sedan at the vermillion gate of the Sun family residence, the crowd of onlookers all exclaimed at how exquisite she looked, like the bud of a peony bursting into bloom.

Lin Xiangfu tossed and turned on the kang that evening, unable to fall asleep. Every time he closed his eyes, he would see that young woman from the Liu family, dressed completely in red, stepping out of her bridal sedan and slowly walking toward him through the main hall. Then it became Xiaomei in a floral qipao, appearing outside the front gate at dusk. Scenes like this passed before his eyes as if they were blowing by in the breeze.

Lin Xiangfu thought of that length of satin. It was because he had taken it out of his satchel and placed it on the table in the main hall of the Liu family's home that he had missed that chance at marriage, leading instead to Xiaomei's abrupt arrival and departure. That length of satin floated around in his mind, impossible to forget. Finally he felt it must all have been predestined—it was his fate.

11.

A month before the wheat was harvested, Lin Xiangfu took a trip into town and had a few scythes made at the blacksmith's in preparation for the harvest. He also bought two lengths of satin—although Xiaomei had gone, he still had to face the future. He continued to follow the matchmaker around meeting potential brides, in search of a woman he could grow old with and who could continue the Lin family line. But this time he had to be sure to marry a respectable girl from a respectable family, and not some mysterious woman with an unknown background.

When he returned home, it was already dark. He saw that the kerosene lamp on the windowsill had been lit, and he heard the creaking sound of the loom. He was so startled at first he dropped the scythes he was carrying on the ground. His heart beat wildly as he walked a few steps into the house, still leading his donkey.

Xiaomei had returned. She was wearing that same floral qipao and sitting upright at the loom. She turned to the side and looked at Lin Xiangfu, the lamplight illuminating half of her lovely face, leaving the other half obscured in shadows.

Lin Xiangfu just stood there staring, still leading his donkey, not realizing he had led it into the house. He had the feeling she was smiling at him, but he couldn't make out her expression very clearly. After a few moments, as if talking to himself, he asked:

"Xiaomei?"

He heard Xiaomei's voice respond: "It's me."

"You've come back?" Lin Xiangfu asked.

Xiaomei nodded: "I've come back."

Lin Xiangfu watched her rise from the stool as he asked, "Did you bring back the big croakers?"

Xiaomei didn't answer, but slowly knelt. Lin Xiangfu continued to ask:

"The little croaker?"

Xiaomei shook her head. The donkey tossed its head, causing the bell to tinkle. Lin Xiangfu turned to look at the donkey, then shouted at Xiaomei:

"What are you doing coming back here? You stole the money my family had saved over generations and now have the nerve to come back here empty handed!"

Xiaomei trembled and kept her head lowered. The donkey tossed its head again, causing the bell to tinkle once more. In a rage, Lin Xiangfu turned to the donkey and shouted,

"Stop tossing your head!"

He turned back to look at Xiaomei trembling and kneeling on the floor. He felt confused. The room was completely silent. After a while, Lin Xiangfu sighed. Waving his hand, he said dejectedly,

"Get out of here now, before I start to really get angry. Go."

"I'm pregnant with your own flesh and blood," said Xiaomei softly.

Lin Xiangfu was shocked. He looked her carefully over and, noticing that her belly had already begun to protrude, found himself at a loss. He saw the imploring look in Xiaomei's eyes and heard the sound of her crying. For a long time he didn't know what to say. Finally he let out another sigh and said harshly:

"Get up."

Xiaomei didn't move and continued crying. Lin Xiangfu said at the top of his voice: "Stand up! I'm not going to help you—stand up on your own."

Trembling in fear, Xiaomei stood up. Wiping the tears from her eyes, she said to Lin Xiangfu: "I'm begging you—let me have the child here."

Lin Xiangfu waved his hand to stop her from saying any more. "Don't talk about this with me; say it to my parents."

In the still darkness of the night, they went to the cemetery at the eastern edge of the village. Lin Xiangfu was still leading his donkey, its bell tinkling crisply through the night air, though he didn't hear it—he had completely forgotten he was still leading the animal. When they arrived at his parents' grave, he pointed at their tombstone standing in the moonlight and said to Xiaomei:

"Kneel."

With one hand on her pregnant belly and the other groping down for the ground, she carefully lowered herself down and knelt. Lin Xiangfu waited for her to get settled and then said, "Say it."

Xiaomei nodded, propping herself up with both hands on the ground. Facing the tombstone of Lin Xiangfu's parents, illuminated by the moon, she began to speak:

"It's Xiaomei. I've come back . . . I would be too ashamed to come see you, but I'm pregnant with the Lin family's flesh and blood. Even though I deserve to die a thousand deaths, I still had to come back—if I broke the Lin family line, that would only add to my guilt. For the sake of this child, I'm asking you to forgive me this once. I'm carrying a descendent of the Lin family, and I couldn't not bring him back. I'm begging you to let me have the child in the Lin family home . . . "

After Xiaomei had sputtered this out through sobs, Lin Xiangfu said to her: "Get up."

She stood and wiped her tears. Lin Xiangfu began leading the donkey home, and Xiaomei followed behind. Only then did Lin Xiangfu hear the donkey's bell and realize he had been leading it all the while. He reached out and patted the animal, and said in a sad voice,

"You're the only one who's stayed with me this whole time."

Lin Xiangfu walked for a bit, then turned around to see Xiaomei struggling along behind, her head down with both hands supporting her belly. He stopped and waited, and when she had caught up, he hoisted her up onto the back of the donkey. At first Xiaomei was shocked; then she began sobbing. As Lin Xiangfu led the donkey forward, he heard her crying quietly on the animal's back. He sighed and said to her gently,

"You tricked me and ran off with my family's gold. I shouldn't take you back—but considering that you're already pregnant with my offspring, a new generation of the Lin family, I suppose . . . "

When he got to this point, Lin Xiangfu shook his head and said, "You never promised at my parents' grave—you never swore that from now on, you'll never leave again."

At that, he stopped and looked up at the starry sky, his mind a complete blank. Not until the donkey moved and jingled its bell did they resume their progress. When they had entered the courtyard, Lin Xiangfu turned around and lifted Xiaomei down off the donkey. As he was about to put her on the ground, he thought of the threshold—he hesitated, and then carried her over it.

Once he had gotten the donkey settled in for the night, he

walked over to the doorway of the inner room and watched Xiaomei's familiar movements as she took a blanket out of the wardrobe and spread it over the kang, where they had made such sweet memories in days gone by. After she had smoothed out the blanket, Xiaomei looked up and, seeing Lin Xiangfu standing in the doorway, was unable to suppress her smile.

"The gold?" Lin Xiangfu asked her.

Her smile vanished in an instant, and she lowered her head without a word.

Lin Xiangfu continued questioning: "Who did you give the gold to?"

She kept looking down in silence.

"Who is Aqiang to you?" Lin Xiangfu asked.

"My older brother," she replied hesitantly.

Lin Xiangfu turned around and left. It was a calm, quiet night. He sat silently on the little stool and stared at the loom, visible in the dim light of the kerosene lamp.

He sat for a long time without moving. Only when the lamp on the windowsill had burned all of its oil and the flame suddenly flickered out did he snap out of his stupor. Only the moonlight remained. Slowly he stood up, poured some more oil into the lamp and lit it, then carried it into the inner room.

Xiaomei was still sitting on the kang, both hands supporting her belly as she watched him uneasily. Lin Xiangfu looked through the hands on her belly and saw the child that would soon arrive in their midst. Softly, he said to her,

"Get some sleep."

"Okay," Xiaomei responded warmly.

She bent over and removed her cloth shoes, and then her socks. As she began to remove her jacket, Lin Xiangfu noticed that her feet were red and swollen. These two tiny bound feet had traveled such a long way, carrying his child back to him.

After Xiaomei crawled in under the covers, Lin Xiangfu put out the lamp, removed his overclothes, and lay down under his own blanket. Lin Xiangfu sensed that Xiaomei was turned towards him, sleeping on her side—that familiar breath had returned, still completely odorless, still fresh and clean as a morning breeze as it lightly brushed across his face. Then those familiar hands returned—one of them reached over under his blanket and grabbed his own hand. It was still soft and supple, only now it was trembling. Lin Xiangfu lay motionless, feeling Xiaomei's hand quivering in his own as if it were pouring her heart out. Gradually it calmed down, and the other hand, just as soft, made its way over and took his other hand.

When he was finally holding both her hands in his, he felt that Xiaomei had truly returned.

Her hands pulled his under her blanket and gently spread his fingers, placing them on her pregnant belly, where something struck the palm of his hand through the warmth of her skin. Startled, he cried out,

"Ah!"

"It's kicking you," Xiaomei said.

"Kicking me?" asked Lin Xiangfu.

"Your child is kicking you," Xiaomei giggled in the darkness.

Lin Xiangfu felt as if he were awakening from a dream. The baby inside Xiaomei's belly let loose a series of kicks against his palm, and Lin Xiangfu cried out in surprise,

"My god—it's kicking and punching!"

Lin Xiangfu began laughing, but then thought of his parents. If they were still living, they would have been able to share such a happy occasion.

His sadness passed and he said Xiaomei's name a few times, but there was no reply—exhausted from her travels, she had already fallen asleep. He kept one of his hands on her belly, feeling the baby kick, and with the other hand he cradled her face and murmured all of his most intimate thoughts and feelings. He told her how deeply sad and angry he had been after she left, and then said finally,

"Although you ran off with half of my family's gold and

didn't bring any of it back, you also didn't give birth to my child in some wild, faraway place—you brought my child back."

Then, after a little while, Lin Xiangfu added, "You also didn't greedily run off with all the gold; you even left behind more than you took."

12.

The news of Xiaomei's return spread like wildfire. Villagers came to Lin Xiangfu's home in a steady stream to have a look at Xiaomei's bulging belly, and with jolly laughs they offered their congratulations to the young mistress of the house. When she had been gone for months after returning to her parents' house, they had felt it was rather suspicious, but now that she was back, it all seemed only natural—it was a very long journey, after all, and Xiaomei was pregnant, so it seemed perfectly reasonable that the round-trip would take several months.

Beaming from ear to ear, Lin Xiangfu said to them: "When we got married before, we didn't have a bridal sedan or write out horoscope cards, so it doesn't count. So we're going to redo the wedding now—it doesn't have to be anything spectacular, but this time it has to be proper."

Lin Xiangfu went to a neighboring village and invited an old teacher at the private school to his house for an elaborate meal. After three rounds of drinks, the old man carefully took his seat and opened the gold-flecked paper of the folded horoscope card. He ground some ink from his black inkstick, which was bound with a red silken thread. Then he took up a calligraphy brush and wrote the characters "乾造"—"groom's horoscope"—on the top side of the card, followed by Lin Xiangfu's name, the time and date of his birth, and the characters "恭求", meaning that he was requesting a woman's hand in marriage. Then the old man changed brushes. On the bottom side of the card he wrote "坤造"—"bride's horoscope"—followed by Xiaomei's name, the time and date of her birth, and the characters "敬允", meaning that she had accepted the groom's proposal. When the time had come for the old man to write Xiaomei's name, he asked her what her surname was; Xiaomei hesitated and said it was Lin. When Lin Xiangfu exclaimed that Xiaomei was also named Lin, Xiaomei quietly said it hadn't been Lin, but that it would be from now on. Finally, on the side of the card the old man wrote: A hundred years of harmony; a happy couple by nature; forever united by the heart.

Lin Xiangfu took the horoscope card with both hands and reverently placed it on the shelf by the stove, praying to the kitchen god for eternal peace for the Lin family and an unbroken line.

Lin Xiangfu said to Xiaomei: "Most people leave it there for a few days or a week, but we'll leave ours there for a month. During this month, if all is well and everything remains peaceful in the home, and there are no accidents or misfortunes, it means our horoscopes are a good match and our fates are harmonious. But if we even so much as break a dish, it will mean we are ill-paired and have reached the end of our fated relationship."

The season for harvesting the wheat arrived. Lin Xiangfu said now that the wheat had ripened, they needed to make haste and gather it in. While he and the Tian brothers hadn't been going out to the fields every day, they now went out early in the morning and came home late in the evening, working alongside the tenant farmers.

Xiaomei rose early and stayed up late managing the housework. At midday, supporting her increasingly large belly, she would bring lunch out to the fields, but after two days Lin Xiangfu made her stop—he said it was too much in her condition. If she tripped and broke a bowl or two—without even mentioning the possible effects on her pregnancy—it would mean they were not destined to stay together as husband and wife. He warned Xiaomei not to forget about the horoscope card on the shelf by the stove. He said that usually when he harvested the wheat, he would hold the stalks with his left hand and use his right to cut them with speedy, swishing swings of his sickle. Now, though, he didn't dare make such speedy swings, but only carefully-aimed cuts. Why was this? Because of the horoscope card, he was afraid of slicing a finger.

From then on, the two of them were extremely cautious, afraid of having an accident during this crucial period. Although the days of harvest were exhausting, they passed by peacefully. One evening, as Lin Xiangfu lay his fatigued body down on the kang, Xiaomei walked over to him and quietly asked,

"Has my complexion looked okay these past few days?"

Lin Xiangfu said it had; her face looked nice and rosy.

Upon hearing this, Xiaomei said in a worried tone, "Everyone says that when a pregnant woman's complexion is thin and sallow, it means she's having a boy; if her complexion is ruddy and fresh, she's having a girl. You can also tell from the way she walks—if she lifts her left foot first she's having a boy; if she lifts her right foot first she's having a girl. These past few days I've mostly been starting off with my right foot. I'm afraid I'm only able to give you a daughter, not a son."

Lin Xiangfu saw the worried expression on Xiaomei's face and realized that for the past few days her brows had been constantly furrowed. He comforted her by saying they would only know for sure once the baby was born. When he saw her give a resigned nod, he said simply,

"Get some sleep."

With that he fell asleep, emitting deep, audible breaths. Late that night, Xiaomei took some of Lin Xiangfu's clothes out of the wardrobe and put them on, followed by his white headcloth, which she wrapped around her own head. Then she went out to the courtyard and walked slowly around the well, making circle after circle under the moonlight. She looked at the wide shadow her heavily clad figure cast on the ground, which had the appearance of a man. She had always heard about this method of changing the baby's sex in the womb—if she donned her husband's clothing and walked around the well while looking at her shadow, as long as she never looked back or let anyone know, the fetus would change from female to male.

For the next two nights, after Lin Xiangfu was asleep, Xiaomei would put on his clothes and go out to the courtyard. On the third night, Lin Xiangfu woke up. He reached over for Xiaomei but didn't feel her there; he groped around some more, but still came up with nothing. He bolted upright and discovered she was not in the kang. In shock, he thought she must have left him again. He leapt off the kang and ran barefoot into the courtyard, where he found her dressed in oversized clothes and walking around the well under the light of the moon. He immediately called out,

"Xiaomei!"

Xiaomei turned her head in surprise and stared at him. Lin Xiangfu walked up to her, saw the way she was dressed, and asked what she was doing. Xiaomei sighed and said she was changing the fetus—she wanted her baby girl to turn into a baby boy. With a disappointed smile, she said,

"Once someone sees you trying to change the fetus, it won't work."

Now that Lin Xiangfu understood, he hit himself on the head and let out a cry of regret. Xiaomei smiled and took his hands, then sat down on the edge of the well and said to him,

"Actually, changing the fetus only works during the first trimester—people say that during those months the fetus is just starting out; it hasn't yet taken shape and can still be changed. I'm nearly at seven months now, so even if you hadn't seen me, it would still have been very difficult to change the sex. But I just couldn't help myself—I still wanted to have a boy to carry on the Lin family line.

Lin Xiangfu was still kicking himself. He'd been sleeping so nicely—why did he have to wake up and ruin things? Xiaomei stood up and anxiously asked him,

"When you called out for me just now, did I turn my head to the left or right?"

Lin Xiangfu thought for a moment, then hesitated before saying, "I think you turned to the right."

Xiaomei hung her head and drew closer to him. Then she sat back down on the edge of the well and said, "Turning to the left would have indicated it's a boy, turning to the right means it's a girl. Now I'm sure of it—I'm pregnant with a girl. It's a shame I can't give you a boy, and I can't continue the Lin family line."

Lin Xiangfu hesitated again as he carefully thought things over. "On second thought," he said, "I think you might have turned to the left."

Xiaomei smiled, and Lin Xiangfu took her hands and said, "Actually, a girl would also be good; she will still be a descendant of the Lin family. Besides, you can always have a boy later on—having a boy later won't be too late. Take a look at the Tian family. There are five brothers—you could still give birth to five boys!"

Hearing this, she lowered her head in silence. The two of them sat for a while on the edge of the well; then Lin Xiangfu pulled Xiaomei up by the hand and they went back inside. After they lay down on the kang, Xiaomei took Lin Xiangfu's hands and held them in front of her chest—this was her preferred sleeping position. Lin Xiangfu told her that when he had woken up and discovered she was not on the kang, he broke out in a cold sweat, thinking she'd left again for good. As he said this he felt her hands tremble. He continued,

"You returned, but you didn't bring back a single bar of gold you took, and you haven't mentioned a word about where it might be. I assume it must be related to some difficult situation, so I haven't asked any more about it. But sometimes I still get the feeling you might leave again . . ."

Lin Xiangfu paused, then said in a firmer tone, "If you disappear again without saying anything, I'll come find you. I'll bring the child with me to the ends of the earth if I have to, but I'll come and find you."

After saying this, he realized that Xiaomei had brought his hands up to her face, and her tears were running down in between his fingers. They seemed to trickle down hesitantly, as if trying to find their way.

That afternoon, as Lin Xiangfu stood in a wheat field with a sickle in his hand, watching his shadow slowly lengthen under the sunlight, he estimated the time and figured it must be getting on in the afternoon. He put down his sickle, strode to the edge of the field, and headed home.

As soon as he went in the door, he eagerly asked Xiaomei: "Were there any accidents at home today? Did you break any dishes? Did any thread snap when you were using the loom?"

Confused, Xiaomei shook her head: "I didn't break any dishes, and no thread snapped on the loom."

Relieved, Lin Xiangfu picked up the horoscope card on the shelf by the stove and told Xiaomei that a month's time had already passed, and thankfully no accidents had occurred.

"It looks like our horoscopes match and our fates are harmonious," he said to her.

Supporting her belly with her left hand, Xiaomei slowly stood up from her stool at the loom and walked over to Lin Xiangfu. She took the horoscope card from him. As her eyes drifted over it, she heard Lin Xiangfu's relieved voice exclaim over her head:

"I was on pins and needles this whole month!"

13.

After the wheat had been harvested and laid out to dry, Lin Xiangfu and the Tian brothers selected some nice large stalks with big ears loaded with grain, threshed them, and spread it all out in the courtyard to dry in the sun. Xiaomei sat in the doorway making baby clothes, looking up from time to time to see them working. They burned the stalks, mixed the ashes with the seed grain, and poured the mixture into vats. Then Lin Xiangfu stood up and said to Xiaomei, "After the White Dew, which falls around the eighth month, we'll spread the seeds in the fields." Xiaomei held up the baby clothes she had just finished and said,

"By that time, these clothes will have a little one in them!"

Lin Xiangfu walked over and took the clothes from Xiaomei as gingerly as if he were receiving the child itself. He held them up and examined them, then broke out into laughter.

Lin Xiangfu and the Tian brothers moved the vats inside and arranged them neatly; then they went out to the fields and planted some sorghum and corn. After that, Lin Xiangfu felt everything was in order, and the next few days could be devoted to preparing for the wedding.

Lin Xiangfu stayed home and once again took up residence in his wood shop. He had the Tian brothers move all of the finished items out so he could set to work on the old furniture in the house—the tables, chairs, stools, wardrobes, and chests. When he had finished his banging and pounding, everything looked brand new. When Xiaomei looked up from her perch in the doorway where she was still making baby clothes, she exclaimed in surprise,

"Oh my!"

Lin Xiangfu hired two painters from a neighboring village. They sanded all the furniture and covered it with several coats of paint until everything shone. Xiaomei said it was as smooth and shiny as a mirror.

Lin Xiangfu wanted to have the wedding when it looked like the White Dew was just about to arrive, before they sowed the wheat. He hired a tailor to make Xiaomei a red top, red pants, a red skirt, and red embroidered shoes. When the tailor saw that Xiaomei was nine months pregnant, he shook his head. He said the embroidered shoes he could make, but not the top, pants, or skirt—they would just come out ill-fitting and unpresent-able. Xiaomei said don't bother with the top, pants, or skirt—just make a red robe big enough to cover her whole body.

The tailor made the red robe and embroidered shoes. After he left, Lin Xiangfu said to Xiaomei, "This time you have to ride in a bridal sedan."

Lin Xiangfu summoned the Tian brothers, and the six of them together flipped over a square table and fashioned it into a sedan chair. The four table legs became the four posts of the sedan, while the tabletop became the floor. Bamboo poles were lashed along two sides, and on the ends of those were lashed two carrying poles to hoist the sedan. A red cloth was hung around on all sides from the feet of the table, which were adorned with red decorative toppers. Lastly some wheat straw was spread over the floor of the sedan, on top of which was placed a square cushion. In under four hours—or less than two *shichen*—a bridal sedan with four carriers appeared before Xiaomei's eyes.

Lin Xiangfu chose an auspicious date for Xiaomei to mount this bridal sedan made from a table. A small stool had been placed inside, and although it was quite difficult, with Lin Xiangfu's support she was able to enter and sit down. Four of the Tian brothers then lifted the sedan and went out through Lin Xiangfu's gate.

The sunlight that day was radiant. Lin Xiangfu said they should go to the main road outside the village. They continued on for some distance, Tian Da leading the way, the sedan chair creaking as they followed the little path. Lin Xiangfu followed behind the sedan, and the villagers followed behind him. When the procession made it to the main road, the dust began fly-ing—there were over a hundred villagers crowded together as they made their way toward Lizhuang. A surprised passerby inquired,

"Who is in this bridal sedan?"

"It's the legendary beauty Diao Chan," the Tian brothers responded.

As they approached Lizhuang, Xiaomei began moaning loudly inside the sedan—*aiyo, aiyo!* The Tian brothers immediately stopped and called back for Lin Xiangfu. They said the young mistress couldn't hold it in any longer; she was about to give birth—all women moan like that when they're in labor.

That can't be right, said the passerby—women in labor sound more like "*aiya.*"

You know shit, said Tian Da, they only say "*aiya*" after they've given birth.

Lin Xiangfu anxiously ran up and stuck his head inside the sedan. His face was beet-red when he looked in, but pale white when it brought it back out. With a quiver in his voice, he said, "She's having it."

The four Tian brothers ran like mad down the main road with the bridal sedan, with Tian Da and Lin Xiangfu leading the way. They ran toward Lizhuang, where there was a particularly well-known midwife.

Xiaomei kept on moaning in the sedan as sweat poured like rain from the six sprinting men. Lin Xiangfu spurred them on as he ran in front, shouting to the four sedan carriers that they were slower than turtles. The four men didn't utter a word, but merely panted through strained faces as they ran. After running about two *li,* Lin Xiangfu was growing so impatient he called for the sedan carriers to halt; he then hoisted Xiaomei out of the sedan himself and flew with her down the road. Tian Da had his four brothers follow behind with the empty sedan. Then he said he would switch off with the young master and ran on ahead.

Tian Da wasn't able to catch up. Even with Xiaomei in his arms, it was as if Lin Xiangfu's feet had sprouted wings; Tian Da, who wasn't carrying anyone, couldn't go fast enough to reach them. The four Tian brothers running with the sedan receded even farther into the distance. Lin Xiangfu ran past a patch of forest and turned a corner, at which point he could no longer see any of the others.

By the time the five Tian brothers made it to the door of the midwife's house in Lizhuang, Lin Xiangfu was already standing there drenched in sweat, looking like he'd just been fished out of the water with two puddles pooled around his feet. He stared at the Tian brothers as they ran up to him, set down the sedan chair, and collapsed one by one on the ground, gasping for breath like they were working a bellows. Just then, a baby's cry came from the room. Lin Xiangfu's face twitched a few times, as if he were trying to laugh and cry at the same time. A little while later, the midwife emerged with a smile on her face and announced,

"It's a beautiful baby girl!"

14.

Three days after Xiaomei gave birth, the midwife brought some mugwort and prickly ash over to Lin Xiangfu's house and cooked up a medicinal soup. She poured the hot soup into a wooden bowl and sprinkled in some peanuts and dates. Then she added the baby, which she washed in this herbal concoction. The midwife said it was necessary to cleanse the baby and ward off misfortune.

After one month, the midwife came again, this time with a barber in tow, as well as a large number of villagers. With a shiny blade, the barber shaved the baby's hair and eyebrows, which Xiaomei carefully gathered up in a piece of red cloth. Lin Xiangfu carried the hairless infant into the courtyard, where the sunlight glinted off the baby's smooth head like a ball of glass. The villagers were full of laughter and smiles.

Summer slipped away and autumn quickly approached. One morning in the tenth month, Lin Xiangfu awoke before dawn to the sound of the baby's incessant crying. He called out a few times for Xiaomei, but when there was no response, he got up and lit the lamp. His heart gave a thud as he looked over at the kang and discovered Xiaomei wasn't there. He picked up the lamp and went outside calling for her, but to no avail.

He realized it had happened again. He opened the wardrobe and saw that her clothes were gone and her cloth shoes were no longer under the bed. He immediately took out the wooden box from the interior wall and found that the ten big croakers and three little croakers were all still there, wrapped in their red cloth—this time, Xiaomei hadn't taken a single bar of gold.

The baby was crying so hard she began choking, and Lin Xiangfu rushed over. He saw that the headscarf with the "phoenix and peony" pattern was tucked around the baby's swaddle, and a bowl of congee had been placed beside her. Lin Xiangfu scooped up the baby, took a drink of congee, and then fed it to her from his own mouth.

When his daughter had fallen asleep again, Lin Xiangfu went outside and sat on the edge of the well until daybreak. He thought of his past with Xiaomei—how she had worn his clothing and walked around the well under the moonlight in hopes of changing the baby's sex; how she had sat on the edge of the kang and carefully collected the baby's hair that the barber cut off . . . When the first rays of the morning sun touched Lin Xiangfu's face, he got up and went inside, scooped his daughter up off the kang, and took her out the back door to Tian Da's place so they could watch her for a bit. Then he returned home, took the red-wrapped parcel of gold bars out of the wooden box, and set off for town, walking briskly in the morning sunshine.

In town, he went to the *qianzhuang* bank and mortgaged his 476 *mu* of land for a wad of cash. He exchanged his gold bars for cash as well, except for one little croaker, which he exchanged for silver yuan. Then he went to a tailor and had some baby clothes made—two sets for each season, made slightly on the large side. He also had them make a couple of bags and said he would be back in two days to collect it all. It was already late in the evening by the time he returned to the village. He went to Tian Da's house to fetch his daughter and had Tian Da follow him home. When the two men reached Lin Xiangfu's house, they sat by the weak light of the kerosene lamp while Lin Xiangfu told Tian Da everything that had happened. Tian Da was so shocked he could hardly close his gaping mouth.

Lin Xiangfu said that in three days, he would take his daughter and go searching for Xiaomei. He said he had already taken a three-year mortgage out on his land; he hadn't mortgaged his house, but instead wanted Tian Da to move in with his family and look after the place. He told Tian Da that after he found Xiaomei, he would send a letter. If he didn't receive one within two years, it meant he had died in some distant place, and the house would become theirs; after the three-year mortgage period, the land would have a new owner. After saying all this, he passed the deed to the house over to Tian Da.

As Tian Da—this man who had once carried Lin Xiangfu all over the village on his back—listened to what Lin Xiangfu said, his eyes filled with tears. Holding the deed in his hand, Tian Da said,

"Young master, take me with you—have someone to look after you on your journey."

Lin Xiangfu shook his head and said, "You just look after the house and fields for me."

A tear from Tian Da's eyes fell onto the deed, which he carefully dried with his worn sleeve. Again he begged Lin Xiangfu,

"Young master, take me with you—my brothers and I will be too worried about you out there all alone."

Lin Xiangfu held up his hands and said, "You can go home now."

"Yes, young master," Tian Da answered and respectfully stood up, wiping the tears from his eyes as he left.

Three days later, Lin Xiangfu placed his sleeping daughter in a cotton sack and strapped a large bundle onto his back. He set out before sunrise, leading his donkey. The first place he went was his parents' grave at the eastern edge of the village, where he knelt down and said to them,

"Father, Mother, I've wronged you, and I've wronged our ancestors. I've mortgaged our family's land, and I'm setting out to go find Xiaomei. Father, Mother, your granddaughter wants milk; she can't be without a mother—I'm going to go find Xiaomei and bring her back. Father, Mother, I swear to you right here, right now, that I'll be back . . ."

15.

Lin Xiangfu headed south, carrying his daughter in a cotton sack at his chest. His bundle he placed on the back of the donkey, which he led by the reins down the dusty, bumpy road. He searched for any information about Xiaomei's whereabouts, asking if anyone had seen a young woman wearing a grayish blue tunic and skirt. He also sought out nursing mothers, from whom he could beg a little milk for his hungry daughter.

After two days of traveling, Lin Xiangfu came to the banks of the Yellow River. An old ferryman informed him that he could take people across the river, but not donkeys: the wind and waves were too high, and the donkey wouldn't be able to stand on the goatskin raft—it would fall overboard. Lin Xiangfu watched the river water flowing by, carrying some chunks of ice that were bobbing up and down and crashing into each other. The goatskin raft was also bobbing up and down in the water, coming in and out of view. He looked down at his infant daughter sleeping soundly at his chest, a bit of drool hanging from the corner of her mouth. Lin Xiangfu looked up and asked the ferryman where he could find a courier station with donkeys. The ferryman said there was one nearby, along the river about one *li* to the east.

Lin Xiangfu took his donkey and sold it to a man at the courier station. Then he said he would also like to buy some fodder. The man gave Lin Xiangfu a strange look—he just sold his donkey, why did he want to buy fodder? Lin Xiangfu said that the donkey had been with him for five years; it had been his companion, and he wanted to feed it one last time. The man took out some wheat straw, but Lin Xiangfu shook his head and said he didn't want those coarse stalks—he wanted the premium selection. The man gave him another strange look and asked what kind of premium selection—green grass? Hay? Wheat bran? Lin Xiangfu passed him a copper and said he would take some of each.

As the sun set in the west, Lin Xiangfu squatted on the ground, his daughter still strapped to his chest, and stirred the feed into an even mixture. The man stood beside him and chuckled, saying he had never seen anyone mix fodder for so long.

Lin Xiangfu laughed as well and replied, "There's an old saying—'whether or not you've got a lot, mix well every bit you've got.'"

Then Lin Xiangfu turned and spoke to the donkey: "I would never have sold you, but you can't make it across the river, so I have to leave you behind. You've stayed with me for five years: plowing fields; turning the grindstone; transporting people; pulling carts; carrying loads—you did it all. From now on, though, you'll follow someone else. Take good care of yourself."

Night had nearly fallen by the time Lin Xiangfu left the courier station and boarded the goatskin raft to cross the Yellow River. As the raft bobbed up and down with the waves, he used one hand to hold on tightly to the cotton sack holding the baby at his chest, and with the other he gripped his bundle. The ferryman knelt in front, wielding his oar as he rowed them along. Waves buffeted the raft and soaked Lin Xiangfu's clothes. Looking out through droplets of water, he could see that night was about to envelop the endless stretches of land on both sides of the river, and that a crescent moon rose in the boundless sky. From time to time, the baby's cries broke through the sound of the crashing waves.

After crossing the Yellow River, Lin Xiangfu continued south. From that point on, the sound of horses' hooves marked his travels as he changed from one horse-drawn wagon to another, ranging from twelve horses harnessed in three groups of four to just three horses with one in front and two behind. The cracking of the drivers' whips and their shouts of "*Jia! Pa! He!*" were constant. Without so much as looking, Lin Xiangfu knew that when the driver shouted "*Wu, wu!*" they would turn left; when he shouted "*E, e!*" they would turn right; when he shouted "*Yue, yue!*" they were headed up a slope; and when he shouted "*Dai, dai!*" they were crossing over a stone threshold in the road.

He stayed in countless inns with a wide variety of names. He stayed at a small, spartan inn with a wicker strainer hanging out front, where he had to share a sleeping mat with some traveling peddlers; he stayed at an inn with a round frame with cloth streamers attached hanging out front, where he sat cross-legged with some carters and porters; he stayed at an inn with a sign advertising pear-shaped buns hanging out front, where he chatted with some men who were transporting draft animals; he stayed at a large inn with seven round frames with red streamers hanging out front, where he had a polite exchange with a man who sold gold teeth.

He crossed numerous hanging bridges, pontoon bridges, beam bridges, and stone arch bridges, following the Grand Canal south; he arrived at the Yangtze along with winter. After crossing the river, he no longer continued due south, but began wandering the area, going from one Jiangnan river town to another. He passed through over twenty towns, and through winter and spring. Everywhere he went, he would ask about a place called Wencheng—Xiaomei's town. Yet everyone he asked looked completely baffled.

One day after spring had turned into summer, he made his way to a town called Shendian. He aimlessly wandered down the flagstone street until it abruptly ended at the wharf.

A young boatman was standing on the stern of his boat, loudly talking and laughing with a young woman on the shore. Their rapid cadence struck a chord with Lin Xiangfu—although he didn't understand what they were saying, he could tell it was the same accent Xiaomei and Aqiang had spoken in when they first appeared at his door. He had the feeling he had arrived in Wencheng. The boatman saw Lin Xiangfu standing there and asked if he needed a boat. Lin Xiangfu mounted it unsteadily, stooped under the bamboo awning, and sat down in the cabin. He saw a grass mat spread on the red-painted planks of the deck, along with two pillows made of bamboo and wood. The young boatman asked where he was headed, and Lin Xiangfu replied:

"Wencheng."

"Wencheng?"

A confused expression spread over the boatman's face; it was a look to which Lin Xiangfu had already grown quite accustomed. He knew the boatman had never heard of such a place, but the accent he'd heard him speaking in just then gave him cause for hope. He asked the boatman where he lived.

"Xizhen," he replied.

Lin Xiangfu asked, What kind of place is Xizhen? The boatman said that as soon as you opened your door, there was water; if you wanted to go anywhere you had to use a boat. This struck another chord with Lin Xiangfu—he recalled that Aqiang had once described his hometown the same way. So he said,

"Take me to Xizhen."

16.

As the evening light reflected on the surface of the water, Lin Xiangfu sat in the boat holding his infant daughter. He thought about removing the large bundle from his back, but it provided him with some comfortable padding when he leaned back, so he left it on. He instead took off the cloth sack hanging around his chest and let his daughter lay stretched out on his legs. He reached up and pulled back the bamboo awning, letting the evening summer breeze blow against him.

The boatman sat in the stern, his back leaning against an upright board and an oar tucked under his left arm, slicing through the water and helping him steer as he peddled with his two bare feet. Lin Xiangfu listened to the smooth swishing of the paddle wheel and watched the other small boats with bamboo awnings as they made their way over the waves. In his right hand the boatman held a wine flask, from which he would take a drink of rice wine as he wiggled and stretched his feet. Then he would reach his left hand over to a plate sitting on the edge of the boat, pick up a soybean, and drop it in his mouth.

The evening rays turned the clear sky a fiery red. Plow oxen mooed on both sides of the river as they returned home from the fields, and the smoke from cooking fires curled upwards. Lin Xiangfu began to let his imagination take flight—he saw Xiaomei sitting on the threshold of a northern courtyard, holding their daughter, her grayish blue tunic and the baby's swaddle both turned red by the light of the setting sun. Lin Xiangfu was returning from town, leading his donkey with one hand and holding a stick of candied haw berries in the other. He walked up to Xiaomei and handed the haw berries to her, and she held them up to their daughter's lips. This was the last memory Lin Xiangfu had of Xiaomei—before the sun had come up the next morning, she was gone.

A loud noise suddenly shattered Lin Xiangfu's reverie. What had moments ago been a clear sky pierced by rays of evening sunlight had now turned black with cracks of thunder and bolts of lightning. As the wind and rain descended on them, he saw the boatman's frightened eyes darting around through the pelting rain. Then Lin Xiangfu looked up and saw the funnel-shaped cloud of a tornado barreling toward them, dust and debris whirling through the air; it was almost as if the rain was pouring upwards from the earth into the sky. Just then the two folded-up bamboo awnings tore away from the boat and sailed through the air as if they had taken wing. The boatman cried out, "tornado!" and jumped in the water, his right hand still gripping his wine flask.

The boatman had fled for his life, but Lin Xiangfu couldn't jump in the water with a baby strapped to his chest. He could only remain in the boat and hold on to her tightly with both hands. He felt his clothing lift up from his body, as if it were trying to pull him up into the air. He crossed his legs, shut his eyes, and bent forward, protecting his daughter at his chest and resisting the pull of his clothing. The large, heavy bundle at his back now became his staunchest ally, united with him in resisting flight.

The little boat flew into the air like an arrow shot from a bow. After remaining airborne for a time, it dropped back down on the water and skidded forward. His daughter's wails from the sack at his chest disappeared in the roar of the tornado, along with the sound of his pounding heart.

The boat no longer glided forward, but knocked and bumped its way along. When he opened his eyes, Lin Xiangfu saw that trees were uprooted, and debris was still flying through the air—the other little boats with bamboo awnings had blown up on land, while roofs from the houses on shore were now in the water. The boat was in tatters—the deck had split apart in the wind. She knew he wasn't actually sitting in the boat, but on a floating plank of wood. Then that plank broke apart and his body rose up in the gale, his clothing billowing out like a sail. He felt like he was flying, but also like he was charging forward, leaping over roofs and walls as if he were in a martial arts novel. Finally he crashed into something, fell down, and passed out.

The tornado had moved on, and the summer night gradually receded. Lin Xiangfu found himself waking up in a field of flattened rice, greeting the dawn with the rest of the earth as the sky gradually lightened, a few scattered clouds vigorously racing across it.

With a start, Lin Xiangfu moved his hand to his chest and realized that neither the cloth sack nor his daughter were there. He stood up with a cry, but a heavy weight on his back pulled him back down to the ground; he reached back to discover his enormous bundle was still there. Propping himself up with both hands, he managed to get to his feet. Anxiously he looked around, but saw no sign of the cloth sack or his daughter—only a piece of broken plank from the boat stuck in the paddy field. The field itself was a total mess of vegetation: the trees at the edges had all flown away, with only a few muddy pits left behind as markers of their misfortune.

Lin Xiangfu began running around and shouting frantically, desperately searching for his daughter. He saw that the wind had carried him about two or three *li* from the water, and that a rooftop and a few large, broken trees had accompanied him on this journey.

He could not find her. Wailing loudly, he made his way over those large trees, blown in from who knows where, tangled together and propping up an empty roof frame. He walked toward the distant water, looking around in every direction; yet he felt as if he were wandering blindly, unable to see anything at all. He ran screaming and crying to the water's edge, where he stopped and looked out over the vast expanse glistening in the morning light. Trees, pieces of boats, furniture, and clothes floated everywhere . . . He stood facing the water and shouted, but the only thing he heard in return was his own echo. He noticed that clothing and household objects were slowly sinking beneath the water's surface, while the trees and boat planks remained floating on top.

Lin Xiangfu stood there for a long time, his loud wails gradually giving way to quiet sobs. He wiped the tears from his eyes and walked away, feeling in that moment that he had lost his daughter. He trembled all over, staggering as he walked.

Continuing to look around in every direction, his vision blurred by tears, he kept trying to call out, but every time he opened his mouth no sound would come out. He stumbled and fell over some sort of structure, and when he tried to crawl up, his hands could find nothing to grip. He fell again, and this time after groping around he found the rough trunk of a tree; finally he was able to prop himself up. Standing once again, he blinked a few times and wiped his eyes, then discovered he had circled right back to where he'd started. He walked over to the trees that were propping up the roof and realized that this hollow frame of a roof was what had initially caused him to trip.

That was when he spotted his cloth sack hanging from a branch of one of the fallen trees, just under the roof. He blinked a few times; the sack was still there. A gust of wind blew a few of the roof's remaining strands of thatching past the top of the sack. He smiled nervously and looked around as if he were seeking a second opinion, then carefully stepped in the empty roof frame and unevenly made his way step by step to that branch on which he'd hung all his hope. He took the sack and held it in front of his chest.

His daughter was in the sack, her eyes tightly closed. He nervously reached out a finger and held it under her nose, at which point the sleeping baby yawned. Lin Xiangfu smiled through his tears.

He hung the sack in front of his chest and carefully protected it with both hands. Standing with both feet inside the roof frame, he looked at his surroundings—it seemed as if everything around him had been rinsed clean. This was the first time he really looked at this vast expanse of land known as the Wanmudang. The rising sun bathed the scene of destruction in a red light.

Lin Xiangfu left the roof and started with big strides down a small path. An enormous smile on his face, he unconsciously imitated the tone of the matchmaker back in his hometown and said to his sleeping daughter,

"So it's possible for such a thing to happen—you can yawn while you're sleeping."

With the giant bundle on his back and both hands protecting his baby daughter in the sack at his chest, Lin Xiangfu set off over the flattened rice and weeds toward a collection of buildings off in the distance.

Lin Xiangfu entered the town of Xizhen, where the trees had lost their leaves and the roofs had lost their tiles. He took out the "phoenix and peony" headscarf Xiaomei had left behind and wrapped it around his daughter's head. The first person he came across in Xizhen was Chen Yongliang. Because Lin Xiangfu was still so elated at having found his daughter, the man Chen Yongliang saw approaching him in the morning light did not look like a man fleeing disaster, but a joyous father.

17.

Lin Xiangfu kept his hands around the sack containing his daughter as he walked through the ruined streets of Xizhen. When he listened carefully to the accent of the villagers, it was as if he were listening to a conversation between Aqiang and Xiaomei.

He noticed blue calico headscarves and lots of wooden clogs on the street. After the young women washed their feet in the river, they would put on their wooden clogs and clop down the flagstone street. The sound made Lin Xiangfu think of Xiaomei walking across the floor of his northern home. Xiaomei had said the sound was like a xylophone, and during the evenings in Xizhen Lin Xiangfu often heard this xylophone-like sound.

Lin Xiangfu felt this place was very much like the Wencheng that Aqiang had mentioned, and several times he asked people, "Is this Wencheng?"

The response he got was always the same: "This is Xizhen."

"Where is Wencheng?" Lin Xiangfu would then ask.

Lin Xiangfu would then be met with a perplexed look, followed by a decisive shake of the head—no one here knew anything about a Wencheng. After crossing the Yangtze on his search for Xiaomei, every place he went he'd been met with this same puzzled look and this same shake of the head—no one knew where Wencheng was. As he stood there on the street in Xizhen looking lost, a feeling of failure enveloped him.

A familiar-looking figure drifted past amongst the crowd, like the fallen leaf of a tree blowing across a patch of weeds. A few moments passed, and, as if waking from a dream, Lin Xiangfu realized the figure seemed a lot like Xiaomei. He turned around and immediately set off after it, the head of his sleeping daughter lightly bumping against his chest. He slowed his pace a bit and proceeded more carefully, cradling the baby's head with his right hand.

The figure came in and out of view in the crowd ahead, and several times she looked back at Lin Xiangfu. He couldn't get a clear look at her face, but what he could see was a floral patterned qipao, which had a different color and pattern from Xiaomei's. Yet her figure was that of Xiaomei's, though slightly skinnier and more delicate. As he followed her, he thought to himself: Xiaomei's grown thinner.

By the time Lin Xiangfu had made his way to the wharf and entered a narrow lane, the figure was gone—he had seen her turn in this lane, but now she had suddenly disappeared. He stood for a while at the entrance to the lane before entering. As he walked past a door that was slightly ajar, he heard a creak, and the door opened—the woman in the floral qipao was standing there in the dim light just inside the doorway. She smiled at Lin Xiangfu and said something, but he couldn't understand her rapid accent. He knew that she was the figure he'd seen, and he also knew that it wasn't Xiaomei.

As Lin Xiangfu stood there glumly, the woman repeated what she'd just said: "Come in."

This time Lin Xiangfu understood, and he stared woodenly at the smiling woman standing inside. Again she repeated, "Come in."

Lin Xiangfu didn't know why she was greeting him so warmly, but he went in anyway. There was a strong smell of fish as he followed her up the stairs and into a room. She shut the door and bolted it, then invited Lin Xiangfu to have a seat.

Lin Xiangfu didn't realize he was with a prostitute. He sat in the chair and looked at her in confusion. She looked at the baby in the sack in front of his chest and smiled—it was the first she'd ever seen someone bring a baby with them to visit a prostitute. She opened the wardrobe and took out a cotton blanket, which she spread on the table. Then she smiled and said to Lin Xiangfu:

"Give the little one to me."

She removed the sack from the flummoxed Lin Xiangfu, took the baby out, and placed her on the blanket. Then she smiled at Lin Xiangfu and removed her floral qipao, folded it, and placed it on a stand by the bed. When she started taking off her underwear, Lin Xiangfu realized where he was. Just then the baby started crying—she was hungry.

This woman with Xiaomei's figure was then faced with a very flustered man. Lin Xiangfu practically leapt from his chair and scooped up the baby crying on the table. In two steps he was at the door, which he tugged at a few times before realizing he hadn't unbolted it. After sliding open the deadbolt, his anxious footsteps could be heard flying down the stairs; then they anxiously came running back up. Red-faced and clutching the baby to his chest, he went back in the room and placed a few copper coins in the chair he'd just been sitting in. Then he turned around and left, his anxious footsteps once again pounding down the staircase and disappearing into the small lane outside.

18.

For several days afterwards, Lin Xiangfu continued wandering the streets of Xizhen, constantly searching. He spotted a few familiar-looking figures, but he never laid eyes on Xiaomei's face.

The battered houses in Xizhen had battered, waist-high gates in front of their doors, now mostly in bits and pieces from the tornado. Lin Xiangfu had heard Xiaomei speak of these short gates, so he knew their purpose was to keep pigs and dogs out of the house. He saw that many people had placed bowls of fresh water outside their doors, and some had hung black gauze from their doorframes. These homes had lost someone to the tornado.

Seeing these bowls of water brought back painful memories of Lin Xiangfu's parents. He had once placed two bowls of water outside his own door: one for his mother, and one for his mother to give to his father.

After the disaster, life in Xizhen returned to normal. Although Lin Xiangfu could still hear the quiet tears of women and the sighs of men, their sadness seemed as serene as a gentle breeze. He felt that Xizhen treated people kindly—whenever his daughter became hungry and cried, someone would always come forward and lead them to the home of a breastfeeding woman. When he was leaving town, a woman he didn't recognize approached him with a basket and gave him some red silk clothing for the baby, along with a hat and shoes. Before Lin Xiangfu had recovered from his surprise to say something, the woman had already gone. He watched as she hurriedly walked away without looking back, guessing that she had lost a baby in the tornado—now she had passed down its clothing to him.

Outside the town, people were harvesting what was left of the damaged crops; they were standing fallen trees back up in the muddy soil, pulling their boats back into the water, and rebuilding their thatched roofs. Although the brick houses in town hadn't collapsed in the tornado, the tiles on their roofs had all blown away, so a number of ceramic kilns had sprung up outside town, their chimneys stretching upwards like a stand of fir trees.

When autumn winds began blowing down the first leaves from the trees, Lin Xiangfu carried his baby daughter out of Xizhen. For the next three months he traveled south, resuming his search for Wencheng. All along the way he continued asking, but still no one had heard of it. Wencheng became a purely imaginary place in Lin Xiangfu's mind. He continued traveling south, but the further south he went, the stranger the accent became, sounding less like Aqiang and Xiaomei. So he decided to stop this southward journey. He sat down on a bridge and carefully thought things over for a long while. Of all the places he had been, he felt that Xizhen seemed most like the Wencheng that Aqiang had spoken of.

He realized that Aqiang's Wencheng wasn't real, and that, in all likelihood, neither were the names Aqiang and Xiaomei.

After all of the untold hardship he had suffered, Lin Xiangfu hadn't found Xiaomei. A feeling of desolation crept over his heart, and he thought of returning home. He thought of his donkey with its red tassel and tinkling bell, and he thought of his fields and his house. He felt the cash hidden in his daughter's clothing and patted the silver yuan hidden in his, and he imagined crossing the Yellow River, finding the courier station, buying back his donkey, and redeeming the mortgage on his land.

But then his daughter changed his mind. As he was standing on the bridge, supporting her with his right hand and trying to move her over to his left, he felt her legs stiffen as if she were trying to stand on her own. Standing there on the bridge, he let out a laugh. It was only the second time he had laughed since leaving his home for the south—the first had been when he found his daughter after losing her in the tornado.

Lin Xiangfu decided he would return to Xizhen. His

daughter needed a mother, he needed Xiaomei, and he believed that the Wencheng Aqiang had told him about was actually Xizhen. Even though he had no idea where Aqiang and Xiaomei were at the moment, he believed there would always come a day when they would return to Xizhen, and he would wait there, day in and day out, for them to appear.

Lin Xiangfu turned around and headed back north. By the time the first snowflakes of winter were fluttering through the air, he had made it back to Xizhen.

19.

This snow turned into a blizzard that lasted for eighteen days. When the first flakes started falling, no one in Xizhen realized it was the beginning of another disaster—they simply thought it was the first snow of the season. Although the snowflakes fell like goose down and quickly covered the roofs and streets in a layer of white, everyone assumed it would stop before the next morning, when the sun would come up and slowly melt the accumulated snow. But the snow did not stop, and the sun did not shine on Xizhen. For the next eighteen days, the snow fell without ceasing. Sometimes it was heavy, sometimes it slackened off, and sometimes it even stopped for a few brief moments, but the gray pallor of the sky never changed, and it enveloped Xizhen for days on end.

Lin Xiangfu clutched his daughter as he trudged with increasing difficulty through the ever-deepening snow, searching for milk. After rolling up the lower hem of his long padded coat, he held his daughter in the cotton sack at his chest and set off, his calves sinking down in the snow as flakes flew through the air and clung to his hair and clothing, silently engulfing him in white.

Lin Xiangfu made his way down the deserted street, his daughter hungry and crying at his chest. As he forced his way through the snow, he listened carefully for the sounds of a baby crying in any of the houses along the street—if he heard it, he would go knock on the door.

After entering a house he would hold out his right hand, a copper coin laying in his palm, and look imploringly at the breastfeeding woman. The woman's husband would take the coins from his hand, indicating their agreement, and a look of gratitude would flash briefly over Lin Xiangfu's face. He would then remove the baby from the sack at his chest and pass her over. When he saw his daughter finally reach the warmth of the woman's breast, he would feel a warm current pass through his own body. The sight of her little hands moving over the woman's breast would bring tears to his eyes; he knew she had latched on, like someone who'd just found their footing.

In this frozen Xizhen, each morning unfolded under a gray sky, and each evening faded into a black night with neither moon nor stars, as if the whole town had fallen into a dark abyss.

The people of Xizhen began to feel like the swirling snow-flakes would never stop coming down, like they would persist for the rest of their lives. A general mood of depression seeped into their houses and took hold of them, and they began to wonder aloud if they would live long enough to see the sun again. This feeling spread like the plague, and when Lin Xiangfu would enter people's homes, the men of Xizhen would ask him pitifully,

"When will this snow ever stop?"

Lin Xiangfu could only shake his head; he didn't know. He walked all over Xizhen carrying his daughter at his chest, tapping on door after door. The women of Xizhen faced the snow with a bit more strength and composure than the men. While their faces wore the same numb expressions, they still managed their households just as before. It was their activity in their homes that gave Lin Xiangfu the feeling there was still some life in this frozen town.

One day, Lin Xiangfu came to the home of the head of the local chamber of commerce, Gu Yimin. Gu Yimin's business ventures were expansive and varied—not only was he the head of the local *qianzhuang* bank and the goldmine in the western hills, but he had also opened a number of silk shops in Xizhen and Shendian that were frequented by silk brokers from Shanghai, Suzhou, and Hangzhou. These shops had a leg up on the competition, because they would send the sales clerks parading through the streets with sample fabrics to drum up business.

The first time Lin Xiangfu laid eyes on this man in his thirties, he hadn't known he was such a figure of authority in Xizhen. The cries of a baby had lead Lin Xiangfu to this imposing courtyard mansion. After passing a long, high wall that surrounded the residence, he saw that snow was piled high on the giant trees on the other side. The large red door was slightly ajar, leaving a crack that allowed him to see that the interior courtyard had been swept clean of snow. The baby's cries were still coming from inside, so after hesitating for a moment, he decided to go in.

He entered the cavernous main hall, where two sturdy round pillars held up the beams overhead. Around a dozen people were sitting in chairs on either side, and six charcoal braziers had been set out in two rows providing them with some warmth. A thin, swarthy man was seated in the position of the host. They were discussing something, but when they saw Lin Xiangfu enter they all stopped talking and looked with surprise at this uninvited guest. Lin Xiangfu held out a copper coin in his right hand and stated the reason he had come. Gu Yimin— that thin, swarthy man—turned his head and said to a servant,

"Call in the wetnurse."

The servant left and the wetnurse appeared. A well-endowed woman walked up to Lin Xiangfu and looked indifferently at the copper coin in his hand. She took the baby from him and went into another room. Lin Xiangfu continued to hold out his hand; the wetnurse hadn't taken the money. No one in the main hall paid him any more attention, and they resumed their previous conversation. Listening to their rapid speech, Lin Xiangfu could tell they were discussing the snow that had been falling for fifteen days.

Everyone sitting in the main hall was a prominent resident of Xizhen. They said three draft animals should be sacrificed to heaven and seemed completely confident that after that, the snow would stop. Then they sighed and said the livestock had all frozen to death; they weren't sure who had any animals that were still alive.

As the men talked, Lin Xiangfu noticed that they were all bent forward toward the braziers except for the thin, swarthy man, who remained sitting perfectly upright in his chair. Instead of holding his hands out toward the heat, he kept them back on the armrests, while the warm breath escaping his mouth dispersed in front of his face as he listened attentively.

The wetnurse reappeared and returned Lin Xiangfu's daughter, who had eaten her fill and fallen asleep. The copper coin remained in Lin Xiangfu's outstretched hand, leaving him a bit uneasy. Noticing Lin Xiangfu's awkwardness, Gu Yimin gave him a slight nod, indicating he should return the coin to his pocket.

Then Gu Yimin spoke. The words of this serious man carried a natural authority as he announced: "The firewood and three draft animals have already been prepared, and I have spoken with the Daoist priests at the temple of the city god. Tomorrow we can do the sacrifice, and we'll see how long we can carry it out. This isn't like a typical sacrifice to the sun, moon, earth, or ancestors—it's not a simple matter of getting results after one day. 'Time reveals a person's heart,' as the saying goes—it's the same with heaven."

For the next three days, Lin Xiangfu carried his hungry daughter through the deserted, snow-covered streets to the plaza in front of the temple of the city god, where he saw the source of Xizhen's vitality.

On the first day of the sacrifice, a long table was set up with dozens of people sitting around it, shivering in the snow. A sheep was placed on the table. Lin Xiangfu looked at its eyes, which appeared crystal clear on the verge of its slaughter; after the sharp blade entered the animal, its eyes clouded over. Then a boar was brought to the table, on which a thin layer of ice had already formed. It was set down on one side and promptly slid off the other. After several attempts, the boar's struggling and squealing changed to a low grunting, which sounded like jaded laughter. The people busying themselves with the sacrifice broke out into fits of laughter—it was the first time Lin Xiangfu had heard anyone in Xizhen laugh since the snowstorm began. It eventually took eight strong men to hold down the boar's feet. The butcher's knife plunged in, and the pig's blood spurted out over the snow and splattered the people nearby. Finally they got an ox up on the table. Because they had already taken so long, the animal had become stiff from the cold; its eyes had a docile look and were only half open, as if it were about to fall asleep. The butcher's knife plunged into the ox's chest—it twitched as if it had been suddenly awakened, then let out a long, mournful sigh.

On the second day of the sacrifice, when Lin Xiangfu passed by the temple of the city god, he saw that it was packed full of people kneeling in prayer. A large altar had been set up inside the temple for burning the three sacrificial animals, and the fragrance of incense filled the air. Daoist priests stood along both sides of the temple holding *di* flutes, *xiao* flutes, *suona* horns, and wooden fish. As a rhythm was beaten on the wooden fish, graceful music from the flutes and horns rose up among the beams and pillars of the temple and floated out amongst the snowflakes. Inside, the kneeling supplicants kowtowed with their hands flat on the ground, their bodies undulating like even waves amidst the music.

On the third day of the sacrifice, the number of supplicants increased, and over a hundred men and women knelt in the plaza outside the temple of the city god, praying to heaven. Their bodies rose and fell as the lovely sounds of the music floated out of the temple. Before the sacrifices, the area had been swept clear of snow, but now after three days it was back. The snow had accumulated up past their knees, and Lin Xiangfu could no longer see their lower legs, as if they had been erased by the snow. The warm breath they exhaled gathered in a fog that rose up into the sky, where it dispersed like cooking smoke.

20.

It was on that day that Lin Xiangfu met Chen Yongliang. Chen Yongliang's second son was three months old then, and it was the cries of this child that led Lin Xiangfu to their home. Lin Xiangfu sensed a certain warmth in the atmosphere of this two-room house. Chen Yongliang, his face covered with a full beard, was holding his two-year-old son, while his wife, Li Meilian, was breastfeeding the three-month-old baby. The whole family was sitting around a charcoal fire.

When Lin Xiangfu appeared, Chen Yongliang pulled out a stool and invited him to sit by the fire. Unlike the blank expressions of the other women in Xizhen, when Li Meilian brought Lin Xiangfu's daughter to her breast, he could see a mother's warmth. Li Meilian praised the baby's looks, along with the red silk clothes and hat she was dressed in. She took off the baby's silk hat and admired its fine hand stitching, and she kept leaning down to sniff the baby's hair. Cheng Yongliang, who was now holding both of his sons, looked over at his wife and smiled. It had been a long time since Lin Xiangfu had experienced the warmth of a family, and observing this scene made a strange thought come to his mind—if something were to happen to him, could this family take in his daughter?

Now that he was somewhat familiar with the Xizhen accent, he could tell that these people had come from elsewhere. Chen

Yongliang told Lin Xiangfu their hometown was about five hundred *li* to the north, but continuous drought had forced them to pack up everything and head south. They had relied on temporary work as they traveled, carrying loads, pulling carts, and even driving boats—Chen Yongliang said he rowed by hand, unlike the boatmen from the Wanmudang, who paddled with their feet. Then, two years ago, they met Gu Yimin, and ceased their itinerant life to settle down in Xizhen. In a calm and even tone, Chen Yongliang described how they had managed with their newborn son through all the hardships and uncertainty of their precarious existence.

Chen Yongliang's family met Gu Yimin in Shendian. Gu Yimin needed to transport a large load of silk from Shendian to Xizhen, so he hired four porters, one of whom was Chen Yongliang. As he carried the silk toward Xizhen with the other three temporary workers, his wife and child followed behind. Like Chen Yongliang, Li Meilian also had a carrying pole, but on one end of hers was the family's clothing and blankets, and on the other end was their son—this was the pole that Chen Yongliang usually carried, but it had now temporarily passed to her shoulders. Riding in his sedan chair, Gu Yimin carried on a conversation with Chen Yongliang as they went along. He learned of the family's experiences, and that the reason Chen Yongliang's wife and son were following them was because they had nowhere else to go. He saw the petite Li Meilian wearily following her husband with their carrying pole—in order to keep up with the brisk pace of the men, she had to break into a trot. At some point along the way their son started wailing, so she took him in her arms. To balance out the carrying pole, she moved the blankets to the spot he had vacated and then opened the front of her shirt to begin feeding him. With her right hand she supported the baby, and with her left she held onto the pole, maintaining her trot all the while. The sound of her panting was like a bellows and her hair was soaked with sweat, which ran down her face and blew off in droplets as she ran. Yet she smiled the whole time. When they made it Xizhen, Gu Yimin paid the three other porters and sent them home, while he invited Chen Yongliang's family to stay.

From Chen Yongliang's story, Lin Xiangfu knew that this Gu Yimin was the thin man he had seen four days before. He thought of the long, high wall that surrounded his residence, and asked how big the place really was. Chen Yongliang shook his head and said that although he went there often, he usually only went to the main hall, and occasionally the study, but he had no idea what sort of world lay beyond that. After Chen Yongliang had finished speaking, he looked calmly at Lin Xiangfu, who knew he was waiting to hear his own story.

"I'm also from the north," he quietly offered.

After saying this, he noticed a puzzled look on Chen Yongliang's face, so he added a phrase, saying that in the past he had studied woodworking. Chen Yongliang asked what kind of woodworking.

"Hardwood," Lin Xiangfu answered.

A look of admiration appeared in Chen Yongliang's eyes. He said he had also studied woodworking, although he had only learned the lowest-level trades of sawyer and carrying pole maker.

Lin Xiangfu shook his head and said, "Woodworking only has different categories; one is not necessarily better or worse than the other. A good sawyer has to be able to make a perfectly straight cut and not ruin the lumber, while a carrying pole maker has to be very careful not to hurt the shoulders of the person carrying it."

When Li Meilian had finished feeding Lin Xiangfu's daughter, she didn't immediately hand her back. As the two men talked, she tried to get the baby to stand up on her lap. When she felt the baby's legs making an effort, she let out a cry of happy surprise and said the baby would soon be able to stand and walk. The sincerity of her happiness touched Lin Xiangfu, and as he sat there he felt there was no distance between them.

Chen Yongliang, who had experienced such a vagrant life, developed a good feeling about this man in front of him. He had a miserable appearance and humble way of speaking, but he had experienced a few things in this life. His eyes flashed when he spoke, and he seemed to have a certain vitality within him.

Lin Xiangfu didn't get up and leave as he normally did as soon as his daughter had been fed. Chen Yongliang's sincerity and Li Meilian's warmth kept him sitting there for a long time— it was the first he had felt like this since the snow had come to Xizhen. He had entered a number of peoples' homes, but the gloomy atmosphere always made him feel like the snow and ice had followed him in. At Chen Yongliang's place, though, the icy cold had been kept outside.

Here there was a flaming red charcoal fire, an easygoing man who took hardship in stride, a woman who was happy with her lot, and two young boys. Lin Xiangfu was loath to get up from his stool; a long period of loneliness had increased the warmth he felt now. When Li Meilian offered him a steaming hot bowl of rice porridge, his hand trembled as he accepted it. He knew what it meant to be offered a bowl of porridge during this time of snow and ice—they were sharing with him a little bit of their very own lifeblood. He took their older son on his lap, blowing on the hot porridge and carefully feeding it to the boy, never taking a bite himself. Chen Yongliang and Li Meilian watched him quietly, not saying a word as they slowly drank their own porridge, some white droplets sticking to Chen Yongliang's beard. When the oldest son was finished eating, Lin Xiangfu stood up to take his leave, placing not one but two copper coins on the stool. He suddenly felt a bit sheepish for not holding out the coin in his right hand as he usually did.

"Does the child have a name?" Li Meilian asked.

Lin Xiangfu nodded and said, "She does. She's relied on the milk from everyone's families, so her name is 'Hundred Homes Lin'—Lin Baijia."

Chen Yongliang and Li Meilian were visibly moved by this, and they urged him to stay the night—the snow outside was over two *chi* deep; what would he do if his daughter fell ill from the cold? Lin Xiangfu shook his head and opened the door. Faced with the frigid expanse of white outside, he hesitated. But when he thought of how he had only just met them, he stepped out into the snow. When Chen Yongliang went to shut the door, he saw that Lin Xiangfu's knees had completely sunk down in the snow—it looked like he was kneeling with his daughter, making his way on his knees.

As Lin Xiangfu struggled to make his way forward, frozen birds occasionally dropped from the trees, making soundless dents in the snow. The trees on either side suffered their own misfortune in the cold, creaking and snapping in the frigid temperatures—it was almost like the sound of crackling wood in a forest fire, although these creaks were more drawn out, and the snaps were even sharper.

Cheng Yongliang and Li Meilian begging Lin Xiangfu to stay was almost like fate giving them a hint. Lin Xiangfu never made it back to his place that day. Amidst the creaking of the frozen trees and the shock of the falling birds, he made his way, step by step, back to their home, where he stayed from then on.

His daughter was crying uncontrollably by the time he knocked on Chen Yongliang's door. Without a word, Chen Yongliang pulled Lin Xiangfu inside. Li Meilian took the baby, opened her shirt, and fed her. Chen Yongliang and Li Meilian said nothing; it was as if Lin Xiangfu were meant to come back.

As night approached, Lin Xiangfu's daughter kept crying, and after a few drinks of milk she vomited. Li Meilian reached out her hand and felt the baby's forehead, then cried out that she was burning up. This threw Lin Xiangfu into a panic, and he wasn't sure what to do. Chen Yongliang ladled out a basin of cool water from the vat, then soaked a cloth in it, wrang it out, and placed it on the baby's forehead.

That evening, Cheng Yongliang and Li Meilian gave the

only bed in the house to Lin Xiangfu and his daughter. Chen Yongliang told Lin Xiangfu this was the custom in their home-town—the guest always slept in the bed; they slept on the floor.

Lin Xiangfu said nothing and simply shook his head. He held his daughter as he sat by the fire, his eyes fixed on the flames. As the burning heat from his daughter's body passed through the cotton sack to his hand, terrible thoughts wracked him and he became filled with sorrow. If his daughter left him, his days on this earth would be numbered.

During the night, Lin Xiangfu's daughter let out a few weak cries. When Li Meilian, who was sleeping in the other room, heard her, she immediately threw on some clothes and came out. She took the baby from Lin Xiangfu and fed her some milk, but found she couldn't keep the milk down. Lin Xiangfu looked awkwardly at the milk splattered all over Li Meilian's front, but she told him not to worry—every child got sick and met with accidents. "Getting sick was like crossing a crevasse; having an accident, like crossing a mountain pass."

By the middle of the night, his daughter seemed to have fallen asleep. Lin Xiangfu sat up holding her until dawn. She had been laying quietly for some time, but then suddenly she burst out crying. Her wails were so loud they woke Chen Yongliang and Li Meilian in the other room, who both put on some clothes and came out. Li Meilian said that the baby's cries sounded like the fever had broken. She took the baby and felt her forehead, then announced it had. Then she fed her some milk, which the hungry baby noisily sucked down. Lin Xiangfu couldn't keep the tears from coming to his eyes.

Li Meilian saw rays of light on the windowpane and watched them spread out evenly through the crack around the door, as if they were about to cut through the room like a saw. She cried out in surprise and asked Chen Yongliang if that was actually sunlight she was seeing. Only then did they realize that the street outside was bustling with activity. Chen Yongliang opened the door, and the radiant sunlight greeted him like crashing waves.

21.

Winter passed, spring arrived, and Lin Xiangfu remained in Xizhen. When green buds burst forth from the frozen scars of the trees, Lin Xiangfu put down his own roots in town.

After the tornado had come the blizzard, and the extent of the destruction was evidenced by the state of Xizhen's doors and windows. Lin Xiangfu put his woodworking skills to use on Chen Yongliang's battered, misshapen windows and door—he fixed them up like new and then did the same for the next-door neighbors. The reputation of Lin Xiangfu's woodworking spread, and when he went out on the street, requests for his services would come one after another. Lin Xiangfu became too busy to handle it all, so Chen Yongliang began helping out. Chen Yongliang demonstrated his skills as a sawyer: without a ruler and using only his hand, he could cut the exact length of wood Lin Xiangfu needed with a thin, straight cut. He was also able to apply some of his skills from making carrying poles to the repair of doors and windows. When the two men combined their forces, they worked better and more efficiently, and in one day they could fix a family's door and windows. When neighbors asked how much it cost, the two of them would become flustered, having no idea how much they should charge. Finally Li Meilian came up with an idea. She hung a bamboo basket outside under the eaves by the gate, so people could toss their payment in that—however much they wanted to throw in was fine, and if they didn't want to put in anything, a few kind words would suffice. The neighbors all threw some money in the basket, and they had plenty of kind words as well.

When they realized all of Xizhen was covered in broken, misshapen windows and doors, Lin Xiangfu and Chen Yongliang discussed continuing on with this kind of work. Chen Yongliang said there was no more gold to be mined in the western hills, and the tornado before the snowstorm had ruined their equipment. There weren't even any workers left at the mine besides him, the lone foreman. Because he'd had no place else to go, Gu Yimin hadn't dismissed him from his post, but now Chen Yongliang could go to Gu Yimin and resign.

The two of them went door-to-door through the streets. Chen Yongliang, who had specialized in sawing and carrying poles, now extended his skills to make a cart. It turned out to be very sturdy, although when they pulled it down the street piled high with lumber and materials, it made a strange sound, which served as a hawker's cry. People needed only to hear the rumbling of their cart, which sounded like a bridge on the verge of collapse, to know that the two men who repaired doors and windows had come.

They carried with them a rice sack so dirty it looked like it had been used to hold charcoal, and they would throw their earnings in it. When they returned home in the evening, the first thing they would do was empty the copper coins from the sack into the bamboo basket. Li Meilian had moved the basket under the peach tree in front of the house, so that as the coins piled up, the petals from the cherry blossoms fell in as well. With the coins and flower petals mixed together, she said the money would carry a whiff of happiness.

As the two men pulled their cart through the streets fixing windows and doors, Lin Xiangfu kept an eye out for Xiaomei. He came across five men named Aqiang and seven women named Xiaomei, but he never found the ones he was looking for. He and Chen Yongliang had been to nearly every home in Xizhen, but he still couldn't find a single trace of Xiaomei. The only houses they hadn't entered were the vacant ones, the doors and windows of which were all tightly closed up.

As they were fixing windows and doors for people, when Chen Yongliang wasn't paying attention, Lin Xiangfu would ask the townsfolk why those houses were vacant. For some, they said, the owners had gone away and never returned; for others, the owners had died. Lin Xiangfu couldn't stop thinking about the ones whose owners had left—he felt that one of those abandoned houses held a clue about Xiaomei, and he wanted to find out. When they had nearly finished fixing everyone's doors and windows in Xizhen, Lin Xiangfu said to Chen Yongliang:

"The doors and windows of those vacant houses are also all banged up and broken. Their owners aren't around, but should we help fix them anyway?"

Chen Yongliang nodded when he heard this. He wasn't aware of Lin Xiangfu's real motive and simply thought he wanted to do a good deed. They pulled their rumbling cart up to the first vacant house and found an iron lock hanging on the door. Chen Yongliang hesitated and said to Lin Xiangfu,

"Fixing people's doors and windows is a good deed, but prying locks isn't."

Lin Xiangfu also hesitated. Although he really wanted to go in and have a look, he knew it wasn't right to break the lock on someone's door. So he nodded and said to Chen Yongliang,

"Let's just go on to the next one and see."

They went to several more abandoned houses, but there were locks hung on all their doors. Chen Yongliang didn't say anything, but just looked at Lin Xiangfu.

"Let's keep looking," Lin Xiangfu said.

The two of them pulled their cart around to all the vacant houses in Xizhen. Chen Yongliang had the feeling Lin Xiangfu wasn't really concerned with the locks on the doors; he just wanted to know where the vacant houses were and poke around them a bit. He thought Lin Xiangfu must be waiting for the owners to return so they could come back and fix the doors and windows.

22.

Word of Lin Xiangfu and Chen Yongliang's superb craftmanship spread throughout Xizhen, and people started bringing their old furniture for Lin Xiangfu to refurbish. One piece became ten and ten became a hundred as more and more pieces of old furniture began arriving at Chen Yongliang's door. This gathering of old furniture also acted as a gathering for Xizhen's cockroaches, which came along with the furniture. They brazenly crawled out of the furniture and scurried into the houses on both sides of the street.

In Chen Yongliang's house, the cockroaches would appear one minute and disappear the next. They crawled up the walls, dropped down from the ceiling, and scuttled out of the blankets. When you opened the wardrobe you'd send them hopping and scurrying; when you cooked a meal they'd run around bumping into each other on the shelf by the stove; at night they'd crawl across your face. Li Meilian became paranoid, tiptoeing around the house and constantly looking all over for them, ready to smash one at any moment. She would often get up stealthily in the middle of the night and go to the narrow area of the kitchen where they would congregate to launch a surprise attack.

Later on, people started showing up to order new pieces of furniture. Lin Xiangfu said to Chen Yongliang that if they opened up a workshop, their business would always be booming. Chen Yongliang nodded and said it was really time to start a woodworking business. Hearing that the two men wanted to start making new furniture, Li Meilian was elated, exclaiming that new furniture doesn't have cockroaches.

As they talked, Li Meilian sat in front of the door washing clothes, Chen Yongliang's two sons were sitting on his lap, and Lin Xiangfu was supporting his daughter with both hands. Lin Xiangfu said that down the street to the east was a vacant lot where they could put up two buildings. They could live upstairs, while the ground floors could be used for their workshop, and they could build a wall from both ends to make a courtyard— he just didn't know whether or not the lot was available? Chen Yongliang said all the vacant land around Xizhen belonged to Gu Yimin, so this shouldn't be difficult—he would go ask Gu Yimin, who would offer a fair price.

Building a house—two multi-story houses at that—wasn't something they could do in a day or two; it would take about a year. The sounds of the construction would bother the neighbors, but that shouldn't be a problem, either—they had already fixed up all their doors and windows, but they hadn't painted them, so all they had to do was spend a little money and hire some painters to come paint their doors and windows for free; if they did that, the neighbors would surely be able to accept a little construction noise.

Chen Yongliang said there was only one difficulty—where to get the money to build the houses? They'd already made a good bit, but it was still far from enough to build a house.

Lin Xiangfu set to work undoing his daughter's clothing and took out a little sack. He opened the sack and removed the deed to his mortgaged land and the twelve banknotes he had received in exchange for the gold bars, then passed them over to Chen Yongliang. Chen Yongliang stared in shock at the enormous sum of the banknotes piled in front of him—he had never imagined that someone wandering so far from his hometown like this would be carrying such an astonishing amount of wealth. He passed back the banknotes and watched Lin Xiangfu carefully return them to his daughter's clothing. Lin Xiangfu said that if he lost the money, he and his daughter would have nothing to live on. Chen Yongliang said, so if you lose your daughter, you'll also lose the money? Lin Xiangfu replied,

"If I lose my daughter, what would I need the money for?"

Once the neighbors' doors and windows had been painted, Lin Xiangfu and Chen Yongliang began construction. They hired a bricklayer and a painter, but handled the wooden parts—the beams, pillars, doors, and windows—themselves. They worked on that plot of land from sunup to sundown. Six months later, a pair of two-story gray brick buildings with tile roofs had sprung up, surrounded by a wall. The two families lived in the upstairs of each building; the downstairs of one building was used as the workshop, while the downstairs of the other was comprised of Li Meilian's kitchen and two storage rooms, along with the largest of the rooms, which served as a warehouse.

Chen Yongliang had a fengshui master select an auspicious day for the workshop's grand opening, which would also be the families' moving date.

Over twenty neighbors showed up that day. These men and women, speaking in their rapid accents, merrily crowded into Chen Yongliang's old place and, like a strong wind blowing the last clouds from the sky, cleared everything out. Everyone grabbed something to move, and even the three children were scooped up. When the remaining neighbors looked around and saw there was nothing left to move, they raced on ahead to lend a hand. The group of neighbors proceeded grandly down the street toward the two new houses at the eastern end, followed by a large number of children. Li Meilian, teary-eyed, followed behind them. This woman, who had experienced all the hardships of life on the road, could now finally feel as if she had a stable foundation. She said to Chen Yongliang, walking in front of her,

"This many people coming to help out shows we've been decent neighbors."

Gu Yimin also came, bringing with him a few strings of firecrackers he had a couple servants light in front of the main courtyard gate. Amidst the snapping and popping, Gu Yimin looked at the two brand-new structures and the large crowd of people who had come to help, and said to Lin Xiangfu and Chen Yongliang,

"Your families can put down roots here."

Gu Yimin saw Lin Xiangfu's daughter standing under a table giggling, holding onto one of the table legs as if it were her father's. Gu Yimin asked Lin Xiangfu, what's the child's name? Lin Xiangfu replied,

"She drank the milk from everyone's families, so her name is 'Hundred Homes Lin'—Lin Baijia."

Gu Yimin nodded and said, "That's a good name—very auspicious."

Standing off to the side, Li Meilian heard this and felt a bit sad. After the neighbors had left, she told Lin Xiangfu that he should start searching for a suitable woman.

"Not for yourself," she said, "but so your child can have a mother."

Lin Xiangfu smiled and dismissed the notion with a wave of his hand, saying to Li Meilian, "You're the child's mother."

23.

Lin Xiangfu wrote a letter to Tian Da briefly outlining his experiences over the past two years. He said that he wouldn't be returning home for the time being—he felt that Wencheng was actually Xizhen, and he wanted to wait for Xiaomei's return. He also asked Tian Da to go often to his parents' graves to clear the weeds and add dirt.

That evening, Lin Xiangfu lay on his bed smelling the scent of the new wood and fresh paint, thinking of what Li Meilian had said to him earlier that day. A vision of Xiaomei leapt before his eyes. He remembered every tiny detail of Xiaomei's body—it was as if his memory had sprouted a hand that gently fondled her everywhere. He thought of those searing nights when the two of them had lain together on the kang, his powerful body pounding into her, gently accepting him.

Lin Xiangfu realized it had been a long time since he had been aroused. He tried to think back to when this had started to be the case—perhaps during the snowstorm in Xizhen, or during his long, arduous travels. He couldn't remember exactly. But he knew that for some time now, when he woke up in the mornings, while he used to be rock hard down there and sticking up like a wooden stake, it now just hung there like a wet towel.

Then Lin Xiangfu thought of that figure he'd once seen on the street after the tornado—the one who disappeared down that narrow lane and then reappeared in that dimly lit room. He hesitated for a moment, then quietly got up and walked out of his new home. Under the light of the moon he made his way to Xizhen's wharf. He found the narrow lane and walked down it, although he didn't remember which door it was. With light, cautious footsteps, he passed a door that was slightly ajar and caught a fishy scent. He remembered this smell, so he carefully pushed the door open and went in.

A young woman sitting at a table saw him enter. She smiled and stood up, introducing herself as Cuiping. Carrying an oil lamp, she led him into a room upstairs. She shut the door and slid over the bolt, and then placed the lamp on a dresser by the bed. Smiling at Lin Xiangfu, she began taking off her clothes.

The light of the lamp allowed Lin Xiangfu a good look at her face. Before, he had only been able to see that she wasn't Xiaomei—he hadn't noticed her large eyes and upturned lips.

First she removed her floral-print qipao and folded it neatly on a stool by the bed. Then she took off her striped undergarments. Every article she removed she would fold neatly and place on the stool. When her butt stuck out as she bent over to fold her underwear, Lin Xiangfu could also see the outline of her bones. He realized that this woman was incredibly skinny, and when she lay her naked body down on the bed, he noticed that her smooth lower abdomen ever so slightly caved in.

Lin Xiangfu stood there without moving. He felt his heart begin pounding like a drum and his breathing quicken, but down there it still just hung, limply, like a wet towel.

Then, with a smile, the woman sat up and asked Lin Xiangfu, "Shall I undress you?"

Lin Xiangfu shook his head. By the light of the lamp, he practically tore off his clothes and crawled onto the bed. As he was crawling on, he noticed the pubic hair lightly distributed over her lower region and felt his first twinge of excitement.

Trembling, he crawled on top of her body. Her eyes were closed, and he gently moved his hands over the deep red nipples on her slightly protruding breasts. He heard her breaths lengthen.

But this was not enough to sustain Lin Xiangfu's excitement, and he felt his desire gradually disperse like a puff of smoke. He removed his hands from her nipples and slid them down her smooth, soft body. As he began exploring her lower region, he felt her hands doing the same to him. After a while, he removed his hands and placed them on her shoulders. Regretfully, he told her it wasn't working.

This woman with her upturned lips opened her eyes and moved her hand to his forehead—he was sweating, she said. Comforting him, she told him there was no rush and that he should just take his time; she'd had guests slower than him before.

Lin Xiangfu's hands once more returned to her lower body, to that place of increasing wetness. Quietly he asked her—could he stick it in if it was still soft?

With a gentle laugh, she said she didn't know, but he could try.

She spread her legs, and Lin Xiangfu, clinging on to this last hope, tried again and again. She reached down to help with her hand, but he was still unable to get it in.

Lin Xiangfu was drenched and his confidence was falling as fast as the beads of sweat running down him. He rolled off the bed and quickly got dressed, then sat down in a chair hidden in the shadows. His face red from shame, he watched as the woman meticulously put each item of clothing back on. Then he stood up from the chair in the shadows and passed her a silver yuan. Shocked, she said he'd made a mistake—this was a silver yuan, not a copper coin.

Lin Xiangfu said there was no mistake, and she very gratefully accepted the silver yuan. She picked up the oil lamp and led him out the door. As they went down the creaking steps, the strong smell of fish once again assaulted Lin Xiangfu's nostrils. He asked if her husband was a seafood trader, and she said yes, he had gone to Suzhou. Then he asked if his business as a sea-food trader wasn't enough to support her, that she still had to do this sort of work? She said he was addicted to opium, and he could barely support himself with the money he made.

Lin Xiangfu left her and walked along the deserted streets, feeling a kind of exhaustion he had never experienced before. His legs felt as if they were made of stone, and his body was so stiff it felt like he was about to collapse. When he made it back to his new house, he fell asleep without even getting undressed.

He slept through to the following afternoon. When Lin Meilian put lunch on the table and realized that Lin Xiangfu's breakfast was still there, she had Chen Yongliang go up to his room and check on him. Chen Yongliang said there was no need—he could hear him snoring from downstairs. He said he must be tired, so they should let him sleep.

This long sleep helped to clear away Lin Xiangfu's accumulated fatigue. He awoke to the sound of his daughter laughing downstairs. When he got up and went down, Li Meilian was braiding Lin Baijia's hair as the two-year-old sat on her lap holding a round mirror. After seeing her braids in the mirror, she began giggling uncontrollably.

After dinner, Lin Xiangfu took his daughter out for a walk along Xizhen's seven streets and lanes, out toward the western hills, and then back home. The two-year-old Lin Baijia walked with her father down the first street; for the remaining six, she rode in his arms, then on his back, and then finally up on his shoulders.

Lin Xiangfu talked to her the entire time. He told Lin Baijia he would never marry or take a concubine, and that she would never have any brothers or sisters—from then on, everything he did would be for her. The young girl knew that her father was talking to her, so after everything he said, she would give an affirmative "mmm!"

24.

Lin Xiangfu and Chen Yongliang hung a sign for their woodworking shop at the entrance to the courtyard. That evening, they sat down and figured up the sizes and prices for all different kinds of furniture. Then, using the standard style of writing, Lin Xiangfu copied it all out on *xuan* calligraphy paper, mounted it, and hung it on the wall at the entrance of the business. Lin Xiangfu said this was called "clearly stating the price," so that customers would know how much things cost as soon as they walked in. Chen Yongliang praised Lin Xiangfu's standard script, saying he had better handwriting than the teacher at the school in his hometown.

The woodworking shop became more prosperous by the day. Lin Xiangfu and Chen Yongliang were constantly busy and had more customers than they could handle. They realized they should hire some employees, so Lin Xiangfu wrote out over twenty help-wanted notices in his standard script, and the two men posted them up on all the street corners of Xizhen.

On one of the corners stood a shabbily dressed man leaning on a tree branch he was using as a walking stick. He studied the handwriting on the help-wanted notices for a long time, and then, in a thick northern accent, asked one of the locals passing by—he couldn't read, but he seemed to recognize the handwriting; was the person who wrote this named Lin Xiangfu?

After receiving an affirmative response, this man, a bundle on his back and a pair of straw sandals hanging in front of his chest, made his way to those two newly constructed buildings and stood hesitating at the entrance to the courtyard. The two families were eating supper just then. When Li Meilian walked out of the kitchen and saw this man leaning on a tree branch and holding a broken bowl, she thought he was a beggar, so she went back inside and got another bowl of rice, which she then took out and dumped in the man's bowl. He looked gratefully at the rice in his bowl, but he remained standing there and seemed to have no intention of leaving. So Li Meilian went back in and brought out some other food and put it in his bowl. Still he kept standing there. Li Meilian noticed he kept glancing over toward the house, so she asked him what it was he still wanted.

This time, he opened his mouth and said, "The person talking inside sounds like my family's young master."

Li Meilian smiled and asked, "Who's your family's young master?"

"The one who's speaking," he said.

Li Meilian heard that it was Lin Xiangfu who was talking, so she went back in and said to him, "There's a man outside who seems to know you."

Lin Xiangfu got up and went outside. As soon as the man saw Lin Xiangfu, he began wailing loudly as he leaned on his tree branch. Through his tears he said,

"Young master, you left and we never heard anything more from you—two years, two months, and four days. We thought you were dead!"

Realizing this man was Tian Da, Lin Xiangfu called out as he ran up and grabbed him. He examined him carefully, having not seen Tian Da in over two years. The hair on this man in his forties had already gone gray, and wrinkles crisscrossed his face.

"What are you doing here?" Lin Xiangfu asked.

Through his sobs, Tian Da said, "We got your letter in early spring, and I came as soon as I could."

As he spoke, Tian Da removed a package wrapped in red cloth from a pocket at his chest. His hands trembled as he passed it to Lin Xiangfu and said, "Young master, this is the deed to the house—I've brought it for you."

Lin Xiangfu opened the red cloth and looked at the deed— seeing his grandfather's name written on it brought forth a mixture of emotions. Tian Da then brought out a small cloth bag from the pocket at his chest and handed it to Lin Xiangfu, who opened it to find two small bars of gold. When he looked up at Tian Da with a confused expression on his face, Tian Da said,

"This is two years' worth of profits from the fields. I went to the *qianzhuang* bank in town and had the money changed into two little croakers, which I've brought here for you."

As he looked at Tian Da standing before him, dressed in rags, Lin Xiangfu became overwhelmed with emotion. After staring blankly for a few moments, he took the deed and the small cloth bag and helped Tian Da into the house. When they got to the door, Tian Da sat down on the threshold and removed the worn straw sandals from his feet. Then he took the new pair from around his neck, dried his tears, and said with a smile to Lin Xiangfu that he had prepared five pairs of sandals when he'd started out on his journey—he'd worn through four, and now this was the last pair. He said he'd been reluctant to put on this last pair, but now that he'd found the young master, he could wear them.

Tian Da donned the new straw sandals and entered the house. At once he recognized Lin Baijia, who was in the midst of eating her meal. Again tears came to his eyes, and he asked Lin Xiangfu,

"Is this the young lady?"

The crying Tian Da went to hug Lin Baijia, but his dirty, disheveled appearance caused her to withdraw in fright. Tian Da stopped and said to Lin Xiangfu,

"The young lady has gotten so big—she looks like the young mistress."

The next day, Lin Xiangfu hired a barber to give Tian Da a haircut and a shave, and he also hired a tailor to make Tian Da some new clothes, both unlined and padded. Tian Da was anxious to get back home, but Lin Xiangfu said to him,

"You've come so far, you should stay a few days."

After he'd been there for three days, Tian Da went out and got a bundle of rice straw, sat down on the threshold, and began making sandals. Seeing this, Lin Xiangfu knew he wanted to head back, so he asked Li Meilian to prepare some extra food for him to take on the road. Lin Xiangfu went out himself and bought Tian Da a walking stick.

When Tian Da had finished weaving his fifth pair of sandals, Lin Xiangfu called him into his room and said there were some things he needed to discuss. He handed Tian Da six banknotes and said that as soon as he got back, he should go redeem the mortgage on the land. Then he passed back the deed to the house and said,

"Take care of the fields and the house for me, and tend to my ancestors' graves. You live in the house for now, and you and your brothers take the income from the fields. When I come back some day, the house and land can be returned to me."

Tian Da pulled back his hands and refused to accept, but Lin Xiangfu said sternly, "Take it."

So Tian Da took the money and the deed. Wiping his eyes, he said, "Young master, when will you be coming back?"

Lin Xiangfu shook his head and said, "Right now I don't know, but there will come a day."

Early the next morning, Tian Da set off. He was dressed in his new clothes, the five pairs of sandals hanging around his neck. On his back he carried two new bundles wrapped in blue calico—in one bundle was his clothing, and in the other was the food Li Meilian had prepared for him. He bowed to Chen Yongliang and Li Meilian as he left and asked them to take good care of the young master—he was truly a good person, he said, the best in the world. Then he noticed Lin Baijia tugging at Li Meilian's clothes, so he bent down and walked over to her. Very gently touching her face, he once again noted how big the young lady had gotten, and that she looked like the young mistress.

Lin Xiangfu saw Tian Da off to the wharf. As they walked through the streets of Xizhen, Tian Da cradled his new walking stick in front of his chest. Lin Xiangfu asked him why he wasn't using it, and Tian Da laughed and said he was reluctant to use such a nice walking stick. Before he boarded one of the little boats with a bamboo awning, Lin Xiangfu stuffed five silver yuan into one of his satchels and told him it was for traveling expenses. This time Tian Da didn't say anything. He stooped down and got on the boat, and as the boatman began to push off, he cried and shouted up to Lin Xiangfu on the riverbank,

"Come home soon, young master!"

25.

The years went by without incident, and in the blink of an eye, ten had passed. Lin Xiangfu had never stopped searching for Xiaomei during those ten years—he always kept Xizhen's abandoned houses in the back of his mind, sure that one of them belonged to Xiaomei and Aqiang. So he waited for their return. In the past ten years, eight families had returned to Xizhen. He paid visits to the first five, introducing himself as Lin Xiangfu from the woodworking shop and offering to repair their windows and doors; when they asked how much it would cost, he dismissed the question with a wave of his hand. The last three families came to him—when they returned to Xizhen, their neighbors had told them that Lin Xiangfu from the wood-working shop would fix their windows and doors for free. So they arrived at the shop grinning from ear to ear, asking which one was Lin Xiangfu.

Lin Xiangfu brought one of the shop's employees, Zhang Pinsan, to do the repairs, and as they worked, Lin Xiangfu engaged the newly returned residents in wide-ranging conversation. After getting their backstories, he found that none of these eight returned families had any connection with Xiaomei or Aqiang.

By this time, Lin Xiangfu owned over a thousand *mu* of land in the Wanmudang. The first bit of land he bought with the money he had originally brought with him; after that, he used his combined income from this land and the woodworking shop to buy more land in the Wanmudang. The woodworking shop was thriving and had outgrown its original workshop, so he built a new workshop and warehouse on an empty plot of land further away.

This northern peasant felt a strong attachment to the land, which was hard to describe—it was like a child being immersed in the warm embrace of their mother. He first laid eyes on the Wanmudang in the aftermath of the tornado twelve years earlier, when he had lost and then found his daughter. In the glistening light of the rising sun, he saw its vast fields crisscrossed by rivers and lakes. Trees were uprooted and scattered in all directions; crops in the fields were flattened as if they were nothing more than trampled weeds; broken bits of boats, bunches of thatching, enormous trees, and empty roof frames floated on the surface of the water . . . Despite this scene of destruction, Lin Xiangfu was still able to see the fertile richness of the Wanmudang, as if recognizing the former beauty in the face of an old woman.

After the fall of the Qing dynasty, the country descended into nonstop fighting as warlords and bandits spread over the land. Bandits began flooding into the Wanmudang and kidnapping women, most often capturing young girls from wealthy families and demanding a high ransom. Many families, worried their daughters would be defiled by the bandits, rushed to marry them off, so the roads and waterways of Xizhen and Shendian became constantly filled with *suona* horns heralding bridal processions, folk performers coming and going, and the sounds of wedding music. The bandits' looting and plundering caused all the wealthy families in the Wanmudang to sell their land for cheap and move to either Shendian or Xizhen. Once the wealthiest families had moved, the second-tier families then became the bandits' targets, so they also sold their land for cheap and moved to Shendian or Xizhen. At this point, Lin Xiangfu was still buying up land in the Wanmudang—he wasn't concerned by the unstable situation, or the fact that the bandits were letting the crops go to waste. He felt that, as the saying goes, "so long as the green hills stand, there will always be wood to burn."

Gu Yimin—still thin and swarthy, but no longer as spirited and energetic—was deeply troubled by the deteriorating situation, often forgetting what he was saying midsentence.

"The president of the Republic changes every day," he said to Lin Xiangfu, "no one knows who we're living under."

Lin Xiangfu had also begun to show the signs of life's hardships; this tall and sturdy northerner could often be heard coughing as he walked through the streets.

The two men discussed marriage arrangements for their children. Lin Baijia was twelve, and Gu Yimin's eldest son was fifteen. Gu Yimin said that with all the constant fighting and widespread banditry, it wasn't a good time to arrange a marriage, but they couldn't put it off—they still needed to go on with their lives, and they had to do what they had to do. The two of them settled for an engagement ceremony on the twelfth day of the twelfth month.

26.

Gu Tongnian attended a boarding school in Shendian, where he had already gained quite a reputation for his devilry. No flies were allowed in the school's dining hall, and if there were, the kitchen staff would be punished. Gu Tongnian would catch flies and throw them into the vegetable bin, causing the kitchen manager to be punished several times. The kitchen manager, who was over fifty, didn't know who was doing it, but one day he went as far as kneeling in front of the students and pleading with them,

"We put everything we've got into our operation—we can't make up the loss!"

Over the years, the little hooligan had become quite good at the pole vault. His school was across the river from a theater, outside of which prostitutes would gather looking for customers. One night, Gu Tongnian found himself a long, sturdy pole, and, just as it was getting dark, he vaulted himself across the river, then dragged his pole into the theater and watched a performance. From the age of twelve on, though, he no longer had any interest in the theater. This boy, who was not yet through puberty, taught himself how to chat with prostitutes as he dragged his vaulting pole back and forth in front of the theater's doors. He also learned how to haggle with them over their price. This twelve-year-old Gu Tongnian started getting a room at a nearby hotel and sleeping with prostitutes, spending the whole night until the sun came up.

This scion of the Gu family, wealthy as he was, was not generous with his spending. He would only pay half price for a prostitute, his reason being that he was only half the size of a full-grown man. At first, none of the prostitutes in front of the theater paid any attention to this little runt who hadn't even grown any facial hair. But Gu Tongnian dragged his pole back and forth in front of the theater shouting and cursing as he argued his case, and his loud, shrill voice attracted a number of onlookers. He shamelessly ranted on and on, complaining to anyone he saw about how he had been wronged. Eventually, he began to wear the prostitutes down, and they began to feel a bit sheepish. Gu Tongnian may have been young, but he had a big appetite, so he hired two prostitutes at a time. Although he was only paying half price, the prostitutes thought that two of them handling this little smooth-faced pipsqueak should be easy enough, so they followed him and his vaulting pole to a room in the hotel. Once they got on the bed, though, they began begging for mercy—they never imagined the thing on that little runt would be as hard as that bamboo pole of his. He also liked to innovate, and had them flipping, flopping, and crawling all over the place. After a night of rendering their services, the prostitutes felt like they had put in a full day's work carrying heavy loads at the wharf. After that, whenever the prostitutes in front of the theater saw Gu Tongnian vaulting over the little river on his pole, they would run for cover—they said this little hooligan really was like an evil demon king.

Acting like he had achieved some great victory, Gu Tongnian started hiring three or four prostitutes at a time. One night he hired five, had them all strip naked and lay crosswise on the bed, and then drilled them one by one. When he'd tired himself out, he lay down across all five of their bellies and took a little nap, then woke up again and continued drilling them. Only after the prostitutes had become so exhausted they couldn't take it anymore and left did he feel satisfied enough to fall asleep. He woke up at noon feeling sapped of his strength as he dragged his bamboo pole out of the hotel. As he was preparing to vault over the river, his hands and feet were shaking so badly he plunged headfirst into the water. He crawled out of the river and sneezed a few times, then started running a high fever that wouldn't recede. So he returned to his home in Xizhen and stayed in bed for twenty-three days. On the twenty-fourth day, he rode in a sedan chair back to his school in Shendian, then got his pole and vaulted over the river that very evening. From then on he never again got four or five prostitutes at once, and usually assaulted just two or occasionally three at a time.

Gu Yimin sent his three other sons in succession to the boarding school in Shendian. Gu Tongnian taught his three younger brothers, Gu Tongyue, Gu Tongri, and Gu Tongchen, to become experts at the pole vault. The prostitutes in front of the theater saw not one but four little demon kings vaulting over the river. The four of them would approach with their bamboo poles looking like authentic whoremongers, their four pairs of gleaming, shifty eyes glancing left and right. Each one would chose a prostitute to take to the hotel. They would get only one room, and once the four prostitutes were laying on the bed naked, the brothers would have a physiology class, offering a wide-ranging comparative commentary on the prostitutes' breasts, faces, legs, and butts. This would last about an hour, until the prostitutes on the bed began yawning. When the comparisons were finished, they would climb on the bed in the order of their ages. First would be Gu Tongnian, followed by Gu Tongyue and Gu Tongri, and then finally Gu Tongchen. Gu Tongnian would usually do all four before getting of the bed, while Gu Tongyue and Gu Tongri would be spent after just one. The prostitutes feared Gu Tongchen the most—the seven-year-old's interest in breasts surpassed that of the others, and he would climb onto their chests and start pinching and rubbing, sucking and biting, grabbing and pulling. Their screams of pain nearly broke the windows.

27.

Lin Xiangfu didn't send Lin Baijia to school because there were none within a hundred *li* that accepted girls. So she stayed home, and he taught her himself.

Lin Baijia grew up together with Chen Yaowu and Chen Yaowen in these two two-story houses. As children, they ran up and down the stairs, their feet thundering on the upstairs floorboards, causing dust to fall through the cracks and into the dishes Li Meilian was cooking. Li Meilian would holler at them while she cooked, telling them not to run around upstairs. When the three children heard her shouts, they would immediately jump around, causing more dust to fall. They started to pull pranks, getting wood shavings from the workshop and stuffing them in the cracks between the floorboards, then resuming their hopping and jumping. Li Meilian would yell loudly in the kitchen beneath them, and the children upstairs would jump with even more glee. There was nothing she could do but call the two men over from the workshop and have them paste paper over the ceiling to cover the cracks and keep the dust and shavings from falling through.

Lin Xiangfu saw the three children running around wildly all day, and he felt the sound of their pounding footsteps should be accompanied by the sound of lessons being recited. He and Chen Yongliang tidied up one of the downstairs storage rooms, hung a small blackboard on the wall, pasted the Yongzheng Emperor's *Amplified Instructions on the Sacred Edict* beside it, and set up three small desks and stools. Lin Xiangfu summoned the three children.

"Now you're going to start learning how to read and write," he told them. "From this day on, you'll sit upright and walk straight."

Lin Xiangfu began instructing Lin Baijia, Chen Yaowu and Chen Yaowen. Ten days later, Lin Xiangfu moved in two more desks and stools, and Gu Yimin sent over his two daughters, Gu Tongsi and Gu Tongnien.

The sisters from the Gu family were aged ten and seven. Lin Xiangfu led them into the classroom and, with a broad smile, told Lin Baijia, Chen Yaowu and Chen Yaowen their names.

"These are your classmates, and also your sisters," he said.

Dressed in light green and pink qipaos, Gu Tongsi and Gu Tongnien blushed as they looked at the three older children. Walking over to Lin Baijia, the elder sister Gu Tongsi held out three little cloth sacks and passed them to her. Filled with curiosity, Lin Baijia opened one and discovered that it contained candy—she knew this was the Gu sisters' gift upon their first meeting, so she distributed the other two sacks to Chen Yaowu and Chen Yaowen. The two boys opened them greedily and devoured the candy, while Lin Baijia took a few pieces in her palm. She placed one piece in Gu Tongsi's mouth, one in Gu Tongnien's mouth, and the third she placed in her own mouth.

After consuming their candy like it was water, the boys looked on hungrily as Lin Baijia and the Gu sisters slowly savored theirs. Standing silently at the blackboard watching the girls enjoy their candy, Lin Xiangfu forgot what he was going to teach. Seeing them get along so well on their first meeting filled his heart with joy.

The arrival of Gu Tongsi and Gu Tongnien brought about a change in Lin Baijia. She no longer ran around all day like a tomboy with Chen Yaowu and Chen Yaowen, but now began acting more like a typical little girl and older sister. On breaks from class, while Chen Yaowu and Chen Yaowen would be playfighting in the courtyard with wooden knives and daggers, Lin Baijia and the Gu sisters would kick around a shuttlecock. The seven-year-old Gu Tongnien would often lose her balance and fall over when she raised her leg to kick. So Lin Baijia tied a rope on the shuttlecock, helped Gu Tongnien up with her left hand, and then held the rope out with her right, so that Gu Tongnien could kick the shuttlecock without it flying away. When class was over, Lin Baijia would see the Gu sisters to their sedan chair waiting outside the courtyard. Although they would be seeing each other the next day, they were still reluctant to part as they waved their goodbyes. In the mornings, Lin Baijia would wait in front of the courtyard gate for their sedan to arrive.

Lin Xiangfu fell in love with teaching. He let Chen Yongliang handle the woodworking shop while he completely devoted himself to the classroom. He proceeded according to the standards of traditional private schools and taught the Confucian classics, including all the essentials: *The Analects, The Classic of Filial Piety, The Great Learning, The Doctrine of the Mean, The Mencius,* and *The Book of Rites.* Then he heard that a modern-style of education was becoming popular, so he paid a visit to the boarding school in Shendian to see what he could learn.

That evening, Lin Xiangfu saw Gu Yimin's four sons walking out of a restaurant with their vaulting poles, wiping the shiny oil from their mouths. He watched them get a running start for four or five meters, then use the poles to launch themselves over the river. They seemed as light as sparrows as they flew over the water, their poles pausing briefly at the moment they stuck straight up into the air. The youngest, Gu Tongchen, even hummed a little tune as he vaulted over.

28.

On the twelfth day of the twelfth month, the engagement ceremony for Gu Tongnian and Lin Baijia went on as planned. Lin Xiangfu hired a barber to come over and give him and Chen Yongliang a haircut, shave, and eyebrow trim. Then they donned their padded *mianpaos* and headed out to the main street. According to the custom in Xizhen, the bride-to-be needed at least two people from her side to participate in the engagement ceremony, although beyond that, there was no specific number of participants required. So Lin Xiangfu had Chen Yongliang come with him, and the two of them went to the Gu residence. The front entrance was decked in festive lanterns, and the place was teeming with guests. Two *suona* horn players filled the air with a loud tune, while four people on the gong and drums beat a rousing rhythm. Gu Yimin stood on the steps in front of the gate, smiling and bowing as he greeted the guests.

Everyone who had received an invitation from Gu Yimin was one of Xizhen's prominent residents, and naturally they all arrived in sedan chairs. Every sedan chair in Xizhen was hired out that day—even those who lived nearby hired sedans and had the carriers take them for a turn around town so everyone would know they had received an invitation from Gu Yimin. Lin Xiangfu and Chen Yongliang were the only ones who arrived on foot that day. They tucked their hands up in their sleeves and walked quickly under the rays of the winter sun. When they walked up to Gu Yimin and bowed in greeting, Gu Yimin noticed the sweat on Lin Xiangfu's ruddy face.

The engagement ceremony was held in the main hall of the

Gu residence. Twenty "eight immortals" tables were set up with eight seats each, and dozens of charcoal braziers were placed around the perimeter of the hall, aglow with deep red flames. All the noise of the guests filled the Gu family's main hall with a lively spirit, as if it were a scene at the theater. After the guests had been seated, the ceremony began. First, the groom-to-be's family invited a scholar to read out the family's list of gifts. This consisted of a single sum of betrothal money amounting to five thousand taels of silver, which elicited gasps from the seated guests. In addition to this, there were silks, rings, earrings, bracelets, necklaces, and the like. Then Chen Yongliang read out the list of gifts on behalf of the family of the bride-to-be: five hundred *mu* of fertile land in the Wanmudang, along with all sorts of useful household items and clothing for every season. When Chen Yongliang finished, the main hall of the Gu mansion was abuzz.

The meal was served, and Gu Yimin's servants filed in with dish after dish of exquisite cuisine, encompassing nearly everything edible that flew, swam, or lived on land. Dozens of jugs of alcohol were lined up, containing dozens of southern wines and liquors, all with varying hues, aromas, and flavors. There was yellow rice wine from Shaoxing; "fortune and faith" from Hangzhou; "three whites" from Songjiang; "red pal" from Yixing; quince wine from Yangzhou; "hundred flowers" from Zhenjiang; *xiaruo* from Tiaoxi; *lahuang* from Huai'an; *pujiu* from Pukou; *xunjiu* from Zhexi; *sharendou* from Suqian; and *wujiapi* from Gaoyou.

29.

Li Meilian dressed Lin Baijia in a red skirt, red pants, red silk embroidered shoes, and a red silk embroidered *mian'ao* jacket. Bursting with happiness, she said to her,

"Today is a great day for you—you're now part of the Gu

family. You'll sit primly in your chair with no fidgeting, and you'll take care not to get your clothes dirty. There's no dust on the Gu women's clothing and no dirt on their shoes; their teeth are all nice and white; and their hair is shiny, black, and fragrant."

Li Meilian had the red-clad Lin Baijia sit in a chair, then moved a charcoal brazier over by her feet. She instructed her two sons to wait on Lin Baijia, putting more charcoal in the brazier when the flames went down and getting her some tea when she was thirsty. When she had said this, she picked up her basket and went out to buy some food. Lin Xiangfu and Chen Yongliang had gone to the banquet, so she wanted to give the three children a special lunch as well.

As Lin Baijia sat in the chair, Chen Yaowu kept an eye on the flames in the brazier, muttering to himself: go out, go out so I can put more charcoal in. Chen Yaowen got some tea and came to stand by Lin Baijia's side. He kept asking if she was thirsty, but each time she would shake her head.

"Sitting here unable to move—being a member of the Gu family doesn't seem that great!" said Lin Baijia.

Just then, two strange men entered the courtyard. Their faces flashed by the window, and then they entered the house. One had a rifle, the other had a pistol, and they both looked overjoyed when they came in the main hall and laid eyes on Lin Baijia. The one carrying the rifle said,

"Who's this young lady, dressed up pretty as a flower?"

"She's a young lady of the Gu family," Chen Yaowen answered assertively.

The man with the pistol said, "Judge a tree by its leaves and branches, judge a person by their looks—from the way she's dressed up, I'd say she's worth five hundred silver yuan."

Chen Yaowu and Chen Yaowen stood there dumbstruck. Lin Baijia asked Chen Yaowen why he didn't offer their guests some tea. The man with the pistol said forget the tea, you're coming with us right now. The man with the rifle said a cup of tea won't make us late. Chen Yaowen quickly got up and served the tea, and the two bandits sat down and drank. They looked at Lin Baijia, they looked at Chen Yaowu and Chen Yaowen, and they looked all around the room. When they had finished their tea and were done looking around, Lin Baijia got up and said to them,

"Let's go."

Chen Yaowen didn't understand what was happening. "Where are you going?" he asked her.

Chen Yaowu understood and said to his brother, "They're bandits—they're kidnapping her."

As Lin Baijia followed the two bandits out the door, she turned back to Chen Yaowu and said, "Brother, go now and tell my father to prepare five hundred silver yuan for my ransom."

Having said this, Lin Baijia asked the bandit with the rifle, "Where should the exchange take place?"

"We'll send out a notice," said the bandit.

30.

On her way home from buying food, Li Meilian heard that a group of bandits had entered Xizhen kidnapping people for ransom. When she thought of the three children at home, she scampered back on her tiny bound feet and was immediately met by Chen Yaowu and Chen Yaowen, who told her that Lin Baijia had been taken by the bandits. Li Meilian's legs went limp and she plopped down on the threshold, thinking of all the horrible things she'd heard about the bandits. To the men they kidnapped, they would do a "crank grind," which meant ramming a bamboo stick up their ass and twisting it back and forth; to the women they kidnapped, they would "work the bellows," which meant shoving a bamboo stick up their vagina and poking around.

"Go quickly and take the place of Lin Baijia," Li Meilian

said to her eldest son, Chen Yaowu. "You're a man, so the 'crank grind' will just hurt you a bit. If they "work the bellows" on Lin Baijia, she'll be shamed for the rest of her life!"

The fourteen-year-old Chen Yaowu went out the door and asked some panic-stricken people on the street which way the bandits had gone. They said they had gone to the south, so Chen Yaowu rushed south after them. He flew over Xizhen's main street, raced through the town's south gate, and ran so fast down the main road outside of town that his chest felt like it would burst and the sweat poured off him like rain. As he ran, he took off his padded jacket and held it in his hand as he continued on; he then felt like it was dragging him down, so he threw it down and lost the jacket altogether. Up ahead he saw over twenty kidnapped prisoners, all tied together with a rope and making their way down the road, surrounded on all sides by gun-toting bandits. As he ran closer, he saw that Lin Baijia was in the very front, accompanied by the two bandits who had come to their house. He ran out in front of them and stood in the middle of the road, blocking their path as he said through gasps of air,

"Our bandit guests! I have something I need to discuss with you."

The bandit carrying the pistol stepped forward and slapped him. "You must want to die!" he growled.

Shielding his face with his hands, Chen Yaowu said, "I don't want to die; I want to take my sister's place."

Then he pointed at Lin Baijia and said to the bandit with the pistol, "Today's the day of her engagement, so she's all dressed up, but usually I'm dressed more nicely than she is. She's just a girl, so she's not worth as much as I am. I'm the heir of the family, so if she's worth five hundred taels of silver, I'm worth a thousand. Would you rather get five hundred, or a thousand?"

Hearing this, Lin Baijia quickly said to Chen Yaowu, "Brother, don't try to take my place. We're not a rich family—we can't afford an extra five hundred."

Chen Yaowu nodded at her reasoning and said to the bandit with the pistol, "Forget it—take my sister. Five hundred's no small sum!"

Chen Yaowu walked over to the side of the road, but the bandit with the pistol shouted at him, "Get the fuck over here! I don't want her five hundred taels, I want your thousand."

The bandit untied Lin Baijia's rope and tied up Chen Yaowu. Lin Baijia saw that Chen Yaowu was shivering in only a thin, sweat-soaked shirt. She asked what happened to his jacket, and he said it was slowing him down, so he'd tossed it aside. Lin Baijia took off her red silk embroidered *mian'ao* and put it on him. It was a little small and he struggled to get it on, so the bandit carrying the rifle reached out a hand and helped him get his arm through the sleeve. The bandit with the pistol swore at him,

"You're a bandit, not a monk. No one wants to see your Bodhisattva's heart."

Without a word, the bandit with the rifle grabbed hold of his dagger and stabbed Chen Yaowu's left arm. Chen Yaowu cried out in shock, then realized that the blade sliced through his clothing but didn't pierce his skin. The bandit then slipped the rope through the gash he'd just cut in the sleeve and tethered Chen Yaowu to the other hostages.

The bandits shouted for the hostages to get going, and Lin Baijia ran up to Chen Yaowu and whispered in his ear, "Brother, stay close to the one with the rifle—he seems a little nicer."

31.

The banquet at the Gu mansion was just getting underway. The guests looked on with excitement as Gu Tongnian made his appearance, wearing a deep red *mianpao* and a black silk six-paneled pointed hat. Amidst the din of the guests, a steward accompanied the fifteen-year-old Gu Tongnian around the tables and up to Lin Xiangfu. Smiling happily, he offered a gift to Lin Xiangfu and Chen Yongliang in honor of their first meeting.

Gu Tongnian knelt down. Lin Xiangfu helped him up, took a small envelope from Chen Yongliang, and pressed it into Gu Tongnian's hand. Lin Xiangfu carefully examined Gu Tongnian. He was as swarthy and thin as his father, but he had a cynical, irreverent look on his face without a trace of Gu Yimin's seriousness, which caught Lin Xiangfu a little off guard.

Just then a servant hurried up to Gu Yimin, bent down, and said a few things into his ear. Gu Yimin's smile immediately vanished and his face turned to stone, as if it had instantly frozen over. In a low voice, he leaned over and told Lin Xiangfu and Chen Yongliang that bandits had just entered the town and taken hostages, including Lin Baijia.

Lin Xiangfu stared at Gu Yimin in disbelief, and Gu Yimin repeated himself—this time his words came down like a sledgehammer, and Lin Xiangfu jumped up as if he were avoiding it. He squeezed between the tables and chairs and rushed outside, causing the guests—winecups in their hands and mouths full of food—to look on in shock. Then they saw Chen Yongliang jump up and race out of the hall after him. No one had any idea what was happening—they all looked nervously at Gu Yimin, who forced a smile and said as casually as possible,

"Some bandits entered the town and took hostages—don't be alarmed, they've already left."

As Lin Xiangfu ran wildly down the street, Chen Yongliang, following behind him, realized he was headed toward their home. Chen Yongliang called out for him to stop. He pointed to someone on the side of the street and told Lin Xiangfu they'd said the bandits had already left town through the south gate. Lin Xiangfu froze, then nodded and turned and ran toward the south gate. He felt a stinging in his eyes as he ran, and when he reached up to rub them he realized that sweat had been pouring into them. Passing through Xizhen's south gate, he noticed a child in red clothing flash by him. He heard Chen Yongliang call out behind him, so he stopped and turned to see Chen Yongliang standing by a young girl. Chen Yongliang waved at him, and he wiped the sweat from his eyes to see that the girl was Lin Baijia. He ran to his daughter, knelt down, and hugged her to his chest. Her body felt thin and light, and he realized she was only wearing a thin red silk shirt, so he asked where her padded *mian'ao* was.

After learning that Chen Yaowu had been taken away by the bandits, Lin Xiangfu noticed a bewildered look flash across Chen Yongliang's face. His eyes followed the main road as it trailed off to the south, disappearing into the vast, watery stretches of the Wanmudang. Lin Xiangfu said they should quickly continue after the bandits, but Chen Yongliang shook his head and hugged Lin Baijia.

"Let's go home," he said.

Li Meilian was standing out in the street looking for them. She saw Lin Xiangfu and Chen Yongliang appear from around a corner, at which point Lin Baijia jumped out of Chen Yongliang's arms and ran toward her. Li Meilian held her hands to her chest and let out a long sigh.

When they got home, Li Meilian pulled Lin Baijia in front of her and examined her closely. When she saw that her hair was just a bit ruffled and nothing more, she could finally relax. She asked for a brush so she could brush Lin Baijia's hair, but Chen Yongliang suggested getting her a jacket first. Only then did Li Meilian realize Lin Baijia was wearing only a thin shirt—she smiled and said she must have become flustered with joy, then went into the next room and fetched a *mian'ao*.

But as she was putting it on her and fastening the top button, she suddenly burst into tears. She told them she had bade Chen Yaowu to go take Lin Baijia's place, fearing the bandits would "work the bellows" on her—she had two sons but only one daughter, so she'd made Chen Yaowu go.

Li Meilian's tears filled Lin Xiangfu with sadness, and he

lowered his head and walked out of the room. Chen Yongliang followed him out, placed his hands on his shoulders, and said,

"She's right—we have two sons, but only one daughter."

32.

News of the bandits coming into town and taking hostages hit Xizhen like a clap of thunder. The townsfolk were thrown into a panic and had no idea what to do; when they discussed their options, they only succeeded in scaring themselves more. Normally accustomed to a peaceful existence, now that they were scared, their talk became more and more exaggerated—according to them, the future of Xizhen was doomed.

Some people who had been captured by the bandits in the Wanmudang and had escaped from their lair to Xizhen now came forward to tell about their experiences. As they talked, their ruddy faces became white as sheets. They told the people of Xizhen all about the bandits' varied methods of torture—they would dig out hostages' eyeballs and cut off their ears; they would do the "crank grind" and "work the bellows"; they would also do a "pole press," "cut the carp," "sit on the happy chair," and "plow the field." As the escaped hostages spoke, they forgot which things they had actually experienced themselves and which they had merely heard as rumors.

From their descriptions, the people of Xizhen learned that "cut the carp" meant using a knife to slice rows of slanted squares down a person's back, just as one would prepare a carp before putting it in the pot to cook. "Sitting on the happy chair" meant spreading nails over the seat of a chair with the tips pointing up, and then making the hostages sit. The most complicated was "plowing the field"—after the explanation still left some people confused, several of those who had been tortured by the bandits walked out on the street to demonstrate: one person had to lay face-down on the ground and have two wooden poles strapped to their legs, while two others then stood the poles upright, forcing the person to crawl forward. Three of the former hostages demonstrated "plowing the field," then began crying out in pain as they crawled forward, calling out to stop before they'd even made it a full meter. They collapsed on their bellies, large beads of sweat rolling off their foreheads.

This demonstration of "plowing the field" quickly turned into a "plowing the field" competition. A number of people began practicing in earnest, vying for the title of "plowing" champion. In the end, three of them were deemed the winners—Gu Yimin's servant Chen Shun; Zhang Pinsan, an employee from the woodworking shop; and the boatman Zeng Wanfu. All three of these sturdy young men had made it about five meters, but no one could determine which one of them had actually gone the farthest. They weren't content to leave it there, however; they wanted to see who was really the best.

Using the torture methods of the bandits to hold a contest right when Xizhen was suffering from their marauding seemed completely inappropriate to the town's more high-minded residents, so they went to the head of the chamber of commerce, Gu Yimin, to ask him to personally put a stop to the competition.

Gu Yimin was getting ready to establish a local militia. The bandits coming into town and taking hostages had truly scared him, and he feared they would continue to wreak havoc in Xizhen. He ran back and forth between Xizhen and Shendian, looking for some government troops who could come to help protect Xizhen, but in such tumultuous times, there were no troops to be found. His only option was to use his position as head of the chamber of commerce to raise a militia, so he sent people out into the surrounding countryside to buy up guns. Gu Yimin had heard tell of this "plowing the field" competition, and when these gentlemen described it to him in more detail, he just shook his head slightly—but he didn't agree that he should put a stop to the contest.

"While this 'plowing the field' competition is entirely

inappropriate," he said, "everyone is in a panic right now, and this contest can help them alleviate some of their stress."

With that, the chamber of commerce arrived on the scene to officially commence the competition, and the residents of Xizhen gathered in the plaza in front of the temple of the city god. A good number of them also climbed trees and went up on roofs to get a better look, and the windows of the surrounding buildings were all open and filled with faces squeezed together looking out.

The contestants Chen Shun, Zhang Pinsan, and Zeng Wanfu were all dressed in martial arts attire, with tight-fitting black shirts, harem pants, and protective belts. The crowd was fired up, and the faces of the three contestants were glowing red. When Gu Yimin slowly raised his right hand, the three men immediately got face-down on the ground and raised their left legs, like urinating dogs, so that wooden poles could be tied onto them; then they switched and raised their right legs for the same purpose. When Gu Yimin lowered his hand, six burly men rushed forward in pairs and took up the wooden poles as if they were plowing, forcing the three men to crawl forward. All three of them surpassed five meters without making a sound, gritting their teeth as they crawled. Their faces turned from red to purple, then from purple to blue, finally looking as if they'd all been beaten up.

Amidst waves of encouraging cheers from the crowd, the three men crawled ten meters. They crossed the ten-meter line marked in lime and kept going. Zeng Wanfu was the first to succumb to the pain. Once he started screaming "Ow, ow!", Chen Shun and Zhang Pinsan quickly followed suit; then cries of "Ow, ow!" began spread through the crowd like a plague. In no time at all, the shouts of "Go, go!" had all turned to "Ow, ow!" The three men crawled past the twenty-meter line. No one had expected them to make it this far, so beyond twenty meters there were no more line markings. Still the three men continued to crawl forward, their cries changing once more—this time from "Ow, ow!" to a low "Ooh, ooh," like cats in the middle of the night. This too infected the crowd, who were soon crying "Ooh, ooh" as well. When the contestants had crawled about thirty meters, Chen Shun was the first to collapse, his head thudding on the ground like a wooden bucket thrown in a well. He was followed shortly by Zhang Pinsan. The boatman Zeng Wanfu, whose arms and legs were better conditioned through their daily use, held on the longest. Finally he lay down on the ground, too, as the "plowing" champion.

The three men lay paralyzed on the ground. Even after the wooden poles were removed, their legs remained totally unresponsive. When others tried to help them up, their limp legs simply folded like paper; their bodies rocked back and forth a few times and then fell back down. Gu Yimin called for three sedan chairs to carry them home.

Over the next three days, whenever the people of Xizhen spotted any of these three men, they saw them staggering along like toddlers just learning to walk, holding onto a wall for support, stopping to rest every few steps. They had all scraped their faces when they fell on the ground at the end of the competition, and they now wore bitter smiles amongst their injuries.

33.

The bandits sent out a notice eleven days after taking the hostages. The family members of those who had been captured went outside that morning amidst swirling snowflakes to find a gleaming dagger stuck in each of their doors, pinning to them a snowflake-covered paper with the amount of the ransom and the location of the exchange written on it.

Li Meilian had passed eleven sleepless nights with Chen Yongliang tossing, turning, and sighing beside her. Sometimes she would drift into a light sleep, but then the sound of footsteps on the street outside would startle her awake, and she would sit up and listen carefully to determine if they stopped in front of their gate. That night, she heard footsteps come up to their gate, followed by the thwack of something being stuck in the door. When the footsteps had gone, Li Meilian jumped out of bed, threw on some clothes, and opened the door to find the bandit's note. With difficulty she pulled out the dagger and went back inside, where Chen Yongliang was sitting up in the bed.

He looked at the dagger and piece of paper in Lin Meilian's hands and asked in a whisper, "Did the notice arrive?"

Li Meilian nodded. "It did," she said.

By the light of the kerosene lamp, the two of them read the bandits' note several times. Lin Xiangfu had also heard something, and he knocked on the door of their room. He came in and joined them, carefully reading the note. When he was finished, he let out a long sigh and said Chen Yaowu could now be freed—he had already prepared a thousand taels of silver. He asked if they should send their employee Zhang Pinsan, but Chen Yongliang shook his head and said he would deliver the money himself.

That afternoon, Gu Yimin gathered the most prominent members of the chamber of commerce at his house for a meeting. He said that the money for the ransom shouldn't be raised by the families of the hostages, but should come out of the chamber's annual tax revenue—they might be the ones captured today, he said, but tomorrow it could be you. As Gu Yimin spoke, the sound of gunfire could be heard in the distance. Seeing the panicked looks on everyone's faces, he told them not to worry, it wasn't the bandits—where would the bandits get cannons? This was the Beiyang Army and the National Revolutionary Army fighting in Shendian. Then he raised his voice and said,

"In these unsettled times, it's imperative that the people of Xizhen band together and protect themselves against disaster."

Gu Yimin and the chamber members decided that the chamber of commerce would indeed put up the ransom money, and to ensure against any problems, the members themselves would select the ones to deliver it. The three contestants in the "plowing" contest—Zeng Wanfu, Chen Shun, and Zhang Pinsan—received the broadest support and were chosen as the best candidates to deliver the money. Gu Yimin also favored these three men, although he did wonder if after the contest their legs would still be able to run.

That afternoon in the plaza in front of the temple of the city god, under the expectant gaze of the crowd and to the sound of their cheers, the three men kicked and stretched their legs and demonstrated how they could run away in retreat. Gu Yimin was completely satisfied and said these were really six good legs—they could kick like cats and run like dogs.

On the morning of the twenty-seventh day of the twelfth month, on the steps in front of the temple of the city god, Gu Yimin, his hair white with snow, gave twenty-three banknotes of differing amounts to Zeng Wanfu, Chen Shun, and Zhang Pinsan. Then he gave them a formal send-off amidst the swirling snowflakes. He raised a bowl of wine high above his head, and the three "plowing" champions did the same, followed by the representatives from the hostages' families. Brushing the snowflakes from their faces, they drained their bowls in one shot. Then Gu Yimin said to the three men,

"Go quickly, and come home quickly."

The three men, with belts fastened around their black padded jackets and wrappings around their legs, walked amongst the crowd with their heads high and their chests out. They were perhaps a little overly excited, their grand plans causing them to break out in foolish giggles.

They left Xizhen and headed in the direction of Shendian. After walking about ten *li,* they turned onto a small road toward Five Springs, where they then took a winding mountain path. That would lead them to the location the bandits' notice had specified for the exchange, where there was a temple to the bodhisattva Guanyin.

As they were passing Five Springs, they came across a peasant headed in the same direction with an empty carrying pole,
who told them that the day before he had seen the Beiyang and
National Revolutionary Armies fighting. They fought the entire
day, while the peasant hid under a bridge listening to the gunfire—his ears were still ringing from the noise.

Just as they were about to arrive at the Guanyin temple, they
heard the thundering sound of footsteps behind them. When
they turned to look, they saw dozens of troops with rifles running towards them. Then they heard the same sound of footsteps coming in front of them and saw roughly the same number
of men charging forward. The two units stopped about thirty
meters apart, raised their rifles, and aimed at each other, with
the four men standing right in their line of fire. The swirling
snow kept each side from getting a clear look at the other, and
they each asked the four men standing between them who the
other side was. As a mix of northern and southern accents came
toward the men, the peasant pointed to the unit in front of him
and spoke up:

"You have northern accents, so you must be the Beiyang
Army. The other side has southern accents, so they must be the
National Revolutionary Army."

As soon as he finished speaking, gunshots rang out like
strings of firecrackers, and bullets began flying in both directions. Before Zeng Wanfu understood what was happening, the
peasant fell to the ground; then, as if hit by cudgels, Chen Shun
and Zhang Pinsan did the same. Finally Zeng Wanfu realized
what was going on and began flailing his arms and shouting,

"Don't shoot! Don't shoot! Just wait a minute!"

Zeng Wanfu's shouts didn't stop the shooting. He watched
the armies on both sides continue firing as they dispersed along
the side of the small path. As the bullets whizzed around him,
he broke into a sprint and started running away, waving his
hands in the air as if he were trying to stop the bullets. Just as
he was about to escape from the line of fire, a bullet tore off

the middle finger on his right hand, but he was completely un-aware—he only knew he must run for his life. His belt snapped as he was running and his pants slid down, so he reached down and held them up by the crotch as he continued on.

Zeng Wanfu ran for over ten *li* without having any idea where he was going; he only knew that sometimes he made a turn or sometimes crossed a bridge. He continued holding up his pants with his right hand as he ran, staining the crotch red.

Zeng Wanfu continued running until he made it back to Xizhen, where he went straight to Gu Yimin's door. Only then did he realize there were no longer any bullets whizzing by him. As he stood there gasping for breath and holding up his pants, he looked fearfully all around him.

Gu Yimin was in the study when he heard his servant tell him that Zeng Wanfu had returned. This surprised him, be-cause Zeng Wanfu and the others had only been gone no more than three *shichen*. He had the feeling something was wrong, so he left the study and went to the main hall where Zeng Wanfu was standing, still holding up his pants, looking scared out of his mind.

When he saw Gu Yimin emerge, Zeng Wanfu began sputter-ing out a few words—fighting, bullets, Beiyang Army, National Revolutionary Army. He felt like Gu Yimin was staring at his crotch, so he also looked down. As soon as he laid eyes on that sea of red, his head felt dizzy, and he collapsed on the ground with a thud.

After narrowly escaping death, Zeng Wanfu remained deliri-ous for the next few days. If someone asked him a question, he would just stare at them blankly, as if he didn't even recognize the person who was talking to him. When he was alone, he would often raise his right hand with its missing middle finger and stare at it in a daze, as if he were contemplating the reason there were only four fingers. No one was able to get any infor-mation from him about Chen Shun or Zhang Pinsan, and when they checked his pockets they were unable to locate the stack of twenty-three banknotes. Gu Yimin remembered personally handing them to him in front of the temple of the city god right before they set off; some people said they had seen him pass them to Chen Shun, while others said they had seen him pass them to Zhang Pinsan. Most people said they hadn't paid any attention—they had been absorbed in the majestic atmosphere of the occasion. The three men had displayed such a heroic spirit as they set off, yet the result had been Zeng Wanfu losing his wits and returning like a fool, with no sign of the other two.

34.

Before the search party Gu Yimin had sent out for Chen Shun and Zhang Pinsan had returned, a terrifying piece of news arrived. A regiment of the Beiyang Army stationed in Shimen, over two hundred *li* from Xizhen, had been defeated, and as they were retreating they ran into another branch of the National Revolutionary Army—the defeated troops turned around and were now headed toward Xizhen. These ragtag remnants looted and plundered as they went. Chickens flew away, dogs ran, and the people who lived in the army's path fled for their lives—refugees appeared intermittently for a ten *li* stretch, traveling over the frozen land with no particular destination.

One morning, when the people of Xizhen opened their doors, they were met with over a hundred refugees who had entered through the town's north gate. These people, having abandoned their homes, were carrying bundles, satchels, sons, and daughters; some were wrapped in blankets, some had children on their backs, some were pushing the elderly in single-wheeled carts. They headed down the main street of Xizhen and on out the south gate, looking utterly exhausted. They told the people of Xizhen that the retreating Beiyang Army was headed straight for them.

The scene from that morning continued the rest of the day, as refugees traveling in small groups of threes and fours kept appearing on the streets of Xizhen. Some went to the homes of relatives and friends in town, where they would drink a bowl of hot rice porridge and tell through bitter smiles how the Beiyang Army had burned, murdered, stolen, and raped—they were better at banditry than the bandits, they said. Other people stood on the street telling their stories of how they'd fled—some hid under upside-down baskets and waited for the horror to pass; some climbed up in their rafters; some splattered themselves in mud and played dead. One woman holding a baby described her husband's death: as she hid in the cellar, her nipple stuck in the baby's mouth to keep it from crying, she'd heard his final screams. At the time she hadn't dared utter a peep, but as she recounted this now, she burst out in loud wails.

Some townsfolk gathered up their belongings and followed the refugees out the south gate, planning to go stay with friends and relatives elsewhere. The fear the refugees brought with them spread across town, and as more of them came in the north gate, more residents of Xizhen followed them out through the south gate.

Some felt that fleeing wasn't the best option. Although the retreating Beiyang Army was acting like bandits, they weren't actually bandits, and they weren't going to settle down somewhere and put down roots—they were just wreaking havoc as they retreated. If you just hid from them as they came through, you could simply wait for them to move on, and Xizhen could remain intact. Some people thought of the vast expanse of marshland in the Wanmudang and said that was a good place to hide. Many agreed with this, but how would they manage it? Some suggested boats, but others immediately said that would never work—how many people could those at the wharf hold? Someone suggested having Lin Xiangfu's woodworking shop quickly build a few boats, but everyone shook their heads. The Beiyang Army was practically staring them in the face—there was barely enough time to make a wash basin, let alone a few boats. The person countered by asking how there could not be enough time to make a wash basin; it only took an afternoon. The crowd then asked, could a wash basin hold all of Xizhen's twenty thousand residents? You'd have to make at least twenty thousand wash basins, and moreover, fitting a full-grown adult in a wash basin wouldn't be easy.

Then someone suggested they could make bamboo rafts. As soon as they said this, several clever people ran back to their homes and got axes, then rushed off to the bamboo forest in the western hills. By that afternoon, the western hills were covered in men from Xizhen, the sound of their shouts mingling with the chopping of bamboo. In no time at all, a sizeable chunk of the luxuriant forest had been decimated. While still out in the hills, they cleared the branches and leaves from the bamboo, then used cleaving knives to cut the bamboo into poles of equal length. Then they carried the poles back down to Xizhen and spread them out along the water's edge, which quickly became completely covered with them. First they used rope to lash together a frame, then lined the bamboo poles up one-by-one and lashed them on to complete the raft. Xizhen's waterside was bustling with activity, and excited children ran this way and that. This was the first time many of the townsfolk had made a bamboo raft, so they learned as they went—they bound the bamboo poles together with only one layer of rope, binding their rafts the same way they bound their kindling.

Two days later, the water was covered in bamboo rafts, like rice drying in the fields after the harvest. After making the rafts, the men returned home, their faces covered in sweat and their hands covered in blisters; their wives had already packed up their things, ready to board the rafts and hide in the marshes of the Wanmudang. The fleets of rafts eased the minds of those still in Xizhen. They planned to wait until just before the Beiyang Army arrived to get on their rafts and flee into the marshes.

Some people worried the Beiyang Army would attack Xizhen

by surprise during the night, so they prepared their luggage in advance and carried their bundles down to the water after nightfall, where they boarded their rafts and set out for the marshes. The sight of their shadowy figures gradually retreating in the moonlight filled the remaining townsfolk with anxiety. They assumed they must have heard something, so they quickly followed suit, loading their children and elderly relatives onto rafts and joining the shadowy figures floating away in the darkness.

Then word came that the pillaging Beiyang Army was only about ten *li* from Xizhen. In no time at all, the waterside became crammed with fleeing townsfolk, each pushing and shoving their way to their own family's raft. Some rafts fell apart before they even set sail, while others splintered out in the middle of the water. Many people plunged into the bone-chilling water—some elderly people and children succumbed to the cold after only a minimal struggle, while the stronger adults climbed up onto neighboring rafts. This caused more rafts to break apart under the added weight, so more people plunged into the water, and more people drowned.

The night sky over Xizhen rang out with cries for help.

35.

Neither Lin Xiangfu nor Chen Yongliang went to the western hills to cut bamboo for rafts; they had prepared to flee by land. When the news came that the Beiyang Army was ten *li* from Xizhen, they had already prepared their luggage and loaded it on that noisy cart of Chen Yongliang's. Lin Xiangfu lifted Lin Baijia and Chen Yaowen up onto the cart, Li Meilian locked the door, and Chen Yongliang started pulling. But just then, Li Meilian unlocked the door and, standing in the doorway, announced to the two men:

"I'm not going. I'll stay behind—you all go ahead."

"The bandit army's almost here, and now you're wanting to stay behind?" asked Chen Yongliang.

"I can't go—what if our son comes back and can't find anyone—what will he do?" said Li Meilian.

Chen Yongliang shook his head and said, "We can't worry about him at a time like this."

"You all go on," said Li Meilian. "I'll stay here and wait for our son."

"If you're not leaving, none of us are," said Chen Yongliang.

Li Meilian shook her head resolutely. "I can't go," she said.

"You must want us to all stay here and die!" shouted Chen Yongliang.

Li Meilian began crying. "No," she said.

Chen Yongliang pointed to Lin Baijia and Chen Yaowen on the cart and said, "We've got two children here—if you don't want them to die, lock the door and come along!"

With that, Chen Yongliang picked up the cart and started walking. "I can't lock the door," said Li Meilian. "If our son comes home, he needs to be able to get in the house."

"Don't lock it, then," said Chen Yongliang. "Let's go."

Li Meilian wiped her tears and started following after the cart. After walking about ten meters, they realized that Lin Xiangfu wasn't with them—now he was standing in the doorway.

"I'll wait for Chen Yaowu to come back," he called after them. "You take Lin Baijia and Chen Yaowen and go."

Chen Yongliang shook his head and said to Lin Xiangfu, "If one of us isn't going, none of us are."

Lin Xiangfu pointed to Lin Baijia and Chen Yaowen on the cart and said, "Go on now, for the sake of the children."

Chen Yongliang put down the cart, walked over to Lin Xiangfu, and said, "I'll stay—you two take the children and go."

Li Meilian followed Chen Yongliang over and said to Lin Xiangfu, "I'll stay, too—you take the children and go."

With a bitter smile, Lin Xiangfu said, "With Lin Baijia in your care, I know I'll have nothing to worry about."

"And we won't have anything to worry about with Chen Yaowen in your care," argued Chen Yongliang.

Just then, one of Gu Yimin's servants came running up and said his master requested the presence of Lin Xiangfu and Chen Yongliang to discuss an urgent matter, so the two men ended their stalemate and told the servant they would be there at once. The servant said he needed to go tell some others and ran off. Chen Yongliang went over to the cart and pulled it back into the courtyard, where he watched Lin Baijia and Chen Yaowen hop off. Then he told Li Meilian to wait at home, and he and Lin Xiangfu set out.

It was already evening in Xizhen as Lin Xiangfu and Chen Yongliang walked through the deserted streets. As they approached the south gate, they noticed that many people who had already left were now streaming back in. The returning people told them that the Beiyang Army was still over a hundred *li* from Xizhen.

When Lin Xiangfu and Chen Yongliang entered Gu Yimin's main hall, they saw that nearly all the important people in Xizhen were gathered there. Gu Yimin was speaking:

"I went down to the wharf this afternoon to have a look and saw that nearly half the rafts had broken apart, and the water was covered with pieces of bamboo. Many people had fallen into the water, and a number of them drowned. I never felt that running and hiding was a good option. When the retreating Beiyang Army sees something they want, they take it; when they see a house, they burn it. People might be able to avoid them, but the town can't. The Beiyang army will rob Xizhen clean and burn it to the ground, and when the people who fled come back, I'm afraid they'll only be returning to piles of rubble. This would be the biggest loss. I think everyone should stay put, give the Beiyang Army a warm welcome, and treat them well. Even though they're fleeing in retreat, they're still the military—not bandits."

36.

Xizhen descended into a state of grief. Over a hundred people had drowned in the water, and nearly a thousand had fallen in and been saved, only to then fell seriously ill with high fevers. Between the fear and the hypothermia, illness spread quickly through Xizhen, and the sound of coughing and sneezing could be heard all up and down the streets and lanes.

Gu Yimin sent people from the chamber of commerce to reserve all the taverns and restaurants in town and have them ready to greet the Beiyang Army with a feast. There were still a few refugees passing through Xizhen, but the townsfolk no longer followed them. The disaster of the rafts had caused them to give up on fleeing, and they felt like Gu Yimin was right—they only need welcome the Beiyang Army and treat them well, and Xizhen would be spared.

The skies over Xizhen were overcast for two quiet days, and then the sun came out, glinting off the snow and making Xizhen sparkle. By the afternoon, some people noticed that no refugees had passed through that day. When Gu Yimin heard this, he sent out word that the restaurants and taverns should prepare all their best dishes along with some local yellow rice wine—the Beiyang Army would soon be there. One *shichen* later, the faint sound of hoofbeats could be heard. Gu Yimin immediately stood and led the members of the chamber of commerce, along with a large number of townsfolk, to welcome the Beiyang Army outside the town's north gate.

A cavalry unit came galloping forward, the sound of the horses breaking through the winter air. The group assembled outside the gate to welcome the army trembled with fear. When the cavalry unit was about two *li* away, they pulled back on the reins, looked at the group standing outside the gate for a few moments, and turned around. As they rode away, the horses' hooves kicked up so much snow the townsfolk could no longer see the horses or their riders. Roughly another *shichen* passed, and the main unit of the Beiyang Army appeared. Making no distinction between road or field, they approached like a giant swarm, coming in waves. One group of over a hundred led eight horses pulling two large cannons. They rumbled over the fields, trampling everything underfoot.

A handsome young officer brandishing a whip came riding over to the gate and shouted, "Who's the leader?"

Gu Yimin stepped forward and introduced himself as the head of Xizhen's chamber of commerce. He said the people of Xizhen had come out to welcome them, and that all the restaurants in Xizhen had already laid out a banquet in honor of the esteemed army's arrival. The officer nodded, then rode away. Then the brigade commander, surrounded by dozens of cavalrymen, rode up to the gate and dismounted his horse. He walked up to Gu Yimin and bowed with both hands clasped, then said with a big smile,

"Many thanks to all for the kind reception."

Over a thousand troops proceeded to flood through the north gate of Xizhen, which took half a *shichen*. Even though it was the middle of winter, most of the soldiers were wearing only one thin layer of clothing. Some wore clothing they had stolen along the way—some were in long *changpao* gowns; some were in short *duan'ao* jackets; some were in inside-out fur coats; some were in women's floral *hua'ao* jackets; some had formal hats on their heads; more still had floral headscarves wrapped around them. After entering Xizhen, they immediately squeezed into the restaurants and taverns and greedily devoured the food. The sounds of chewing, laughing, and shouting seemed like they would go on forever—it sounded as if all the livestock from the surrounding area had converged on Xizhen and were making a continuous racket. The brigade commander and the handsome young lieutenant, along with over twenty other officers, had been invited to Gu Yimin's house for a meal, with the brigade commander and his aides-de-camp sharing a more intimate family-style meal with Gu Yimin himself. After they had eaten and drunk their fill, he invited them to another room to relax and had some opium sent in. As the brigade commander smoked the opium, Gu Yimin ventured,

"Commander, in the cold of the twelfth month, many of the soldiers in your illustrious army seem to be dressed in a single layer of clothing. If hunger and cold drives the soldiers to make some mistakes, and if your higher-ups were to investigate things, wouldn't you have to bear the responsibility as their commander?"

"These days, everything seems like it's headed to a dead end," said the commander as he smoked. "What am I supposed to do?"

"Within the next three days, I'd like to make new winter uniforms for the entire army," Gu Yimin said. "I'd also like to feed them and pay their wages for the month. If the commander would be so kind as to call in the quartermaster, I can ask him how we might best go about this, and how many taels of silver we'll need."

"There's no need to ask the quartermaster," the commander replied. "I'm very familiar with the situation. Sixty thousand taels should be enough for the winter clothing and one month's provisions."

Gu Yimin immediately agreed, and promised that within three days he would have over a thousand winter uniforms ready, as well as the pay and provisions. Gu Yimin knew that the few tailors in Xizhen could never make over a thousand uniforms in three days, so he had them only make the uniforms for the officers. For the regular soldiers' uniforms, he had the chamber of commerce organize the housewives from over a thousand families to make them.

Over the next three days, the housewives stayed inside to cut the materials for the uniforms and went outside to do the sewing in the sun. They were all quite skilled at this task, as they were usually the ones who made the clothes for their families.

Gu Yimin encouraged the chamber of commerce to make

some room in all the inns, warehouses, and shops so they might
be used as barracks. To prevent the women from respectable
families from being violated, Gu Yimin had the chamber of
commerce hire out Xizhen's two brothels, which would be given
over to soldiers to quench their lust. He also sought out the
good-looking independent prostitutes. There were over twenty
of them, and they were different from those in the brothels—
they all wore clothing made of blue calico, and they didn't wear
make-up or lipstick. While usually they would quietly receive
their guests in their homes, they now lined up for the brigade
officers, regimental commanders, battalion commanders, and
company commanders to choose from. Each of these prostitutes wore a bashful expression and smiled the whole time,
from the battalion commanders right down to the company
commanders.

The first battalion commander to pick couldn't seem to make
up his mind—he said he liked the fat ones as well as the skinny
ones, and wasn't sure which one he should choose. The other
commanders said battalion commander, if you like fat ones and
skinny ones, just take one of each—draw your bow on both
sides, shoot with two guns!—show everyone the heroic nature
of your position. The battalion commander smiled and nodded
in agreement, saying that maybe he should draw his bow on
both sides. After he chose his two, the other commanders made
their selections. The ones who liked breasts chose ones with big
breasts; the ones who liked butts chose ones with big butts; the
ones who liked slender figures chose skinny ones; the ones who
liked fuller figures chose fat ones; the ones who liked the classic "melon seed" face chose ones with oval faces; the ones who
liked a "goose egg" face chose ones with round faces; the ones
who liked eyes chose ones with bright, black eyes. Then they
each took their selections and led them away like goats.

The platoon leaders and squad leaders had no choice but
to wait on the streets outside in the cold with the regular soldiers. Of course they were not going to stand there freezing

their legs off with the ordinary troops, so they ordered the soldiers crowded in front of the brothel doors to let them through. Even livestock knows how to make way, they cursed—you're all dumber than a bunch of fucking cows.

Once inside the brothel, burning with desire, they each rushed for a room and had the prostitutes spread their legs. Take it easy, commanders, said the prostitutes. The commanders swore at them: even dogs know how to spread their legs—you're more fucking worthless than a bitch! When the platoon leaders and squad leaders finally emerged from the brothel, the soldiers began elbowing their way in, one after another, like a bunch of starving maniacs.

That afternoon, the battalion commander crawled out from between the fat prostitute and the skinny prostitute. He donned his uniform and took the handsome young lieutenant and some guards to go walking along the streets of Xizhen to inspect the troops. When they passed the brothels, they saw that the streets around them were crowded with soldiers, waves of heat emanating from their bodies. The battalion commander asked his lieutenant—"what's going on here?"

"We're at the brothels," answered the lieutenant.

The battalion commander became angry and said to his lieutenant,

"Outrageous! This is supposed to be an army? It looks more like starving peasants raiding a granary. Send out the order: no more pushing and shoving in a clump. Give me two nice straight lines, and enter the brothel in a civilized manner. The orderly conduct of our military extends to visiting prostitutes."

After the lieutenant called over the platoon leaders and squad leaders and issued the orders, the leaders started shouting and cursing, and eventually the clump of soldiers formed into two straight lines. The lines were so long they snaked through the streets and lanes, causing the soldiers at the end to hang their heads in disappointment. When they were all in a clump, they said, they could at least still see the brothels' lanterns; now that the lines stretched down the street and went around several corners, they couldn't even see the brothels' roofs, let alone the lanterns.

By evening, the prostitutes in the brothels were exhausted. They had each dealt with dozens of soldiers, and they complained to their madams that their breasts were swollen from all the squeezing, and their legs felt like they'd been dislocated. They begged for mercy and asked for the doors to be shut. With sullen faces, the madams said they couldn't shut the doors—all the customers waiting outside had guns, they said, and if we shut the doors and they start shooting, we'll all have more holes in us than a honeycomb.

So the scene continued late into the night. The hands and feet of the soldiers who had been standing out in the cold wind all day were numb. When some of them got close enough to see the brothels' doors, they rubbed their frozen bodies and said that even if they were to make it inside now, they wouldn't be able to do anything, so they might as well just go to bed. Frozen stiff and cursing to themselves, they walked away. When the soldiers who held out to the end finally made it into the brothels, they saw the naked prostitutes lying motionless on their backs as if they were dead. The soldiers still had the desire but not the strength, and they desperately rubbed their hands, legs, and the rest of their bodies. The soldiers still waiting in line began shouting and swearing, so the ones inside decided they had to get things over with as quickly as possible. They groped the prostitutes' bodies, but their hands were so cold they could hardly feel a thing. It was as if they were holding wooden sticks in their hands and groping the prostitutes with those.

The next day, both brothels had to call a truce. The prostitutes had struggled valiantly all day and all night, but now some were bleeding, some had dislocated joints, and others were barely breathing. The thought of the whole experience made the madams of the two brothels tremble like frightened little birds—the Beiyang Army was large and vicious, they said.

At another banquet with the battalion commander, Gu Yimin said through a bitter smile, "Xizhen used to have such a flourishing red-light district, but after suffering this onslaught, I'm afraid it will take it a while to recover."

The battalion commander said to his subordinate, "Chamber President Gu has shown us every consideration and done everything he could. Put out the order to all the troops that no one is permitted to disturb the townsfolk—any looting, pillaging, or raping will be punishable by immediate execution."

37.

The situation at the brothels made the independent prostitutes who had serviced the commanders flee out of fear. For the next two days, the soldiers would eat and drink their fill in the restaurants, then go out with their rifles in groups of three or four and find a spot to sun themselves. Unable to find any women, the commanders could only pass the time by lying around smoking opium.

After one such occasion, a company commander went out in the middle of the night and knocked on the doors of five houses until he found a passably attractive young woman. He crawled on top of her trembling body and didn't stop until dawn, when he finally fell asleep and slept until noon.

The young woman's parents suffered through the night and bit their tongues. The next morning they went to Gu Yimin and told him everything through a flood of tears. Gu Yimin offered them some words of comfort and went to tell the battalion commander. After hearing what had happened, the battalion commander became enraged and issued an order for execution on the spot. The battalion commander's lieutenant took two guards with him to go rouse the company commander and drag him out of bed.

That day, the seventeen-year-old lieutenant spotted the

twelve-year-old Lin Baijia down by the Xizhen wharf—she was taller and more slender than other girls her age, looking more like thirteen or fourteen. As the lieutenant and the two guards dragged the offending commander into a tavern, a group of children followed behind them, including one particularly lovely young girl. The lieutenant couldn't help but keep glancing over. Once the men had been seated, Lin Baijia and the rest of the children stood outside the window and looked in. The lieutenant ordered a full spread of food and drink and said to the company commander, who was still a bit groggy,

"Commander, this meal is the battalion commander's treat— eat your fill!"

The company commander, a man in his thirties, knew his death was fast approaching. He said to the lieutenant, "Lieutenant Li, my parents died young, and I'm about to go meet them in the netherworld. Please promise me one thing."

The lieutenant looked over at Lin Baijia on the other side of the window, then turned back and said, "Please continue."

The company commander pointed at his face and said, "Don't shoot me here. If you do, I won't be able to face my parents."

The commander then pointed to his heart and said, "Shoot me here."

The lieutenant nodded and raised his glass. "You have my word," he said.

The company commander drained his glass, and then three more. His face flushed the color of a pig's liver and he began shoving huge bites of meat into his mouth and chewing loudly. The lieutenant kept toasting him, all the while continuing to glance out the window at Lin Baijia. He smiled at her, and when she saw the kind face of this handsome young officer, she couldn't help but return his smiles. Then he got up, walked over to the window, and asked Lin Baijia her name and where she lived. Lin Baijia answered his questions one at a time, but when she said she was from the Lin family, Chen Yaowen, who was standing beside her, piped up,

"No she's not—she's a member of the Gu family."

The lieutenant saw Lin Baijia blush, and as he walked away he couldn't help but look back at her once more. Then he sat back down at the table and continued toasting the company commander and encouraging him to eat.

That afternoon, the lieutenant got the offending company commander drunk as a skunk, then had the two accompanying guards help him out of the tavern. The lieutenant saw that outside the tavern was a mass of bobbing heads—the news of the commander's execution was buzzing around Xizhen like a swarm of flies, and everyone had gone down to the wharf and crowded around the tavern. When the lieutenant and his party left and headed north, the crowd followed them to the north gate like a giant wave.

The seventeen-year-old lieutenant, in high spirits and full of energy, waved his hand and signaled for the crowd to make way. The drunk company commander staggered along, causing the two guards supporting him to work up a sweat. The commander giggled like a fool the whole way, singing and shouting:

"*Dang li-ge-dang, dang li-ge-dang, dang li-ge dang li-ge dang li-ge dang;* the northwest wind blows, *hu-hu,* freezing my bones; sister, sister, help me out; use that pussy to warm up a dick!"

A few of the residents of Xizhen were able to understand what the commander was singing and burst out in gales of laughter. The lieutenant and the two guards also started laughing, and the lieutenant explained to the crowd,

"The company commander is reciting a Shandong *kuaishu* clapper rhyme—he's from Liaocheng in Shandong province."

As the commander kept on with his "*dang li-ge-dang,*" the crowd kept growing and continued on out through Xizhen's north gate. The two guards dragging the commander told the lieutenant that they had walked and laughed so much, they were too exhausted to make it much further. So the lieutenant stopped and waved his hand, indicating for the crowd to give them some space. He saw a large tree by the side of the road, so he had the two guards pull the commander over and lean him against it. The commander's head slumped over as he continued to sing,

"*Dang li-ge-dang;* sister, sister, help me out . . . "

The lieutenant told the guards, who were also the executioners, to aim for the heart, not the face. The two guards raised their guns, the lieutenant gave the command, and two bullets went into the commander's stomach. The commander reacted as if he had been kicked—he slid down to the ground, his eyes opened wide from the pain. He stared at the lieutenant and the rest of the crowd with a surprised look on his face, and then he uttered his final "*dang li-ge-dang.*"

The lieutenant scolded the two guards, "I clearly ordered you to shoot him in the heart, and you shoot his belly instead."

Panting, one of the guards said, "The commander's big and heavy—after dragging him such a long way and laughing the whole time, we don't have any strength left. We could only raise our guns to the level of his belly; we couldn't get them up to his chest."

The lieutenant took a rifle from one of the guards and walked up to the commander. He could see all the food he had just eaten spilling out along with his intestines, slowly slithering down the side of the road.

By this point the commander was no longer singing. He had sobered up and was gazing sorrowfully at the lieutenant as he aimed the barrel of the rifle at his chest. As the lieutenant pulled back the trigger, a single tear fell from the commander's eyes. The gun sounded, and the commander's body jolted; then his head slumped down further to the side. Finally, his body fell over next to the tree.

The lieutenant, his clothes splattered with fresh blood, turned around and saw Lin Baijia. Her face appeared through a break in the crowd, her eyes fearful and utterly bewitching.

38.

Just as Gu Yimin had promised, over a thousand winter uniforms and one month's pay and provisions were delivered to the soldiers. One morning the battalion commander took his lieutenant and guards over to the woodworking shop, which made Lin Xiangfu and Chen Yongliang incredibly nervous. Once the commander and his entourage had been seated, the two of them remained standing obsequiously off to the side. The battalion commander invited them to sit and asked which one was Lin Xiangfu. Then he pointed to the lieutenant and said,

"This lieutenant is my nephew; his name is Li Yuancheng. He's from a poor family, and his parents died when he was young. He was apprenticed to a tailor, but when I passed through his hometown the year before last, he put down his needle and thread, took up a gun, and came with me. Today in Xizhen he saw a young woman as lovely as Xishi, the famous beauty—it turns out she's the daughter of this house. My nephew would now like to put down his gun and take up his needle and thread once more, to join with your daughter in everlasting harmony."

When Lin Xiangfu heard what the battalion commander had to say, a dark cloud passed over his face, and he stammered, "Having the opportunity to join families with the battalion commander would be the greatest honor of three lifetimes. But my daughter is only twelve years old, and hasn't yet reached the age for marriage."

"They wouldn't have to get married now," the commander said. "My nephew could first get engaged to your daughter, and after the engagement he could set up a tailor shop next to your woodworking business. When the time for their marriage comes, I'll return and drink the wine at their wedding."

Lin Xiangfu had no choice but to reveal the truth of the matter: "My daughter has already been promised to Gu Tongnian, the oldest son of the president of Xizhen's chamber of commerce, Gu Yimin."

After he said this, the battalion commander's face took on a blank expression. Lin Xiangfu began to tremble, and Chen Yongliang quickly added,

"They've already had the engagement feast."

The commander smiled and said, "My congratulations on joining families with Chamber President Gu."

Upon saying this the commander stood up, turned to his lieutenant, and said, "The young lady is already spoken for, so you'd best put her out of your mind. Continue following your uncle—a life of wandering is your fate."

Li Yuancheng nodded and said to his uncle, the commander: "I'll keep my gun and follow my uncle."

Lin Xiangfu and Chen Yongliang bowed and said, "Please excuse this impropriety on the part of your inferiors."

As they went out to the courtyard, they saw Lin Baijia and Chen Yaowen. The handsome young lieutenant stopped and said to Lin Baijia,

"Remember me, Li Yuancheng. In the future, if you come across a heroic Li Yuancheng in the newspaper, it will definitely be me. If you ever run into any trouble, come find me."

Lin Baijia had never heard anyone speak like this before, and she couldn't help but smile. The battalion commander let out a big laugh and took his leave from Lin Xiangfu and Chen Yongliang with a bow, then led his nephew and guards out of the woodworking shop.

The defeated army occupied Xizhen for three days. After lunch on the third day, the troops gathered in the plaza in front of the temple of the city god and made a grand exit through Xizhen's north gate. Gu Yimin had the chamber of commerce mobilize the citizens to line the streets and bid the army farewell, while he and the battalion commander walked in front of the troops. When they parted outside the north gate, the commander said to Gu Yimin,

"Truth be told, our army had originally intended to loot and pillage all the wealthy families in town. But when you extended such benevolence toward us, we could not do it."

The Beiyang Army followed the main road as it snaked its way out into the distance, their warm breath rising up over the snowy ground and into the cold winter air like a cloud of steam. The battalion commander and his lieutenant rode on horseback. Their cavalry quickly rode up through the fields and surrounded them, the horses' hooves kicking up the snow and obscuring their figures as they departed.

After Gu Yimin bowed and bid his farewells with the crowd at the north gate, he got in his sedan chair and had his carriers head straight for the western hills. After the road had taken them up a mountain slope, Gu Yimin got out of the sedan and looked out over the whole of Xizhen. He stood there for a long time gazing at the buildings and streets below, covered in snow and still completely intact, even dotted with a few pedestrians. Gu Yimin let out a long sigh, then got back in his sedan and told the carriers,

"Go home."

39.

Some people down at the wharf spotted Zeng Wanfu in a little boat with a bamboo awning, calling out loudly to solicit customers just as he had before—the Zeng Wanfu who had been scared silly was suddenly no longer silly. Out of curiosity, some people went to the wharf to talk to him, and he answered their questions clearly and fluently. When someone asked him what happened to his finger, though, he looked completely baffled—he had no idea. When they asked about Chen Shun and Zhang Pinsan and what happened when they went to deliver the ransom money, he simply eyed them suspiciously, with no recollection of anything to do with ransom money.

The two servants Gu Yimin had sent out to search for Chen Shun and Zhang Pinsan had long since returned. They searched along the road as they went, and when they were about to reach the Guanyin temple, they discovered a large number of corpses covered over with snow. They searched through them and found Chen Shun and Zhang Pinsan, and in Chen Shun's pocket they found the wad of cash. The servants returned just as the Beiyang Army was about to enter the town, so Gu Yimin kept the information to himself. Now that the army had left, he was considering what to say to the townsfolk, and how to once more try to ransom the hostages.

Then a barber strolled into Xizhen with his carrying pole, asking around for Lin Xiangfu and Chen Yongliang. When he made it to their door, he opened a little drawer built into the stool he carried, took out a letter, and held it up in the air as he called out,

"Letter for Chen Yongliang! Letter for Chen Yongliang!"

Li Meilian came out of the house, and when the barber handed her the letter, he said he'd been sent by the bandits who had taken the hostages. As soon as she heard the letter was from the bandits, Li Meilian grabbed the letter and ran inside, calling to Lin Xiangfu and Chen Yongliang,

"The bandits sent a letter!"

Chen Yongliang took the letter, opened it, and pulled out a piece of paper and an ear. The ear fell on the table. Chen Yongliang's face turned white as a sheet, and the hand holding the letter began trembling. Li Meilian looked at the ear on the table and asked in horror,

"What is that?"

Lin Baijia, who was standing nearby, picked it up and carefully examined it. This ear has a mole on it, she told Li Meilian—Chen Yaowu had a mole on his left ear, and this one looks exactly the same as that one.

Li Meilian looked at the letter in Chen Yongliang's hand and asked in a trembling voice, "What does it say?"

Lin Xiangfu took the letter. After reading it over, he told Chen Yongliang and Li Meilian that because the ransom money wasn't received at the appointed time and place, the hostages each had an ear cut off. If the ransom money wasn't received within ten days, the bandits would be sending the hostage's heads.

As soon as he said this, Li Meilian grew dizzy and fainted. It was already dark by the time she regained consciousness, and she began crying with long, drawn-out sobs. Her crying sounded like the repetitive tune of a traditional *changshu* story, and her long howls were interspersed with mournful sighs.

Over the next two days, one after the other, a peddler, a dentist, a cobbler, an elderly traveling pharmacist, and a peasant who had been out cutting firewood came to Xizhen delivering letters from the bandits to the families of the hostages. Each letter contained an ear and the same basic message Chen Yongliang had received. But the handwriting and sentence length of the letters was all different, and each one specified a different location for the delivery of the ransom money. According to the people who delivered the letters, they had all met with different bandits at different places, some in groups of two or three, others in groups of five or six—the bandits had robbed them and then forced them to carry the letters to Xizhen. The dentist and the elderly traveling pharmacist said that the bandits they met didn't know how to write, so they dictated their letters.

Eventually all the letters made it to Gu Yimin, and the families of all the hostages met in his main hall. After reading over each letter carefully, Gu Yimin said that before, there had only been one location for the delivery of the ransom money, but now they were spread all over the place; the Beiyang and National Revolutionary Armies had been fighting a lot recently, so the bandits hadn't had many opportunities to loot and plunder—their main group had likely splintered apart, so the collection points for the ransom were all different.

Gu Yimin told them that the corpses of Chen Shun and

Zhang Pinsan had already been found, along with the money. "This time," he said, "The best method will be for the family members to each deliver the ransom themselves, as carefully as possible. There's just one point I'd like to emphasize: if you discover there's been a mistake, don't say anything and just go with it—no matter whose family the hostage is from, just bring them back. If we can get all the hostages back safely, even if everyone brings back the wrong one, we'll have the right outcome."

40.

As the moon was rising, Chen Yongliang exited the north gate with the ransom money tucked in his chest and headed toward the location specified in the bandits' note.

Night had already fallen before he left. Li Meilian was worried, and she begged Chen Yongliang to wait until the next morning to deliver the ransom. Chen Yongliang looked up at the sky and said that the moon was bright that night, so he wouldn't get lost. Lin Xiangfu said he would go with him; the two of them should be able to look after one another. Chen Yongliang didn't agree, saying it was too dangerous—one of them had to remain at home. Lin Xiangfu said in that case, he should be the one to go, and Chen Yongliang should stay behind. Chen Yongliang shook his head and said that with Chen Yaowu gone, he was already worried about one person; if Lin Xiangfu went to deliver the ransom, then he would be worried about two people and would feel too anxious just sitting at home—so it was better for him to just go himself.

The two of them kept quietly arguing as they went out the door. When they got out to the road, Lin Xiangfu no longer held back—if something were to happen to Chen Yongliang, how would he and Li Meilian manage with the children? He should be the one to deliver the ransom. But Chen Yongliang held firm, saying that the only way he could feel at peace would be for him to deliver the money himself. As they neared the north gate, Lin Xiangfu had no choice but to give up and watch his friend continue on alone.

When Chen Yongliang exited through the north gate, he saw about a dozen people walking silently ahead of him. One of them looked back and saw him, then said something; the rest of the group stopped and waited for Chen Yongliang to catch up. Chen Yongliang saw that they were all the fathers or brothers of the hostages. When he caught up to them, they continued standing there looking back at the north gate they'd just exited. Chen Yongliang turned to look and saw other fathers and brothers of hostages coming out to join them. When the group delivering their ransoms to the bandits had finally assembled, someone counted them up; when they reached twenty-three, they announced that everyone was there.

They walked ahead in the darkness, the silent moonlight illuminating their quiet group. They knew they were walking into an unknown fate, yet they all wore slight smiles on their faces. Not one of them had waited until morning to deliver the ransom, so they felt encouraged by one another's presence.

When they arrived at a large intersection, seven of them turned left, while the rest of the group stopped and watched them walk away, as if seeing them off. When they had gone about twenty meters, the rest of the group turned right and continued on their way. This pattern continued as they went—a few, or sometimes just one, would branch off on another road, and the rest of the group would stop and watch them go. The group grew smaller and smaller, and by the time Chen Yongliang turned off on a small road, there were only four left. The group of four stood and watched Chen Yongliang walk away. When he had gone about ten meters, Chen Yongliang turned back and saw they were still standing there; he waved to them and they waved back, then he turned and continued on.

41.

The bandits who entered Xizhen and took hostages on the twelfth day of the twelfth month belonged to three different factions, known by the nicknames of their bandit leaders: Floater, Leopard Li, and The Monk. Floater's was the largest, with seven members, then Leopard Li's with five, and finally The Monk's with only three. These fifteen bandits captured twenty-three hostages in Xizhen and took them out the north gate into the frozen expanse of snow.

Chen Yaowu, wearing a red silk embroidered *mian'ao* jacket, was walking in the front; behind him were Li Zhanggui of the soy sauce shop, Blacksmith Xu, the fried dough-stick seller Chen Sanhe, and the clerk at the tofu shop Big-Eyes Tang. To reduce the tracks they made in the snow, the pistol-carrying bandit called Floater had the hostages step in the same set of footprints as they walked. So the twenty three hostages proceeded with their heads down, careful to stay within the single set of footprints—they stretched out in a line as they trudged ahead on the snow-covered road, like a long, wriggling worm. When the soy sauce seller Li Zhanggui accidentally stepped outside a print, the bandit called Leopard Li hit him over the head with the butt of his rifle; he cried out and fell down on the snowy ground, pulling down Chen Yaowu, Blacksmith Xu, and a few others along with him. Floater and Leopard Li began kicking them viciously until they each got up. Only Li Zhanggui remained lying on the ground without moving, so they started beating him again with the butts of their rifles. He didn't move, so they began kicking his head.

"He's probably dead," said the bandit called The Monk, carrying a rifle on his back.

"He's fucking playing dead," said Floater. "Shoot him."

Leopard Li pointed his rifle at Li Zhanggui's forehead and pulled back the bolt. As soon as Li Zhanggui heard the gun being cocked, he jolted upright and immediately stammered,

"Master! Master! I can walk!"

They continued following in the footsteps in front of them, slowly making their way up a mountain path until they came to a babbling brook. Then the bandits made them walk in the water and follow the stream—this would prevent them from making any footprints. At first, the freezing water of this wintry stream pierced through to their bones, but eventually their feet became numb and lost sensation.

By evening, they passed through a stand of forest on the mountain, where they came upon a dilapidated thatched cottage. Inside was an old man sitting on his bed, so poor he was dressed in rags and huddled under a blanket. Several of the bandits went in and snatched his blanket, even though the old man clung to it desperately and begged them not to take it, saying it was so tattered it was basically worthless. But without another word, Leopard Li went in and hit the old man in the face with the butt of his rifle. The old man crawled to the door, his face covered in blood and tears streaming down from his eyes, and watched as the bandits tore his blanket into strips, which they then tied around the eyes of the twenty-three hostages. Chen Yaowu saw the old man looking at him just as The Monk tied one of the strips over his eyes.

The blindfolded hostages staggered up one mountain slope and down another, the bandits both walking in front and bringing up the rear. When they heard the barking of dogs, they knew they had entered a village. The tofu seller Big-Eyes Tang whispered to the dough-stick seller Chen San,

"This place looks like Liucun."

As soon as he said this, the butt of a rifle smashed his face and they heard Leopard Li's ferocious voice say,

"The next person to open their motherfucking mouth dies!"

After nightfall, the bandits led the hostages into a damp room and took off their blindfolds. By the light of an oil lamp, they found themselves standing in a large, windowless room. Then they noticed Big-Eyes Tang's black-and-blue face—this clerk at the tofu shop who was known all over Xizhen for his large eyes now had such a swollen face that his eyes could only peek out from two tiny slits.

The bandits tied up each individual hostage with a rope and then connected them all together. They were all seated with their backs against the wall, with the end of the rope hanging from the ceiling in the middle of the room—this made it easier to keep an eye on them. One of the bandits called Li'l Five came in with a load of rice straw and spread it in the middle of the room. Then he spread a blanket over it, draped another blanket around his shoulders, and sat down. Beside him he placed a whip, then greedily began gnawing on a pig's trotter.

The twenty-three hostages sat on the cold, hard ground. The straw beneath them was molded and rotten, and they were hungry, thirsty, and exhausted. As they watched Li'l Five practically making love to his trotter, their empty stomachs began to rumble, but their thirst prevented them from producing any saliva; all they could do was stick out their parched tongues to lick their lips. The other bandits were all playing drinking games in the next room, where the sound of their laughter mingled with the sounds of their chewing. One after another they would get up and come into the room where the hostages were to urinate against the wall. The hostages didn't dare make a peep. Finally Blacksmith Xu couldn't stand it any longer and ventured quietly,

"If there's nothing to eat, that's fine, but could we please have a bowl of water?"

Holding his trotter in his left hand, Li'l Five picked up the whip with his right hand and stared at Blacksmith Xu. When he determined that he was the one who had spoken, he raised the whip and brought it down on the man, leaving a gash on his face.

"Anyone who talks is clearly trying to plot something, so they get their head chopped off."

After saying this, Li'l Five put his whip back down and

started licking the grease off his fingers, then returned to his passionate engagement with the trotter. The hostages, hungry and cold, hung their heads and listened as the bandits ate and drank their fill in the next room, then began smoking opium, playing dominoes, and rolling dice.

42.

The next morning, the bandits took each hostage out to beat and interrogate them. The first one to be taken was the soy sauce seller Li Zhanggui. With a sinister laugh, Floater asked him—how much silver did his family have? Two thousand taels? Li Zhanggui knelt on the ground with an anguished look on his face, kowtowing and begging.

"I just have a small-time business; usually what I make doesn't even cover my costs—please have mercy on me, masters, and let me go."

That gave the bandits a good laugh. "Have mercy on you?" said Leopard Li. "Go find a monk in a temple! We're selling human flesh, and anyone who wants it has got to pay."

With that, Leopard Li kicked over Li Zhanggui as if he were kicking over a stool. Li'l Five and another bandit picked him up and stripped off his clothing, then tied his arms across a carrying pole and hung him from the rafters. Li'l Five and the other bandit stood on either side of him whipping his chest and back; with each crack of the whip, a new welt would raise on Li Zhanggui's body. When the lashes broke the skin, blood would run down in rivulets, and Li Zhanggui would let out bloodcurdling screams. The bandits gave him forty lashes, and Li Zhanggui cried out forty times. Floater said he was tired of hearing his screams, so he took some ashes from the cooking fire and shoved them in Li Zhanggui's mouth. The screams immediately subsided, as did Li Zhanggui's breathing; his face became so pale it looked as if it had been whitewashed, his eyes bulged out, and his body trembled for a few moments before he was able to catch his breath again. The next time he screamed, blood sprayed out of his nose and mouth and splattered over the hostages sitting against the wall.

Floater laughed and asked him, "So you've got two thousand taels?"

Li Zhanggui nodded eagerly as a whimpering sound came from his mouth. Floater said to The Monk, who was sitting beside him acting as the accountant: "Have his family put up two thousand taels."

The next to be taken out was the clerk from the tofu shop, Big-Eyes Tang. Floater asked him how much silver his family had, and Big-Eyes Tang shook his head and said they didn't have a single piece. Floater looked at his swollen, black-and-blue face and said to the two bandits beside him,

"Beat his ass—beat it to a pulp so it looks just like his face."

The two bandits stripped off his pants, pressed him down on a stool, and began striking him viciously with their whips. Big-Eyes Tang gritted his teeth and kept himself from screaming, allowing only heavy breaths to escape his nose. One of the bandits, after giving over a hundred lashes, put down his whip, wiped the sweat from his face, and said he needed to rest for a while and get a drink of water. So the other bandit took his whip and gave another hundred lashes. Big-Eyes Tang's butt swelled up like a drum, the surface of which no longer had individual whip marks, but instead looked like the scales of a fish. Still Big-Eyes Tang remained silent, so Floater had Li'l Five go into the other room and get some spicy noodles, which he dumped over Big-Eyes' butt. Finally he cried out in pain, and beads of sweat the size of beans began raining down from him, mixed with tears.

Floater took a look at his butt and said, "It's been beaten to a pulp, but it still doesn't look like his face—it's missing a pair of eyes."

Li'l Five got a pair of red-hot tongs and branded an egg-sized mark on each one of Big-Eyes' buttocks—a sizzling sound was soon accompanied by the smell of burning flesh. Big-Eyes Tang let out a series of low, long "ow's," which sounded like the cries of an injured wolf in the wild.

"Now this ass looks more like a face," Floater said with a smile. "Switch back to his face now, and beat it till it looks like his ass."

The two bandits pulled Big-Eyes up and shoved him into a corner. "Have him sit on the stool against the wall," said Floater.

The two bandits brought over the stool and had Big-Eyes Tang sit. As soon as his butt, which was completely drenched in blood, touched the surface of the stool, he immediately stood up again as if he'd been scorched. The bandits laughed uproariously.

Li'l Five cracked his whip and said, "Sit the fuck down."

Big-Eyes Tang gingerly sat back down on the stool, but the piercing pain made him stand right back up. The bandits laughed so hard they started coughing. Through his swollen eyes, Big-Eyes Tang looked at the other bandits sitting along the wall—he saw a line of trembling bodies and a row of fearful eyes. With a bitter smile, he locked his jaw and sat back down on the stool, his face distorted with pain.

Li'l Five picked up his whip and gave it a crack—it swished past the wall and struck Big-Eyes Tang in the face. He gave a heavy groan, and the snapping and cracking sounds of the whip resumed. His face became an indistinct mess of blood and flesh, until finally he collapsed on the floor and fainted.

Floater walked over. "Okay," he said, "You can't really make out any part of his face—it looks like his ass."

Li'l Five coiled his whip and said with a smile, "Red and raw, like a monkey's butt."

When the bandits were done laughing and Big-Eyes Tang had regained consciousness, Floated squatted down, patted him on the shoulders, and said,

"Now tell me—how much silver does your family have?"

Big-Eyes Tang opened his mouth slightly, spit out some

blood, and said through a gurgle, "We don't have any silver. I'm a poor man."

Leopard Li, who was standing off to the side, picked up his rifle and pointed it at Big-Eyes Tang's head. "Are you really that fucking poor?"

Big-Eyes weakly nodded his head. "What's the point of living if you're so poor?" Leopard Li said, "Might as well die."

Leopard Li pulled the trigger and fired, and Big-Eyes Tang's head was blown to bits. Fresh blood splattered all over the wall and sprayed on Floater's face.

Floater wiped his face and cursed, "You could have fucking said something before you shot him!"

The Monk couldn't bear to look. "Some hostages are rich, some are poor," he said. "If we got a poor one, that's just bad luck—it doesn't mean we have to kill him."

"You're still acting like you're some kind of monk," said Floater, "when you're a fucking bandit!"

Then Floater turned to the hostages sitting along the wall and said, "We didn't make any mistakes here—you should all be worth some money."

Li'l Five went for Blacksmith Xu next. His thick arms and sturdy physique trembled as he walked out, his face bearing a mark from when he was whipped the night before. Before the bandits said anything, he spoke:

"I'm a rich man, master—I'm not poor."

Among the hostages was a teacher at a private school named Mr. Wang. Before he was even summoned, he said, "Master, I'm a rich man."

All the remaining hostages proclaimed they were rich, and the bandits were all smiles as they assigned their ransoms. When it came to Chen Yaowu, he said:

"I told you yesterday."

Floater thought for a minute, then smiled and said, "Right—you, young man, are a thousand taels."

43.

The hostages from Xizhen remained shut up like pigs and dogs in that damp, dark room for fifteen days. Each day, they each got only two bowls of thin rice porridge and one pancake, with the occasional pickled vegetable. To keep them from plotting amongst themselves, the bandits had them sleep head-to-feet, one on their back and the next on their front. The ones sleeping on their backs were okay, but the ones on their fronts had to have their faces next to the moldy, decaying straw—after a few nights, their skin had begun to rot and stink. Every morning they would get up at six o'clock and go outside for some fresh air; if they were slow getting up, they would feel the sting of Li'l Five's whip. This time out in the fresh air was also their only time for defecating and urinating, and they were only allowed out once each day—after this one time each morning, they weren't permitted outside again, so they would just have to hold it. One hostage had such trouble holding it in he started holding his belly and groaning. Li'l Five said,

"This is a hostage prison, not your own home—you can't just go whenever you want!"

The man had no choice but to go in his pants. Over the course of fifteen days, all the prisoners' pants became full of feces, which froze like rocks in the winter temperatures. During the day, the hostages had to sit up straight, their buttocks festering in their excrement. Their hands and feet had become so swollen and frozen they started bleeding, and the dampness of the room caused their clothing to begin mildewing. The ropes that bound them wore through their clothing and began to cut into their arms, staining the ropes red with blood. The hostages stunk from head to toe, and their hair was all matted in clumps and full of lice.

On the sixteenth day, as snowflakes fluttered through the air, the bandit factions led by Floater and Leopard Li went down the mountain, leaving The Monk behind to keep an eye on things. The Monk said to the hostages,

"Your suffering is almost over—the ransoms will be delivered today, so you can return home tomorrow."

That afternoon, the snow stopped and the sun came out. The Monk led the hostages outside with the rope, as if he were leading a group of cattle or sheep. Then he had them sit down against the wall and said to them,

"You've all started growing moss—sit here and get some sun so you can dry off and go home."

As the sunlight shone on their bodies and the dry winter wind blew against their faces, the hostages looked at one another and found that they were all wearing the same happy expression. The fried dough-stick seller Chen San squinted his eyes in the sunlight and took in big breaths of fresh, clean air, and the other twenty-one hostages did the same—they gulped the air so greedily it was more like eating than breathing. Blacksmith Xu lowered his head and started giggling, and his giggles spread to the other hostages. When they reached Chen Yaowu, the giggling turned to crying, and soon they all began shedding tears until their faces were completely wet; then the sunlight gradually dried their tears. They looked at the snow-covered forest in front of them and knew they were on a mountain, but the trees kept them from seeing any of the other hills or ridges. They could only see the empty bit of land between the building and the forest, with some scattered decaying trees sticking out of the snow here and there.

By evening, the two groups of bandits who had gone down the mountain returned. They had waited all day near the Guanyin temple until their hands and feet had frozen stiff, but Zeng Wanfu, Chen Shun, and Zhang Pinsan never showed up with the ransom. They came back shouting and cursing like an angry pack of rabid dogs. Li'l Five brandished his whip and lashed the hostages as he screamed at them,

"Fuck! We've held you here for over two weeks! . . . Fuck!

None of your families brought any money, or even showed up! . . . Fuck! You've just been sitting around here eating, getting fat and doughy! Fuck, you've got it better here that back in your own homes!"

Then Floater had one of his bandit assistants carry each hostage out one by one. The first one out was Blacksmith Xu. After he was taken, none of the remaining hostages heard a sound, and they all began trembling with fear as they tried to guess what was happening. Then they heard Blacksmith Xu let out a bloodcurdling scream. After a little while, he returned with his head bent over to the side, and the other hostages saw that he was missing an ear—the place where his ear had been was now covered in cookstove ashes, and his neck and shirt were stained red with blood. His face ghostly pale, he unsteadily sat on the ground and stared down at his feet. The next one taken out was Chen San—he still hadn't understood what had happened and turned to look at Blacksmith Xu as he left. Once he was outside, the hostages in the room heard him sobbing and begging; then he let out a scream like a pig being slaughtered. When Chen San returned, he was also missing an ear, and the place where it had been was also covered in black, sticky ashes; his face, too, was white as a ghost, and he was wobbly, staring straight ahead.

Chen Yaowu was the seventh one taken out. He squinted as he saw the sun setting in the west, its red light reflecting off the snow-covered branches of the trees. Li'l Five pushed him in front of The Monk, who held his left ear in a pair of chopsticks and tied the ends together tightly with a piece of thin twine. Chen Yaowu saw Floater's blood-soaked hand pick up a blood-soaked shaving knife. As The Monk tied the twine tighter, Chen Yaowu began to cry from the pain. Through his tears he begged The Monk to loosen the chopsticks, but The Monk responded,

"The tighter the better—if I loosen them, it will hurt more when it's cut off."

Chen Yaowu could feel Floater pinching his already numb

ear. The shaving knife was brought up next to his forehead and sawed back and forth a few times; Chen Yaowu heard some crunching sounds, and then The Monk pressed a handful of ashes into the spot to stop the bleeding. With his other ear, he heard Floater say,

"This boy's ear is so tender—it came off as soon as we touched it."

Chen Yaowu felt like his left side had become lighter, while his right side had become heavier. A cold wind blew against his left side and chilled him to the bone. As he hobbled back into the room, he could feel warm, fresh blood running down his neck, and a sharp, searing pain. Chen Yaowu felt as if his body were growing thinner and thinner, until it seemed he would float away. When he sat down, it was as if he slowly dropped to the ground. When he looked at the other hostages, they all appeared blurry. Then he shut his eyes and passed out.

44.

The next morning when they were taken out for some fresh air, the twenty-two hostages missing twenty-two ears looked at one another and felt they all seemed a lot thinner. Floater and a few other bandits walked past them and gleefully showed off the severed ears. Floater said,

"Look at your ears—fuck! If we don't get some ransom for you now, we'll chop off your heads."

Several of the bandits went down the mountain to find some passersby who could deliver the ears to Xizhen. When they had gone about twenty paces, they heard a gunshot and immediately came running back, shouting as they ran,

"Bad news—the army's coming!"

Leopard Li stood out in the open and shouted, "Quick! Distribute the ears and take the hostages into the woods—each person take two hostages, and run as far away as you can!"

The bandits cut the rope that tied all the hostages together, distributed the severed ears, and ran with the hostages through the clearing next to the building and into the woods. As Leopard Li was running to the woods with his two hostages, he kicked the bandits beside him and swore,

"For fuck's sake—split up!"

Floater, who had been running ahead with Chen Yaowu, shoved him over to The Monk and tossed his ear over as well.

"Monk," said Floater, "I'm giving this valuable one to you. You're good with a gun—take your men and fight with all you've got, and we'll circle back around from the north."

As gunfire snapped and popped like beans in a frying pan, Leopard Li and Floater raced into the forest with their men and hostages.

Floater turned back and shouted to The Monk, "You hear that, Monk? They've got fucking machine guns! We can't fight machine guns—we won't circle back around. Take good fucking care of yourself—we'll meet again some day!"

"Bastard," cursed The Monk.

The Monk and his two men shoved Chen Yaowu along as they hunched down and ran forward, bullets whizzing all around them. The Monk yelled for them to duck, and the four of them lay down under a rotting tree as bullets flew over their heads. The short, rapid bursts of sound were like chattering flocks of sparrows.

They lay under the tree for a while listening to the bullets, which were clearly firing over them from both sides. The Monk gave a little laugh and said to the two other bandits,

"They're not shooting at us—the Beiyang Army and the National Revolutionary Army are fighting each other."

After laying there for nearly a whole *shichen,* the gunfire stopped and they stood up. One of the bandits asked The Monk if they should go find Floater and Leopard Li.

"They've been running this whole time—do you think we could catch them?"

The Monk and his group didn't dare take the main road, but instead stuck to the small mountain paths; Chen Yaowu followed them over all the ridges and hills. He hadn't eaten or slept enough in the preceding days, plus he'd had his ear cut off, so he staggered unsteadily as he pressed onward. With his left ear cut off, his body tilted to the right, so he leaned as he walked—he walked and walked, until he finally walked off the path and slid down the mountainside. The Monk and his men had no choice but to crawl down after him and pull him back up.

The two bandits with The Monk started cursing and complaining up on the road, saying they could barely catch their breath after climbing over so many hills, and having to pull along this kid was just about the last straw. One suggested digging a hole and burying him alive, but the other asked where they would get the energy to dig a hole—it would be easiest just to shoot him. By evening, Chen Yaowu once again rolled down a slope and was unable to stand up. The two bandits kicked him, but he could only shake his head in silence. The Monk saw that Chen Yaowu really couldn't walk anymore, so he said he would have to be carried. The other two bandits shook their heads, saying they wouldn't even be able to carry their own fathers—how could they carry this kid?

The Monk gave a bitter smile and put Chen Yaowu on his own back, then began staggering onward.

Laying on The Monk's back, Chen Yaowu quickly fell asleep.

In the middle of the night he was awoken by the bark of a dog, so he knew they had entered a village. They went up to a building and The Monk knocked on the door. After a while, an oil lamp was lit inside, and an old woman's voice asked,

"Who is it?"

"Ma, it's me," said The Monk, "Xiaoshan."

The Monk's mother put on a jacket and came out with an oil lamp. When she saw Chen Yaowu, she asked, "Whose child is this?"

"One of the hostages from Xizhen," replied The Monk.

Over the next few days, Chen Yaowu ran a high fever and stayed in The Monk's woodshed, where he slept nearly the entire time. His vision was blurry and he heard a gurgling sound in his ears, as if they were filled with water; his whole body felt like it was made of stone. He dimly perceived that The Monk and some others had come in the room a few times and stood beside him talking. What he remembered most from this period of fever-induced delirium was the presence of The Monk's mother. Every time this old woman entered the room she was carrying something—water, porridge, sometimes even ginger soup. Then she would say in a raspy voice,

"Drink some water . . . have some porridge . . . try some ginger soup."

Chen Yaowu made it through these four days, his life hanging in the balance. Then on the fifth, he woke to the birds chirping and sunlight streaming through the window of the shed. The fog had receded from his vision, the strange sound had left his ears, and his body no longer felt so heavy. He felt his stomach rumbling and heard it grumble, and he realized he was hungry. To his surprise, he discovered a red rope tied around his wrist.

The Monk's mother came in with some rice porridge. When she saw him sitting up, she reached out and felt his forehead.

"By the protection of Guanyin Bodhisattva—his fever's broken."

The old woman asked his name and which family he came from in Xizhen; he replied that his name was Chen Yaowu, the son of Chen Yongliang of the woodworking shop. The old woman told him she had tied the red rope on his wrists, which was meant to protect him.

She proceeded to boil two eggs for Chen Yaowu, which he gobbled right down, stuffing so much in his mouth that his cheeks bulged out. After that he drank down a bowl of rice porridge, and the sound of his gulping was like throwing rocks into a well.

While Chen Yaowu had been burning up with fever, The Monk and one of the other bandits went out to issue the ransom note. When they got to the main road, they detained a traveling barber and had him take the note to Xizhen and deliver it to Chen Yongliang at the woodworking shop.

45.

Chen Yaowu spent ten days in this village at the foot of the mountains. He slept on the floor of the woodshed, on which The Monk's mother had laid a thick bed of straw for him; she also gave him a cotton-padded mattress and a blanket. The Monk had removed the ropes that had been tied around him, allowing him to move freely among several rooms of the house. He was even able to go outside, so he would sometimes tuck his hands up in his sleeves and go out to enjoy the sunshine. He helped the old woman with the housework, and when she cooked or prepared meals, he would sit in front of the stove and tend the fire. The old woman taught him how to do it, keeping the flames lower when she was cooking rice and making them hotter when she was stir-frying. When she told him the fire was too big, he would quickly grab some ashes and throw them on to tamp down the dancing flames; when she said it was too small, he would grab the blower pipe and blow until the flames were leaping high and filled the stove. Every time she was done cooking and the flames gradually died out, she would give him a sweet potato to bury in the hot coals. During these few days in The Monk's house, Chen Yaowu always had a baked sweet potato waiting for him after his meals.

One morning, The Monk and one of the bandits left the village to go collect the ransom, leaving the other bandit behind to keep an eye on Chen Yaowu. When they returned in the afternoon, they found Chen Yaowu squatting by the corner of a wall and enjoying the sunshine. They waved at the bandit standing beside him and went inside. A little while later they came out, and one of the bandits walked over to where Chen Yaowu was squatting, gave him a kick, and shouted,

"Get up."

Chen Yaowu stood up and saw The Monk smiling—he had no idea what they were up to. The bandit who kicked him said,

"You've been here so long, you little brat, we can't keep looking after you. We've given you food and drink, we've given you a place to sleep, and we even let you come out and enjoy the fresh air—what did we get out of it?"

"Get going," said the other bandit, "the hole's already been dug for you."

When Chen Yaowu heard that the hole had already been dug, he wondered to himself—were they going to bury him alive? His legs suddenly went limp and he began to tremble.

The Monk smiled at him and said, "Go on."

Chen Yaowu tried moving his legs, but they wouldn't budge. He saw The Monk smiling at him, as was the old woman, who was standing in the doorway and waving. Chen Yaowu remembered that the bandits also smiled when they killed people. With a distraught look on his face he said,

"I can't lift my legs."

The Monk took a strip of black cloth and tied it around Chen Yaowu's eyes, and the two bandits picked him up and carried him off. When they left the village gate, they turned up a small mountain path, huffing, puffing, and swearing as they dragged him up the mountain. Dejectedly, Chen Yaowu said,

"You can stop now; don't make more work for yourselves. Just do it here and get it over with."

The Monk and the bandits didn't answer and kept dragging him along. They went up hills and down hills, and after a while they made it to a main road. Chen Yaowu's legs had gone completely numb and felt like tree stumps. He started crying and begged The Monk,

"I really can't walk—no matter where we go, I'm still going to die, so just do it here."

The Monk stopped, and the two bandits who were dragging Chen Yaowu loosened their grips. The Monk warmly said to Chen Yaowu,

"We're not burying you alive, we're letting you go home."

They removed Chen Yaowu's blindfold, and he found himself standing in the middle of a large road. One of the bandits pointed ahead and said,

"Run."

Chen Yaowu looked at the three of them in disbelief. The bandit aimed his rifle at Chen Yaowu and said,

"Run."

Chen Yaowu felt his legs come back to life. Just as he was about to turn around, The Monk stopped him, and Chen Yaowu felt his legs go weak once more. The Monk put a sack over his shoulder and said,

"Here are some things my mother made you—to eat on the road."

Then The Monk told him, "Follow the main road straight ahead, and you'll make it to Xizhen. Don't go on any side roads, or you'll get lost."

Chen Yaowu nodded, then turned and carefully began making his way forward. After a few steps, he heard one of the bandits behind him say,

"Run—we're going to shoot!"

As soon as Chen Yaowu heard this, his legs kicked into gear. Missing an ear, his center of gravity was off, so he kept going crooked as he ran. The other bandit called out after him,

"Just go straight—don't make any turns!"

Chen Yaowu knew he couldn't go straight—he couldn't give them an easy target to shoot from behind, so he kept running this way and that. He could hear The Monk and the other bandits laughing loudly behind him; he ran as fast as he could, and their laughter followed him the whole time. When he had gone about ten *li,* he couldn't go any further, yet The Monk's laughter seemed like it was still following him. He stopped and heaved a few sobs, then turned back and said,

"You might as well shoot."

Chen Yaowu stood in the middle of the street gasping for breath. He wiped the sweat from his eyelids and looked carefully down the street, but it was completely empty. Confused, he blinked a few times, but still he didn't see anyone. The Monk and the bandits must have really set him free, he thought. Then he feared they would surely regret their decision and come after him, so he began running again. The sound of The Monk's laughter followed him once more, but when he turned to look, there was no one there. He realized it wasn't their laughter he was hearing, but the sound of his own panting. As he continued to run, he began laughing himself.

He ran for nearly five more *li* until his legs ran out of steam, so he began walking slowly. He continued walking for a while—he wasn't sure how long—until he really couldn't go another step and collapsed on the ground. After laying there on his back for some time, he knew that was no good—if he wanted to live, he had to get up and keep going. So he stood up and walked for a bit, then stopped to rest; when he felt like he had gathered a little strength, he started running again.

After dark, Chen Yaowu became lost. He couldn't remember when he had strayed from the main road and gotten on a small mountain path through the forest. The rustling of the leaves made the winter wind seem especially bitter, and when he raised his head to look at the sky, he saw the stars coming in and out of view behind a layer of clouds. He had no idea which direction was which, and he had no idea where Xizhen was—all he could do was continue following the small path he was on.

Chen Yaowu walked through the mountain forest for a long time. In the moonlight he spotted a thatched cottage, and he went up to it and knocked on the door. There was no sound from within, so he pushed on the door, but discovered it was bolted from the inside. He knocked again and said,

"Whoever is the kind soul inside, I'm Chen Yaowu from Xizhen. I was taken hostage by the bandits, and I've just escaped—and now I'm lost."

The door to the cottage creaked open, and an old man stood in front of Chen Yaowu.

"Come in," he said.

Chen Yaowu went in, and the old man lit an oil lamp. Chen Yaowu saw the old man's kind, gentle eyes.

"There's no stool," said the old man. "Have a seat on the bed."

Utterly exhausted, Chen Yaowu sat down on the bed. His right ear felt heavy, and his whole body involuntarily leaned to the right until he lay down and fell into a dizzy sleep. He slept until the next morning, and when he awoke the sunlight was already shining through the crack around the door. Sitting up, he saw that the old man was standing in front of him holding a bowl of hot rice porridge.

"Have some porridge," he said.

The two of them sat on the bed and drank their porridge. The hot substance entered Chen Yaowu's mouth and slid down his throat like a warm fire slowly spreading throughout his body. He noticed there was a cloth bag with him, and he recalled that The Monk had given it to him; when he opened it, he found two eggs and two pieces of flatbread, so he took them out and shared them with the old man. They ate the flatbread first, then cracked the eggs on the sides of their bowls and carefully peeled them. Chen Yaowu devoured his egg in two bites, while the old man slowly savored his, taking a drink of porridge from time to time to help him swallow the egg. As Chen Yaowu felt his strength returning, he looked around at his surroundings—there was nothing in the room other than the old creaky bed, which didn't even have a blanket. The old man told him the blanket had been stolen by the bandits.

As Chen Yaowu thought about it, he realized it was here that the bandits had torn up the old man's blanket and blindfolded them with the strips of cloth. He remembered Leopard Li hitting the old man in the face with the butt of his rifle—he looked closely now at the old man's face and saw that the scar was still visible. Chen Yaowu lowered his head and said it was time for him to go.

The old man saw Chen Yaowu off as far as the mountain slope, then pointed to a main road down below the mountain. He told Chen Yaowu that if he followed the road south, it would lead him to Xizhen. Chen Yaowu headed down the mountain, and when he made it to the main road, he looked back up and saw the old man standing there, waving and calling after him to head south. Only once he began walking south did the old man let his arm drop.

As Chen Yaowu walked along the main road, the sun was shining brilliantly and glinting off the snow, and instead of a cold, winter wind, there was a gentle breeze. Peasants with carrying poles appeared on the road, along with women in headscarves and small-time traders. Chen Yaowu walked amongst them.

Then he noticed someone walking ahead of him who seemed to keep veering off to the right. When he noticed the person was also missing his left ear, he ran up to him and found it was Chen San, the fried dough-stick seller. He tugged at Chen San's clothing and said,

"You've also escaped!"

When Chen San saw it was Chen Yaowu, he broke into a surprised smile and took his hand. The two of them continued on hand-in-hand, unconsciously veering off to the right and then every so often taking a few corrective steps to the left.

As they continued on to Xizhen, they kept seeing others in front of them veering one way or the other as they walked. They eventually joined up with Blacksmith Xu, the soy sauce seller Li Zhanggui, the school teacher Mr. Wang, and two others. Of the seven of them, four were missing their left ear, and three were missing their right. They were surprised and delighted to come upon each other, and they naturally joined hands and continued on together. Hand-in-hand, the seven of them walked forward; with four of them veering right and three of them veering left, they started to achieve a balance.

They were the first of the hostages to return, and when they entered through the north gate hand-in-hand, Xizhen erupted in happiness. The news of their return swept through the town like the wind, and people gathered around them calling their names. The seven of them continued holding onto each other as people crowded around them in all directions. As countless voices called out their names, they neither smiled nor cried, but merely nodded their heads continuously while numbly issuing a series of "mm-hmms." Finally they went their separate ways when their family members appeared, shouting and crying, and led them away.

When Chen Yaowu saw his mother, Li Meilian, she was sobbing; even the handkerchief she was holding seemed to shed its own tears. He saw that his father, Chen Yongliang, had a huge smile on his face, although he was also crying. Lin Xiangfu, Lin Baijia, and Chen Yaowen were all sobbing.

Chen Yaowu finally laid eyes on his home. He walked inside and sat down on a stool, silently staring at his family members, who surrounded him as they continued to cry. Lin Baijia sat down beside him, tugged his arm, and asked through her tears,

"Why aren't you crying?"

Chen Yaowu answered, "Nothing will come out."

46.

For a period of time after the hostages had returned to Xizhen, their bodies continued involuntarily leaning to the side. Blacksmith Xu slept for three days, then woke up and went back to work. He picked up his hammer, aimed it at a chunk of red hot iron, and delivered his first blow, but was startled by a terrible shriek—he saw that the hammer hadn't landed on the chunk of iron, but had instead struck the left hand of his apprentice Sun Fengsan, whose fingers were now all smashed into an indistinguishable pulp. So the fire in his forge went out and he spent the whole day sitting in his shop, staring blankly; his apprentice Sun Fengsan sat by his side wearing a long face, bandages wrapped around his smashed hand.

The soy sauce seller Li Zhanggui knew it was difficult to maintain his balance while standing—if he let up his vigilance for even a moment his body would start leaning, so as soon as he got out of bed he would sit in a chair, both hands pulled up into his sleeves, and shake his head from time to time when it had begun to slant to the right. Once he'd adjusted his head back to the left, he would cough and give directions to his shop assistant.

Out on the street, the fried dough-stick seller Chen San would fry his dough-sticks while adjusting his position according to the wind, standing so that the winter wind blew against his right side and acted as a cane, propping him up and keeping him from leaning too far to the right.

Mr. Wang, the teacher at the private school, had enjoyed an excellent reputation and had seven regular students. Now that his right ear had been cut off, it was like he was being pulled by an invisible rope. He squinted his eyes as he expounded upon the Confucian classics, and just as he was beginning to discuss the notion of forgetting the self, he unconsciously started moving to the left until he ended up at door, where he stood and lectured on *The Doctrine of the Mean*. Once he realized where he was, he lowered his head and moved wordlessly back to the middle of the room, looking sheepishly at his students. They saw their teacher's face had gone pale, while his left ear, which fortunately remained, turned as red as a hot coal. One of the students picked up his desk and left, and soon the other students followed suit, moving their desks over to Mr. Zhang's room. When Mr. Wang once again shifted over to the door while lecturing, the last student finally moved out his desk.

Mr. Zhang's reputation and caliber were beneath that of Mr. Wang, and only by charging a minimal tuition had he been able to get four students. Now that Mr. Wang's seven students had all come over to his classroom, he was clearly very pleased with himself. When he passed by Mr. Wang's door, he would pause for a moment and look in at Mr. Wang, who was sitting in the empty room looking sad and lonely. Mr. Zhang would then offer a few words of greeting and then walk off with a laugh.

Naturally, Mr. Wang picked up on Mr. Zhang's scornful overtones. One day he walked up to his door and, in front of a crowd of people, angrily pointed his finger at Mr. Zhang and said,

"You take advantage of others' misfortune."

Because Mr. Wang was so worked up, he had gotten off kilter and was veering sharply to the left. This caused the aim of his finger to be off, so when he delivered his line, he pointed not at Mr. Zhang, but at Chen San, who just happened to be walking by. Mr. Zhang walked out looking completely unconcerned, as if he had nothing to do with the matter. The dough-stick seller Chen San saw Mr. Wang angrily pointing at him, and when he turned to look behind him and found no one else, he could only offer up an innocent smile.

After Chen Yaowu returned home, he became sullen and rarely spoke, often sitting silently in the corner for long stretches of time. When Chen Yongliang and Li Meilian tried to talk to him, his eyes would float past them as if he were looking off into the distance. The smiles disappeared from his parents' faces and were replaced by worried expressions. This in turn influenced Lin Xiangfu, who lost his smile as well. One day Lin Baijia went over and sat by Chen Yaowu, and from then on she would accompany him whenever he was alone in the corner—if he sat there silently for the entire day, Lin Baijia would sit there silently as well.

Their quiet lives resumed, and Lin Xiangfu began teaching again. Gu Yimin's daughters, however, did not reappear. After the bandits had come to Xizhen taking hostages—and had in fact taken one from the home of Chen Yongliang and Lin Xiangfu—Gu Yimin was concerned with his daughters' safety, and didn't send Go Tongsi or Gu Tongnien back.

After Lin Xiangfu resumed teaching, Chen Yaowu no longer sat in the corner—he now sat in front of the window staring outside, while Lin Baijia would sit beside him, often turning her head to do the same. Chen Yaowen, rather than looking around, would just sit there yawning. Even Lin Xiangfu's mind would wander as he taught, so he tried to wrap things up quickly each day.

The room where Lin Xiangfu held class was directly across from Mr. Wang's school. As he stared out the window, Chen Yaowu saw the seven students move their desks out of Mr. Wang's classroom, and he saw Mr. Wang standing dejectedly out on the street. Over the next several days, Chen Yaowu would see the open door of Mr. Wang's room, but not Mr. Wang—although in the afternoons, the angle of the sunlight would cast the shadow of the teacher, sitting up straight, on the ground in front of the door.

One day as Lin Xiangfu was teaching, Chen Yaowu suddenly got up and began moving his desk. After bumping against Chen Yaowen's desk, he went out the door and over into Mr. Wang's room.

When Mr. Wang, who had spent the past few days sitting and staring blankly with his hands tucked up in his sleeves, saw the similarly one-eared Chen Yaowu move his desk into his room, at first he was puzzled. He lowered his head and looked down for a while, but when he looked up again and saw Chen Yaowu sitting shyly in the corner, he beamed with happiness. He walked over to the boy and moved his desk to the middle of the room, then took out a book and began lecturing loudly.

Chen Yaowu's actions had taken Lin Baijia and Chen Yaowen by surprise, and they stared at Lin Xiangfu walking up to the empty space that was now left in front of the window. Lin Xiangfu looked across the street at Mr. Wang's open door and saw that the shadow cast on the ground now included two figures. He heard their voices, first one and then the other, back and forth—Chen Yaowu, who had been silent for so long, now sounded like a rooster crowing in the morning, his voice loud and clear.

Chen Yongliang happened to be out of town at the time, and when Li Meilian learned what had happened she rushed to Mr. Wang's classroom and softly called Chen Yaowu's name from outside the door. Chen Yaowu turned to look, then turned back around as if he could no longer hear her. Then she saw Lin Baijia and Chen Yaowen moving their desks over to Mr. Wang's school. She turned to see Lin Xiangfu standing in the courtyard gate, smiling. He wasn't really cut out to be a teacher, he told her—he was a woodworker.

Mr. Wang was bursting with pride. Although he'd lost seven students and only gained three, his voice rang out in the classroom as if he were lecturing to a sea of pupils. Then he made a curious discovery—he was standing in the same place he'd started out, and after a while, he realized he hadn't moved. He eyed the doorway suspiciously, then cautiously asked the three students—had he moved at all in that direction? They said he hadn't gone over to the door, but had remained standing in the same place. Mr. Wang's face turned red as he realized he had unknowingly corrected his leaning problem. He opened his mouth, but no sound came out; he held out his hand, but he wasn't sure what to do with it. After an awkward few moments, he picked up *The Analects* and began rhythmically reading aloud.

Mr. Wang kept the students late that day. When Mr. Zhang passed by, the sound of his hoarse voice stopped him in his tracks. Mr. Wang glanced over at Mr. Zhang a few times as he continued talking, and each time Mr. Zhang got the feeling that Mr. Wang was pretending to ignore him. As soon as Mr. Zhang left, Mr. Wang, clearly exhausted, put down the book in his hand and said,

"Class dismissed."

Once the class was over, Mr. Wang stood in the entrance to the school, his hands tucked up in his sleeves, and remained there until evening. When he saw Lin Xiangfu pass by, he respectfully called out his name and bowed.

47.

To guard against the bandits, Gu Yimin established a Xizhen militia, just as Shendian and other towns had done. After the defeat of the Beiyang Army, many of their guns made their way into the hands of the general populace, so Gu Yimin bought some of these guns and ammunition on behalf of the chamber of commerce. At the same time, the bandits were trying to increase their own strength and were rampaging all over the place and accumulating weapons. People trafficking contraband firearms sprouted up like bamboo shoots after a spring rain—this included peasant farmers, shop owners and street vendors, men and women, elderly people and children. These gun traffickers braved the winter winds and trudged through the snow, looking to acquire the firearms cheaply and sell them at inflated prices to either the bandits or the Xizhen and Shendian militias. As this trade in weapons flourished, the only thing people were talking about along the streets and down the alleys was guns, guns, guns—from the sound of things, it was as if Xizhen were some kind of arsenal. Everyone was discussing who got what kind of gun and what price they could get for it. The prices skyrocketed—a Hanyang rifle went for seventy-eight silver yuan; long barrel rifles and .38 calibers could get over a hundred; and

Mausers could get over two hundred. Gu Yimin paid an astronomical price for a Browning pistol.

As the number of gun traffickers increased, the number of available guns decreased. Blacksmith Xu with his missing ear and Sun Fengsan with his hand wrapped in bandages both joined the ranks of those buying and reselling guns. They went out with a sack of grain for three days, and they returned with one weapon—it wasn't a Hanyang, a long barrel rifle or a .38, but a rusty old spear.

The apprentice with his bandaged hand supported his master by the arm, keeping him from veering off to the side so that he could make a dignified entrance into Xizhen, although in fact his master no longer suffered from this problem. The rusty spear rested between them on their shoulders. While others laughed and pointed, they remained in high spirits, as if they were carrying a shiny new .38.

Blacksmith Xu and Sun Fengsan never actually got into the gun business, but instead decided to join the militia. One earless and unsteady, the other with a smashed hand, they could no longer carry on as blacksmiths, so after much consideration, they felt their only option for making a living was to take up arms and fight. So they went one morning to the plaza in front of the temple of the city god to sign up for the militia. When they wrote down their names at the "eight immortals" table, they saw that there were already 127 names in front of theirs.

Gu Yimin had only intended to set up a militia with around thirty people; he never expected that over two hundred would come to sign up. When the forest is big, you get all kinds of birds—there were the wealthy sons of elite families alongside homeless beggars, respectable young men alongside bullies and thugs. Of the twenty-two residents who had been kidnapped by the bandits, nineteen of them showed up to join.

The people gathered in front of the temple of the city god stood on their toes and craned their necks to see the four-carrier sedan chair approaching with Zhu Bochong, the man Gu Yimin had hired from the provincial capital to lead the militia. Zhu Bochong had served as a squad leader in a Yong Ying division of the Qing army as well as a regimental commander in the northwest army of the Anhui Clique. When he emerged from his sedan, the people of Xizhen saw a tall man of about fifty with white hair, a silver beard, and lively, piercing eyes. Immediately the crowd erupted with surprise,

"He really looks like a big official!"

Zhu Bochong, with the appearance of an important official, trotted out with his Mauser and leapt up onto the "eight immortals" table, eliciting more surprised exclamations from the crowd. In a booming voice, he announced that the militia was not a general store, and not just anyone could join. He looked over at Gu Yimin, with his Browning pistol at his waist, and said the militia was more like a pharmacy—only the best products should be selected for inventory. He said only those who were tested and qualified could join. How would they be tested? Zhu Bochong got down off the table and asked who wanted to see first.

A young man wearing a quilted *mianpao* skittered forward— it was the Young Master Guo from the Chinese medicine shop. Young Master Guo assumed he would be tested on the breadth of his learning, but when he got up to the "eight immortals" table, he found there was no brush, inkstone, or paper. Zhu Bochong took a bowl of out a bucket, filled it with water, and placed it on Young Master Guo's head. Then he had him stand still as he walked about twenty meters away, picked up his Mauser, and aimed it at Young Master Guo.

All noise from the crowd stopped at once, and even the birds fell silent. They now knew what the test was—a bullet was going to fly straight at the top of Young Master Guo's head. Young Master Guo also knew that a bullet was headed for him, and his legs began to tremble, followed by his hands, and then his lips. Zhu Bochong aimed and saw a bunch of heads bobbing in the background behind Young Master Guo. He lowered his pistol and yelled,

"Bullets don't have eyes—please clear a path!"

The people behind Young Master Guo started scrambling as if the bullet had already been fired, shouting as they pushed and shoved their way to either side. The area around Zhu Bochong was also cleared, as everyone tried to get as far away as they could. Zhu Bochong shook his head and said,

"It's a bullet, not a bomb—there's no need to back so far away."

Zhu Bochong raised his Mauser and once again aimed at Young Master Guo. He looked through the scope, but couldn't find him; he moved his gun up and down, left and right, but still no Young Master Guo. He heard the crowd erupt in laughter, then put down his gun to discover that Young Master Guo had already fled. Zhu Bochong stood there motionlessly and waited for the laughter to subside. When it had finally died down, he shouted:

"Next!"

He waited for a bit, but when no one appeared, he yelled again, "Who's next?"

Blacksmith Xu strode out of the crowd and walked over to the place where Young Master Guo had just been standing. His apprentice Sun Fengsan also walked out and stood by his master's side, still supporting his arm out of habit. When Zhu Bochong saw the two of them standing there perfectly straight, he nodded to indicate that two bowls of water should be placed on their heads; he then raised his gun and took aim. Two shots rang out, and the bowl on Sun Fengsan's head shattered. Blacksmith Xu instinctively retracted his neck, causing the bowl of water on his head to fall on the ground and shatter.

The crowd marveled, thinking that Zhu Bochong had hit both bowls. Blacksmith Xu and Sun Fengsan both stood there without moving, their faces covered in water.

Zhu Bochong raised his left arm and waved at them. "We'll take them," he said.

As if waking from a dream, the two men looked around

and touched the water on their faces. As they stood facing the noisy crowd of people clustered together, Sun Fengsan asked Blacksmith Xu,

"Did you see the bullets, master?"

"No," he said, "I shut my eyes."

"I saw them," said Sun Fengsan. "The bowl on my head broke, and then I saw the bullet fly. How did the bullet come afterwards?"

Zhu Bochong fired twenty-eight more shots, and twenty-seven bowls of water shattered—mostly because they fell off of trembling heads. Only Chen San didn't tremble. He was the last one, and after the gun sounded, the bowl of water remained on his head. The crowd cried out in approval, thinking Zhu Bochong had simply missed. The bullet, however, had actually brushed over Chen San's head like a winter wind, leaving him jumpy and skittish for the next several days. He kept having the sensation that bullets were skimming over his head, making his scalp numb.

The Xizhen militia was established, including all nineteen of the one-eared applicants. The other eleven members included farmers and laborers, loafers and petty criminals. They were all fully armed, carrying long barrel rifles, .38 calibers, Hanyang rifles, and shotguns, and would train from early in the morning until late at night.

Zhu Bochong had them practice marching with their firearms, carrying them on their right shoulders. The men who were missing their left ears had already regained their balance, but now with the added weight of a gun they began veering to the right. Zhu Bochong saw the situation and had those men switch the guns to their left shoulders. Now as they trained, some men carried their guns on the left, while others carried them on their right, so whenever they turned left or right, their guns would knock into each other. Zhu Bochong saw this and shook his head. Next, he had them aim while laying down, aim while squatting, aim while standing, and aim while running. He only allowed them to aim, though, and not shoot—bullets were too expensive, he said, worth their weight in silver and gold. The people of Xizhen said they were all just farting without shitting—all day long they listened to commands of "shoot!" and "fire," but never actually heard the sound of a gun.

48.

Chen Yaowu began to experience a new sense of unease. Ever since he had come home, Lin Baijia had stuck close by his side—if she wasn't sitting by him, she was walking with him. At first he didn't think anything of it. But then one evening, he turned his head and saw her radiant face illuminated by the rays of the setting sun. In that moment, he realized that this was no longer the Lin Baijia of before, tugging at his clothes and running around with a snotty nose calling him "big brother."

Sometimes Chen Yaowu would go into a trance as he stared at Lin Baijia, especially in Mr. Wang's classroom, when he would turn to see her sitting to his left. By now the air was warming up and the flowers were blooming, and Lin Baijia was sitting at her desk wearing a short jacket with mid-length sleeves and loose-fitting pants. Chen Yaowu had noticed her slightly protruding bosom, and his gaze started to travel from her face down her slender neck to her chest, where it lingered for a long while. Lin Baijia didn't move a muscle, but a rosy tint slowly appeared on her face.

Grasping his disciplinary ruler in hand, Mr. Wang was now basking in his own success. The seven students who had left had now all returned, and he had become stricter than ever—if he caught anyone daydreaming in class, he would raise his ruler and bring it down hard on the student's hands, then warn them that the next time it would be like a string of firecrackers. When Chen Yaowu would enter a daze, however, Mr. Wang tended not to notice—sometimes he would actually not see, while other times he would deliver a light little tap on Chen Yaowu's desk.

Lin Baijia also began to feel uneasy. Chen Yaowu's gaze was as scorching as an oven—she knew he had changed, and that she had changed as well. Her face would often turn red and her heart would beat faster, and sometimes her lips would even begin to tremble.

Spring turned to summer, and one afternoon Lin Baijia, dressed in a pleated skirt, was napping on a bamboo bench in the courtyard under the shade of the trees. As Chen Yaowu passed by the sleeping girl, he saw her milky white thigh peeking out of her skirt. His heart began racing and his breath quickened as he stood there staring at her leg. Then he placed his hand on it—the coolness of her skin surprised him, and he withdrew his hand in fear. A few moments went by, and he touched it again—it was just a cool as before. He started lightly stroking it, and it felt as smooth as silk.

Lin Baijia awoke with a start. At first she was surprised to see Chen Yaowu, but then she shyly closed her eyes and felt his hand moving on her leg. His hand trembled with excitement and nerves, and this feeling soon transferred to her, who also started trembling. They stayed like this for a time, until Lin Baijia remembered they were under the trees in the courtyard, and so she stood up and pushed Chen Yaowu away. Before he could understand what was happening, he heard Li Meilian, who had appeared in the doorway, exclaim:

"Scoundrel!"

Chen Yongliang appeared in the doorway alongside Li Meilian. Immediately he grabbed a carrying pole beside the door and started beating Chen Yaowu. Chen Yaowu fled like an unbridled horse, running wildly down the street as his father followed him, seething with rage, shouting as he ran,

"I'll skin you alive!"

The people on the street stared in shock—no one dared to intervene. Just then Lin Xiangfu happened to be passing by, and when he saw Chen Yongliang running down the street brandishing a carrying pole, he ran to grab hold of him and ask what was going on. Chen Yongliang struggled to break free, but Lin Xiangfu held him tightly until he calmed down. Finally, with his head hung low, he turned around and headed home, dragging the carrying pole behind him. Lin Xiangfu walked beside him and asked him once more what had happened. Still he said nothing. When they got home, he shut the gate to the courtyard and went in the main hall. Finally, he glumly said,

"We've wronged you."

Li Meilian then told Lin Xiangfu what had happened. Lin Xiangfu turned to look at Lin Baijia, who was standing in the corner like a frightened bird. He didn't say anything, merely nodding his head slightly to indicate he understood. Then he sat down in a chair, lost in thought.

Chen Yaowu ran all the way to the western hills, and only when he looked back and saw that Chen Yongliang was no longer chasing him did he stop. Panting, he walked into a patch of forest, where he sat until the sky became filled with stars. Mosquitoes were buzzing and biting him until he itched all over. When he finally emerged from the trees, Xizhen in the valley below was already dark. He was hungry and thirsty as he walked down from the western hills to Xizhen's wharf, where he lay down by the river and drank a bellyful of water. Filled with uncertainty, he started walking away as he heard the night watchman sound the third *geng*. Then he went home and pushed on the front door, but it was latched from the inside; the thought of knocking crossed his mind, but he didn't dare. After standing there for a while he sat down, at which point he fell asleep leaning against the door.

In the morning when Li Meilian opened the door to the courtyard and found Chen Yaowu asleep, she gave him a shove to wake him and then pulled him inside the main hall, where Chen Yongliang, Lin Xiangfu, Lin Baijia and Chen

Yaowen were all sitting. Chen Yaowu rubbed his eyes and saw that they were eating breakfast. Li Meilian dragged her son over to his father, who nodded, got up to get a rope, and then led Chen Yaowu outside. Lin Xiangfu got up to stop him, but Chen Yongliang shook his head and said, "The country has its laws, the family has its rules."

"First let him eat something and get some sleep," said Lin Xiangfu, "then carry out your rules."

Chen Yongliang looked at the missing ear on the left side of his son's face, and a pain rose up in his heart. "He can have something to eat," he said, "but no sleep."

Chen Yaowu sat in front of Lin Baijia and hungrily devoured his breakfast. Then he followed his father outside, where he stood under an elm tree hanging his head; because he wasn't fully awake, he kept yawning. Chen Yongliang tied him up with the rope and hung him from the tree. He saw Chen Yongliang get his whip. Chen Yaowu said,

"Pa, please take me down and let me take off my shirt before you whip me—I've only got two shirts."

Chen Yongliang hesitated, but took him down and loosened the ropes so he could take off his shirt. Then he tied him up again and hung him back on the tree. The whip in Chen Yongliang's hand struck Chen Yaowu's body with loud thwacks as Chen Yaowu cried out in agony. His skin rose up in long welts, and thin streams of blood trickled out where the skin had broken.

Sitting in the main hall, Lin Baijia could hear Chen Yaowu's wails. Her whole body shivered, and tears came to her eyes. She wore a pained expression on her face, and Lin Xiangfu knew why—the incident that had transpired wasn't merely one-sided, but had involved them both. Chen Yaowu's cries were like arrows piercing her heart. First her cheeks went pale, and then her lips; then, during one of Chen Yaowu's more anguished howls, she fainted and collapsed on the floor.

Lin Baijia's fainting threw the main hall into a uproar. Even

Chen Yongliang dropped his whip and came running inside. Li Meilian ran up shouting for him to go at once and get a doctor, so he turned right around and ran back out.

Lin Xiangfu carried his daughter upstairs and laid her on the bed, where she lay for half a *shichen* without making a sound. When Chen Yongliang rushed in with Mr. Guo, the Chinese medicine doctor, Lin Baijia had just woken up. Mr. Guo checked Lin Baijia's pulse and said it was a bit weak, but that everything seemed to be fine now. Everyone breathed a sigh of relief; then they remembered that Chen Yaowu was still hanging from the tree.

Lin Xiangfu and Chen Yongliang went immediately to get him down and discovered that he, too, had fainted. Once again everyone was thrown into a tizzy, and Chen Yaowu was carried upstairs and laid on a bed. Mr. Guo took his pulse and said it was also a bit weak, but when he checked again shortly afterwards he reported it had regained its strength. He stood and said the boy would wake soon; then he looked at the injuries on Chen Yaowu's body and said,

"Take some ashes from the stove and put them on the lacerations—that will keep poison from attacking the heart."

Li Meilian got some ashes and carefully spread them over Chen Yaowu's injuries. The searing pain of the ashes on his open wounds caused Chen Yaowu to wake up, and he cried out twice, thinking that he was still being lashed by the whip. When he saw that it was not Chen Yongliang but Li Meilian, and that he was laying on a bed, he stopped crying out and began moaning.

Li Meilian looked the marks of the whip on her son's body and the missing ear on the left side of his face, and couldn't help but cry. Shaking her head, she said,

"The young mistress already belongs to the Gu family—if word of this gets out, how will she ever be able to hold up her head?"

After Chen Yaowu had fallen asleep, Li Meilian went into

Lin Baijia's room and gave a heavy sigh as she sat on her bed and looked at her pale face. When Lin Baijia saw her, a bellyful of grievance welled up within her, and she clutched Li Meilian's sleeve and began weeping loudly. Li Meilian stroked her hair and said,

"This fate was determined in a previous life."

49.

Lin Xiangfu and Chen Yongliang sat by the light of the flames flickering on the wick of the lamp until late that night. They had consumed two *jin* of rice wine, but hadn't touched any of the four dishes Li Meilian had made for them. Counting on his fingers, Chen Yongliang determined that he and Li Meilian had been away from their hometown for fifteen years; Lin Xiangfu realized it had been thirteen years since he had put Lin Baijia in that sack and headed south. The two men were filled with a thousand different feelings. Chen Yongliang told Lin Xiangfu that he wanted to return to their hometown, and that he had already made up his mind. Lin Xiangfu knew what Chen Yongliang was thinking—he wanted to take Chen Yaowu far away from Lin Baijia. Lin Xiangfu said many things to Chen Yongliang, but he didn't try to stop him from leaving; he only said that he hoped they wouldn't go far—the country was in turmoil, and who knew what sort of disaster might befall them; the two families still needed to look out for one another. Lin Xiangfu said that he already had over 1300 *mu* of land in the Wanmudang, and that after Lin Baijia's dowry of five hundred *mu,* there were still over eight hundred left.

Then he put a finer point on things, saying that as long as Lin Baijia and Chen Yaowu didn't see each other, that was enough—there was no need to make a big production of going all the way back to their hometown. Even though this place wasn't where they were from, it hadn't been easy to accumulate all this property.

Lin Xiangfu's words made Chen Yongliang think for a long time. Finally he nodded and accepted Lin Xiangfu's suggestion. They finished the rice wine but still felt they had more to say, so they went out and walked through the quiet nighttime streets of Xizhen, making it all the way to the south gate before they managed to find a tavern that still had its lamps lit. They went in and ordered two plates of food and two more *jin* of wine, then sat down by a window and started haggling. Lin Xiangfu wanted to give all the remaining eight hundred *mu* of land to Chen Yongliang, but Chen Yongliang would only accept a hundred. Lin Xiangfu repeatedly tried to convince him to take more, but the most he was willing to accept was two or three hundred.

That night, Lin Xiangfu revealed his past to Chen Yongliang. He told him that the reason he had made the long journey to Xizhen was in search of a woman named Xiaomei—Lin Baijia's mother. Although he had increasingly come to the conclusion that Aqiang and Xiaomei were husband and wife, he still referred to them as brother and sister as he told his story.

Chen Yongliang listened calmly as Lin Xiangfu told his story. Having been so close with Lin Xiangfu over the past thirteen years, he had long felt that for him to have carried his baby daughter all the way from the north and settled in Xizhen, he must have had some business there that was too painful to speak of. Now, he had revealed it.

Chen Yongliang said he had only come to Xizhen two years before Lin Xiangfu, and that he was about as familiar with Xizhen as he was with Lin Xiangfu. He had known three women in Xizhen named Xiaomei, and two men named Aqiang, but none of them quite matched the age and appearance that Lin Xiangfu described.

Lin Xiangfu said that back when they were pulling their cart around town fixing doors and windows, he'd come across seven women named Xiaomei and five men named Aqiang, but none of them had been the Xiaomei and Aqiang he had been searching for. Then he said to Chen Yongliang,

"If Wencheng isn't real, then the names Xiaomei and Aqiang are also probably not real."

Chen Yongliang nodded. He thought back to Lin Xiangfu's insistence that they repair the windows and doors of all vacant houses in town, but because the doors had been padlocked they hadn't been able to enter. Afterwards, whenever someone returned from elsewhere to Xizhen, Lin Xiangfu had always taken the initiative to go fix their windows and doors. Now Chen Yongliang knew the reason—he had been waiting for Xiaomei and Aqiang to return. Chen Yongliang said to Lin Xiangfu,

"Everyone within a hundred *li* of Xizhen knows about the woodworking shop in Xizhen and Lin Xiangfu—so this Xiaomei and Aqiang would also probably have heard."

After a pause, Chen Yongliang added, "They probably won't be returning to Xizhen."

Lin Xiangfu gave a bitter smile. He said that thirteen years had passed and he'd never found Xiaomei and Aqiang; not even a trace of them had appeared. He thought he'd originally felt so strongly that Xizhen was actually Wencheng, simply because he'd so desperately wanted it to be. But now he felt he was wrong—Wencheng was not Xizhen, it must be some other place. Lin Xiangfu told Chen Yongliang that he wanted to return home, to his hometown in the north—but because Lin Baijia was not yet married, and was not yet officially part of the Gu family, he couldn't leave. Hearing this stirred Chen Yongliang's emotions, and he told Lin Xiangfu that someday they would all return to their hometowns.

After that, the two men stopped talking. They raised their winecups again and again, not knowing when the next time would be that they could drink together. Each time they raised their cups, they exchanged a smile.

The next morning, Chen Yongliang put a sack of grain on

his back and went out the door to Xizhen's wharf, where he got a small boat with a bamboo awning. From there he sailed into the Wanmudang to see where he would live. After Chen Yongliang left, Li Meilian started getting their belongings together. As she was going through their clothing, she came upon that old sack made of coarse cotton cloth—the scene of Lin Xiangfu carrying Lin Baijia into their home during that terrible blizzard immediately flashed before her eyes. She took the sack over to Lin Xiangfu and told him it wasn't of much good to anyone anymore, could he give it to her? Maybe someday in the future she would find a use for it. As she said this her eyes filled with tears. Lin Xiangfu knew she wanted something to remember Lin Baijia—spending thirteen years together day and night had given them a bond of mother and daughter. Lin Xiangfu nodded and said,

"Take it with you."

Lin Baijia sat in her room in a daze. She had the premonition that Chen Yongliang's family was going to leave, and she would sporadically start crying. When Chen Yaowu was able to get out of bed, he once again sat staring just as he had when he had returned from the bandits. Only at meals did they lay eyes on each other. Sometimes Lin Baijia would raise her head and glance at Chen Yaowu, but he always kept his head down. The injuries from the whip were still painful, and he didn't dare cast a look toward Lin Baijia.

Two days later, Chen Yongliang returned. He told Lin Xiangfu that in the village of Qijiacun, there were over two hundred *mu* of fields that belonged to him, and that's where he had chosen to settle—he had even gone ahead and bought a brick house with a tile roof. Lin Xiangfu called Mr. Wang over from the school and had him act as a witness as he signed the two hundred *mu* of land in Qijiacun over to Chen Yongliang.

Chen Yongliang then pulled out that rumbling old cart, which had sat idle in the woodworking shop for so many years now, and loaded it up with their luggage. He looked over at

Lin Xiangfu, who was squinting in the summer sunlight, then lowered his head and pulled the cart out through the main courtyard gate. Lin Xiangfu was walking to the side and about two paces ahead of Chen Yongliang, while Li Meilian walked along holding Lin Baijia's hand; Chen Yaowen pushed the cart from behind, and Chen Yaowu walked behind him, hanging his head. At first Chen Yaowu seemed to be walking straight enough, but after continuing for a while on the main road, his head suddenly began to tilt to the right, and he began veering off to the side.

When they reached Xizhen's wharf, Chen Yongliang jumped on a boat, and Lin Xiangfu passed the luggage to him piece by piece. After Chen Yaowen and Chen Yaowu had climbed aboard, Chen Yongliang went back on shore to bid farewell to Lin Xiangfu. As he stood in front of Lin Xiangfu, he wanted to say something, but nothing would come out—he could only scratch his head and smile. Lin Xiangfu didn't know what to say, either, so he simply nodded and patted Chen Yongliang on the shoulders.

At that point, Li Meilian, who had bravely worn a smile on her face the whole time, burst into tears. She held Lin Baijia's face in her hands and took a good look. When Lin Baijia started crying, she wiped her tears and told her not to cry, although she herself had tears streaming down her face. Chen Yongliang pulled Li Meilian over and helped her onto the boat. He told her not to cry, although he was unable to keep from shedding tears himself. He then told the boatman to push off and stood on the prow waving at Lin Xiangfu. Finally, he was able to get out a few words of parting:

"Take care of yourself."

As Lin Xiangfu, his eyes filled with tears, watched the boat drift away over the vast expanse of water, he felt that he had truly become a part of Chen Yongliang's family. He looked at his daughter—her face tearstained, she stared woodenly at the boat as it sailed away. She was watching Chen Yaowu standing on the bow of the boat, his head tilted to the side, giving her the feeling that he could drop into the water at any moment.

50.

When Gu Yimin learned that Chen Yongliang's family had moved to Qijiacun, he was shocked. "The bandits are all over the Wanmudang," he said to Lin Xiangfu, "There are over ten bands of them, of all sizes. Anyone with a little bit of money has already moved into Xizhen—why would Chen Yongliang move out to the Wanmudang?"

Lin Xiangfu didn't respond immediately. Then, as if to himself, he said, "One can only follow the will of heaven."

For the first several days after they left, Lin Baijia spent much of the time crying by herself. She would sit staring out the window in the room that had once been the classroom, looking sad and beautiful, as motionless as a rocky cliff. Then one day a thought occurred to her. She walked up to Lin Xiangfu and asked him who her mother was.

Lin Xiangfu was caught off guard. Only then did he realize what an important spot Li Meilian had held in his daughter's heart. For thirteen years, Lin Baijia had never once asked about her mother. Only now that Li Meilian was gone did she think to ask.

An image of Xiaomei sprang to Lin Xiangfu's mind. Her face, her voice, and the heat of her body seemed so near he could almost feel her—but then it all began to fade like a wilting flower, and in the blink of an eye a feeling of loss spread over him. Once again he had the feeling that Xizhen was not Wencheng, and that he had waited here for Xiaomei in vain for thirteen years. He had the sad feeling that he would never see Xiaomei again in this life. The Xiaomei that had just appeared before his eyes had now gone far away—her face became indistinct, her voice became faint, her warmth gradually dispersed.

Lin Baijia saw her father's lips quiver. He then proceeded to tell her about her mother. The person Lin Xiangfu described, however, was not Xiaomei—it was Liu Fengmei, the woman the matchmaker had taken him to see: that beautiful young woman who hadn't said a word when he met her, and who could have been his partner in a happy marriage had he not let the opportunity slip by. He desperately tried to remember Liu Fengmei's appearance, but when he started describing her, he kept changing it, so that in the end he realized that everything he'd said was a description of his past with Xiaomei. Finally, he told his daughter that her mother's name was Liu Fengmei, and that she had died shortly after she was born.

Lin Baijia asked: had the three blue calico headscarves in the wardrobe been her mother's? The question took Lin Xiangfu by surprise, but he nodded. He saw a look of sadness spread over his daughter's face.

Lin Baijia was sad for ten days. For ten days her mind was elsewhere, and everything she put in her mouth tasted like dust. Then one day Lin Xiangfu suddenly heard her laughing—she was carrying her books and walking out of the school across the street, her cheeks glowing like the setting sun. Lin Xiangfu felt as if a heavy burden had been lifted from his shoulders. He thought about how good it was that she was still young, able to forget about things and move on. He was thrilled that this was now all in the past, and that she was once again the same joyful Lin Baijia as before.

51.

After the sixteen-year-old Chen Yaowu was separated from Lin Baijia, he felt utterly dispirited. Every day he would stand by the water in Qijiacun and stare in the direction of Xizhen. One day, the cargo vessels that came and went through the waters of the Wanmudang gave him an exciting idea—he stripped off his clothes and jumped into the water, holding his clothing up with one hand and using the other to propel himself out into the water. When he swam up to the side of one of the cargo boats, he grabbed hold of it and asked the boatman, could he hitch a ride to Xizhen? When he received a response in the affirmative, he hoisted himself on board and stood there naked on the prow, letting the summer sun dry the water on his body until he could put his clothes back on.

As soon as he got on shore at the Xizhen wharf, he headed straight for Mr. Wang's school. When he appeared, he heard a shriek of surprise and saw that Lin Baijia's face had turned beet red. Mr. Wang asked him how he had gotten there, and after he'd told them, he saw that Lin Baijia was biting her lip as tears streamed from her eyes. He sat beside Lin Baijia and kept looking over at her, and she kept looking over at him. In Lin Baijia's eyes, Chen Yaowu could see a boundless love—it was a look unlike any he'd ever seen.

Sometime in the afternoon, Chen Yaowu ran out of the school back to the wharf, where he got on another cargo boat to head home. As the boat sailed through the Wanmudang and approached Qijiacun, Chen Yaowu once again stripped off his clothing, jumped in the water, and held up his clothes as he swam to shore. When he climbed up on land, he jumped around to shake the water off his body. Then he put his clothes back on and went back home as if nothing had happened.

As Chen Yaowu continued these trips between Qijiacun and Xizhen, he started becoming familiar with the boatmen. Standing naked on the prow of the boat, the boatmen would look at him curiously. One day one of them asked why he was always going to Xizhen.

"To see my woman," he said.

The boatmen looked down at the sparse smattering of hair around his groin and couldn't help but burst out in laughter. From then on, whenever he stood on the prow of a boat drying off in the breeze, the boatmen in other boats would wave to him and ask,

"How's your woman?"

"Good," Chen Yaowu would answer simply.

One day Lin Xiangfu thought he saw a figure that looked something like Chen Yaowu coming out of Mr. Wang's school, walking briskly down the main street; at the time he didn't think much of it. Around a month later he saw the figure again, and this time he recognized it as Chen Yaowu—Chen Yaowu didn't see Lin Xiangfu, but Lin Xiangfu caught sight of his face as he turned a corner and noticed his joyful expression. After that, Lin Xiangfu became very worried—he now knew why the color had returned to Lin Baijia's face, and why she'd once again begun to laugh.

52.

One afternoon, Gu Yimin came over with a copy of the Shanghai newspaper *Shen Bao* to discuss the current political situation with Lin Xiangfu. He forgot to take the paper with him and left it on the table.

That evening, Lin Xiangfu picked up the copy of *Shen Bao* and happened to read an article about the McTyreire School. He learned that Shanghai had schools for girls, and that in addition to the education generally offered at local private schools, the McTyreire School included instruction in Western music and the basic principles of Christianity. A thought flashed through Lin Xiangfu's head—this school would be a good fit for Lin Baijia. He didn't pursue this thought any further, though, and as soon as he put down the paper, he forgot about it. He returned to thinking over his conundrum—how to keep Lin Baijia and Chen Yaowu from seeing each other. He started lying awake at night, thinking that since the two of them were meeting at Mr. Wang's school, the neighbors must all know about it.

Suddenly, Lin Xiangfu realized it was possible that Gu Yimin had already caught wind of it. Perhaps Gu Yimin had visited that afternoon and left the copy of *Shen Bao* intentionally, so that he might get the idea to send Lin Baijia to the McTyeire School in Shanghai.

Two weeks later, Lin Xiangfu took Lin Baijia and her luggage on a small boat with a bamboo awning to Shendian, where they got a horse-drawn carriage to Shanghai. Lin Xiangfu wore a stern expression the whole trip, and Lin Baijia felt anxious. She didn't know where they were going, and she didn't dare ask—she had the feeling her father had learned of Chen Yaowu's secret visits. When they got to Shanghai and went to the McTyeire School, Lin Baijia finally understood where her father was sending her.

Her second day at the school happened to be the school's "sisters day." Lin Baijia wore her uniform, which had an orange flower embroidered on the lapel, indicating her class. Other new students with red, yellow, green, blue, and purple flowers stood on the lawn, and as a gramophone played some Western music, a group of smiling upperclassmen girls walked toward them—they would each choose a new girl and become her "big sister." Each of the older girls carried a fresh cut flower, and when a younger girl accepted their flower, they became "sisters." The beautiful Lin Baijia attracted a number of older girls, who approached her with their flowers. Lin Baijia blushed, and just as she was hesitating and wondering which flower to accept, two younger girls came up to her with flowers and called out,

"Sister Lin!"

Lin Baijia saw that it was Gu Tongsi and Gu Tongnien, both of whom had grown much taller. The unexpected nature of their meeting caused Lin Baijia to forget her manners, and without a word she turned away from the expectant older girls and walked away with Gu Tongsi and Gu Tongnien.

Gu Tongsi walked up and gave her flower to Lin Baijia. Gu

Tongnien also walked up with her flower, but when she saw that her sister was offering her flower, she took a step back and let Lin Baijia take the flower from her older sister.

Lin Baijia accepted the flower from the smiling Gu Tongsi and walked over to Gu Tongnien, who was feeling a bit shy. She also took the flower from Gu Tongnien's hand, which brought an smile to her face. As Lin Baijia embraced the Gu sisters, from whom she'd been separated for so long, she couldn't help but weep; the smiling Gu sisters were soon shedding tears as well.

The Gu Tongsi bowed her head in prayer. "Thank you Lord for delivering to us my beautiful sister Lin."

Gu Tongnien followed suit, saying, "Thank you Lord for allowing me to see my sister Lin again."

Lin Baijia began a completely new life. She shared a room with the Gu sisters and joined a prayer group. In the evenings, she would sit around the dinner table with her classmates and sing,

"Father, we thank Thee for the night, and for the pleasant morning light; for rest and food and loving care, and all that makes the day so fair."

In the evenings, after Lin Baijia and the Gu sisters got washed and ready for bed, they would go to the foot of their beds and softly pray, "Thank you Lord for the peace You bring."

After the lights were supposed to be out, Go Tongsi would hang a blanket over the window, light a candle, and secretly do some embroidery. Gu Tongnien adhered to the school's regulations and obediently crawled under her blanket and lay down, looking over at Lin Baijia sitting by her bed in the dim candlelight. Lin Baijia would watch Gu Tongsi embroider as she thought over the things that were weighing on her mind. From time to time, Gu Tongsi would look up from her embroidery and cast a smile over to Lin Baijia, who would smile in return. Then she would look over at Gu Tongnien, who still had her eyes open and was looking back at her. In a soft voice she would tell her to go to sleep, and Gu Tongnien would nod and close her eyes.

The McTyreire School had a crying room, which was opened on Friday afternoons. The new students who were not yet used to life at school could go there and cry for as long as they liked. After her first week at school, Lin Baijia finally entered the crying room. With both hands over her mouth, she sobbed for a long time, her face flooded in tears as if a levee had burst. She was filled with a hundred different emotions, all tied together by sadness. She thought of Chen Yaowu; she thought of Li Meilian and Chen Yongliang; she thought of Chen Yaowen; and she thought of many events from the past. She thought of her dead mother and tried to imagine her appearance, although the image that always floated before her eyes was that of Li Meilian. She thought of her father, who had always been by her side for the past thirteen years, but from whom she was now separated.

Her eyes puffy and red, Lin Baijia walked out of the crying room. Gu Tongsi and Gu Tongnien were waiting for her outside the door. Gu Tongsi handed Lin Baijia her completed embroidery, which featured three branches of plum blossoms in descending order from large to small, symbolizing the three sisters. The three girls looked at each other and smiled, then joined a nearby group of students who were talking and laughing.

53.

Lin Xiangfu returned to Xizhen and went to see Gu Yimin. When he told him he had sent Lin Baijia to the McTyreire School in Shanghai, Gu Yimin didn't seem at all surprised—he simply nodded and said that his daughters, Gu Tongsi and Gu Tongnien, were also there. This took Lin Xiangfu a bit by surprise—Gu Yimin had never mentioned this, and he had not seen the Gu sisters when he had taken Lin Baijia to the school, although it had been a very quick trip, and he had returned to Xizhen as soon as he dropped off Lin Baijia.

It greatly comforted Lin Xiangfu to know that Lin Baijia would see the Gu sisters at the McTyreire School.

"They should run into each other, then," he said to Gu Yimin.

Lin Xiangfu commenced life on his own. Because of the bandits' kidnappings, all the business that came to the woodworking shop was related to the hasty marriages people were arranging for their children. Customers had come to the shop in a steady stream to order furniture, but now that this brief, hectic period had passed, business had cooled, and the shop was piled high with beds, tables, chairs, chests, wardrobes, cabinets, basins, buckets, and crates, as well as vase stands, basin stands, trivets, and the like. All of it was covered in a layer of dust and cobwebs.

Living by himself in the empty house, Lin Xiangfu's heart also felt empty. One night, he got out of bed and walked out of the house, through the courtyard gate, and down to the wharf where the prostitute lived. He walked up the rickety stairs and sat down across from Cuiping, her slender frame, big eyes, and upturned lips illuminated by the flickering light from the kerosene lamp. Lin Xiangfu remained silent. The scent of fish no longer inhabited Cuiping's home; her husband had died from an opium overdose. Cuiping told Lin Xiangfu her husband had been carried home on a moonless night, his mouth and nose stuffed with mud. The people who brought him home told her that the mud was meant to help save her husband. They said that if someone had eaten crude opium, or "opium dirt," they needed to be given mud—only by mixing dirt with dirt could the person be saved. At the time she'd had no idea what to do, although afterwards she felt it all seemed rather suspicious— what was this nonsense about mixing dirt with dirt, when her husband had clearly suffocated from the mud?

Cuiping was already a faded flower, and she no longer had any customers coming to enjoy her body. She had become even thinner over the years, and wrinkles now crept along the corners of her eyes, which had dimmed from their former radiance. Lin Xiangfu had come to visit her out of loneliness, and she exclaimed in surprise when she saw him—laying eyes on his bashful face, she herself wasn't sure what to do. She would never forget that northern man who had once so easily parted with his money, and then proceeded to make a name for himself in Xizhen over the next ten years. She knew he was second in wealth only to Gu Yimin.

When Lin Xiangfu first began his visits, he would simply sit without speaking for around a *shichen* and then go, quietly leaving ten coppers behind on his chair. Cuiping knew that Lin Xiangfu's body wasn't up for it, so she didn't try to initiate anything. She would pour him a cup of tea, then retreat back to the edge of the bed where she would sit cautiously. When Lin Xiangfu had finished his cup, she would get up and pour him another one.

After Lin Xiangfu had visited a few times, the two of them started engaging in little bits of conversation. Lin Xiangfu would always bring up his daughter, Lin Baijia, and sometimes he would pull one of her letters out of his shirt pocket, read an excerpt, and smile. At one point Cuiping brought up her deceased husband, telling Lin Xiangfu that in her younger years, her husband had spent nearly every bit of money she made selling her flesh on his opium addiction. Yet even as she complained about her husband, her eyes still revealed a sense of fondness as she remembered him. She told Lin Xiangfu that for a woman, to have had any kind of man at all was always better than to never have had one.

One evening, after Lin Xiangfu had been sitting with Cuiping for a long time, he decided not to go home and said he would stay the night. Cuiping immediately got up to make the bed. Lin Xiangfu took off only his outer garments and crawled under the covers in his underwear. He quietly left ten copper coins under his pillow.

Cuiping hesitated by the side of the bed, then proceeded to take off all her clothes and lay down naked beside Lin Xiangfu. After the two of them lay there for a while without talking, Cuiping felt Lin Xiangfu place his hand on her chest, then slowly move it down her body. Then she felt his hand becoming a little naughty, like a kid who was playing around. Cuiping reached a hand into his pants and slowly began to fondle him. Her hand, which had at first been quite cold, gradually warmed up. Lin Xiangfu could feel himself relaxing, like a wrinkled piece of clothing being ironed out smooth.

In the days that followed, when Lin Xiangfu came for an evening visit, he wouldn't go back home. He would instead strip off all his clothes and crawl under the blankets, then fall into a deep sleep under Cuiping's gentle touch. Cuiping caressed him, her fingernails running lightly over his skin, allowing his tense body to relax, like a field once its soil has been loosened by the plow.

54.

The last time Chen Yaowu got a boat to Xizhen, the chill of autumn had already set in, and the waters of the Wanmudang had grown cold. When he crawled up on board the boat, the autumn winds caused him to shiver and sneeze, yet he still stood naked on the prow of the boat, letting the chilly breeze dry his body before putting on his clothes. When Chen Yaowu got to Mr. Wang's school, he didn't see Lin Baijia—her seat was empty, and her desk wasn't even there. So he sat down to the side and stared for a while at the door. After Mr. Wang read a passage from a book he was holding, he put the book down and said,

"She's not coming back."

Mr. Wang told Chen Yaowu that Lin Baijia had gone to study in Shanghai. Chen Yaowu lowered his head, and it started to tilt. He sneezed three times and stood up, looking as if he were frozen, and walked shivering out of Mr. Wang's classroom and back down to the wharf. He stopped in front of a boat that was getting loaded up with sacks of soybeans and stood there holding himself and shivering. When the cargo was all loaded, Chen Yaowu boarded the boat. The boatmen all recognized him, and when they saw the dismal look on his face and the way he was shivering, they asked with a laugh,

"How's your woman?"

"I don't have a woman," he answered, broken-hearted.

This time Chen Yaowu didn't stand on the prow of the boat, but instead huddled up amongst some sacks of soybeans. A few of the boatmen tried to tease him playfully—how could there be no women to be had in this world, they asked. Never mind the daughters from noble families and the beautiful daughters from regular families—even if you just counted widows, there were still more of them than there were soybeans in those sacks. Plus, there were always prostitutes. A three-legged hen might be hard to find, they said, but two-legged women were everywhere.

Just as these boatmen were laughing and joking, several small boats with bamboo awnings sped right up next to the side of the cargo boat. A man with a Mauser hanging over his shoulder and an ax in his hand leapt on board, followed by several other gun-wielding men. One of the boatmen tried to knock one of them off with his oar, but the first man who had jumped on rushed forward brandishing his ax and hacked off half the boatman's shoulder, killing him instantly. The remaining four boatmen knew their boat had been taken by bandits, and they each knelt down as the helmsman pleaded, bowing with his hands folded,

"Masters, the boat and the cargo are yours—please spare our lives."

Without saying a word, the man with the ax walked over and hacked up the four boatmen one by one, kicking their corpses overboard. As the four boatmen were being chopped, only the first one managed to scream; none of the other three made a sound before they were killed. Sitting amongst the sacks of soybeans, Chen Yaowu saw that one of the bandits who had hopped on board was The Monk. He called out in a low voice:

"Monk—Monk—save me!"

The Monk heard Chen Yaowu call him, and he stared blankly for a moment as he carefully looked him over before finally recognizing him. As the man with the ax approached Chen Yaowu, The Monk said,

"Leave this one to me."

The Monk tied a rope around Chen Yaowu, wrapping it around loosely a few times, and shoved him off the boat. In the water, Chen Yaowu was able to struggle free from the rope and make it to the surface. The water was stained with the fresh blood of the four boatmen, which turned his hair and face red. It was their blood that now saved him, his face blending in with the gory scene in the water. When the man with the ax saw him, he thought he was just another floating corpse. Once the bandits had sailed the stolen cargo boat away, Chen Yaowu climbed up on one of the small abandoned boats and wept. The boatmen who had just been so happily talking and laughing had already returned to the Yellow Springs—the ax had sliced down through their shoulders, and as their bodies floated in the bloody water, their shoulders began to separate from their bodies. Only their waists remained intact as they drifted and spread out over the surface of the water.

Over the next three years, Chen Yaowu never left Qijiacun—he stayed there and grew up to become a strong young man. From time to time he would think of Lin Baijia, but she remained the same thirteen-year-old girl in his mind, and he no longer felt much excitement. He had no idea that for three years, she had been writing him letters. She had sent the letters to Mr. Wang to pass along to him, but Mr. Wang hadn't seen Chen Yaowu for three years. He had hidden them all in his wardrobe—there were so many he began to complain he'd soon run out of room for his own clothes.

55.

A bandit named One-Ax Zhang began gaining notoriety. Over the past three years, he had been all over the Wanmudang, stealing a total of fifty-seven cargo boats and slaughtering a total of eighty-nine boatmen with his ax. When the bandits under his direction docked the stolen boats and unloaded the cargo to sell, it was always covered in blood—so bloodstained rice, soybeans, cloth, and tea started showing up in shops in Xizhen and Shendian. As the blood-spattered merchandise began spreading, so did the rumors about One-Ax Zhang.

Not only did he terrorize people with his ax, but he was also an excellent marksman who could shoot a willow leaf at a hundred paces. He was incredibly quick and nimble—he could run like the wind, vault over walls, and leap onto boats. When he was young he'd followed around a fortune teller and learned his trade, so he could also tell fortunes through "finger divination." On the waters of the Wanmudang, One-Ax Zhang robbed and killed, ransacking all the nearby villages. He loved to eat human liver fried in rice wine—if no one came to pay a hostage's ransom, he would cut open the hostage's chest while they were still alive, pull out their liver, and fry it up for his dinner.

Over seven years, One-Ax Zhang married seven wives and killed seven wives. The last one to die was mending some clothes and dropped her needle. She couldn't find it, so One-Ax Zhang helped her look. He saw it after merely glancing down, so he picked up it for her. You really have the eye of a thief, said his wife with a laugh. "Eye of a thief," however, was a prohibited phrase, so One-Ax Zhang grabbed his Mauser and shot her right there on the spot.

One-Ax Zhang's ruthless violence made the once-formidable Floater, Leopard Li, and the other bandit leaders now tremble at the sight of him, and so one by one they all came under his command. Once One-Ax Zhang amassed his forces, he planned to attack Xizhen. He gathered Floater, Leopard Li, and a few others and said to them,

"There aren't any more cargo boats left in the Wanmudang, and all the wealthy families in the surrounding villages have fled to Xizhen. There's nothing left around here for us—it's all in fucking Xizhen."

As word got out that the bandits were planning to attack Xizhen, Zhu Bochong, the leader of the Xizhen militia, made preparations. He stationed sentries atop the city wall and ordered the city gate to be closed after dark. He distributed ammunition and took the militia out to the western hills for target practice. Finally the citizens of Xizhen heard real gunshots—the militia that only farted but never shit was now actually shooting. The people of Xizhen, though, were on tenterhooks, wondering if this militia of one-eared men would suffice. Would these nineteen men who'd had their ears cut off by the bandits simply shit their pants once they faced them again?

56.

One day in the fourth month, One-Ax Zhang led over a hundred bandits—along with two scaling ladders, two carts of wet blankets, and a rudimentary cannon—rumbling toward the south gate of Xizhen.

Zhu Bochong sent some men to guard the other three gates, while he stationed himself and seventeen men at the south gate—ten of them up on the city wall, and seven at the gate below. To prevent the bandits from entering, they piled up sacks of mud at the gate.

The bandits arrived outside the city gate and noisily came to a halt. They were all talking at once, and a few of them pulled down their pants and took a piss. One of the bandits called up to the men on the wall,

"Brothers in town! We're the men of One-Ax Zhang, and we've come to spend the night in Xizhen. Please open the gate."

When the militiamen up on the wall heard the bandit speak, they weren't sure how to respond—they all looked to Zhu Bochong, who shouted back at the bandits,

"Xizhen's too small to accommodate you. Please leave."

One of the bandits who had just finished urinating shook his pants and shouted,

"Fuck—we carry a gun for a living, and so do you. Tell us how much money you want to open the door, and we'll give it to you."

A few of the one-eared militiamen on the wall recognized him and exclaimed in surprise,

"Li'l Five—that one's Li'l Five!"

Li'l Five heard them and looked up—after examining them for a minute, he laughed and turned to say something to the other bandits. Then he looked up again and shouted,

"It seems my brothers up on the wall are all missing an ear!"

The bandits below the wall all burst out in laughter, while the eight earless militiamen on top of the wall all hung their heads. Li'l Five continued shouting up from below:

"Are they naturally like that, or did someone chop them off?"

Zhu Bochong saw the faces of the eight militiamen turn red with embarrassment. They looked dispirited, hanging their heads and holding their rifles as if they were walking sticks. Zhu Bochong was afraid these eight might not be very dependable, so he shouted to them,

"Those rifles aren't canes—hold them up!"

One-Ax Zhang was growing impatient, and he shouted: "Open the fucking gate! If you make us attack, we won't cut off your ears—we'll dig out your hearts!"

Suddenly a gunshot rang out, and Li'l Five fell to the ground. It was Blacksmith Xu who'd fired the shot, and when he saw that he had killed Li'l Five, his face flushed with excitement and he began to stammer the old saying,

"Wh-wh-when enemies come f-f-face to face, th-th-their eyes turn r-r-red with h-h-hate."

Blacksmith Xu's shot bolstered the courage of the seven other one-eared militiamen, and they all raised their guns and fired down from the wall. When they saw several bandits fall to the ground, they became as excited as Blacksmith Xu, and began reciting the same phrase as they continued to shoot,

"When enemies come face to face, their eyes turn red with hate!"

The bullets fired from up on the wall sailed through the trees below and sent their leaves rustling to the ground. The bandits below dispersed and returned fire, sending a barrage of bullets flying up toward the wall.

Chen San's left hand was hit, and he began waving it as if it were on fire and yelling,

"It burns! It burns!"

When the other one-eared militiamen saw his hand covered in blood, they were stunned. Zhu Bochong shouted at them to kneel down, and they did so at once, taking shelter behind the wall. The bandits' firepower quickly overcame that of the militiamen on the wall, and two teams of bandits came running toward the city wall with their scaling ladders.

Zhu Bochong yelled at the men on the wall to fire, and he joined them with his Mauser. Once again a concerted attack rained down from the wall.

Just then Blacksmith Xu spotted Floater running behind one of the scaling ladders and shouted,

"Floater! I see you, Floater—I'll fucking kill you!"

When the other one-eared militiamen heard this, they ran up to Blacksmith Xu and asked,

"Where is he, where is he?"

"Behind the ladder," Blacksmith Xu replied. "Don't you see?"

"We see, we see!" they shouted. "Kill him, kill him!"

All the bullets on the wall fired toward Floater, kicking up a cloud of dust. When Floater realized they were all aiming at him, he knew it wasn't good—he fled like a dancing monkey and hid behind a large tree.

A one-eared militiaman on the other end spotted Leopard Li. He announced his discovery, and the other one-eared men rushed over to him. Leopard Li was shouting and gesturing for a group of bandits to get the ladders up on the wall. Around ten bandits with brightly-colored wet blankets over their heads started climbing up, swords and Mauser pistols in their hands. Other bandits started firing toward the top of the wall. Together with the bandits climbing the ladders, they shouted:

"We're invincible! We're invincible!"

When Zhu Bochong saw the bandits climbing up the wall shouting "we're invincible," and that the one-eared militiamen were all huddled in a group pointing and trying to locate Leopard Li, he shouted:

"Fire your fucking guns! Your supposed to be fighting, not watching an opera!"

When the one-eared men saw the bandits climbing up, they quickly aimed their guns at the brightly-colored blankets and fired. The bullets made a thudding sound against the blankets, and cotton wadding began flying out. The bandit's shouts of "we're invincible" stunned the militia—the bullets had clearly hit them, yet they still kept climbing up.

"Fuck—they really are invincible!" the militiamen cried.

Two bandits made it up the wall and leapt out from under their blankets. One of them ran at Zhu Bochong brandishing his sword, and Zhu Bochong shot him in the face. Then he shot the other one and killed him, too. The one-eared militiamen suddenly realized what had happened and shouted,

"They weren't invincible—it was just the blankets!"

Just then, four more bandits leapt off the scaling ladder and onto the wall. When they threw off their blankets and prepared to shoot, the one-eared militiamen all raced forward, threw them to the ground, and began biting them. As the bandits screamed out in pain, Blacksmith Xu's apprentice Sun Fengsan ran up with his gun, held it up to each of the bandits' chests, and fired, killing all four.

"Push off the ladders! Push off the ladders!" shouted Zhu Bochong.

Zhu Bochong ran up and pushed one of the ladders down himself. Chen San ran up to the other ladder just as a bandit had made it to the top and discarded his blanket. Chen San raced forward, tackled him, and bit his face. He bit off a huge chunk of flesh, then kicked hard at the wall with both legs, causing both himself and the bandit to fall down with the ladder.

Chen San hit the ground and scrambled to get up, dazed and disoriented. His cheeks bulging out, he raced toward another bandit in front of him. Several bandits fired at him—both his legs went limp and he knelt on the ground, spitting out fresh blood. He spit out the chunk of flesh he had bitten off, then picked it up and examined it carefully—he'd bitten off an ear. Staggering to his feet, he turned around and, with a pleased look on his face, held the ear high above his head to show the men on the wall what he was holding. A spray of bullets tore through his body—the hand holding the ear dropped to his side, and he fell to the ground.

One of the one-eared militiamen on the wall began wailing loudly at Chen San's heroic death. He picked up a sword, leapt down off the wall, and rushed toward the bandits carrying one of the scaling ladders.

When the bandits saw this wailing man, unafraid to face

death, rushing at them with a sword, they threw down the ladder and ran away. Other bandits fired at him. This one-eared militiaman ignored the bullets and hacked with all his might at the ladder until he had broken it. Despite the fact that he had been hit several times, he rushed toward the other ladder and began hacking at it.

"Hold your fire," shouted One-Ax Zhang.

One-Ax Zhang then sprinted forward himself. He raised his ax and chopped off the militiaman's left arm. Still, the man continued hacking at the ladder with the sword in his right hand. By the time One-Ax Zhang sliced off his head, the scaling ladder was already in two pieces.

When One-Ax Zhang saw that both the ladders had been cut in two, he knew there was no way to scale the city wall. He ordered the bandits to pull back and bring out the cannon.

As the bandits pulled back, they could hear sobbing coming from the top of the wall—the men on the wall were crying over the brave sacrifice of their two fellow one-eared fighters.

When Zhu Bochong saw the bandits bringing the cannon forward, he ordered the men on the wall to disperse and the seven men guarding the gates below to withdraw twenty meters. The men on the wall squatted down with their guns and listened to the din of the bandits below. When Zhu Bochong waved his hand, they immediately stood up and fired, then squatted back down to reload. As they reloaded, they could hear the sound of the bandits' groaning below—this caused Blacksmith Xu to snicker, and the other men soon joined him.

Just then an explosion sounded, and the cannon blew a hole in the wall. Bits of rock and dust flew through the air, and men on the wall were deafened by the sound. As they crawled to their feet, completely covered in dust, they saw that their leader had been injured.

A chunk had been blown out of Zhu Bochong's midsection, out of which his warm, steaming intestines were pouring. The militiamen surrounded him in shock. Zhu Bochong shouted at them to get back, while at the same time attempting to stuff his intestines back inside his body, together with bits of debris. He ordered them to guard the opening in the wall and then called forth the seven men stationed at the gates, continuing to give orders as he sat on the ground. The bandits rushed toward the breach in the wall, and he raised his hand and ordered the militiamen to shoot. The bandits rushed forward three times, and retreated under the militia's fire three times. Zhu Bochong felt he wouldn't be able to hold on much longer. When there was a break in the fighting, he called over Blacksmith Xu, who summoned the rest of the militia. They squatted down around Zhu Bochong, their faces covered in dust and blood, as Zhu Bochong counted them up—there were still twelve of them left, and as he gazed at their faces he smiled and said,

"I can't tell who's who."

Zhu Bochong said he was on the verge of death. He saw tears gathering in the dusty eyes of his men and streaming down their dusty faces. He passed his Mauser to Blacksmith Xu and appointed him as the militia's new leader. Gesturing below the wall, he told them:

"Remember the depth of your hatred. Defend the city wall to the death—no matter what, you can't let the bandits in."

Just before he died, Zhu Bochong had a final moment of clarity and bid his farewell: "My whole life has been spent in the military, from the Qing army, to the Northwest Army, to commanding your Xizhen militia. I never imagined that the most gallant and courageous of these would be the Xizhen militia—being your leader has been the greatest honor I could hope for in three lifetimes, and I can die with no regrets."

The twelve militiamen on the wall once again broke down in tears. Then Blacksmith Xu sat on the ground like Zhu Bochong, and when the bandits rushed forward again, he raised his hand like Zhu Bochong, and the militiamen all stood up immediately and fired.

After the militia had engaged in bloody battle for over two

shichen, only Blacksmith Xu and his apprentice Sun Fengsan were left. Sun Fengsan had suffered a number of wounds, and Blacksmith Xu's eyeball had been blown out. Master and apprentice each lay on their bellies on top of the wall over the breach, defending Xizhen to the death. Every time Sun Fengsan would shoot a bandit, he would ask,

"Master—was that one Leopard Li?"

At first, Blacksmith Xu had been able to see clearly, but that was no longer the case. He felt like there was something hanging in front of his eyes, so he asked Sun Fengsan,

"Is there something hanging in front of my eyes?"

Sun Fengsan took a look and replied, "Master, it's your eyeball."

Blacksmith Xu yanked it out and felt the other eye gradually go dark. He passed his Mauser over to Sun Fengsan and said,

"I'm blind now, so I'm entrusting you with Commander Zhu's gun—you are now the leader of the militia."

Himself on the verge of death, Sun Fengsan accepted the gun. Just then they heard a loud boom outside the city wall.

One-Ax Zhang had led a hundred bandits in a vicious attack on Xizhen. But after fighting for an entire day they still had not been able to capture the town, so they were beginning to grow dispirited. On-Ax Zhang was left with no choice but to use the cannon again to blow open the city gate. But this time too much gun powder had been loaded in the cannon and it exploded, killing three bandits and injuring five more. When One-Ax Zhang took stock of the dead and injured, he saw there were less than sixty men left.

Suddenly an earth-shaking sound of shouting erupted in Xizhen, and a mass of bobbing heads began to appear atop the city wall. One-Ax Zhang knew something bad was about to happen, so he ordered the bandits to retreat.

As the one-eared militiamen were fighting to the death, some of Xizhen's courageous young men climbed up onto their roofs to watch the battle. When they saw how bravely the militia fought, and how they all risked their lives to guard the city gate, it energized them and made their blood run hot. So the young men climbed down and ran through the streets and alleys of Xizhen telling everyone what they'd seen. People began running out of their houses with kitchen knives, kindling knives, wooden clubs, iron clubs, and spears, congregating in the main street, and shouting, "Kill the bandits!" A short time later, all the knives had been taken from the butcher shop, all the blades had been cleared out of the blacksmith shop, and even the tailor's scissors were gone. Hundreds of men rushed toward Xizhen's south gate—some, who had originally intended to flee once the bandits broke in, still carried bundles on their backs, although now they were shouting and running with everyone to the gate.

They came pouring out through the breach in the wall like water. When the bandits heard their thunderous din and saw the dark mass of people rushing toward them, they became frightened and scattered in all directions; some of them even threw down their guns so they could run faster. The slower bandits and those who were injured were all hacked up and beaten to death, and one particularly unlucky bandit was even cut to death by scissors.

The bandits' desperate retreat boosted the morale of the citizens of Xizhen, and they continued attacking wildly in hot pursuit, until in no time at all they had chased them over ten *li*. By this point many of the men couldn't run any longer, so they gave up the chase and stopped, until eventually there were only about ten pursuing the bandits. As they ran along shouting, they could tell their shouts were growing fewer and farther between; only then did they realize there were only a few of them left. At that point the twenty or so bandits they had been chasing turned around and rushed back toward them, so that they became the ones fleeing. But the bandits were still worried that more men from Xizhen might turn up, so after firing a few shots they turned and fled south.

After driving away the bandits, the men of Xizhen headed back to the south gate. They searched through the piles of rubble on top of the wall and below the wall for the remains of Zhu Bochong, Blacksmith Xu, Chen San, and the others of the seventeen militiamen. Only Sun Fengsan, holding the Mauser to his chest, still had some faint breath left in him. The people of Xizhen laid down seventeen door planks and placed the militiamen's corpses on them, then combined their forces to carry them to the temple of the city god. Both sides of the street were crowded with onlookers, and once the seventeen door planks passed by, they fell in behind and followed them to the temple.

Sun Fengsan, who was still hanging on by a thread, was taken to Mr. Guo's pharmacy. Gu Yimin summoned all the doctors of Chinese medicine in town, but when they saw the numerous injuries Sun Fengsan had suffered, they either sighed or shook their heads. They told Gu Yimin there were eight bullets in him they couldn't get out, and there were so many other wounds they couldn't even count them all.

Some of the doctors noticed that Sun Fengsan was still bleeding, so they fried up some cattail pollen and spread it on the wounds—the said all they could do was apply some cattail pollen to stop the bleeding, relieve the pain, and prevent inflammation. Crowds of people had gathered outside the pharmacy door, waiting for news on Sun Fengsan's condition.

Sun Fengsan had passed out, but right before he died he suddenly opened his eyes and saw that he was still holding the Mauser to his chest, and that Gu Yimin was standing by his side. A smile appeared on his face, and with both hands he lifted the gun to offer it to Gu Yimin. In a weak voice, he said,

"Before he died, Commander Zhu made my master the commander, and before my master died, he made me the commander. Now I'm about to die, so I appoint you as the commander . . . Please carve 'commander of the militia' on the graves of my master and me."

Gu Yimin accepted the Mauser and then reached out and

closed Sun Fengsan's eyes. Then he took the Mauser outside and announced to the waiting crowd that Sun Fengsan had died. The lively crowd immediately fell silent as Gu Yimin raised the gun in his hand and said,

"Three years ago I went to the provincial capital to invite Zhu Bochong to come to Xizhen to organize and lead a militia. Before Zhu Bochong died, he appointed Blacksmith Xu as the next commander, and before Blacksmith Xu died, he appointed Sun Fengsan. Before Sun Fengsan died, he passed his gun to me and said that I was to be the next commander. I stand before you now as the fourth commander of Xizhen's militia."

The eighteen brave members of the militia who had sacrificed their lives were not buried in the western hills. Instead, Gu Yimin had them buried in the plaza in front of the temple of the city god—he wanted the people to remember who had defended Xizhen. Eighteen tombstones were erected in front of the temple. On Zhu Bochong's were carved the words, "First Commander of the Xizhen Militia"; on Blacksmith Xu's were carved the words, "Second Commander of the Xizhen Militia," and on Sun Fengsan's were carved the words, "Third Commander of the Xizhen Militia."

57.

The fame of Xizhen's one-eared militia spread far and wide. When news got out that Gu Yimin was once again establishing a militia, people came from all over to sign up. Gu Yimin went to the provincial capital and purchased twenty Hanyang rifles, some of the wealthier families in Xizhen donated their own privately owned firearms, and Gu Yimin set up a new, thirty-man militia. From that point on, Commander Gu Yimin's gun never left his side—wherever he turned up, he would always have Zhu Bochong's Mauser slung over his shoulder, even if he were receiving guests or attending a banquet. He modeled himself on Zhu

Bochong—he had his men practice marching with their firearms in front of the temple of the city god; then he had them practice aiming while laying down, aiming while squatting, aiming while standing, and aiming while running. Like Zhu Bochong, he took them to the western hills to practice shooting, where he shouted at them like Zhu Bochong. Zhu Bochong would shout encouragement while the men were target shooting, so when Gu Yimin heard them firing their guns, he couldn't keep from yelling,

"Nice shooting!"

Militias from nearby towns came to strike mutual defense agreements with the Xizhen militia. Even well-fortified Shendian sent someone over to make a defense pact—aside from a militia, they also had troops sent by the provincial military governor to root out bandits.

Gu Yimin saw himself as the leader of all the militia commanders. He called all the militia commanders to Xizhen for a summit to discuss the eradication of the bandits. Now that the people's hearts were stirred, he said, they should not let up in their efforts against the bandits. From this day forward, the purpose of the militia would not merely be to defend the town, but to strike out on the offensive. Whenever there was a report of bandit activity, Gu Yimin would lead the militia out to squash them. Over the next three months, Gu Yimin gleefully led the militia out of Xizhen thirteen times. Although they never actually encountered any bandits, the militia's reputation grew even more illustrious. Zhu Bochong had always led his men in front, but when Gu Yimin took his men out after the bandits, he still bore his status as the head of the chamber of commerce—while he had usually traveled in a sedan chair with four carriers, to boost the morale of his men, he now rode in a sedan chair with eight carriers. When his sedan ostentatiously paraded through town on those summer days, a militiaman would walk on each side of him waving a fan. When he alighted from the sedan, someone would be ready with a parasol to shield him from the beating sun.

58.

The battle at Xizhen had caused One-Ax Zhang to lose about half his men. Furthermore, Floater, Leopard Li, and some others had broken with One-Ax Zhang, taken some of the remaining men away with them, and recommenced their highway robbery.

Not quite twenty bandits remained with One-Ax Zhang. He knew he couldn't achieve anything big with just twenty-some guns, so he started recruiting more men in the Wanmudang, forcing villagers to throw in their lot with the bandits. When he was starting out, One-Ax Zhang had gone after cargo boats, but they had since all but disappeared from the waters of the Wanmudang; the wealthy families of the Wanmudang villages had also nearly all fled. Previously, One-Ax Zhang had ignored the slim pickings that remained in these little villages, but after his defeat at Xizhen, his interest in them returned. So one day, he led a group of bandits to the village of Qijiacun, where Chen Yongliang and his family lived.

The bandits approached in a disorderly manner through the rice paddies, carrying long blades and hacking through the rice as they went. It pained the villagers to see the bandits whacking their way through the rice, which was just on the verge of harvest, but they dared not say a word. Only the hotblooded, impetuous Chen Yaowu ran toward the bandits shouting,

"Do you people live on grass? Why are you chopping down the rice?"

One of the bandits raised his blade toward Chen Yaowu and said, "Fuck—it's not just rice I'm going to cut; I'm going to chop off your head!"

Chen Yongliang tugged at his son's arm to keep him from saying anything more. One-Ax Zhang and his bandits emerged from the rice paddy, a Mauser slung over One-Ax Zhang's left shoulder and an ax in his right hand. Chen Yaowu recognized him at once—this was the bandit who had hacked off the shoulders of those five boatmen. Chen Yaowu felt his scalp tingle.

One-Ax Zhang walked up to the villagers and said to them, "This is my territory, and whatever I say goes. This a big village, so choose twenty young men to come join up with me. You also have to supply us with provisions."

Chen Yongliang stepped forward and said, "Our village depends on farming for our livelihood, and we can't spare that many hands; as for food and money, we're willing to provide you with as much as we can."

One-Ax Zhang looked down for a while, then very slowly said, "Give us the food and money first."

The bandits then proceeded to ransack Qijiacun. They went from house to house searching through cabinets and chests, took everything worth any money, and loaded it all onto their boats, filling four of them with food, clothing, and other items. Then they set up a cookfire in Chen Yongliang's courtyard, killed some pigs and sheep, and started cooking. They ate meal after meal, littering Chen Yongliang's courtyard with scraps, which the chickens and ducks that hadn't yet been slaughtered walked around pecking at. They remained in Qijiacun for two days, eating and drinking. When they had consumed all the food and livestock they were unable to take with them, they stood up and dusted off their butts, issued some belches from their grease-smeared mouths, and headed for their boats. Before he boarded, One-Ax Zhang snickered and patted Chen Yongliang on the shoulders, saying,

"We'll be back to pay a visit next month."

After the bandits left, the women of Qijiacun wept and wondered aloud how they would make it through the days to come. Chen Yongliang called all the households together and said,

"It seems like we'll no longer be able to enjoy any peace. Everyone be extremely careful and hide anything you have left that might be of any value—that goes for all of your food as well."

Finally, he warned the villagers: "Don't stir up any trouble—stay calm and remain patient, and we might be able to avoid disaster."

59.

Over the course of a year, One-Ax Zhang had managed to gather together around fifty bandits, but because they lacked firepower, they restricted their activities to the villages in the Wanmudang. When Gu Yimin took his men out to eradicate the bandits, the show he made of himself in his eight-carrier sedan chair made One-Ax Zhang thoroughly jealous. He wanted to ride in an eight-carrier sedan chair with throngs of bandits shouting and crowding around on all sides—it would be enough to make his whole life seem like it had been worth living.

He began to set his sights on Gu Yimin. He gathered together some of his most capable men and said that to kill a snake, you have to strike it near its head—if they took Gu Yimin hostage, they would not only knock the wind out of the Xizhen militia's sails, but they could also exchange him for the militia's guns and increase their firepower.

One-Ax Zhang prepared a coffin and hid some guns in it. Then he chose about ten capable bandits, dressed them in mourning garb, and set off with them. They docked their boats in the Wanmudang village of Dangxicun, where they took a land route to Xizhen. They didn't take the main road, but a circuitous series of smaller roads that led them through Xizhen's western hills.

Several residents of Xizhen who were in the hills gathering kindling spotted the funeral procession coming up the mountain path, consisting of eleven men dressed in mourning, carrying a coffin as they cried and wailed like a bunch of crows. The townsfolk thought this was all a bit curious, and as the strangers approached, they asked them where they were from.

The bandits didn't reply, but carried the coffin right up to Gu Yimin's ancestral family graves, where they set it down, took out their mattocks, and starting digging a hole in his family plot.

The townsfolk from Xizhen were shocked and quickly rushed forward to stop them. This was Gu Yimin's family's ancestral plot, they said—if they dug it up, they would go to jail. Still the bandits said nothing, and simply carried on with their crying and digging.

One resident of Xizhen said to the bandits, "Do you know Gu Yimin? He's the commander of Xizhen's militia, and also the head of the chamber of commerce."

One-Ax Zhang turned around and replied, "Our Zhang family just purchased this burial plot—look, we've got the deed."

One-Ax Zhang held out a paper for them to see, which they saw did have some writing on it, along with a thumb print. Then he returned the paper to his breast pocket, turned around, and began wailing:

"Pa! Pa! Don't leave us!"

The Xizhen townsfolk had no idea what to do. One of them suggested they should go at once and tell Gu Yimin, and two of them immediately started running down the mountain.

Gu Yimin was in his study when they made it down the mountain and stood in front of him panting. From their stammering, he learned that around ten people had come with a coffin to the western hills and were digging in his family plot, and that they had shown a deed. His head started buzzing— without even bothering to get in his sedan chair, he held up his long *changshan* with his right hand, summoned two servants, and ran for the western hills.

Gu Yimin and his two servants ran as fast as they could, and when the remaining three townsfolk saw them coming, they said to the bandits smugly,

"Commander Gu, head of the chamber of commerce, is here—let's see what you have to say."

When Gu Yimin drew near and saw that his family's burial

plot had been dug up, he was fuming. Trembling with anger, he pointed at the bandits and said,

"You . . ."

Before Gu Yimin could say anything else, the bandits threw down their mattocks, opened the coffin, and took out the guns. One-Ax Zhang grabbed hold of Gu Yimin while another bandit fired three shots, felling two of the Xizhen townsfolk and one of Gu Yimin's servants. As the bandits ran off with Gu Yimin down the mountain path, they turned around and shouted to the two people left standing there in shock:

"Go back and tell your fellow townsfolk—we're One-Ax Zhang's men, and we've captured Gu Yimin. Wait for our note!"

When word got out that the illustrious head of the Xizhen chamber of commerce and the commander of the Xizhen militia, Gu Yimin, had been kidnapped, it was like a bolt of lightning had struck right to the heart of Xizhen. The townspeople were scared out of their wits and had no idea what to do. The previous victory of their one-eared militia had allowed them to hold their heads up with pride for the last year, but now they felt that something very bad was lurking on the horizon. Several other leaders of the chamber of commerce came up with a plan—after an anxious discussion, they immediately closed all four of the city's gates and sent the militia to guard them. Then they asked Lin Xiangfu to go comfort Gu Yimin's family.

That day, wailing and crying filled every corner of Gu Yimin's grand courtyard mansion. Among his wife and concubines, some fainted, some beat their chests and stamped their feet, some wailed and sighed, and some could barely catch their breath. After Lin Xiangfu entered the home, Gu Yimin's primary wife gathered everyone together in the main hall to discuss what they should do. The discussion, however, mostly amounted to them surrounding Lin Xiangfu and weeping until their tears ran down through their makeup, creating patterns like butterfly wings.

Gu Yimin's two daughters were still in Shanghai at the McTyreire School, and three of his four sons were still at the boarding school in Shendian. Gu Tongnian, his oldest son engaged to Lin Baijia, had met a young woman from Shanghai. He'd stolen a thousand taels of silver from his father's study, kept there for the purpose of importing goods, and used it to go off traveling with her.

The speech of this young woman was a mixture of Shanghainese and English, and she claimed to be the daughter of a wealthy family, saying that her father owned a number of silk shops in Shanghai. As they were on their travels, she let Gu Tongnian buy her numerous pieces of jewelry and commission three new qipaos.

By the time Gu Tongnian had spent nearly all the money, they arrived in Shanghai. The young woman said that through her father's connections, she had found Gu Tongnian a good job working for a foreign company down at the docks that did business with the warehouses there. Gu Tongnian followed her to a foreigner's office at the wharf, where a bearded foreigner passed him a contract written in English. Gu Tongnian didn't know English, so the young woman translated for him—she said the main gist was that he would first be an assistant, and his monthly salary would be fifty silver yuan. She added that the shopkeepers in her father's silk shops didn't make more than eight silver yuan a month.

Gu Tongnian happily signed the contract, and the foreigner filed it away in a cabinet. He beckoned him in English, but Gu Tongnian didn't understand and looked to the young woman for help. She had propped up her legs and lit a cigarette, and after lazily taking a drag and blowing a few smoke rings, she said that the foreigner wanted to take him to have a look at his office. She would wait there for him to return.

Gu Tongnian followed the foreigner out of the building there on the wharf and walked over to a large ship, thinking it was a bit strange that his office would actually be on a ship.

The foreigner opened up a metal door on the deck and gestured for Gu Tongnian to please proceed. The scene before Gu Tongnian was pitch black, with what seemed like a large number of people sitting in the darkness. By the time he felt that something wasn't right, the foreigner had already shoved him forward, causing him to tumble down the stairs. Before he could get up, the metal door above had already been closed.

There was only one dim kerosene lamp lighting the hull of the ship, allowing Gu Tongnian to see that most of the people seated around him were dressed in rags. After talking with them, he learned that he had been sold to work as a laborer in Australia. After a moment of shock, he burst out in tears, shouting,

"Pa! Pa! Save me! . . . "

But no amount of shouting or crying could change his fate. He was to be forced into labor in the Australian mines, without enough clothing to cover his body or food to fill his belly.

60.

It was the middle of the night by the time One-Ax Zhang and his bandits reached the Wanmudang village of Qijiacun with the kidnapped Gu Yimin. The bandits made a ruckus as they entered the village with their torches raised high, startling the villagers awake. The bandits rounded up the villagers and told them to gather their food and start some fires for cooking and boiling water. One-Ax Zhang had driven Chen Yongliang and his family out to live in the goat barn, while he and some other bandits moved into their brick, tile-roofed house; the other bandits moved into other villagers' homes nearby.

Chen Yongliang didn't realize the tied-up hostage was Gu Yimin. By the light of the torches, he could only see that the bandits had deposited someone in the woodshed, and that their hands and feet had been bound and a cloth had been shoved into their mouth. That night the bandits didn't pay any attention to Gu Yimin—after they'd had their fill of food and drink, they smoked and played cards for a while, then passed out and began snoring.

The next day, the bandits went to the woodshed. One-Ax Zhang had one of his underlings loosen Gu Yimin's ropes and take the cloth out of his mouth. After being bound for the whole night, Gu Yimin, who was accustomed to living in comfort and being treated with the utmost respect, felt stiff and sore all over. The cloth stuffed in his mouth was of unclear origins and emitted a nauseating stench of urine that kept his stomach roiling the entire night. Once the piss-scented cloth was removed, Gu Yimin felt the urge to vomit, and a sour liquid began pumping up from his stomach and into his mouth. But keeping in mind his status, he steeled himself and swallowed it all back down. After his ropes had been loosened, he straightened his *changshan,* took two steps forward and went to sit down on a stool in front of One-Ax Zhang. The bandits standing behind him, however, moved the stool out from under him, causing his butt to fall on the floor. The bandits burst out in laughter, while One-Ax Zhang, seated in a chair, pretended to reprimand them:

"You mustn't forget your manners."

Gu Yimin stood up and once again went to sit on the stool; the bandits again pulled it out from under him, he again plopped down on the floor, and the bandits again burst out in laughter. One-Ax Zhang again admonished them to remember their manners—this was a very important person, he said—this was Commander Gu, President Gu of the Chamber of Commerce! He pointed to the stool and invited Gu Yimin to have a seat. Amidst roars of laughter from the bandits, Gu Yimin cautiously reached out and grabbed onto the stool before sitting down.

With a laugh, One-Ax Zhang said to Gu Yimin, "You're a valuable item!"

Gu Yimin sat up straight on the stool and looked at One-Ax

Zhang and the other bandits. "You know my position," he said to them, "please say how much silver it will take to set me free, and I'll write at once to my family and have them send the ransom."

One-Ax Zhang shook his head and said, "We don't want your shiny silver. We don't want your shops, your women, or your house. What we want are the Xizhen militia's guns."

"The militia's guns aren't my personal property," said Gu Yimin, "so it's difficult for me to grant you this."

One-Ax Zhang laughed coldly and stood up. "Once we start torturing you," he said, "they'll become your personal property."

One-Ax Zhang stepped forward and kicked Gu Yimin over. The bandits rushed forward and gave him a "pole press"—this involved pressing his knees on the ground with a wooden pole, while bandits on either side of the pole tramped on it with all their might. Then they "cut the carp," which involved stripping off Gu Yimin's *changshan* and undershirt and slicing rows of slanted squares down his chest and back with a knife. They then spread chili powder all over Gu Yimin's body, which had become drenched in fresh blood. Finally, they stuck a bamboo stick up his anus and began twisting it around.

Gu Yimin passed out several times, but would wake up when the torture intensified. During the "pole press" he felt like his bones were breaking; when they "cut the carp" he felt like his skin was being peeled off piece by piece; when the chili powder was spread over him he felt like he was being fried in oil; and when they did "the crank grind" he felt that armies were fighting a battle inside of his body. Barely retaining the will to live under so much pain, Gu Yimin begged in a low voice,

"I'll write it, I'll write it . . . "

As Gu Yimin pleaded sporadically amidst groans of pain, One-Ax Zhang ordered his underlings to pull the bamboo stick out of his anus. Then he bent down and asked Gu Yimin,

"Are the militia's guns your personal property?"

"Yes," he groaned, "They're mine."

Gu Yimin, the most respected man in Xizhen, dipped his finger in his own blood and wrote a humiliating letter asking the Xizhen militia to surrender all of their guns in exchange for his life.

One-Ax Zhang took the letter, looked it over, and said, "You might be bent and banged out of shape, but your writing is perfectly fucking straight!"

Then One-Ax Zhang thought of how Gu Yimin would ride in an eight-carrier sedan chair when he went out on his bandit eradicating missions. So he had Gu Yimin add an eight-carrier sedan chair to the letter.

61.

After One-Ax Zhang's bandits delivered Gu Yimin's letter written in blood, Xizhen was thrown into an uproar. Everyone of status in the town went around discussing what their next move should be. One group, headed by Lin Xiangfu, advocated for doing just as the blood letter requested and ransoming the guns in exchange for Gu Yimin—as the saying goes, it's easier to recruit a thousand soldiers than it is to find a good general to lead them. Lin Xiangfu recalled a series of past events, including the defeated Beiyang Army's rampage through the countryside—Gu Yimin had remained calm and reasonable, which had saved Xizhen.

"Xizhen can exist without a militia," said Lin Xiangfu, "but not without Gu Yimin."

Another faction also advocated paying a ransom in exchange for Gu Yimin, but they were opposed to using the militia's guns for the exchange. They said that without guns, Xizhen would be left with no militia, and without a militia, the bandits would be given free rein to come strutting into town, looting, plundering, killing, and burning; Xizhen would be destroyed and its people reduced to utter misery.

"Of course we want to save Chamber President Gu," they said, "but we can't ransom everyone's lives or the entire city's heritage."

With the two sides in a stalemate, someone suggested they go to the provincial capital and buy some guns that could be used for Gu Yimin's ransom, so the militia would get to keep theirs. Everyone agreed this was a good idea, but it would be too difficult to arrange—it would probably take a couple months. The bandits had only given them ten days. Someone else suggested going to the government troops stationed in Shendian and buying guns from them, which should only take two or three days, or a week at the most. This idea met with unanimous approval.

Because the people of Shendian had been worried their own militia would be unable to defend them against the bandits, they had paid the provincial military governor to send troops to eradicate them. Once the government troops arrived, the people of Shendian learned first-hand what it meant to "invite a wolf in for tea." About once a month the troops would march grandly out of the city with their guns, proclaiming they would exterminate the bandits. But when they actually met up with the bandits, they would drop their weapons, pick up the silver the bandits had left for them, and then run home. The bandits, on the other hand, would drop their silver, pick up the troops' guns, and continue on their way.

The residents of Shendian noticed that the troops would leave the city carrying their guns, then return without a single person missing and their clothing just as neat and clean as when they left—the only difference was that the weapons that had been on their shoulders were now nowhere to be found. The more bandits they "eradicated," the more guns they lost; when they needed to buy more to replace them, the cost fell to the city's chamber of commerce.

The principal trustees of Xizhen's chamber of commerce discussed the matter and decided that the chamber would put up the money to buy thirty guns from the government troops in Shendian. Of course, this would have to be a secret transaction—they already knew of the troops' arrangement with the bandits. One of the members of the chamber had already had some business with the troops in Shendian, so he volunteered to go to Shendian first.

Then the discussion turned to who would go deliver the ransom for Gu Yimin. They all felt that this ransom of thirty firearms was no ordinary ransom, nor was the hostage an ordinary hostage, so the person who went should be a prominent citizen of Xizhen. They had to carefully consider their candidate to deliver the thirty guns—it had to be someone who held some sway.

At this point, everything fell quiet as the thoughts of these esteemed gentlemen turned to the violent savagery of One-Ax Zhang, the mere thought of which gave them goosebumps. As silence enveloped them, someone turned their eyes toward Lin Xiangfu, and soon others did the same. Lin Xiangfu knew what they were thinking—he knew he was the most likely choice to shoulder this responsibility. He lowered his head and remained silent, thinking of the warlord's cruelty. An image of his daughter, Lin Baijia, suddenly floated before his eyes, which filled him with anxiety. Then Lin Xiangfu thought of Chen Yongliang—if Chen Yongliang were there, he would undoubtedly stand up and volunteer to go. Furthermore, if Chen Yongliang were there, Lin Xiangfu wouldn't let him go—he would insist that he go himself. Lin Xiangfu raised his head and saw all the eyes looking at him, which quickly averted their gaze. Softly, he said, "I'll go."

62.

For the two days that the eminent members of Xizhen's chamber of commerce were discussing how to handle the situation, the members of the militia were on tenterhooks. They had heard that Commander Gu's blood letter stipulated that the militia turn its guns over to the bandits; they weren't sure if this also included the members of the militia themselves. They discussed the matter while clutching their guns—some of them thought yes, while others thought no. The ones who thought yes said it was because the bandits in the Wanmudang were recruiting members, and since the militiamen were well-trained, high quality fighters, the bandits would naturally be eager to have them. Those who thought no based their thinking on their faith in Commander Gu's character, saying he would never sell out his own men. They went back and forth like this for two days, until someone ran into Lin Xiangfu on the street and learned that the ransom note did not ask for the militiamen themselves. This provided them with some measure of comfort, although they soon began asking one another,

"Without guns, what will we do when the bandits come?"

"Without guns, we're not a militia—we're just regular townsfolk. What will we do when the bandits come? We'll flee, just like regular townsfolk!"

After word spread that Gu Yimin had been taken hostage by the bandits and that the militia's guns were to serve as his ransom, some residents of Xizhen packed up their families and left. The preemptive flight of these people upset other residents and made them feel all the more nervous. Some people even stood on the street and pointed at the ones with bundles on their backs leaving town, shouting,

"The militia hasn't even given up their guns, and you're already fucking running away! If everyone did that, who would be left to look after Xizhen?"

After the people fleeing in broad daylight were taunted and embarrassed like this, the next ones to flee decided to leave quietly after dark. Ever since Gu Yimin had been taken hostage, the city gates had been closed at nightfall, and the militiamen standing guard knew how to squeeze some profit out of the situation. The people fleeing only needed to quietly slip them some money, and they would open the gates and let them out. The men Gu Yimin had recruited for this reconstituted militia were mostly from out of town, and many had been idlers who joined up simply as a way to feed themselves. When they first sensed that disaster was looming and saw that it was every man for himself, they hadn't realized it would also present them with an opportunity to rake in no small amount in bribes.

"With money coming at us like this," they said, "there's no way we can keep the doors closed!"

Four days later, the Hanyang rifles and .38's that had been secretly purchased from the government troops were loaded into a sedan chair carried by eight militiamen and transported from Shendian to Xizhen.

Some members of the chamber of commerce suggested sending some militiamen along with Lin Xiangfu for protection, but Lin Xiangfu didn't agree. He didn't think they would be of much use, and if too many accompanied him, it would be hard to keep things from escalating into a battle, which would further endanger Gu Yimin. He said all he needed was a boat and someone to sail it.

63.

On the afternoon of the day before he left, Lin Xiangfu leaned back in a recliner and shut his eyes. A vision of his home in the north appeared before him; he saw his mother and heard her voice. His father was there, too, blurry at first, but gradually coming into focus. Then Xiaomei appeared, leading Lin Baijia by the hand. He heard his mother calling his name and woke up, realizing he had fallen asleep.

Lin Xiangfu got up from the recliner and went over and sat at his desk. He wrote a letter to Tian Da back up north, asking him to come to Xizhen with his brothers and take him home. He didn't say anything else in the letter, which he concluded with the line, "as leaves fall back down to their roots, so must a man return to his hometown." When he read the letter over after he finished it, he felt a jolt of fear when he got to this final line. So he picked up his writing brush and blacked it out. He remained seated at his desk for a while, then wrote a letter to Gu Yimin. The letter said that if he were to meet with some sort of misfortune, he would ask that Gu Yimin still proceed with the wedding of Lin Baijia and Gu Tongnian on their previously agreed upon date. Finally, he wrote a letter to his daughter. There were a thousand things he wanted to say, but he was unable to write a single word. After sitting there for the longest while, he finally just wrote that there were five containers buried under the floor in the study, each one containing a thousand silver yuan. Then he took out the account book for the woodworking shop and the deeds for his land in the Wanmudang and wrapped them together in a cloth, on which he wrote the three characters for "Lin Baijia." He then put this in a hiding spot in the wall that Lin Baijia knew about.

Lin Xiangfu took the other two letters to Cuiping. She had long since stopped receiving customers, but when he walked up those creaky stairs, she opened the door to greet him. She knew from the familiar sound of those footsteps on the stairs who had come.

Lin Xiangfu entered Cuiping's apartment and watched her shut the door and slide the bolt. He sat down by the table, lost in thought. Cuiping poured him a cup of tea and sat on the edge of the bed. Neither of them spoke. The news that Lin Xiangfu would be delivering the guns to the bandits for Gu Yimin's ransom had already spread throughout Xizhen, so Cuiping already knew. She watched him anxiously and wanted to ask about it, but stayed quiet.

After sitting there for a long time, Lin Xiangfu told Cuiping he wanted to stay for dinner, so she immediately set to work. This was the first time he had asked to stay for dinner, so it took her a bit by surprise. She went at once to the wardrobe, stuck her right hand in a stack of folded clothing, and pulled out a cloth bag. She opened it, but only then did she remember there were no copper coins left. Standing with her back to Lin Xiangfu, she paused for a moment and then put the sack back in with the clothing. She turned around with an embarrassed look on her face and smiled awkwardly at Lin Xiangfu, then proceed to crawl under the bed. While she was under there, there was a noise that sounded like a brick being moved, and when she reemerged, she was holding a silver yuan.

Lin Xiangfu looked at the silver yuan in her hand and asked what it was for. She said she was going to go out and buy some fish and meat to prepare for dinner. Lin Xiangfu asked since when was a silver yuan needed to buy fish and meat. Her face went red and she told him she didn't have any coppers, not a single coin. Lin Xiangfu took some out of his pocket, but then put them back in and asked what she had in the house to eat. She uneasily told him that all she had was some cold rice and a few pickled things; Lin Xiangfu said then that's just what he'd eat. She shook her head and went to the door, but Lin Xiangfu grabbed her hand and pulled her back before she could open it. He asked her if there was enough cold rice for two people to eat, and she nodded. She then added that to save kindling, each time she cooked rice she would make enough to eat for two days—because it was already past mid-autumn festival, the rice would keep for that long without spoiling. Lin Xiangfu once again said he would eat some cold rice with some pickled veg- etables, and this time his tone was firm. Still Cuiping hesitated, but then came up with a compromise.

"I'll make some fried rice in soy sauce," she said.

Cuiping picked some scallions from a pot on the windowsill and then went downstairs. Lin Xiangfu stood in the doorway at the top of the stairs and watched her begin chopping the scallions on the counter by the stove. Then she lit a fire, heated a pot, and threw in the scallions along with some lard. After frying them up for a few moments, she stopped stirring to add the cold rice and pour in some soy sauce, then began stir-frying it all together.

As the lard, scallions, and soy sauce fried up with the rice, a delicious scent wafted up to Lin Xiangfu, making his mouth water as he stood at the top of the stairs. When Cuiping brought the dish upstairs, she noticed Lin Xiangfu wiping the corners of his mouth.

She and Lin Xiangfu sat across from one another eating the fried rice and pickled vegetables. Since Chen Yongliang's family had moved to Qijiacun and Lin Baijia had gone to Shanghai, this was the first that Lin Xiangfu had shared a meal with someone, and this rice fried with soy sauce tasted delicious. He praised Cuiping's cooking, saying the rice was excellent, as were the vegetables she had pickled. Cuiping ate only a couple bites and held her chopsticks for the rest of the time without eating. She watched Lin Xiangfu with a look of shame on her face, feeling sorry that she hadn't been able to provide him with a good feast.

As it grew darker, Cuiping got up and lit the kerosene lamp, which she placed on the table between them. When Lin Xiangfu had finished eating, he looked at Cuiping's face, illuminated by the flickering lamplight. He told her that the next day he would go to Liucun to deliver the guns to the bandits. As he said this, he drew the two letters from his pocket. First he passed her the one to Gu Yimin—he said that if he didn't return, but Gu Yimin did, that she should give this letter to him; if Gu Yimin didn't return, either, then she should give it to his wife. Cuiping nodded uneasily, and Lin Xiangfu passed her the second letter. He said that if he didn't return, she should mail this letter for him. Out of another pocket, Lin Xiangfu then took out a hundred taels of silver and placed it on the table—that was for Cuiping.

Cuiping's eyes turned red as she looked at the money on the table. Holding the two letters in her hand, she gingerly asked Lin Xiangfu,

"And what if you come back?"

"If I come back," he said, "you can just return them to me."

64.

One-Ax Zhang only allowed certain bandits to enter the woodshed, so Chen Yongliang had no idea that the hostage being tortured in his family's shed was Gu Yimin. Although he had worked under the man for so many years, he had only ever heard him speak kindly, and had never heard him shout or give angry reprimands. Chen Yongliang would never recognize these earsplitting cries and gut-wrenching wails in the woodshed as coming from Gu Yimin.

On the evening of the ninth day, the bandit watching over Gu Yimin let down his guard. Forgetting that One-Ax Zhang had forbidden any of the villagers to enter the woodshed, he had Li Meilian deliver some food to the hostage. Before this, the bandits had always just given Gu Yimin whatever food they had left over after they'd eaten their fill, like throwing scraps to a dog—they would howl with laughter at the image of him lying on his stomach, hungrily gobbling them up. But today there hadn't been any scraps, so they had Li Meilian prepare some food and take it to him.

Carrying a bowl of rice porridge, Li Meilian entered the woodshed and walked up to the hostage, who was nothing more than a disfigured mass of bloody wounds. Softly she called out to him to come take a few sips of the hot porridge. After calling out about ten times, the hostage finally raised his head slowly, and Li Meilian got a good look at his face. When she saw that it was Gu Yimin, she gasped,

"Master—Master, it's you."

Gu Yimin looked at Li Meilian with his lifeless eyes. Li Meilian called to him again several more times, but Gu Yimin still didn't recognize her. When Li Meilian held the bowl up to his mouth, though, he recognized the porridge and sucked it down like a baby at its mother's breast.

Her eyes brimming with tears, Li Meilian made her way back to the goat barn. When Chen Yongliang learned that the hostage in the shed was Gu Yimin, he stood in a stunned silence for a long while, then sat down on the ground. He lowered his head and listened as Li Meilian quietly wept and repeated again and again,

"The Master was completely covered in blood—they've nearly beaten him to death. He seems to have lost his mind . . . "

One-Ax Zhang didn't know that Chen Yongliang had once worked for Gu Yimin, and was unaware of their relationship. After spending ten days in Qijiacun, he led the bandits to Liucun, where they were to collect the guns for Gu Yimin's ransom. Two bandits were left behind to keep watch over Gu Yimin.

Once the bandits went roaring out of town, Chen Yongliang felt the moment had come. Quietly he gathered together the village's prominent elders and made very clear to them that no matter the consequences, he was going to rescue Gu Yimin. The elders of Qijiacun praised Chen Yongliang and said,

"Even if he weren't Gu Yimin, president of the Xizhen chamber of commerce—even if he were just an ordinary hostage, how could we not try to save him?"

Chen Yongliang said that as soon as the bandits discovered Gu Yimin had been rescued, they would seek revenge. He had everyone in the village pack their bags and take everything with them they would need—those who had friends or relatives in neighboring villages should go stay with them for a while; those who had nowhere else to go should take to the water and hide amongst the reeds of the Wanmudang for a time. Then he and Chen Yaowu went and rounded up some strong young men to help them discuss a plan for rescuing Gu Yimin. They decided to use the sunlight as a signal—when the afternoon sun illuminated the western wall of the courtyard, the young men would hide quietly outside the courtyard gate. Chen Yongliang and Chen Yaowu would be the first to act—they would grab the guards, and when the young men heard them shout, they would rush in to tie them up.

"Why do we need to tie them up?" asked Chen Yaowu. "Just kill those two disgusting bandits and be done with it."

"Absolutely not," said Chen Yongliang, shaking his head. "We save people; we don't kill them."

65.

That morning, Lin Xiangfu went down to Xizhen's wharf, followed by eight militiamen carrying a sedan chair. He stood on a stone step that was dripping with water and faced about a dozen boats, both large and small. Then he said to the boatmen sitting in them:

"I need to go to Liucun to deliver the ransom. Who will take me?"

The boatmen all sat there silently in the morning sunlight. They had all heard of the vicious cruelty of One-Ax Zhang, and the mere thought of it made them tremble with fear. Lin Xiangfu stood there and called out three times, but the boatmen either looked down, shook their heads, or turned around and went into their cabins. Lin Xiangfu shouted a fourth time,

"Who will take me to Liucun?"

Lin Xiangfu listened to the sound of the water slapping against the boats, and the sound of the boats bumping against each other. Zeng Wanfu—the one who had been scared silly after failing to deliver the initial ransom—rowed his little boat with its bamboo awning through the midst of the other boats until he came right up beside the stone step where Lin Xiangfu was standing.

"Master Lin," he said, "please get on board."

Once all the guns had been loaded, and as the brilliant

sun rose higher in the east, they set off rowing through the Wanmudang toward Liucun. Lin Xiangfu sat solemnly on the prow, while Zeng Wanfu rowed strenuously from the stern, cleaving the waves as they pushed forward.

A thousand different thoughts swirled around Lin Xiangfu's mind. He thought back to seventeen years ago when he took a boat to Xizhen looking for Xiaomei, a bundle on his back and Lin Baijia at his chest. That was also on this same expanse of water, on a small boat with a bamboo awning just like this, driven by the same sort of boatman. Lin Xiangfu suddenly felt that this Zeng Wanfu before him now was possibly the same one who had brought him to Xizhen seventeen years earlier. Lin Xiangfu asked, and Zeng Wanfu nodded and affirmed that it was—he remembered that enormous pack Lin Xiangfu had been carrying on his back. Lin Xiangfu gave a faint smile and said he never would have imagined that seventeen years later he would once again be sitting in Zeng Wanfu's boat. He then told Zeng Wanfu that he would be paid two silver yuan for transporting him, and that to keep the bandits from stealing it, the money was being held in the chamber of commerce—when they returned to Xizhen with Chamber President Gu, he could go retrieve it. Zeng Wanfu said that two silver yuan was too much; the fare at most shouldn't be more than a few coppers. Lin Xiangfu shook his head and said this was no ordinary trip. After that, Lin Xiangfu didn't say anything else. He listened to the waves wash past the sides of the boat, like the sound of sanding furniture in the woodworking shop.

It was the time of the autumn harvest, but Lin Xiangfu couldn't spot a single person for as far as the eye could see—there were only wild, uncultivated fields, dilapidated thatched cottages, and even a few sun-bleached bones scattered eerily along the shores. He thought back to the flourishing abundance he had once seen there—rice, wheat, cotton, and canola; wild grasses and reeds; stands of bamboo—the whole land was covered by it. Smoke from cooking fires curled up above the rooftops; oxen lowed as they plowed the fields; farmers walked in twos and threes between the fields . . . now, however, war and bandits had left the people poor and homeless, and death and destruction had wiped out nearly all traces of human life in the Wanmudang. Lin Xiangfu saw an elderly person with white hair holding the hand of a child—they were standing atop the riverbank, looking out at them.

Around noon, they reached the wharf at Liucun. Several bandits were waiting there with a cart. They called out to Lin Xiangfu, who was standing on the prow,

"Did you bring the guns?"

Gesturing toward the cabin of the boat, Lin Xiangfu replied, "they're in there."

When the boat reached the dock, one of the bandits said, "pass them up."

"And Chamber President Gu?" asked Lin Xiangfu.

"Pass up the guns and we'll take you to see him," answered the bandit.

Lin Xiangfu nodded to Zeng Wanfu, who docked the boat and tied it to a willow tree growing at the water's edge. Then he went into the cabin and began passing the weapons out to Lin Xiangfu on the prow, who then passed them to the bandits. After the guns had been loaded onto the cart, Lin Xiangfu went ashore, while Zeng Wanfu returned to the back of the boat and squatted down, watching as Lin Xiangfu followed the bandits and the cart down a little path.

When Lin Xiangfu entered the village, several armed bandits smoking opium pipes looked at him and snickered. They were holding bowls in their hands and stuffing rice in their mouths as they spoke with the bandits Lin Xiangfu had followed there.

"Did they send the guns?"

"They sent them."

The bandit who had been leading the way took Lin Xiangfu over to a brick house with a tile roof and had him sit down on the threshold.

"Take good care of our guest," he said to the other bandits standing there.

Lin Xiangfu squinted in the sunlight as he sat on the threshold. A dozen or so bandits were standing around eating rice, smiling, laughing, and swearing. One of the bandits carried over a bowl for Lin Xiangfu. When he stood up to accept the bowl, several bandits came up to him and said,

"Eat up—eat with us!"

Lin Xiangfu nodded and sat back down on the threshold. As he began eating, he noticed that there were a few pieces of fried liver in his bowl, so he put one in his mouth. As he chewed, he had the feeling that it wasn't really like pig's liver; it wasn't like cow's or sheep's liver, either, and it certainly wasn't like duck or chicken liver—he wasn't sure what kind of liver it was. He furrowed his brow and swallowed it down, just as he recalled the rumors that One-Ax Zhang often ate human liver. A wave of nausea surged through his stomach, and everything he had just swallowed came back up into his mouth. Lin Xiangfu dared not vomit, so he forced himself, eyes watering, to re-swallow every sticky, sour particle that had come back up. He didn't eat any more after that. Holding his bowl, he watched the bandits in front of him gulping down their food with big bites and chewing it loudly. One of the bandits said to him,

"Eat, eat! Why the fuck aren't you eating?"

"I'm full," replied Lin Xiangfu.

"He only took one fucking bite and he says he's full," another bandit said. "Eat the whole fucking thing."

Lin Xiangfu looked in his bowl at the rice and the dark pieces of fried liver. He didn't intend to put any more of it in his mouth, so he said to the bandits,

"I really have eaten my fill."

The bandits started shouting: "Eat, eat, eat! Eat it, for fuck's sake!"

Just then One-Ax Zhang's voice came from inside the house:

"Don't be impolite," he said, "this old gentleman from Xizhen is used to eating the finest delicacies—how could he possibly force down your pig slop? Invite him in."

The bandits shoved Lin Xiangfu inside the house, and he walked into the western wing. There he saw a man reclining on a couch smoking opium.

"This gentleman must be the well-known One-Ax Zhang?" inquired Lin Xiangfu.

One-Ax Zhang put down his opium pipe and nodded, then stood up and sat back down with his legs crossed. Lin Xiangfu looked all around and said to One-Ax Zhang,

"I've brought the guns. Please return Gu Yimin to me."

One-Ax Zhang looked at Lin Xiangfu, who was still standing there holding his bowl of food, and said to one of his underlings, "You haven't offered the gentleman a seat."

A bandit who was peeling a sweet potato with a dagger kicked over a stool, and another bandit forcibly pressed Lin Xiangfu down on it.

One-Ax Zhang asked Lin Xiangfu with a smile: "Did you bring the eight-carrier sedan chair as well?"

"All I could find in my hurry to get here was a small boat," said Lin Xiangfu, "and there was no way to fit the sedan on it. As soon as we get Gu Yimin safely back to Xizhen, we'll send it here on a larger boat."

One-Ax Zhang's smiling face quickly turned fierce. "Your Chamber President Gu is dead," he said.

Lin Xiangfu immediately stood up and looked at One-Ax Zhang as if he hadn't quite heard what he'd said. One-Ax Zhang saw that Lin Xiangfu was still holding his bowl of food, and the fierce look on his face changed back to a smile.

"Is the fried liver good?" he asked.

Lin Xiangfu continued standing there with no reaction. One-Ax Zhang said to him playfully,

"What you're eating there is the liver of your Chamber President Gu."

Amidst the laughter of One-Ax Zhang and the other bandits,

Lin Xiangfu remained standing there motionlessly with the bowl. The bandits started shouting,

"You ate one fucking bite and then stopped—have you done right by Chamber President Gu's liver? Do you feel like his liver doesn't fucking taste good enough for you? Let me tell you, you don't get fresh fucking liver like this every day! It's called 'live-cut liver'—they cut it right out of the living person and drop it in a pot of oil, then stir-fry it with rice wine, soy sauce, and scallions. Your Chamber President Gu wasn't even dead yet by the time his liver was all fried up, and you still don't want to fucking eat it. You'd better swallow down every last fucking bite!"

Lin Xiangfu's eyes went red, and he stared at One-Ax Zhang through his bloodred glare as if nailing him to the spot. One-Ax Zhang looked at the bizarre expression on Lin Xiangfu's face and burst out in laughter, calling some other bandits over to take a look. A few of them rushed over, and they too broke out in laughter when they saw Lin Xiangfu's strange, motionless expression.

But then the bandits uttered a cry of alarm—the bowl in Lin Xiangfu's hand was now sailing toward them through the air. The bandit who had been peeling the sweet potato discovered that he was still holding the potato in one hand, but that the dagger in his other hand was now gone.

Lin Xiangfu charged at One-Ax Zhang, and the bandits standing in front of him instinctively got out of his way. Dagger in hand, Lin Xiangfu aimed for One-Ax Zhang's eyes. One-Ax Zhang leapt off the couch, but Lin Xiangfu continued charging toward him, still trying to gouge out his eyes. One-Ax Zhang rolled on the ground and once again avoided Lin Xiangfu's assault, while Lin Xiangfu pounced and hit the floor, the blade of his dagger sticking in a crack between the bricks. Rolling on the ground, One-Ax Zhang shouted at the bandits standing dumbly to the side. Finally they reacted, and by the time Lin Xiangfu had extracted his dagger from the floor and once again charged toward One-Ax Zhang, the bandits rushed forward, pressed him down on the ground, and confiscated the dagger.

One-Ax Zhang stood up, a series of "fuck's" coming from his mouth. He reached up and rubbed his eyes, then shouted to the bandits,

"Tie him up!"

After the bandits had gotten a rope and tied up Lin Xiangfu, One-Ax Zhang had two of the bandits pull him upright. Then he had another bandit pick up the dagger that was laying on the floor and hand it to him. Holding the dagger, he walked up in front of Lin Xiangfu and said with a cold laugh,

"So you like using a dagger."

At that point, Lin Xiangfu's eyes stopped processing the scene before him, and he spread his legs and stood firmly. One-Ax Zhang grabbed his hair with his left hand, and with his right hand thrust the dagger into Lin Xiangfu's left ear, then twisted it around forcefully. Blood spurted out of Lin Xiangfu, and the bandits who had been holding him screamed and jumped out of the way, using their hands to wipe the mess of blood from their faces.

Although he was now dead, Lin Xiangfu was still standing, his body trussed up and looking like a mountainside cliff, the dagger still sticking out of his ear as his head slowly began tilting to the left. His slightly opened mouth and squinting eyes made it look as if her were smiling. Right before the last flicker of life left his body, he saw an image of his daughter—Lin Baijia, an orange flower embroidered on her lapel, was walking toward him down a hallway in the McTyreire School.

The bandits in the room fell silent. They looked at Lin Xiangfu in shock, wondering why he hadn't fallen over. After a few moments, one of the bandits said to the others,

"Fuck—he's smiling."

"Did he turn into a ghost?" another bandit asked.

"How could he turn into a ghost so quickly?"

"You're a fucking ghost as soon as you die."

"Well fuck me—we've just seen a living person turn into a ghost."

The bandits felt spooked, and one by one they all went outside. When One-Ax Zhang discovered he was the only one left in the room, he gasped. Then he went up and gave Lin Xiangfu a kick, causing his body to fall heavily onto the floor. One-Ax Zhang went outside and announced to the bandits who had just fled the room:

"He's down."

The bandits went back inside, where they saw Lin Xiangfu laying on the floor. The ones in the back asked the ones in front,

"Is he still smiling?"

The ones in the front looked down and called back,

"Well I'll be fucked—he's still smiling!"

Zeng Wanfu, who had been squatting in the stern of the boat until his legs had gone numb, heard two bandits running toward him and shouting. He wasn't sure what they were saying, but he felt they looked particularly fierce. Trembling, he rose to his feet, bowing and nodding to the approaching bandits. As the bandits drew nearer, he could tell that they were calling for him to get off the boat.

"Get out of your fucking boat," they shouted. "Come get that ghost and take him out of here!"

Zeng Wanfu didn't understand what they meant, so he continued nodding and bowing. "Masters," he said, "what ghost should I take out of here?"

"The one you fucking came here with!" the bandits replied.

Zeng Wanfu followed the bandits and ran up to the brick house with the tile roof. He saw the jittery appearance of the bandits standing outside; several of them were gesturing for him to hurry up and go in. Nervously Zeng Wanfu entered the house, and in the western room he saw Lin Xiangfu lying on the floor with a dagger plunged in his left ear. Lin Xiangfu's smiling countenance startled Zeng Wanfu, who leaned down and whispered,

"Master Lin—Master Lin."

There was no movement from Lin Xiangfu's body on the floor. Not knowing what to do, Zeng Wanfu walked back to the door and nodded and bowed to the bandits outside.

"Excuse me, gentlemen," he asked, "What is the situation with Master Lin?"

"Dead," the bandits replied.

"If he's dead," said Zeng Wanfu, "how is he still smiling?"

"Just get him the fuck out of here!"

Zeng Wanfu bowed to the bandits and ran back inside. A few moments later, he once again appeared in the doorway with a nod and a bow:

"Excuse me, gentlemen," he said, "Can someone please help me lift him—I just need to get him up on my back."

One of the bandits raised his rifle, cocked it, and said to Zeng Wanfu as he aimed it at him,

"You'd better get him on your fucking back yourself, and don't come back out here for another fucking chat."

Zeng Wanfu bowed once more and went back inside, where he remained for a long time. The bandits outside waited and waited. Why wasn't he coming out, they wondered—did a ghost snatch him? Just as they began speculating, Zeng Wanfu reappeared with Lin Xiangfu on his back. After stepping over the threshold, he stopped to nod and bow to the bandits.

"Stop nodding and stop bowing," said the bandit holding the rifle, "and get out of here before I shoot you, you fucking idiot!"

So Zeng Wanfu set off with Lin Xiangfu on his back and several bandits following behind. After he finally got Lin Xiangfu's body in the cabin of his swaying little boat, he stood panting on the stern and saw the bandits waving their hands on the shore nearby. He didn't realize they were motioning for him to get going, and instead thought they were waving goodbye. So he raised his hand and waved back, which was quickly followed by a series of gunshots; the bullets whizzed through the leaves and branches of the trees on shore, and Zeng Wanfu screamed. Then he sat down and began rowing away as quickly as possible.

66.

The two bandits who had stayed behind to guard Gu Yimin noticed that Chen Yongliang and Chen Yaowu didn't return for a long time after they'd gone out, and they began to get suspicious. They took their guns and went to have a look around outside the courtyard, and when they didn't see anything out of the ordinary, they came back in and bolted the gate.

"If nothing's going on, don't go out wandering around for no fucking reason," they said to Chen Yongliang and Chen Yaowu.

The two bandits sat in the courtyard with their guns until afternoon, when they began yawning. Wiping the tears that had formed in their eyes from the yawns, they got up and went inside, where they reclined partially on the bed and began smoking opium.

Chen Yongliang and Chen Yaowu walked out of the goat barn with the food that Li Meilian had prepared and entered the room where the bandits were smoking.

"Masters, have some dinner," they said.

Neither bandit reacted. They'd just had lunch not too long ago, they thought—how could it already be dinner time? And anyway, shouldn't it be Li Meilian bringing the food? What were the Chen father and son doing here? The bandits once again looked around outside the courtyard—the sun was shining brightly. They knew something was off, so they quickly reached for their guns. Just then, Chen Yongliang and Chen Yaowu threw the bowls of food they were carrying in the bandits' faces, and each of them charged toward one of the bandits. The four of them wrestled on the bed and then rolled onto the floor, and then on out the door. As Chen Yongliang and Chen Yaowu struggled with the bandits, they shouted:

"Come help! Come help!"

The gate to the courtyard was bolted, so when the men waiting outside the courtyard heard the shouts, they were unable to come in. They pounded on the gate and yelled,

"Open the door! Open the door!"

Li Meilian and Chen Yaowen burst out of the goat barn and into the courtyard. A brick in his hand, Chen Yaowen ran up to his older brother—by this time the bandit had broken one of Chen Yaowu's fingers, but Chen Yaowu was still entangled with him and wouldn't let go. He saw Chen Yaowen come over with the brick and shouted for him to smash the bandit's head. Chen Yaowen aimed to the left, and then to the right, but didn't dare strike, afraid he would hit his brother's head by mistake. Li Meilian was scared silly by the scene before her, and she cried as she pleaded with the men outside the courtyard,

"Come in right now!"

The men outside tried ramming into the courtyard gate and shouting, "open the gate!"

Too startled to open the gate, Li Meilian stood there shouting, "Come in here quick! Why aren't you coming in?"

As Chen Yaowu was wrestling with the bandit, he managed to flip over and let the bandit pin him down on the ground. Then he shouted to Chen Yaowen,

"Hit him!"

Chen Yaowen hurled himself forward and brought the brick crashing down on the bandit's head. The bandit was knocked out by the blow, and Chen Yaowen himself fell hard on the ground. When he crawled to his feet, he saw that the bandit wasn't moving. Chen Yaowu rushed toward the other bandit and helped his father pin him to the ground. The bandit was struggling with all his might when Chen Yaowen ran over and knocked him out with the brick—this time, the blow was enough to shatter the brick itself into pieces. After Chen Yaowen got to his feet this time, he heard the shouts of the men on the other side of the gate as they tried to ram their way through it, so he ran over and undid the bolt. Suddenly the gate flew open as the men rushed into the courtyard, charging in with such force that they fell over when they met with the empty courtyard, knocking Chen Yaowen down with them. When they stood up and looked around, they saw the two bandits lying motionless on the ground, while Chen Yongliang and his two sons were all sitting on the ground and panting. Li Meilian was now smiling through her tears.

After they'd tied up the bandits and dragged them inside, Chen Yongliang went in the house and got a blanket to drape over his shoulders. Someone asked him why he was doing that, and he responded that the master was covered in injuries, so he wanted to provide him with a layer of cushioning.

Chen Yongliang then had his two sons carefully lift Gu Yimin up onto his back, and he carried him down to the village wharf. Before they got on the boat, Chen Yongliang passed Gu Yimin over to his two sons. He the boarded the boat and spread out the blanket in the cabin before helping his sons move Gu Yimin inside. As Chen Yongliang began pushing the boat out, he warned the villagers on shore that One-Ax Zhang and his bandits would be sure to seek revenge once they returned, so they should all leave the village at once.

As Chen Yongliang gradually rowed away across the waters of the Wanmudang, he could see that on the road that stretched beyond the village gate, a number of villagers had appeared with bundles on the backs, fleeing with their families. Several boats were making their way to the thick stands of reeds and marsh grasses, and even from such a distance he could make out the silhouettes of Li Meilian and their two sons on one of the boats. Then he looked down at Gu Yimin, his body covered in bloody injuries as he lay there unconscious. He thought back to the first time he met Gu Yimin in Shendian, when he and three other porters carried a load of silk for him from Shendian to Xizhen. So many years had passed in the blink of an eye, and now Gu Yimin, who once seemed infinitely regal, was now struggling to breathe.

Amidst the crisp sounds of the oars cutting through the water and the gentle rocking of the boat, Gu Yimin gradually regained consciousness. He saw a familiar-looking face which he slowly began to recognize. In a weak voice, he asked:

"Are you Chen Yongliang?"

As he was rowing the boat, Chen Yongliang heard Gu Yimin call out his name. Immediately he put down the oars and bent down close to Gu Yimin and said,

"It's me, master—you're awake!"

"Where am I?" Gu Yimin asked.

"Master," said Chen Yongliang, "You're on a boat, and I'm taking you home."

Gu Yimin saw the evening sky filled with the glow of the sunset; he heard the sound of the water; he felt the little boat rocking to and fro. Then he remembered the bandits torturing him. He thought for a while, then gradually understood.

"You're rescuing me?" he asked.

Chen Yongliang nodded. "Yes, master," he said.

Chen Yongliang continued rowing the little boat, while Gu Yimin shut his eyes and didn't say anything else. Chen Yongliang saw a smile spread across Gu Yimin's face, and tears began to gather in the corners of his eyes. The sky grew darker as the sun continued to set, and Chen Yongliang continued to row. In the distance, he could see the lights of Xizhen.

The water route into Xizhen went in through the east gate. After dark, the sluicegate was closed, and Chen Yongliang's boat couldn't pass through. He shouted up to the militiamen guarding the east gate, telling them it was Chen Yongliang and asking them to raise the gate. The militiamen up on the wall were all from out of town, and they didn't know who Chen Yongliang was. They said they couldn't raise the gate—there was no telling whether or not he was actually a bandit. Cheng Yongliang told them he was Chen Yongliang of the woodworking shop, and that he had Gu Yimin with him, president of the chamber of commerce, who was severely wounded—so could they please raise the gate. When the militiamen on the wall heard that Gu Yimin was on the boat, they all burst out into laughter. Stop trying to trick us, they said—if you had said it was anyone else, we might have believed you. But who the fuck would believe you've got Gu Yimin—he's been captured by One-Ax Zhang and his bandits.

Chen Yongliang asked them to take a closer look, but they said it was too dark for them to see anything clearly. Chen Yongliang was growing anxious, and he began angrily shouting at the militiamen. If anything happened to Gu Yimin while they were out there, he said, they'd lose their heads. The men on the wall said that this was clearly the talk of a bandit. Chen Yongliang had no choice but to beg them—even if he were a bandit, he said, he was still only just one bandit, and they outnumbered him, so they had no reason to fear.

"Who's afraid?" they asked.

Chen Yongliang waited for about a *shichen* outside the sluicegate. He continued cursing and begging, but the militiamen still wouldn't raise the gate. Eventually they grew tired and stopped responding to Chen Yongliang. Then they sat down, leaned against the wall, and went to sleep. Chen Yongliang was also exhausted. When he heard the militiamen snoring, he wondered how he was ever going to get past the gate; although Gu Yimin was awake, he didn't have the strength to call out. In a soft, weak voice, Gu Yimin comforted Chen Yongliang, saying that when morning came and boats needed to leave the city, they would raise the gate.

Just then, a family fleeing town quietly rowed a small boat up to the east gate and slipped the militiamen some money—finally the gate was raised. The family recognized Chen Yongliang and Gu Yimin, and they shouted up to the militiamen that they knew the two people waiting to get in.

The news that Chen Yongliang had rescued Gu Yimin and brought him back spread quickly through Xizhen, and Xizhen's prominent residents all rushed to Gu Yimin's home. Gu Yimin's wife and concubines, who had long since ceased their crying and wailing, once again filled the grand home with their sobs.

67.

Zeng Wanfu rowed without stopping across the boundless waters. The bullets the bandits had fired brought back that long forgotten memory of bullets whizzing through the cold air on that winter day; Chen Shun and Zhang Pinsan falling to the snowy ground; a bullet slicing through his middle finger as he ran wildly through gunfire coming from every direction.

This scene continued to haunt him. By the time he guided his little boat with its bamboo awning into the docks at Xizhen, the sun was already setting in the west. Zeng Wanfu felt exhausted as he climbed up on shore. Everyone at the wharf gathered around and looked in the boat's cabin at Lin Xiangfu, the dagger still stuck in his left ear, his blood and brains spilling out and mixing together. Exclaiming and murmuring all at once, they asked Zeng Wanfu what had happened.

"What happened?" Zeng Wanfu asked himself as he wiped the sweat from his face. Slowly he raised his left hand and showed them the missing segment of his middle finger. In a raspy voice, he said, "I'll tell you . . . it was blown off by a bullet."

Lin Xiangfu's body was moved into the temple of the city god, and the people of Xizhen all came to see him laid out there in his gruesome condition. Some cried silent tears, some heaved deep, sorrowful sighs, and some remained silent.

Zeng Wanfu sat on the stone steps outside the main door of the temple, recounting again and again how he had carried Lin Xiangfu's dead body over to his boat, and how he rowed away as the bandits shot at him. When someone asked him how Lin Xiangfu died, he just looked confused and gazed down at his finger with the missing segment.

Late that night, after the steady stream of Xizhen's mourners had left, Chen Yongliang arrived. He and a few others carried Gu Yimin back to his home, and along the way he heard that Lin Xiangfu had been killed by One-Ax Zhang when he delivered the guns for the ransom. When they made it to the gate of the Gu family residence, he didn't enter. After he watched the other men carry Gu Yimin into the house, he turned around and went to the temple of the city god. By that time the Daoists in the temple had already retired, and the hall was empty. Lin Xiangfu was laid out on a table, an ever-burning lamp placed by his feet. Cuiping was also standing to the side, crying softly. Chen Yongliang felt he had seen this woman somewhere before, but he had no idea why she would be experiencing such grief.

When Cuiping heard footsteps enter the temple, she looked up; by the weak light of the flame of the ever-burning lamp, she saw that it was Chen Yongliang. She took a few steps back into the darkness, and Chen Yongliang didn't pay her any more attention. He stood beside the table for a long time, looking at the smile on Lin Xiangfu's face and the dagger that was still stuck in his left ear.

Memories of the past sprouted up in Chen Yongliang's mind like wild grass. Most of them were from the time of the snowstorm—when Lin Xiangfu first came into his house, carrying that enormous bundle on his back and his daughter at his chest. The image was like water dripping off the eaves of a roof—it would appear and stay there for a moment, then drop and reappear . . . Chen Yongliang felt his vision becoming blurry, and only when he reached up his hands to rub his eyes did he realize his face was covered in tears. When he'd dried them, he pulled the dagger out of Lin Xiangfu's ear—at that moment, Lin Xiangfu's slightly open mouth went closed. Chen Yongliang stared at the bloody dagger and said to Lin Xiangfu,

"I'm going to return this dagger to One-Ax Zhang."

These were the last words Chen Yongliang would ever speak to Lin Xiangfu. Once he'd said them, he placed his hand on Lin Xiangfu's ice-cold forehead and slowly moved it down to shut his eyes.

68.

After Chen Yongliang and his family had fled, one of the trussed-up bandits used his teeth to gnaw through the other bandit's ropes. Once the two of them had struggled free, they left Qijiacun and ran through the darkness to Liucun. When they arrived before One-Ax Zhang, they were so soaked with sweat they looked like a pair of drowned dogs. Then they issued their report:

"The villagers of Qijiacun rebelled—they rescued Gu Yimin and ran off with him. There were too many of them for us to handle, and they tied us both up. Once we managed to bite through the ropes, we ran here at once."

Before dawn, One-Ax Zhang gathered together fifty bandits to go exterminate Qijiacun. Before they set off, One-Ax Zhang gave the command:

"I want you to annihilate them—not even a chicken or dog is to be spared."

The next morning, several children who had stayed behind saw that a large group of bandits was approaching the village gate through the fields. They ran back through the village shouting,

"The bandits are here! The bandits are here!"

They were followed by a spray of bullets, which brought each one of them to the ground as if they had tripped. The sound of the bandits' gunfire threw Qijiacun into a panic.

Yesterday when Chen Yongliang left, he encouraged all the villagers to evacuate as quickly as possible. But most of them were still in the process of getting their things together—they hadn't thought that the bandits would come so soon, ready to kill.

When the bandits arrived, they butchered everyone they saw. The villagers scrambled, running for their lives. The women who saw their children fall under the initial gunshots rushed over to them, while One-Ax Zhang came over and chopped the women down with wild swings of his ax, and the other bandits cut them with their swords. Blood spurted everywhere, filling the air with its stench. The women running behind saw the women in front get their shoulders, arms, and heads get chopped off, yet they continued running thoughtlessly toward their children. One woman came running up holding a child, and One-Ax Zhang whacked off its head. Blood sprayed all over the woman's face, but she seemed completely unaware and continued running, clutching her headless child as if they were escaping unscathed out through the village gate.

The bandits went door to door, slaying everyone they saw and stealing anything of value. Once they had finished their killing and looting of each house, they would set it on fire. Soon the entire village of Qijiacun became a sea of flames. Those who ran fast enough to escape scattered out through the fields, while a number of people jumped in the water to swim to some distant stands of reeds. Someone sailed a boat over to them, and around twenty people hiding there swam over and did their best to clamber on. But before they had all made it, the boat flipped over and the people formed a desperate mass in the water, struggling to climb up on the bottom of the overturned boat.

Over two hundred of Qijiacun's villagers had been unable to escape, and amidst the fierce light of the leaping flames, the bandits herded them all over to the threshing ground. Then One-Ax Zhang shouted to them:

"Get into groups of twenty, and stand still! I'm going to 'cut the weeds and pull out the roots'."

As if they were leading lambs, the bandits put the villagers into groups of twenty. Then, waving their knives and swords, they cut off the villagers' heads, young and old alike. Some of the bandits also used spears, which they thrust through the villagers' chests and backs. Unborn children were stabbed to death in their mothers' bellies. When a spear wouldn't come back out, the bandit would use his feet to press against the victim's body, which was often still breathing, and pull out the spear. The fresh blood of two hundred villagers sprayed through the air, splattering the trees surrounding the thresh-ing ground and dripping from their leaves as they blew in the breeze. The dirt was stained red with blood, as was the white hair of the elderly, the eyes of the children, and the pale faces of the women. The villagers in the first group to be slaughtered were chopped up like melons and cab-bage, while the villagers in the next groups stared on. Tears streamed down their faces as they howled in fear and sobbed with grief, their cries ringing out through the sky and caus-ing those who were hiding in the reeds to tremble in horror.

Around ten young women had been saved for last. The fifty bandits rushed toward them, pressed them down on the bloody ground amidst scattered corpses, and raped them. The bandits vied amongst themselves for the women, threatening each other with knives. Two bandits, neither of whom would give in, got into a knife fight and cut each other to a bloody pulp. But when they looked back at the woman, they saw that another bandit was already raping her. This made the two bandits so angry they rushed back over and killed the woman, each of them firing a shot, and then continued their fight. The bandit who had been raping the woman, his face now covered in blood, was so angry he was about to explode. Holding his pants in one hand and using the other to wipe the blood off his face as if it were sweat, he picked up a sword from the ground and joined the fight between the other two bandits, so that all three of them were now chopping and hacking at each other. Another bandit, who was still in the process of raping one of the women, looked around and shouted as he continued his raping,

"Who the fuck is fighting who?"

"No one fucking knows!"

When One-Ax Zhang had finished raping two of the women,
he did up his belt and walked over cursing. He kicked apart the
three fighting bandits and shouted at them,

"You people are so fucking worthless! You leave the ones
that are perfectly alive and well over there, and fight over this
dead one!"

After the ten young women had been gang-raped by all
the bandits, the bandits then chopped off their heads. Flames
roared through Qijiacun, crackling and popping as the village
burned. Of the over six hundred people who lived in Qijiacun,
249 lost their lives. The river water, the grass, the leaves on the
trees, the dirt on the ground—all of it was stained red with
blood. Corpses lay everywhere in clumps throughout the entire village. By day, a foul stench enveloped Qijiacun as blood
seemed to rain from the sky and shrieks and wails pierced the
air; after dark, a strong wind carried mournful cries out into
the night.

The bandits threw forty three of the villager's corpses into
to the small river that flowed through the village, which served
as the main water route connecting the village to the rest of
the Wanmudang. The corpses floated out from the village and
into the Wanmudang's expansive waters, eventually reaching
the Xizhen wharf. Flies swarmed over the bodies, and the boatmen at the docks covered their noses when they met with the
unbearable stench; in order for their boats to pass, they had to
use their bamboo punting poles to push the bodies aside. The
forty three corpses floated around the Xizhen wharf for days.
Schools of fish arrived from the waters of the Wanmudang to
feed on the bodies, nibbling them full of holes and picking off
bits of flesh. Eventually only the white bones were left, which
sank down to the bottom.

A putrid smell hung over Xizhen for several days, while the townsfolk were given over to vomiting and diarrhea. All the anti-diarrheal and anti-nausea medication quickly sold out at the Chinese medicine shop, and for several months, no one would drink the water from the Wanmudang's rivers or eat any fish that were caught in them. When the bellies of some larger fish were cut open, remnants of fingernails and toenails from the bodies were found inside.

69.

The next day, the villagers who had fled Qijiacun started to return. They broke out in loud cries and wails at the scene of devastation before them, and a number of them fainted and fell to the ground. After spending the night in Xizhen, Chen Yongliang rowed himself back. He was met with the sound of crying when he set foot on shore, holding the bloody dagger in his hand. Li Meilian and his two sons ran up to greet him, and when he saw that they were all unharmed, be breathed a long sigh of relief. Then he told them that Lin Xiangfu had been murdered by One-Ax Zhang when he had delivered the guns to Liucun for Gu Yimin's ransom. A dagger had been plunged into his ear, he told them, holding up the bloodstained blade in his hand.

"It was this dagger."

Suffering yet another gut-wrenching blow, Li Meilian and the two boys were stunned at first. Then they began crying bitterly, their wails mingling in the air with those of the other villagers of Qijiacun.

As Chen Yongliang walked through the village, he saw the residents who had returned squatted down in twos and threes by piles of bricks and tiles—the ruins of their homes. They dug through the rubble, crying and cursing, searching for anything that hadn't been burned. The fires hadn't yet gone out in the cellars of several homes, and the food and supplies that the families had stored in them were still burning. So they stuck their hands through the flames and smoke and pulled out whatever they could still salvage.

In what had once been the most prosperous town in the Wanmudang, a center a trade for cotton textiles, livestock, silk, and grain; where houses and buildings had once lined the streets, complete with theaters and pavilions—corpses now littered the ground, and piles of rubble and broken walls were all that remained amongst the smoldering ruins.

They dug graves for the slain villagers. Too many people had died, and there wasn't enough ground in the village to bury them all; in addition, there were also the forty three corpses that had floated away on the waters of the Wanmudang. All they could do was gather the bodies together and bury them in some empty land at the eastern edge of the village, where they piled up 249 grave mounds, forty three of which were empty. At the front of the burial ground, they erected a stone monument. On the front of the stone was the inscription, "The Graves of Two Hundred Forty Nine People," and on the back was carved every name.

Chen Yongliang stood in front of the monument and said to the villagers, "We can't go on eking out an existence like this. We have to fight One-Ax Zhang to the death."

He strapped the dagger to his left arm and dug out a small firewood hatchet from the ruins of his house. Chen Yaowu found a sword one of the bandits had left, and Chen Yaowen picked up a spear. Other villagers digging through the ruins found shotguns, swords, and cudgels. Forty-one young men of the village had survived the massacre, and they decided to follow Chen Yongliang and seek revenge. With faces of steel, they walked out of the village.

Qijiacun's revenge brigade visited two nearby villages trying to learn of the bandits' whereabouts. By evening they'd heard that some of them were spending the night in the nearby village

of Qiancun. Chen Yongliang had everyone sit down by the side
of the road. They'd been on their feet the whole day, he said,
and everyone needed a good rest. They should all drink some
water and eat a little something, and store up their strength
for killing bandits. The forty-four villagers from Qijiacun sat
scattered on both sides of the road holding their shotguns,
swords, and spears. The scene frightened the other people on
the road, who thought they were bandits setting up a roadblock
to shakedown anyone passing by, so they all ran and hid. Chen
Yongliang called out to tell them they weren't bandits—they
were searching for the bandits to get revenge on behalf of the
village of Qijiacun.

The news of One-Ax Zhang's bloody massacre had spread
quickly through the nearby villages, and when the people running away to hide heard that these were in fact villagers from
Qijiacun, they all came forward to hear of the horrible atrocities
that had been committed there—a few even recognized Chen
Yongliang and some of the others. As the sun set in the west,
the road filled up with people. At first, the revenge-seeking men
from Qijiacun had remained dry-eyed—no tears, only hate. But
because others were listening to their story, they now became
choked with sobs as they spoke, and their listeners cried along
with them, tears streaming down their faces.

Then some people from other villages ravaged by One-Ax
Zhang told of the gruesome experiences their own families had
suffered. One man sobbed so hard his body shook. In fits and
spurts, he told of how his wife had been shot and killed by
One-Ax Zhang's bandits, and how they had tossed his young
son up into the air and speared him on a dagger as he fell back
down, his arms and legs still moving. Another man had already
cried himself out when he told of how his wife had thrown herself on the body of their son, who was still weakly breathing.
She protected him as best she could with her own body, until
One-Ax Zhang came around swinging his club and hit her so
hard both her eyeballs were knocked out of their sockets. Then

the bandits took a dagger and plunged it through both his wife and son at once.

A woman spoke up and told of how One-Ax Zhang and his bandits had driven ten or so of the men from her village into the forest, tied them up, and pulled down their pants; then sliced open their anuses and pulled out their intestines. Holding down the slender ends of some tree branches with one hand, they tied the intestines to them and then let go— the intestines were pulled out of the men's bodies by the rebounding branches and then flung up into the trees, where they hung in strands. The ten men howled in agony, then died with whimpering groans.

The people trembled and cried as they recounted these horrific events, and the men from Qijiacun wept along with them. By nightfall, they were all on very familiar terms. Through their tears, some of them said that instead of going home, they would join up with the men from Qijiacun and seek revenge—they would go together and kill One-Ax Zhang.

As Chen Yongliang wiped the tears from his eyes, he tried to find out the situation in Qiancun. A traveling peddler who had passed through told him it was a very small village, less than twenty families, and that he didn't think there could be that many bandits there spending the night. Upon learning this, Chen Yongliang mobilized his men. As the revenge brigade marched forward under the moonlight, Chen Yongliang could tell it was no longer just the original forty-four men he'd set out with. He stood at the side of the road and counted them until he reached sixty-eight. This sudden increase in forces excited him, and he shouted,

"We now have sixty-eight men—sixty eight good men!"

"It's sixty-nine, Pa," Chen Yaowu pointed out from the side. "You forgot to count yourself."

The sixty-nine men headed through the darkness toward Qiancun. They chattered amongst themselves nonstop, asking each other's names and exchanging experiences—it seemed more like a group of people gathering at a market than a bandit-killing brigade.

When they reached a hillside overlooking the village, Chen Yongliang gazed upon it under the moonlight. He stretched out his hand and counted twice, coming up with a total of seventeen houses.

"This is a poor village," he said, "there are no brick-and-tile houses; all seventeen houses are cottages with thatched roofs. All we need to do is surround the cottages, and the bandits will have no way to escape.

Before Chen Yongliang had finished speaking, someone raised a wooden club and shouted, "Charge! Kill the bandits!"

The others quickly joined in and began yelling, "Charge! Kill the bandits!"

The sixty-eight men raised their swords, kitchen knives, clubs, and shotguns and rushed down the hillside; under the moonlight, the chaotic scene looked like a landslide. Only Chen Yongliang was left behind shouting for them to come back—they hadn't yet drawn up any plans of attack. But no one heard him—their ears were filled with only their own shouts and whoops. A few of them fired their shotguns toward the thatched houses below, and the night air was filled with shouting, gunshots, and the sound of blades and clubs striking together. Chen Yongliang shouted from behind until he was hoarse, but not a single one of them turned their heads. He was left with no choice but to follow them down the mountain.

There were only seven bandits spending the night in Qiancun, split up among the homes of four families. Just after they had fallen asleep, they were awakened by the thunderous din of shouting and gunshots charging down the hillside. In their confusion, the bandits pulled on their pants, grabbed their guns, and went outside. By the light of the moon they saw a dark mass of people rushing down the mountain, and they could make out their shouts of "kill the bandits." Frightened, they scurried away from the cottages, but their leader shouted to them,

"Don't run over there—there's a cliff."

So the bandits scurried back and asked, "Where can we find an escape route?"

Their leader pointed to the mountain slope and said, "They're blocking it. Climb onto the rooftops."

So the seven bandits scrambled up onto the roofs just as the sixty-nine men arrived in the village, shouting for the bandits to come out and meet their deaths. The villagers of Qiancun had no idea what was happening and thought these new arrivals were another group of bandits who had materialized out of nowhere. They came out of their homes and begged for their lives—please, masters, they pleaded, don't burn down our houses. Chen Yongliang shouted as loudly as he could and was finally able to get the bandit-killers to quiet down. Then he said to the Qiancun villagers,

"Villagers! We're not bandits—we've come from Qijiacun to kill the bandits."

As soon as Chen Yongliang mentioned Qijiacun, some men behind him piped up with some names of other villages, naming about ten different ones in all. When they were finished, Chen Yongliang continued,

"We've come to seek revenge on One-Ax Zhang and his men. We ask the villagers to please show us where they are."

When the Qiancun villagers heard that these men had come from Qijiacun to seek revenge on the bandits, they calmed down and began talking amongst themselves about how the bandits had obliterated Qijiacun. One of the villagers said to Chen Yongliang and his men:

"The bandits aren't inside—they're laying up on the rooftops. There are seven of them."

Everyone craned their necks and stood on tiptoe to look up on the roofs. There they saw them laying down across the roofs of three cottages. They all shouted up to the bandits:

"Come down right now, or we'll burn you down!"

As soon as the Qiancun villagers heard mention of burning, they immediately pleaded, "Please don't burn down our houses!"

"We're not going to burn down your houses," said Chen Yongliang. "We're just trying to scare the bandits."

Some of the sixty-nine men wanted to crawl up and pull the bandits down.

"Don't bother," said the Qiancun villagers. "They'll end up falling down by themselves. The roofs are thatched with rice straw, and the rafters are made of sunflower stalks. They're okay as long as they don't move, but if they so much as sneeze, they'll break through."

Just as they finished saying that, they heard a crashing sound, and the three roofs caved in at once. The seven bandits fell to the ground, groaning in pain. Over sixty men began pushing and shoving as they eagerly rushed forward to seize each of the seven bandits. Some of the men raised their swords and were about to bring them down when Chen Yongliang stopped them.

"Don't kill anyone here," he said. "Don't defile Qiancun like that. Tie them up, take them to Qijiacun, and kill them there in commemoration of the many we lost."

Then one of the bandits spoke. "We're not part of One-Ax Zhang's forces," he said. "We haven't wronged anyone from Qijiacun, and we have nothing against you. If you're out for revenge, you should go look for One-Ax Zhang."

"If you're not with One-Ax Zhang," asked Chen Yongliang, "then whose men are you?"

"We're with The Monk," one of them replied.

Immediately upon hearing this, Chen Yaowu asked: "Where is The Monk?"

One of the bandits standing behind Chen Yaowu answered: "That's me."

Chen Yaowu turned around and examined him carefully. It really was him. Chen Yaowu repeatedly called out to his father,

"Pa, he's The Monk! He really is The Monk! He's one of the good bandits—he saved my life."

Chen Yaowu untied The Monk's ropes and said to him, "Do you remember me? I'm Chen Yaowu, from Xizhen. You cut off my ear, and you saved my life."

"So it's you," The Monk said. "You're the Chen Yaowu who stayed in my family's home, and who escaped One-Ax Zhang on that boat. You've gotten so tall!"

Chen Yaowu told his father and the rest of his men about The Monk's mother—how she had tied a red rope around his wrist, and how she had boiled him eggs and made him pancakes to eat on the road. Now that Chen Yaowu and The Monk were having this reunion, the other six bandits breathed sighs of relief and said to Chen Yongliang,

"See? This is just a case of friends failing to recognize one another—'waters flooding the temple of the dragon king,' as they say. Please untie us—we're all on the same side here."

That evening, The Monk's group of seven men and Chen Yongliang's sixty-nine men joined forces and spent the night in Qiancun. As they sat around discussing what their next moves should be, The Monk told Chen Yongliang that he and his men didn't approve of One-Ax Zhang's violence, and that they had parted ways with him before his attack on Xizhen.

"If you're fated to be living in these troubled times," said The Monk, "you can't live a quiet life farming the land without facing the bandits' pillaging, and if you become a bandit, you can't live without looting and plundering."

"Becoming a bandit in these troubled times is perfectly understandable," said Chen Yongliang, "as long as you're a bandit with a kind heart."

"We now have more men than One-Ax Zhang," The Monk said to Chen Yongliang, "but going after him and his bandits with a few shotguns and a pile of swords and spears would be like attacking a rock with eggs."

"What's your plan?" asked Chen Yongliang.

"On the waters of the Wanmudang," said The Monk, "One-Ax Zhang holds the advantage, so we can't let ourselves play into his strengths. We should go to the mountain range around Five Springs, which will be the best place for us to hide. Then we can attack One-Ax Zhang when the opportunity presents itself."

Chen Yongliang thought this over for a while and nodded. "The Monk is right," he announced to everyone, "We'll spare the bastard's life for the time being. Don't think we won't get our revenge—it's just that the right moment hasn't come yet."

Over the next month, Chen Yongliang's recruits swelled to over one hundred. But a hundred men had only twenty or so guns, eleven of which were just shotguns. Just when Chen Yongliang and The Monk were really beginning to worry about their lack of weapons, one of Gu Yimin's servants suddenly arrived. He said he had been on the road for four days trying to learn the whereabouts of Qijiacun's revenge brigade.

He drew a letter from his breast pocket and handed it to Chen Yongliang, saying, "This is a letter from the master."

Chen Yongliang took the letter and asked the servant, "How are the master's injuries?"

"They no longer pose a grave danger," said the servant, "but he's still unable to get out of bed."

The servant said he needed to head back at once, as the master was awaiting his report. Chen Yongliang summoned Chen Yaowu and had him gather a few men to escort Gu Yimin's servant through the mountain pass and out onto the main road.

When Chen Yongliang took Gu Yimin's letter, he noticed it was quite thick, and that it was not his handwriting on the envelope. After carefully opening it, he discovered it was not a letter from Gu Yimin inside, but rather ten bank notes, each worth a thousand silver yuan. The surprise registered on Chen Yongliang's face as he passed the money to The Monk, who counted the notes himself and then said excitedly,

"We were just talking about guns and ammunition—well, the guns and ammunition have arrived."

"How do we go about buying it?" Chen Yongliang asked
The Monk.

The Monk told Chen Yongliang about the government
troops stationed in Shendian—how they carried their guns and
ammunition out of the city to go eradicate the bandits, and how,
when they actually met with the bandits, they simply dropped
their arms, gathered up the silver the bandits threw at their feet,
and ran away. The bandits, on the other hand, ran away with
the troops' firearms in exchange for their money.

"I'll go make a deal with the troops in Shendian," said The
Monk.

70.

The injuries on Gu Yimin's chest and back began to fester,
and the bloody pus that oozed out of his wounds stuck to the
bedsheets. Whenever Gu Yimin rolled over, the sheets rolled
along with him, and a servant would have to come gingerly peel
them from his body—it was like removing a layer of skin, and
Gu Yimin would groan in pain. Several doctors of Chinese medicine were of the opinion that if the rotten flesh wasn't removed,
new skin couldn't grow, so they prescribed *shengyao,* a medicinal paste with high levels of toxicity and corrosiveness. They
went to the Chinese medicine shop for a distillation of mercury,
potassium nitrate, and alum and mixed it into a paste to spread
in a thin layer all over Gu Yimin's body. The toxic *shengyao*
caused Gu Yimin's already-rotting skin to become even more
rotten and festering, and as this happened the doctors would
scrape it off; each day, about a bowlful of rotten flesh would be
carried out of Gu Yimin's chamber. His wife and concubines
constantly lamented his state, afraid there was no longer any
flesh left on him. After the *shengyao* had done its job, the doctors crushed up some pungent garlic and spread it all over Gu
Yimin's body to act as an anti-inflammatory and antibiotic.

After experiencing so much pain he no longer wanted to live, Gu Yimin's groans of agony ceased, and he regained his senses and became more clearheaded. Although his voice remained weak, he could now speak with people. When the news spread that Gu Yimin was no longer in critical condition and could receive visitors from his bed, all the prominent residents of Xizhen came to pay their respects.

Now that he was fully conscious, Gu Yimin kept catching whiffs of a terrible smell—it was around that time that the fish had just about finished picking at the forty-three corpses in the river, and the bones were beginning to sink down to the bottom. Gu Yimin asked his visitors what was causing the stink, and that was how he learned of One-Ax Zhang's massacre of Qijiacun after Chen Yongliang had rescued him. He also learned that Chen Yongliang had gathered forces to go take revenge. One visitor told him of all the different sorts of gruesome atrocities he'd heard that One-Ax Zhang had committed, and he fainted before his guest had finished recounting them all. This caused another scare over Gu Yimin's health, and after that no one dared mention Chen Yongliang or Lin Xiangfu's death.

When Gu Yimin awoke from his fainting spell, he opened his eyes and stared at the ceiling. From his recent visitors, he had learned that One-Ax Zhang had held him hostage in a place called Qijiacun, and he also recalled that when Chen Yongliang's family had left Xizhen, they had moved to a village of the same name. Vague memories of the torture he'd suffered under the bandits in Qijiacun surfaced in his mind. At one point in his pain-induced haze he remembered hearing a woman's voice; at the time he didn't recognize it, but now he knew—it was Li Meilian calling out to him. Then, on that swaying little boat, he recognized Chen Yongliang, who had rescued him and brought him back to Xizhen.

Gu Yimin thought of the over two hundred villagers who had been slaughtered in Qijiacun, and his hands clenched into fists; but the thought of Chen Yongliang's revenge brigade relaxed them again. If Chen Yongliang was going to fight One-Ax Zhang to the death, thought Gu Yimin, he would need lots of manpower, and this manpower could not be short on firepower.

Gu Yimin called for his accountant and had him take out ten thousand yuan in bank notes and put them in an envelope. Then he called for his servant and told him to deliver the envelope to Chen Yongliang. The servant saw there was nothing written on the envelope and cautiously asked,

"Master, where shall I find Chen Yongliang?"

Wearily, Gu Yimin answered, "You'll find him out there somewhere."

71.

The Monk took the banknotes Gu Yimin had sent and exchanged them for silver yuan, and then exchanged the silver yuan for guns and ammunition from the government troops in Shendian. He even enlisted a few soldiers from what was left of the Beiyang Army.

One-Ax Zhang was also expanding his power, as bandit leaders like Leopard Li and Floater who had gone out on their own now returned to join forces once more with him. Chen Yongliang built a stage up in the mountains and invited some opera troupes to come perform, which he then used as an opportunity to recruit more men. One-Ax Zhang, on the other hand, set up a gambling joint where he received small groups of bandits who came to join up with him.

The Monk brought his former Beiyang Army recruits to train the villagers. Constant shouts commanding them to run, jump, and lay down ensued, as did the shouts that followed bullets and spears hitting their targets. Some of the villagers often went rabbit hunting in the mountains, and their marksmanship was already quite good; others enjoyed standing on the prows of their boats and spearing fish, so they were already quite skilled with spears.

Chen Yongliang's men and One-Ax Zhang's bandits finally clashed in a village near Xizhen called Wangzhuang. Over three hundred men fought viciously for two days, slaughtering and slaying as if an evil darkness had descended over the earth. Flames rose in all directions around Wangzhuang, and the smoke from gunfire filled the air. The sounds of rifles, pistols, and cannons shook the earth, while swords, axes, lances, and spears met in hand-to-hand combat. The people of Wangzhuang and the surrounding villages fled in droves, taking their families to either Shendian or Xizhen.

The day before the ferocious battle, The Monk told Chen Yongliang that four years ago, Leopard Li and Floater had asked him to join forces with them to fight One-Ax Zhang at Liucun. They lost to One-Ax Zhang, so they temporarily joined up with him. All together, Leopard Li and Floater had a total of thirty-seven men, while he had only three; One-Ax Zhang had forty-three. He and his three men, along with five of Floater's men, lay in ambush at the village gate of Liucun, which resulted in the loss of two of his brothers. One of them was on a rooftop, and when he fired his gun, One-Ax Zhang saw him and shot him . . . his blood ran down the eaves and dripped on the ground. Another fired from up in a tree and was discovered by one of One-Ax Zhang's men—he was also shot and killed, his body left hanging in the tree. His one man who made it out alive set his ambush from the window of a house. When he saw that they would be unable to stop One-Ax Zhang and his men, he hid in an empty coffin in the home, where he was able to evade their detection and escape with his life. As for The Monk himself, he kept fighting and retreating, until he had retreated back to Leopard Li's position. It was an unorganized battle, and the men on both sides became scattered all over the place—no one knew where the others on their side were.

The Monk warned that the next day's fighting would also be

messy and unorganized, and he urged Chen Yongliang to order his men to tie a white strip of cloth on their left arms. This way, if they all got separated, they would still be able to distinguish friend from foe.

Chen Yongliang nodded and said, "You give the command."

"You're the leader," said The Monk.

Chen Yongliang looked back at The Monk without saying anything. The Monk spoke more about One-Ax Zhang—he said cruelty and violence was in his nature, and that he killed people as easily as killing chickens; he was also demanding and very particular. Leopard Li and Floater both brought their men to join forces with him when he rose to power, but when he lost it, they all left, and for many years the only ones who stayed with him were some rogue daredevils who did not necessarily feel much loyalty to him. One-Ax Zhang had excellent marksmanship, but he had the most fun with his ax, chopping off the heads and shoulders of his opponents and frightening everyone with his ruthlessness. It was important not to show fear when confronting him—if you showed the slightest bit of fear, the sharp blade of that ax would come down on you. One-Ax Zhang had a sharp eye and a quick hand, so if you wanted to kill him, you would have to be even quicker.

The Monk wanted Chen Yongliang to tell all of this to the men before they set out, but Chen Yongliang said,

"You're the one who understands One-Ax Zhang, so you should tell them."

Once more The Monk replied, "But you're the leader."

Chen Yongliang thought for a few moments, then said to The Monk, "Although we haven't known each other that long, we already feel like brothers. Tomorrow there will be a terrible battle, and who knows if we'll come out of it alive—so why don't we swear a pact of brotherhood today?"

The Monk smiled upon hearing this and said, "If you make a pact with a bandit, you have to do it according to the bandits' rules."

"What rules?" asked Chen Yongliang.

"Bandits take all of their oaths staring down the barrel of a gun," said The Monk.

The Monk put his Mauser on the table, and Chen Yongliang did the same. The two guns laid there beside one another, pointing at each man. Then Chen Yongliang and The Monk knelt down and kowtowed before the barrels of the guns. Chen Yongliang then repeated after The Monk:

"From this day forward, we are brothers in arms, sharing equally in fortune and hardship. If one of us dies, we'd rather both be dead. Let a gun render judgment on whoever breaks this oath."

72.

Chen Yongliang watched as his sworn brother The Monk engaged in a vicious battle with One-Ax Zhang. By that point, both sides had used up all their ammunition, so it had become a battle of blades, lances, and spears. One-Ax Zhang appeared truly terrifying as he wielded his ax, chopping and hacking. After slicing three people in a row, he spotted The Monk about twenty paces ahead of him and shouted,

"I'm sending you to the underworld, Monk!"

The Monk turned to see One-Ax Zhang rushing toward him with his ax raised in the air. He knew there was no way for him to escape; he would have to face him head-on and fight to the death. Without the slightest hesitation, he met him with the blade of his sword. Both ax and sword were aimed at their opponents' necks, as if they were carrying out a death pact. When The Monk saw the ax coming down, he didn't flinch; when One-Ax Zhang saw the sword coming toward him, he bent backwards and dipped his head to evade it. One-Ax Zhang's ax didn't chop off The Monk's head, but instead hacked off his left arm; The Monk's sword didn't cut off One-Ax Zhang's head, but instead sliced across both his eyeballs.

Chen Yongliang heard the crisp sound of The Monk's sword cutting into the bridge of One-Ax Zhang's nose. Amidst the clashing of swords and spears and the din of hand-to-hand combat, Chen Yongliang could still clearly make out this subtle noise.

His face covered in blood, One-Ax Zhang fell to the ground wailing and holding his hands over his eyes. The Monk, now missing his left arm, was still standing, propping himself up with the sword in his right hand. Then he said to his old associates Floater and Leopard Li,

"One-Ax Zhang will be dead soon—you're now free to go your own ways."

Even now, The Monk, who normally spoke in a soft voice and never shouted, still managed to speak gently and sincerely. He remained standing there with his missing arm, blood running from the place where it had been cut off. When Leopard Li, Floater, and the other bandits saw this, they were completely stunned.

Seeing One-Ax Zhang rolling on the ground wailing and moaning, blood continuing to gush out over his face, Leopard Li and Floater rounded up their men and left, and the other bandit leaders did the same. When the bandits with One-Ax Zhang saw that the situation had turned bleak, they collected One-Ax Zhang and made a hasty retreat. Only then did The Monk fall to the ground.

Right before he died, he saw Chen Yongliang kneeling in front of him, calling out to him, but he couldn't hear a thing. He wanted to say something, and he opened his mouth, but no sound would come out. Everything went dark.

Chen Yongliang wailed over this man who had been his sworn brother for only three days. It was an accumulated sadness beginning with Lin Xiangfu's death, and then the massacre of Qijiacun. Now, at the gruesome death of The Monk, he cried for all of it. Chen Yaowu shed his tears silently—from now on, The Monk would no longer be a part of his life. A feeling of sorrow enveloped the others, who all stood in silence.

Chen Yongliang's men carried The Monk away on a door plank, along with the other dead and wounded, and returned to Five Springs. He sent some men to go find some woodworkers in nearby villages—he worked alongside them to make fifty-eight coffins. The eleven former soldiers of the Beiyang Army were buried in Five Springs, as were the three of The Monk's six men who had died. The others were claimed by people from their home villages, who carried them back, while The Monk and the men from Qijiacun who had died were taken back to Qijiacun. Chen Yongliang distributed the leftover money among the remaining survivors and let them keep their guns—and with that, the brigade dispersed.

Then Chen Yongliang gathered together his sons and asked surviving three of The Monk's men to lead the way as they went down a mountain path to his small village. Along the way, Chen Yongliang asked them what The Monk's real name was. None of his men knew, but Chen Yaowu did—he told his father it was Xiaoshan.

When they arrived at the home of The Monk's mother, Chen Yongliang knocked on the door. The voice of an old woman answered, and after she'd opened the door, Chen Yongliang said to her,

"Ma—I'm Xiaoshan's sworn brother. My name is Chen Yongliang, and we've come to take you to live in Qijiacun."

The old woman looked at Chen Yongliang, Chen Yaowu, Chen Yaowen, and the three of The Monk's men, two of whom she recognized. She knew that her son had died. She had known that sooner or later this day would come, and now it finally had. He had told her that if people came for her after his death, it would mean that he'd had true brothers in that outlaw life of his.

So, the old woman thought, her son had really had true

brothers. She nodded and ushered them inside, and said she'd leave with them once she got some of her things together. As the old woman went into her room to pack up her belongings, Chen Yongliang and the others could hear her crying. Chen Yongliang was thinking of what he should say to her, but when she came out of her room with her things all packed up, she had already dried her tears.

When they had left the old woman's home and made their way to the mountain road, Chen Yaowu took her bags from her and passed them to Chen Yaowen. Then he said to her,

"Grandmother, I'll carry you."

Before the old woman had time to react, Chen Yaowu had already hoisted her up onto his back. As he carried her along, he asked her,

"Grandmother—do you remember me?"

"Who are you?" the old woman asked.

"Think back," said Chen Yaowu.

The old woman noticed there was only a hole where one of his ears should have been. She reached out and touched his ear hole and began crying.

"You're Chen Yaowu from Xizhen," she said. "You've gotten so big."

The old woman then began to sob—the sorrow of losing her child had resurfaced when she saw Chen Yaowu's missing ear, and she could no longer hold it in. Although she tried to temper her grief, it seemed as long and drawn-out as the mountain road they were traveling.

Chen Yongliang and the others remained silent as they went, walking with their heads down as they listened to the old woman's sobs. By the time they arrived at the edge of the waters of the Wanmudang, she had stopped crying. They boarded a boat, and she and Chen Yaowu began to talk. Chen Yaowu spoke of how she had tied the red rope around his wrists, and how she had given him two pancakes and two boiled eggs when he had left; the old woman recalled how he would sit in front of the stove and tend the fire when she cooked. She said that when he would blow on the fire, the flames would leap up high and bright.

Back in Qijiacun, Chen Yongliang established his own militia, dug a moat, repaired the buildings, and constructed a wall around the city complete with twenty embrasures for guns to fire on the enemy. He also helped the neighboring villages establish their own militias and organized a five-village council— as soon as bandits attacked one of the villages, the other four would come to its defense, surround the bandits, and inflict heavy losses. For a long time afterwards, no bandits ever came.

73.

One-Ax Zhang didn't die after the battle at Wangzhuang. After becoming blind, his temper would flare up even more violently than before, and the few men who dared to stay with him could no longer bear it. They said he had become a useless burden, and a grumbling, swearing burden at that, so they might as well just discard him somewhere and forget about him. They discussed what should be done—if they deposited him in the mountains or the forest, he would certainly starve. On the basis of their past friendship, they decided to take him to the wharf at Shendian, where there were always people coming and going. There, at least, he could always beg for a few bites of food.

As One-Ax Zhang was eating his dinner, they suddenly bound him with rope. He swore and cursed as he fought back, so they stuffed an old rag in his mouth. They carried him out to a boat and rowed it to Shendian, where, by the cover of darkness, they deposited him on the docks. They threw a satchel with his belongings down beside him and told him it contained his winter clothing, his Mauser, and twenty bullets. He had quite a few enemies, they said, so they encouraged him to conserve the bullets. Finally they pulled the rag out of his mouth, and he immediately began yelling,

"I'll use these bullets to shoot you bunch of you ungrateful dogs!"

"You'd better save a little energy," they snickered, "so you can call for someone to save you and untie your ropes."

"I'd die before I'd call for someone to save me," shouted One-Ax Zhang.

"Well, just die, then," they said.

Still shouting and cursing, One-Ax Zhang listened as they boarded the boat and rowed off. He didn't know where he was, but he sensed he was sitting on a stone pavement, and he could hear the sound of water beside him, so he guessed he was at a wharf. There were no sounds coming from anywhere around him, so it must be the middle of the night. After a long while, he heard the night watchman strike the drum. One Ax-Zhang shouted,

"Help! Save me!"

One-Ax Zhang never became a beggar. Instead, he gave himself the name Half-Immortal Zhang and became a fortune-teller, which had been his occupation before becoming a bandit.

On a busy street near the wharf, he sat leaning against the wall with a table in front of him. Two sticks of bamboo were tied to two of the table legs, and a banner hung between the bamboo sticks that read "Half-Immortal Zhang Speaks." A white cloth with a yin-yang symbol surrounded by the eight trigrams was spread over the table, while the drawer had been pulled out and set on the ground by his feet; his loaded Mauser pistol occupied the empty space where the drawer had been. To his left sat a barber, and to his right was a cobbler. He quickly made a name for himself in this busy area by the wharf. Everyone said this blind man was very skilled—if you told him the eight characters of your birthdate and horoscope, he could tell you your past as well as your future.

One afternoon, Chen Yongliang came to Shendian in a little

boat with a bamboo awning. He hopped out onto the dock, but instead of going on into town, he stayed there and looked all around the wharf. The news that the blind One-Ax Zhang had been discarded at the Shendian wharf by his own men spread like wildfire among the bandits, and Chen Yongliang learned of it from two bandits who had been captured when they came to rob Qijiacun. Chen Yongliang came as soon as he heard.

As Chen Yongliang walked down a busy street near the wharf, he heard the call of a fortune-teller:

"What is within, and what is without? To know your whence is to know your whither."

Chen Yongliang followed the voice, and there between a barber and a cobbler he saw One-Ax Zhang. Although his beard was scraggly and his hair went down to his shoulders, Chen Yongliang still recognized him at once. Chen Yongliang stood there for a bit, and One-Ax Zhang sensed there was someone in front of him. He raised his left hand from under the table, pointed to the stool in front of it, and said,

"Please have a seat."

Chen Yongliang sat down on the stool and said a random birthdate and horoscope. He looked closely at One-Ax Zhang as he began mumbling some incantations. Then One-Ax Zhang raised his pair of vacant eyes—the eyeballs looked lifeless, and in between them a large scar from a sword rose up across the bridge of his nose. There were also scars at the corners of his eyes on both sides.

One-Ax Zhang said, "The five elements in your horoscope occur in the following amounts: there's one of metal, zero of wood, four of water, one of fire, and two of earth. You lack wood. When you were two years and eight months old, your first cycle of fate began, and every ten years after that you would enter the next cycle. You have many brothers, at least five or six . . . "

"I don't have any brothers," said Chen Yongliang. "I'm an only son."

One-Ax Zhang raised his hand and then smacked it down

on the table. "*Zi wu mao you,* many brothers; *chen xu chou wei,* an only child," he said, reciting combinations of the Earthly Branches.

"I really am an only son," said Chen Yongliang.

One-Ax Zhang smacked his hand on the table once more and said, "Then you've told me the wrong *shichen* of your birth—it shouldn't be the '*zi*' *shichen,* it should be the '*chou*' *shichen.*"

"I was born in between the '*zi*' and '*chou*' *shichens,*" said Chen Yongliang, "so maybe I was born during the '*chou*'."

One-Ax Zhang pointed at Chen Yongliang with his left hand. "A hair's-width off, and you're a thousand *li* away," he said.

"If I was born in the *chou shichen,*" Chen Yongliang asked, "would I still be missing the wood element?"

One-Ax Zhang lowered his left hand below the table and began murmuring to himself. Then he said, "one of gold, zero of wood, three of water, one of fire, and three of earth—you're still lacking wood."

Chen Yongliang noticed One-Ax Zhang's left hand periodically coming up from underneath the table, while his right hand didn't move. He noticed a drawer had been pulled out and placed on the ground by One-Ax Zhang's right foot—he knew there was a Mauser pistol aimed right at him.

One-Ax Zhang began talking at length, starting from Chen Yongliang's youth. Each time he paused to gauge his reaction, Chen Yongliang would nod and voice his affirmation, and One-Ax Zhang would become more animated, his left hand flailing up and down while his right hand remained still underneath the table. Chen Yongliang thought back to what The Monk had told him—One-Ax Zhang was quick, so if you wanted to kill him, you had to be even quicker. When One-Ax Zhang had finished talking about Chen Yongliang's past, he began on his future. One-Ax Zhang could really give himself free rein now that he was talking about the future, and so he described a bright future full of great successes for Chen Yongliang. He also offered him some heartfelt advice, which was to always act with prudence—speaking irresponsibly could have unintended consequences. He urged him to pay particular attention to his relationships with others and to avoid moral compromises in the pursuit of wealth.

As Chen Yongliang looked at One-Ax Zhang's face, he thought back to that evening in the temple of the city god, when Lin Xiangfu was lying dead on the table. After thinking about it carefully, he confirmed that he had pulled the dagger out from Lin Xiangfu's left ear.

One-Ax Zhang finished talking. His left hand retreated back under the table, and his lifeless eyes looked at Chen Yongliang. Chen Yongliang placed a silver yuan on the table, and when One-Ax Zhang heard it hit the surface, he could tell it wasn't a copper coin. Overjoyed, he said,

"That's a silver yuan."

Both his hands came up from under the table. He picked the coin up with his right hand, put it in his mouth, and bit it. Chen Yongliang quietly got up. Out of his sleeve he took the dagger he had pulled from Lin Xiangfu's ear. He came around the table right up to One-Ax Zhang's left ear and said in a low voice,

"I'm returning your dagger."

Shocked, One-Ax Zhang dropped the silver yuan on the ground. As his right hand reached for his Mauser, the dagger had already plunged into his left ear. He pulled the trigger as a conditioned reflex, and the gun went off—the bullet shot out from under the table and hit a wall across the street. The barber and the cobbler both looked over in surprise—the customers who had just been sitting with them jumped away as if they had springs on their feet and stared wide-eyed from a distance.

With his left hand Chen Yongliang gripped One-Ax Zhang's hair, and with his right hand he delivered a powerful smack. The blade of the dagger moved half-way in to One-Ax Zhang's ear, and Chen Yongliang heard a sound like something scraping against a rock. He knew the dagger had reached the skull.

Chen Yongliang pushed One-Ax Zhang's body over to lean against the wall. When he turned around and faced the crowd that had cautiously gathered, his hands and clothing were soaked in blood. He passed through them with a placid demeanor and walked back to the wharf, where he hopped on his little boat with the bamboo awning and sailed away over the vast expanse of water.

74.

Three months later, Gu Yimin was able to get out of bed and, with the help of a servant, walk out to the back garden. While he had been lean and trim before, his wife and concubines saw he was now so thin his bones looked like kindling.

Gu Yimin thought of Lin Xiangfu. While he had been lying in bed all those days, he had received a steady stream of visitors; the only one who hadn't appeared was Lin Xiangfu. So he asked,

"Why haven't I seen Lin Xiangfu?"

Only now did the servant tell him what had happened—that when Lin Xiangfu had taken the guns to Liucun in exchange for Gu Yimin's ransom, One-Ax Zhang had brutally murdered him. Gu Yimin sat in the winter sunlight and stared at his servant as he spoke. The servant said that before Lin Xiangfu set off, he had left a letter for Gu Yimin, which had been delivered by a woman named Cuiping. Gu Yimin reached out his right hand, indicating to the servant that he wanted to see the letter. The servant rushed off to the study and retrieved it, and with trembling hands Gu Yimin opened the envelope. After reading Lin Xiangfu's final wish—that Gu Yimin see to the marriage of Gu Tongnian and Lin Baijia—he gave a slight nod. Then he thought of how Gu Tongnian had stolen all of that silver and run off to who-knows-where, and he began shaking his head.

In his weak voice, Gu Yimin asked his servant where he might find Lin Xiangfu's remains. The servant told him that his body had been laid out in the temple of the city god for three days, during which time the Daoist priests had performed their rites. Unsure of how to manage things afterwards, several members of the chamber of commerce had the body carried to Lin Xiangfu's home to await Master Gu's decision. Gu Yimin remained silent for a long while after hearing this, then asked about the condition of the body. The servant said that the several members of the chamber of commerce were worried the body would start decaying, so they called in two wax workers, who encased Lin Xiangfu's body in beeswax.

Gu Yimin rode in a four-carrier sedan chair over to Lin Xiangfu's house. When the residents of Xizhen saw that Gu Yimin's sedan was out, they starting following it, commenting that Chamber President Gu had recovered; Commander Gu's health had returned. When Gu Yimin alighted from the sedan, he was so frail they hardly recognized him—his once imposing figure was now so thin he seemed barely human. His back was all stooped over and he leaned on a cane as he walked with the assistance of his servants up to Lin Xiangfu's home. When he entered the room where the body had been laid out and walked up to it, he stood leaning on his cane in front of his old friend and wept, burying his head in his sleeves. A servant pulled a chair over and invited him to sit.

When Gu Yimin went to sit down, he fell over. His servants were shocked—a white froth was bubbling from his mouth, and they immediately had the two people standing beside them help lift Gu Yimin into the sedan chair. The four carriers then ran with him back to the Gu residence, while the servants frantically called out the names of several doctors so that some bystanders might quickly go fetch them.

When Gu Yimin regained consciousness that evening, he saw several doctors standing around his bed. One of them said that anger harms the liver, joy harms the heart, thinking harms the spleen, sadness harms the lungs, and fear harms the kidneys—Gu Yimin fainted, he said, because sadness had harmed his lungs. His emotion had become so acute that it had caused his qi to become stagnant. Fluids could no longer enter or exit, so they congealed into phlegm, which caused an obstruction. The doctor used a powder mixture of monkey bezoar, deer musk, greenschist, tabasheer, and borax to reduce Gu Yimin's congestion and ease his sadness.

The next morning, Gu Yimin had a servant go down to the wharf and fetch Cuiping. With much effort, Gu Yimin sat in the study to receive her. When she appeared, he invited her to sit, but she shook her head. Gu Yimin asked her a number of questions regarding the details of the letters Lin Xiangfu had left with her. Cuiping didn't look Gu Yimin in the eye, but answered all of his questions in a soft voice with her head bowed. She told him that Lin Xiangfu had also given her a letter to send to someone named Tian Da in his hometown up north. She had already mailed it—she'd sent it the day Lin Xiangfu's body was moved from the temple of the city god to his home. Gu Yimin mumbled something to himself and then nodded. The letter she mailed to his hometown, he thought, most likely contained Lin Xiangfu's final words.

After Cuiping left, Gu Yimin wondered if he should send a letter to Lin Baijia, asking her to return at once to Xizhen. He had not received any word from Gu Tongnian, so they would have to wait to discuss the marriage.

After going back and forth in his mind, Gu Yimin ultimately felt he should ask Lin Baijia to return so she could see her father one last time, and they could discuss the other matter later. But when he picked up his writing brush he hesitated. When he saw Lin Xiangfu's body all encased in beeswax, it didn't look like Lin Xiangfu; it looked like a fake. Then he thought of the danger of traveling. If she met up with bandits on her way, that would obviously lead to something terrible, and even if she made it back without incident, she wouldn't necessarily be safe in Xizhen. So Gu Yimin decided it would be best for her not to return for the time being—it was much safer in Shanghai at the McTyreire School.

When he thought of Lin Baijia sharing a room with Gu Tongsi and Gu Tongnien and the deep bond of friendship between the three girls, he felt somewhat comforted. Thinking about it some more, he decided he would write a letter after all. He should notify Lin Baijia of her father's death, but tell her the current situation is too unstable to come home and that she should stay at the McTyreire School and continue her studies.

When Gu Yimin had finished writing the letter, he called in a servant and handed it to him, telling him to go to Shanghai the next day and deliver it to Lin Baijia. After the servant left, Gu Yimin envisaged Lin Baijia's devastation after reading the letter, and his heart began racing with anxiety. Then he thought of how Gu Tongsi and Gu Tongnien would be there to help her bear the sorrow, and he felt slightly better.

75.

Carrying the letter at his chest, Gu Yimin's servant set out for Shanghai. As he left the city gate, he saw four northerners in tattered clothing coming toward him pulling a dilapidated cart with a person laying on it. The four northern men stopped at the gate and looked up at the two characters carved in the stone, then began conferring with one another. When they saw Gu Yimin's servant approach, they asked him if the two characters carved on the gate were "Xi Zhen." The servant nodded and said they were. The northerners heard that the servant's pronunciation was different from theirs, but his nod indicated to them that it was in fact Xizhen.

"We're here; we've made it," they exclaimed in joyful relief.

As they entered Xizhen with their cart, the townspeople looked at them with curiosity and went up to talk to them. These four northerners looked at the Xizhen residents with total confusion, unable to understand their rapid dialect. After much talking and explaining, the northerners finally understood that they were being asked where they were from, so they said the name of their town, which the residents of Xizhen had never heard of. Someone asked them where it was, and the northerners looked at each other and repeated the name of the town. Another person pressed on: Was it north of the Yangtze? After several iterations of this question, the northerners shook their heads and said no, it was north of the Yellow River. By that point, the residents of Xizhen had a pretty good idea of where they were from.

Then someone pointed to the person lying motionless on the cart and asked what illness they had contracted. The northerners understood this at once and answered,

"He's dead."

One of the northerners then pointed to the body on the cart and explained to the Xizhen townsfolk that it was their older brother, who had gotten sick along the way.

The townsfolk looked at them in astonishment. They had traveled such a long way, they said—what were they planning to do in Xizhen? A look of polite humility came over their faces as they said,

"We've come to take our young master home."

The townsfolk were a bit confused. You've brought a dead man here, they said, to collect your master and take him home—who is your master? At that point, the northerners realized they still didn't know where Lin Xiangfu lived. So they asked:

"Where is our young master's home?"

Once again, the townsfolk asked, "Who is your young master?"

"Lin Xiangfu," they replied.

When they learned that these northerners were from Lin

Xiangfu's hometown and had come to take him home, the townsfolk all gasped. One of them said to the men,

"Your young master is dead."

The four northerners looked at each other without seeming to have understood. The Xizhen townsfolk all started talking at once, telling how Lin Xiangfu had delivered the ransom and been killed by the bandits. The four of them were able to understand, and three of them began weeping. The oldest among them, Tian Er, didn't weep, because he didn't believe Lin Xiangfu was dead. He took out Lin Xiangfu's letter from his breast pocket and held it out for the townsfolk to see. The young master had written this himself, he said—the young master wanted to return home, and he wanted us to come and take him back.

"If the young master were dead," he said, "he couldn't have written this letter."

The Xizhen townsfolk told Tian Er that Lin Xiangfu hadn't yet died when he wrote the letter, but by the time they had received it, he had. Tian Er still didn't believe it, and he shook his head as he followed the townsfolk to Lin Xiangfu's home. When he saw Lin Xiangfu's body lying there encased in beeswax, he felt it didn't look like their young master. He had his three younger brothers look, and Tian San and Tian Wu agreed it didn't really look like him. Only Tian Si said it looked like their young master—his face was covered in wax, he said, but when you looked closely, you could recognize him. Tian Er drew closer and stared for a while, and when he finally recognized him, he sobbed violently.

"Every day we waited for you to come home," he said through his tears. "When we finally got your letter, we were so happy! Our oldest brother had already fallen ill, and we begged him not to come with us, but he insisted. He said now that the young master finally wants to come home, he had to come and get you. So we had someone make a cart that we could pull him on as we came for you. But he died in the middle of the journey. His illness worsened, so we found a doctor of Chinese medicine, who gave him an eight-ingredient prescription. We finally found someone who could cook up the medicine for us, but our brother died before he was able to finish taking it."

When Gu Yimin heard that five people had come from Lin Xiangfu's hometown to take him back with them, and that one of the five had already died and was laying on a cart, he got in his four-carrier sedan chair and went off to Lin Xiangfu's house. As he was being helped inside, he passed by the dilapidated cart and saw Tian Da lying on it. He shook his head and sighed.

Tian Er was still blubbering as Gu Yimin entered the house, while the other three brothers were wiping their tears. Someone informed them that Master Gu, president of the chamber of commerce, had arrived. They stopped their crying and politely offered their greetings to this frail old master.

Gu Yimin invited them to have a seat. After drying their eyes, they didn't sit on the chairs that had been carried over for them, but instead squeezed in all together on a bench. Gu Yimin looked at them kindly and asked when they had set out and if their journey had been smooth. They said they had left as soon as they had received the young master's letter, and that their trip had gone smoothly enough except for the delays caused by their brother's illness. They once again told of the Chinese medicine doctor and his eight-part prescription, and how their brother had died before he'd been able to finish the medicine. When they reached this point in their story, they couldn't keep from crying.

"We begged him not to come," they said, "but he insisted."

Then Tian Er asked Gu Yimin, "When did the young master die? He was still alive and well when he wrote that letter to us."

Gu Yimin asked about the letter, and Tian Er removed it from his breast pocket and handed it over. When Gu Yimin opened it, he saw that it contained only two simple lines: the first said that Lin Xiangfu wanted to return home, and the second asked them to come get him. Then he saw that at the bottom there was a line that had been blacked out with ink. He held the letter up to the light coming through the window and could faintly make out the line, "as leaves fall back down to their roots, so must a man return to his hometown." Gu Yimin's eyes grew wet. He knew that before Lin Xiangfu took the guns to the bandits for his ransom, he had already made all the necessary preparations. He lowered his head and dried his eyes, then said to the four Tian brothers,

"He died before his letter reached you."

The four Tian brother began crying once more. After they cried for a bit, Tian Er thought of something. He looked all around and asked Gu Yimin,

"And the young mistress?"

"The young mistress is attending school in Shanghai," Gu Yimin replied.

"Is she well?" Tian Er asked.

Gu Yimin nodded. "Very."

The four Tian brothers said they would leave tomorrow to take Lin Xiangfu's body back to their hometown. Gu Yimin thought about it—the body wouldn't be easy to preserve, and it was a very long trip, so it would be best to set out early, while it was still winter.

"Wait a couple days and then go," said Gu Yimin.

Tian Er nodded, and from his breast pocket he withdrew the deeds to the house and land, along with a banknote, and passed them all over to Gu Yimin. This was all of the young master's property, he said. He had already retrieved the land he had mortgaged, according to the young master's instructions. Actually, their older brother had redeemed the land over ten years ago, and they were waiting to return it to the young master in person. Now that he was dead, they would have to ask Master Gu to pass it to the young mistress.

Gu Yimin took the money and the deeds to the land and house. After looking them over carefully, he held up the banknote and said,

"This silver draft is . . . ?"

"That's over ten years' worth of earnings from the fields," said Tian Er.

Gu Yimin passed the banknote and the deeds back to Tian Er and said,

"You continue looking after these. When the young mistress returns to sweep the graves, you can give them to her then."

Gu Yimin then called for two wax workers to come and embalm Tian Da's body in beeswax. Then he called for two tailors to come and make each of the Tian brothers a new set of padded clothes. Finally he called for three former employees of the woodworking shop to come and fix up the old rickety cart. Then, with faltering steps, Gu Yimin made his way through the dust and cobwebs in the storeroom of the woodworking shop and found three coffins that hadn't been sold. He had someone wipe two of them clean and load them on the cart. The cart was just a bit too narrow, and when the coffins were placed side-by-side they wouldn't quite fit. So Gu Yimin hired three woodworkers to make a double coffin that fit the exact width of the cart. The woodworkers worked round the clock, and when Gu Yimin came to see what they had produced, he was quite satisfied. Then he thought of how bumpy the road would be, and he had them attach the coffin directly to the cart.

When all this had been completed, Tian Si respectfully made another request to Gu Yimin: "Would it be possible to put an awning over the cart to block the rain?"

Tian San complained that Tian Si shouldn't be making any more requests. "Chamber President Gu has already shown thorough consideration," he said.

"If rain falls on the coffin," said Tian Si, "the descendants of the deceased will suffer in poverty."

"Our brother died while we were on the road," said Tian Wu. "It's already rained on him several times."

"We didn't have any choice with our brother," said Tian Si, "but we can't let the young master get soaked by the rain. You know the saying, 'If rain falls on the casket, the descendants won't even have a blanket.'"

Tian Er spoke up to reproach Tian Si: "The young mistress is already a member of the Gu family, so how could she end up without a blanket?"

Observing this scuffle amongst the Tian brothers, Gu Yimin smiled and said weakly to the woodworkers,

"Put an awning on the cart to provide some shelter from the sun and rain."

Early in the morning on the day they left, the Tian brothers were all dressed in new padded clothes as they carefully lifted Lin Xiangfu into the coffin on the cart. The deceased Tian Da had been changed into fresh clothing and was already waiting inside for Lin Xiangfu's arrival. The previous day Gu Yimin had sent over a white cloth, which the brothers now spread over the two bodies. Then they closed the lid.

The Tian brothers pulled the cart carrying the coffin through the early morning streets of Xizhen. After getting fixed up by the three woodworkers, the rickety old cart that had noisily entered the town now looked like it had been exchanged for a new one—it didn't even make a sound as they pulled it along, except for that of the wheels rolling over the ground. When the residents of Xizhen heard the cart coming, they opened their doors one by one and stood in the doorways of their houses, murmuring softly that Lin Xiangfu was returning to his hometown in the north. The custom in Xizhen was that only relatives could approach the coffin; everyone else should avoid it, so as to avoid misfortune in the future.

As the Tian brothers approached the north gate, they saw Gu Yimin standing there leaning on his cane, his frail body, hunched back, and bowed head illuminated in the rays of the rising sun. Behind him stood the four carriers of his sedan chair, and beside him stood a servant. The Tian brothers pulled their cart and coffin up to Gu Yimin and bowed while producing four separate greetings of "Chamber President Gu." Gu Yimin took a sack filled with traveling expenses from his servant and handed it to Tian Er. Tian Er accepted the money, and the four brothers bowed to Gu Yimin once more.

Gu Yimin stared blankly at the coffin for a bit and then said to the four Tian brothers: "The road before you is long—please take care of yourselves."

The four Tian brothers nodded: "We will."

They pulled the cart and coffin through the north gate and exited Xizhen, the wheels rolling evenly along. When they got out onto the main road, Tian San looked back and saw that Gu Yimin was hobbling forward with his cane, his servant and four sedan carriers following behind him. Tian San called out for his brothers to stop, and they brought the cart to a halt and all looked back at Gu Yimin slowly making his way forward. When Gu Yimin saw that they had stopped, he waved his hand and motioned for them to continue on, so they did. But when they saw that Gu Yimin was still walking, they stopped again. Gu Yimin waved his hand once more for them to continue, and then Tian Si understood—Chamber President Gu was seeing off the young master. So they continued pulling the cart and coffin forward, looking back periodically to see Gu Yimin still following behind, his figure gradually receding into the sunlight.

With their oldest brother and their young master in tow, the Tian brothers embarked on their long journey under the warm light of the winter sun. Lin Xiangfu had spent his childhood riding on the shoulders of Tian Da, who had carried him countless times up and down the village streets and out through the fields. Now he lay in peace beside Tian Da, traveling down the path that would lead these fallen leaves back to their roots.

The once-prosperous villages along the sides of the road looked bleak and desolate. There were no workers in the fields, and only a few old and decrepit figures could be seen here and there. Fields that had once flourished with rice, cotton, and canola were now uncultivated tracts of weeds and grasses; waters that had once been crystal clear were now muddy and rank.

WENCHENG II

A few of the older folks in Xizhen had witnessed the childhoods of Xiaomei and Aqiang. Other children took their bowls of rice out on the street, laughing and playing as they ate, but Xiaomei and Aqiang stayed inside and sat at the table; other children were always outside frolicking, skipping rope, and playing games, but Xiaomei and Aqiang sat silently in the shop, practicing their mending and patching skills. The two of them were like a single entity, separated from other children, as well as from their own childhoods, by a thin layer of window paper.

Xiaomei came from the Ji family of the Wanmudang village of Xilicun. At the age of ten, she moved in with the Shen family of Xizhen as a child bride. The Shen family ran a business mending and patching clothes, and although it was a small-time operation, it had a well-established reputation. The work of the Shen family's mending shop was always very well done—wool or silk, any color fabric, whether it was burned, torn, or ripped, once it passed through the Shen's mending shop, there was no longer any trace of the damage. Aqiang was the Shen family's only son. His full name was Shen Zuqiang, but his childhood nickname was Aqiang.

No one really bothered to learn the full name of the child bride living with the Shen family. One day when a customer came to settle up their bill, Xiaomei was the only one looking after the shop. The customer saw her primly flip through the account book, clumsily take up a writing brush, carefully dip it in ink, and write down her name in crooked characters: Ji Xiaomei. From then on, everyone in Xizhen knew the full name of the child bride living with the Shen family.

Xiaomei's parents had three sons and one daughter, and Xiaomei was the second oldest. Her family rented fields outside the village of Xilicun in the Wanmudang, which they farmed for their livelihood. Difficult days left her parents exhausted and poor, and they felt they didn't have the energy or resources to raise four children. The traditional preference for sons was a deeply entrenched attitude, and they felt their daughter would belong to another family sooner or later anyway, so they might as well send her off as a child bride. This way they could relieve themselves of the burden of raising her while also helping her find a path for her future. The Shen family in Xizhen, with their well-known mending business, was far from wealthy, but still fairly well off. Because Aqiang was their only son and they had no daughters, a child bride could prove very helpful around the house, while also helping the family save on betrothal gifts and wedding expenses in the future.

So at the age of ten, Xiaomei left Xilicun for the first time. Her mother did as much for her as she could and made her a new set of clothing out of fresh, clean scraps of cloth. Although it was a new set of clothes, because it was made from random scraps, it still looked as if she was dressed in rags. As Xiaomei walked away, tugging at a corner of her father's clothes, she frequently turned to look back, her face full of helpless confusion. Her mother was standing in front of their thatched cottage dabbing her tears, while her three brothers in their tattered clothing looked on enviously, watching her walk away toward the famous Xizhen they'd always heard about.

Her father lifted her up with both hands and placed her in a bobbing little boat with a bamboo awning. She sat down on a grass mat, which shone with a glossy sheen in the few places that weren't covered with patches. The awning overhead blocked her view, and all her hungry eyes could see were the bare feet of the boatman peddling away, along with her father's swaying back. She heard her father telling the boatman about sending her to Xizhen as a child bride to live with the Shen family.

Growing tired of listening to them talk, she peered out through a small gap between her father's back and the boatman's peddling feet at the vast expanse of water. The scene, along with the rocking of the little boat and the sound of the water swishing against the side, filled her with an unexpected happiness.

After about two *shichen,* she found herself once again lifted up by her father's hands, which this time placed her on a dock. With her right hand she held onto a corner of her father's clothing as they walked through the streets of Xizhen, her eyes sparkling like gold. It was the first time she'd seen brick houses with tile roofs, shop-lined streets, and so many people bustling about. Twice she hadn't realized her father had moved on, and she stood with her right hand still extended, as if she were still holding onto his clothing. Then her father would stop and wait for her to catch up. The first time he didn't say anything, but the second time he gave her a quiet reprimand. After that, she held onto his clothing with both hands, although it didn't stop her eyes from sparkling as she looked around.

They came to a halt in front of the Shen family's mending shop. Xiaomei stared curiously at the characters carved on the wooden oblong sign hanging beside the door—in the middle was character *zhi* 織 meaning "weave" or "knit," which she didn't recognize. Inside, Xiaomei laid eyes on her future husband's parents for the first time.

They were both busy in the shop, while at the same time instructing a young teenage boy in his mending work. Xiaomei didn't know that this boy, who was curiously examining her, was to one day be her husband. She maintained her grip on her father's clothing as he stammered out a polite introduction. Her future father-in-law gave a friendly look and got up to offer her father a seat; her future mother-in-law, on the other hand, stared at her coldly without saying a word, which was quite frightening. Just then she heard the rhythmic sound of voices behind her, and she turned to discover the surprising sight of four men panting and running down the street carrying a sedan chair.

Xiaomei stood in the Shen family's mending shop look-ing all around. This displeased her future mother-in-law, who felt her mind seemed a little too active. Yet at the same time Xiaomei did appear clean and pretty. For a while, the stern-looking woman couldn't make up her mind. Then she noticed that Xiaomei's clothes were made from scraps of cloth.

"How could you come into the Shen family home wearing that?" she said.

When Xiaomei's father heard his, he blushed and then turned pale. He leapt up from the stool on which he had just sat down and stuttered out a few words of parting, then took Xiaomei's hand and fled in shame.

Xiaomei's father pulled her so briskly through the streets of Xizhen she staggered to keep up, but her eyes still flashed with wonder as she looked around. They once again boarded the little boat with the bamboo awning, and without a word to the boatman, her father sat with his head bowed for the rest of the way, lost in thought. Xiaomei no longer sat shyly behind her father, but quietly crawled over to sit by his side. As the wide open scene spread out before her, the eyes of the ten-year-old Xiaomei danced with joy, and they continued to shine with that golden light until they reached Xilicun that evening.

2.

One month later, the Shen family of Xizhen sent someone to deliver a new set of blue calico clothes to the Ji family in Xilicun. By that time, the Ji family had already begun looking for a new family for Xiaomei to marry into, thinking that the Shens of Xizhen didn't want her. So they were caught quite off guard when someone delivered a new set of clothing to them from the Shens. Xiaomei's mother cried tears of joy, and her father giggled like a fool. They both went through the village letting everyone know the good news—the Shen family with the well-known mending shop in Xizhen felt their daughter was suitable for marriage.

"They're quite a good family," they exclaimed.

Although it was completely inappropriate, Xiaomei donned the blue calico clothes, and her three shabbily dressed brothers gathered around her. As they strolled through the village, Xiaomei's face flushed with excitement while her three brothers called after her,

"The bride, the bride!"

More of the village's shabbily dressed children ran up to her and joined in her brothers' announcements:

"The bride, the bride!"

A broad smile spread across her rosy, glowing face. Her happiness was not because she would soon become a bride, but because this was the first time she had ever worn brand new clothes.

Xiaomei's parents were in the middle of visiting the neighbors, telling them how Xiaomei would soon be entering into the Shen family who ran the mending shop in Xizhen, when they caught sight of her wearing her new calico clothes amidst calls of "the bride, the bride!" The expressions on the neighbors' faces turned from envy to laughter, while the faces of Xiaomei's parents went completely white. They dragged her home and took off the brand new clothes. But they were careful not to tear them off too quickly, and instead removed them with the utmost care.

Xiaomei's mother held the blue calico clothing up high to carefully inspect it in the sunlight for any specks of dirt, chattering the whole time about how they were going to send Xiaomei back to the Shen family in Xizhen the next day. Only when her mother finally announced that the new clothes hadn't gotten dirty did her father's anger finally cool.

Once again Xiaomei appeared in front of the Shen family's mending shop in Xizhen. The three pairs of eyes looking out of the shop lit up when they saw her. Dressed in the blue calico clothes, Xiaomei looked like a new person—she no longer looked like a country girl from a Wanmudang village, but like a city girl from Shendian. The tightly-pulled face of the stern mother-in-law nearly relaxed into a smile, and a feeling of gratification welled up within her. She finally felt she had made the right choice. Over the past month, she had taken a look at a few other prospective child brides, but they had all been rather average-looking girls with dull, expressionless faces. Upon further consideration she'd finally decided on this girl, whom she'd originally worried might be a bit too spirited.

But the next morning, the mother-in-law once again felt she may have made the wrong choice. When Xiaomei woke up, she discovered that her new blue calico clothing was missing, and that in its place beside her bed was a set of old clothes. She was so sad she began crying. This was different from when she was back in Xilicun and had the new clothes carefully removed from her—this time, she didn't know when she might be able to wear them again. Her mother-in-law sullenly came in and reproached her:

"What time is it? You're not even out of bed yet."

Xiaomei didn't yet know the rules and felt incredibly hurt and wronged. "My new clothing is gone," she said.

"How could those clothes be meant for everyday use?" her mother-in-law answered coldly.

With that, her mother-in-law turned and left. The back of this woman who had only recently entered middle age was as stiff and straight as an old door plank. She feared that Xiaomei beginning her first morning with the family in tears was a bad omen, and she began to feel like perhaps she should send this foolish young girl back to her Wanmudang village.

Over the following days, these sorts of thoughts gradually receded from the mother-in-law's mind. Even dressed in old clothing, Xiaomei was still pretty and clever, but also hardworking and diligent. When she swept the floors or wiped the tables, she never left a trace of dirt. Although her stern mother-in-law said nothing, she saw it all with her eyes and remembered it in her heart.

After a month with the Shen family, Xiaomei began to learn how to patch and mend. The fact that her mother-in-law decided to pass down the family craft to Xiaomei indicated her acceptance of this child bride. Her mother-in-law even discovered that Xiaomei was quite good at it, and after two months, Xiaomei's skills had already surpassed those of her own son, who had been learning for two years.

3.

From the bits and pieces of information she gathered, Xiaomei learned that her kind and agreeable father-in-law had married into the Shen family. He was from a poor family in Shendian, and at the age of twelve he had come to the Shen family's mending shop in Xizhen as an apprentice. Because he was so affable, honest, industrious, and eager to learn, the shopkeeper took a real liking to him—not only did he teach him the art of mending, but he also taught him how to read and write, and even betrothed his daughter to him. When he was seventeen he officially married into the family. In those days, when it was expected that women should always be respectful and subservient to men, he acted as if it were just the opposite—he was always modest and polite with his wife, listening to everything she had to say and doing as she asked. Once a week, this man who had married into his wife's family would go to the chamber of commerce to collect the old newspapers, which he would diligently pore over in his spare time and return back to the chamber of commerce when he was finished. The newspapers were all from Shanghai and had been ordered by Gu Yimin—when he was finished with them, he would take them to the chamber of commerce for others to read. Xiaomei's father-in-law was an avid reader of these old newspapers; it was his only pastime. As Aqiang grew older, he would also let him read the papers. He was afraid that his son would soil them, so he made him wash his hands before reading. Aqiang would always be filled with excitement when he saw the newspapers, although he was less interested in what was written in them than in the pictures and illustrations, which were all in the ads.

Now that Xiaomei was living with the Shen family in Xizhen, the lively, spirited nature of her Wanmudang childhood had to be buried away deep in her heart. Quietly, her desire all became concentrated on the new set of blue calico clothing.

She thought of these clothes constantly. When she dusted the wardrobe in her mother-in-law's room, her movements were filled with the utmost care, as if she were gently stroking the furniture instead of cleaning it. Her mother-in-law was pleased when she saw this, thinking she was a careful and meticulous girl. But Xiaomei was in fact yearning for her calico clothes, which she knew were kept there. This wardrobe in her mother-in-law's room had once been a bright vermillion, but had gradually darkened over time.

Xiaomei wiped it gingerly, thinking all the time of those beautiful clothes. Then one day, both her mother-in-law and father-in-law were out of the house. For the first time, Xiaomei opened the wardrobe. The door made a heavy creak as she opened it, which startled her. Then she sensed someone had come up behind her. Timidly she turned her head and saw it was that boy, the same age as her, standing in the doorway. This future husband of hers looked at her uncertainly, not knowing what she was up to.

Relieved, Xiaomei turned back to the wardrobe and examined it carefully. The clothes inside were all neatly stacked and folded, and her calico clothes were on the very bottom, pressed down by layer upon layer of her mother-in-law's own clothes. Xiaomei pulled out her set. Right there in front of the wardrobe, under the watchful gaze of her future husband, she took off her old, patched-up clothing and changed into the new calico outfit. Then she walked over to the mirror and admired herself as if no one else were there. When she turned to look at the boy standing behind her, he noticed the golden light sparkling in her eyes.

At the age of ten, Xiaomei and Aqiang had already arrived at an unspoken mutual understanding, like that of a married couple. From that day on, if the two adults went out, Xiaomei would immediately go into her mother-in-law's room, take off her shabby old clothes, change into the new calico ones, and indulge herself in front of the mirror. Aqiang would sit dutifully on the threshold of the shop, keeping a lookout for his future wife. As soon as he saw his parents appear in the distance on their way home, he would shout,

"They're coming!"

When Xiaomei heard his warning, she would take the clothes off as quickly as possible, fold them up, and stick them back under her mother-in-law's clothes. By the time her mother-in-law was back home, Xiaomei would already be wearing her old, patched-up clothes, carefully dusting the gradually darkening vermillion wardrobe.

4.

Aqiang was the kind of person who could easily get distracted, which remained the case as he sat on the threshold serving as a look-out for Xiaomei—sooner or later, as they say, the filling would come out of the bun. One day, about two months later, after staring at people coming and going on the street for such a long time, Aqiang somehow failed to realize his parents had returned. Not until his father slapped him on the forehead did he break out of his stupor—he immediately leapt up from the threshold but didn't see anyone. Just as he was beginning to think something strange was going on, he received another

306 · YU HUA

slap on his forehead. This time he turned around to find his father standing inside and his mother about to head into her room—he had no idea when his parents had passed by him. Like a shepherd trying to mend the fold after the sheep are lost, and with a terrible sense of timing, he called out,

"They're back!"

His mother saw Xiaomei wearing her blue calico clothes and admiring herself in front of the mirror. The ten-year-old girl had both of her arms stretched out and was striking a series of simple, innocent poses. To her mother-in-law's eyes, however, they carried a lewd undertone. As soon as Xiaomei heard Aqiang's shout, she quickly began undressing—but when she turned around, she was faced with the cold, hard stare of her mother-in-law. Everything in front of her eyes went dark—she blinked a few times, but once again saw her mother-in-law's shadowy frame standing in the doorway. Xiaomei began to tremble.

Aqiang's shouting had revealed that he was Xiaomei's accomplice, and the punishment started with him. At first, this absent-minded young boy hadn't even realized he was in trouble, and had watched with curiosity as his father bolted the door to the shop, wondering why they were closing up so early. Then his parents moved two wicker chairs out into the courtyard and sat down in them, a cane in his father's hand. Xiaomei stood in front of them trembling, while Aqiang still hadn't caught on to what was happening. His father shouted at him,

"Bring out the bench!"

Only then did Aqiang realize that disaster was about to befall him. Hanging his head, he went inside and came back out with the bench, which he placed in front of his parents. Then he dutifully undid his belt and pulled down his pants, exposing his bare bottom as he lay face-down on the bench. He closed his eyes and heard his father ask his mother in a low voice,

"How many?"

After a moment's hesitation, she answered: "Ten."

A faint smile appeared on Aqiang's face as he secretly said to himself: It's a light punishment. Xiaomei noticed Aqiang's fleeting expression, which surprised her. When she was still in the Wanmudang village of Xilicun, she would often see her father string her three brothers up in a tree and beat them with a switch. Their cries and shouts were like livestock being slaughtered, rising up and echoing into the vast sky. Xiaomei was used to that scenario, and it didn't frighten her—whenever her father was in a foul mood, her brothers would wail in pain. But now she found herself in this narrow courtyard, with her future husband silently lying face-down on the bench as his father whipped him with a switch, and his mother looked on expressionlessly. The nonchalant nature of the violence scared her.

Aqiang never cried or screamed. He clenched his teeth and counted, and when he reached ten, that faint smile reappeared. When his father put down the switch, he got up from the bench and dutifully pulled his pants back up, buckled his belt, and moved the bench back inside. The injuries caused him to waddle back and forth like a duck. Then he waddled back out of the house and stood in front of Xiaomei, waiting for his parents to punish the next offender. Xiaomei assumed it was now her turn, but her future husband had already moved the bench back inside, so they were lacking the necessary requirements. She stood there waiting, afraid and confused.

Her father-in-law and mother-in-law got up and went inside, while Aqiang remained standing in front of Xiaomei. Xiaomei looked at him uneasily. Much to her surprise, he yawned, turned around, and waddled back inside the house. Xiaomei was the only one left in the courtyard, along with the two wicker chairs, as if she had been forgotten. But fear had not forgotten her, and as she stood in the courtyard awaiting her punishment, each minute seemed like an eternity.

5.

Xiaomei's punishment took place indoors after nightfall. By the light of an oil lamp, Xiaomei's future father-in-law drafted a letter and passed it to his wife, who, by the light of the same lamp, carefully looked it over and nodded. Her father-in-law got their seal and ink and placed them in front of his wife.

Xiaomei stood off to the side and watched the whole process of drawing up this document of divorce. She watched them anxiously, sitting there together as if they were conducting routine business. As her father-in-law drafted the letter, he would periodically look up and ask his wife something; she would then respond silently, either nodding or shaking her head. From the few words they exchanged, Xiaomei knew something bad loomed on the horizon—they wanted to send her back to her Wanmudang village of Xilicun. Her shoulders shook as she clenched her teeth and tried to keep from crying.

Her mother-in-law held up the letter for Xiaomei to see, then put it down on the table and said, "Take this letter with you and give it to your father."

Just as her mother-in-law was about to tell her she was sending her back to Wanmudang, Xiaomei suddenly said to her in a low voice, "That's not a letter."

"If it's not a letter, what is it?" her mother-in-law asked.

"A bill of divorce," answered Xiaomei, biting her lips.

This took her mother-in-law by surprise. She carefully examined Xiaomei, who was standing in the shadows. This girl was actually quite smart, she thought.

"You haven't officially joined our family," her mother-in-law replied, "so it can't be considered divorce."

Then she shook her head and corrected herself:

"Well, I suppose you could call it a bill of divorce."

The mother-in-law watched Xiaomei for a while, then slowly began to explain:

"The ancients said there are seven reasons a wife should be

dismissed: if she's unfilial, she goes; if she's barren, she goes; if she's licentious, she goes; if she's jealous, she goes; if she's diseased, she goes; if she gossips, she goes; if she steals, she goes."

As her mother-in-law pressed the seal into the ink, she asked Xiaomei, "Which rule did you violate?"

Her mother-in-law lifted the seal from the ink and held it under the lamplight as she stared at Xiaomei, who answered sorrowfully,

"Stealing."

"No," said her mother-in-law, shaking her head. "You didn't take the clothes out of the room."

Xiaomei nodded and thought some more. Then she lowered her head and said ashamedly,

"Licentiousness."

As soon as she said this, Xiaomei finally burst into tears. Her hands fell down to her sides, and her shoulders shook as she cried softly. Her mother-in-law, still holding the seal up in the air, began to feel some compassion, thinking that it wasn't so easy to come by such a clever girl as Xiaomei. Instead of pressing the seal onto the letter, she got a rag and slowly began wiping off the deep-red ink. When she had finished cleaning the seal, she said,

"Considering that you're still young and don't know any better, we won't send you back just yet."

Xiaomei opened her mouth, but couldn't contain her crying. By the light of the lamp she saw her mother-in-law furrow her brow, and she immediately sucked in her breath. It was as if she had somehow inhaled all of her tears, and her crying ceased.

After this narrow escape, Xiaomei never again opened that dark vermillion wardrobe. From then on, the wardrobe stood like a gloomy mausoleum, the calico clothing she once dreamt of day and night now buried there in its grave.

With the approach of the lunar new year, the children of the well-do-do families of Xizhen all donned new clothing. Aqiang wore a new grayish blue *changshan* and put some pomade in his hair, which gave him the appearance of a young gentleman. Xiaomei, however, was still in an old set of clothes; the only difference was that these didn't have patches. On the first day of the new year, her strict mother-in-law would not allow her to wear her blue calico clothes, indicating that the punishment was not yet over. Xiaomei looked out at the children on the street playing happily in their new clothes, then down at the old things she was wearing, which had been washed clean and white. She couldn't keep from tearing up, and found herself pining for the calico clothes in the wardrobe.

Another year sailed by uneventfully, and Xiaomei passed her second new year in Xizhen. This time her mother-in-law allowed her to wear her calico outfit, but by this point it was too small, and the arms and sleeves were all too short. When she was twelve, she donned a new set of clothes in her beloved calico and walked out from under the watchful eyes of her mother-in-law and into the street, under the gaze of the crowd. By now, though, Xiaomei no longer had that golden light dancing in her eyes.

6.

Xiaomei's mother-in-law molded her in her own image. She taught Xiaomei how to read and write, patch and mend, and look after the accounts. By the time Xiaomei was sixteen, her mother-in-law saw a faint image of herself as a young woman. Xiaomei was clean and tidy, serious and reserved, thrifty and industrious. Now that she and Aqiang had reached a marriageable age, her mother-in-law decided to pick a date for the wedding ceremony.

With their mending business, the Shen family of Xizhen was considered relatively well-off. According to the custom, Xiaomei should return to her family's home in the Wanmudang village of Xilicun and wait for someone from the Shen family to come and fetch her. But her mother-in-law, always looking to economize, decided to skip this tradition and simply invite

Xiaomei's parents for a meal and have a simple ceremony. Then, when the couple went to bed that evening, the marriage would be consummated.

So, on a bright and windy winter afternoon, Xiaomei's parents and her three brothers appeared in front of the Shen family's mending shop, all wearing cotton *mian'ao* jackets covered with patches. All five of them had their hands tucked up in their sleeves, and all five of their faces wore the same obsequious expression.

The letter that the Shen family sent to the Wanmudang village of Xilicun had only invited Xiaomei and her parents for a meal; they hadn't expected that Xiaomei's three brothers would also come. So when her father-in-law first spotted the five people standing outside the shop, he assumed they were customers and didn't think much of it. He said to them politely,

"Today is a day of great happiness for the Shen family, so we are closed for the day."

Upon hearing this, the five people outside the shop exchanged glances and then began giggling. This confused Xiaomei's father-in-law—he had expected them to say a few words of congratulations and be on their way, but they instead continued to stand there grinning.

Then Xiaomei's father announced: "We're the Ji family from Xilicun . . . "

As soon as Xiaomei's father-in-law realized it was the bride's family, he immediately turned to usher them inside the shop.

"After six years, I didn't recognize you," he said.

Xiaomei's father, his hands tucked up in his sleeves, voiced his understanding while ushering in the four others of his party. One by one, they entered the main hall. Xiaomei's parents were invited to sit down in wicker chairs, while her three brothers squeezed onto a bench.

Xiaomei's mother-in-law came out to offer a few words of greeting and took a seat by her husband. Then Xiaomei and Aqiang appeared. Aqiang looked over Xiaomei's parents and each of her brothers. When he saw that they were all smiling ingratiatingly at him, he returned a bashful smile.

Xiaomei stood there in a daze. Six years seemed to have passed in an instant. For six years she hadn't had any contact with her parents or brothers, and now suddenly there they were, all hunched over with their hands pulled up in their sleeves—they seemed so unfamiliar to her she hardly recognized them. Her parents sat in the wicker chairs grinning from ear to ear, while her three brothers eyed her curiously from the bench as if they were observing some strange new thing. She felt that they weren't the eyes of her brothers, but the stares of unfamiliar men.

Then, she saw a tear form in the corner of her mother's eye. As her mother lifted her hand to wipe it away, a distant emotion was finally called forth from deep within Xiaomei's heart. She realized her family had come.

At dinner that evening, Xiaomei saw how reserved and cautious her parents and brothers were, which pained her so much she lowered her head. Her mother-in-law had laid out a sumptuous feast, but these five poor peasants from the Wanmudang nibbled at it timidly. Even though their stomachs were growling, and the luscious scents of all sorts of wonderful dishes filled their nostrils, they all kept their hands tucked up as they sat, as if waiting for something. Only when their father finally reached out a hand, picked up his chopsticks, and placed a morsel of meat in his mouth, did the other four follow suit; when he returned his hand to his sleeve, the other four did the same. Then they waited some more. The next to act was Xiaomei's older brother, who bravely reached out his hand once more. Encouraged by his boldness, the other four did as well, although when he returned his hand, the others did so, too. All their hands continued slipping in and out of their sleeves as if they were pickpockets. Xiaomei remained seated with her head bowed, as her sadness mixed with a feeling of inferiority. When her father-in-law and mother-in-law had finished eating, they put down their chopsticks and sat sullenly. Only Aqiang ate with gusto, smacking his shiny, oily lips.

Finally the long, somber dinner was over, and the ceremony could begin. Xiaomei's mother-in-law hadn't prepared the traditional wedding headdress, red veil, or red silk undergarments, and had only provided a red cotton *mian'ao* jacket, red cotton pants, and a pair of red embroidered shoes. She had economized in every way she should have, and even in ways she shouldn't. The tradition of the twelve eggs she had decided to keep. When she helped Xiaomei change into her red outfit in the bedroom, she brought along twelve eggs and dropped them one by one down through the waist of Xiaomei's pants, letting them roll down the leg and out through the bottom cuff. As Xiaomei felt each of the cold eggs roll from her upper leg down to her shin, it felt as if each one paused to knock on her kneecap. Each egg made it down without breaking. When her mother-in-law had collected them all from the bottom of Xiaomei's pants, she told Xiaomei that the twelve eggs symbolized the twelve months. Because they had all slid down without breaking, it meant that she would be able to give birth to a child in any month as smoothly as a hen laying an egg.

Xiaomei nodded earnestly, as she had become used to doing in her life with the Shen family. For the past six years, whenever her mother-in-law spoke, Xiaomei would listen and nod.

Now, dressed in red from head to toe, Xiaomei entered the main hall. Aqiang was dressed in a long *changpao* gown covered with a *magua* jacket, and she stood next to him, shoulder-to-shoulder. Once they had performed their obeisance to heaven and earth, then to Aqiang's parents, and finally to each other as husband and wife, the wedding of this child bride came to its hasty conclusion.

Xiaomei's parents and brothers then stood up to take their leave. They had arrived like a group of five strangers, and now they were leaving in the same way. Late in the evening, they left the Shen family home after making an obsequious farewell display.

When they left, only Xiaomei's mother looked back, although she was unable to spy Xiaomei. Tears filled her eyes once more.

These five reserved, timid figures left the Shen family home and walked out to the main street of Xizhen. Immediately they recovered their lively spirits, naturally developed through their lives spent out in the open fields. They chattered so loudly through the quiet streets it was like they were shouting to each other across rice paddies rather than walking side by side. Everything out of their mouths was praise—they praised the stately air of the Shen family's stone and tile-roofed house; the lavish spread of delicacies on the table; the dignified look of the groom in his *changpao* and *magua*; and Xiaomei's noble appearance in her red outfit. Xiaomei's mother nodded along while drying her eyes. These were happy tears of gratification—her daughter had married into a good family.

As they walked toward the Xizhen wharf, they got lost three times. Xiaomei's father was the only one who had been to Xizhen before. Each time they got lost, they would stand in the street and have a loud discussion. Then their father would indicate the way he felt they should go, and they would all follow. Their conversation eventually made its way back to that extravagant feast, which got their stomachs rumbling and their mouths watering all over again. The five of them finally arrived at the Xizhen wharf amidst a spirited discussion of the meal's many dishes. Then they woke a boatman from his slumber and boarded his little boat with a bamboo awning, all the while continuing to talk about the meal. About two *shichen* later they arrived back in Xilicun, just as the first pale rays of the morning sun were beginning to shine on their ramshackle thatched cottage.

7.

On that cheerless first night of her marriage, Xiaomei coiled up her braid and bid farewell to her childhood. Then she and Aqiang entered the nuptial chamber.

Xiaomei sat down quietly in a chair and listened to her parents and brothers leave the Shen family home and walk through the streets of Xizhen. Then she heard her father-in-law and mother-in-law go into their room and shut the door with a clack.

Xiaomei waited with her head bowed, unsure of what she should do at this point. She knew no one was coming to their room to tease them and make a fuss, as was the tradition—there would be none of the traditional songs; no one snickering and hiding outside the door or under the window; no one to spread any jokes or gossip about her wedding night to their friends and neighbors.

The groom, still wearing his *changpao* and *magua,* sat on the edge of the bed and yawned. Then he got up and walked over to Xiaomei. Although they had spent the past six years growing up together, and although for six years she had known that this person would become her husband, as he approached her now on their wedding night, she became nervous, and her heart began pounding. This young master of the mending shop fixed his eyes on Xiaomei as he casually strolled around her. Like a dog on the hunt circling its prey, he considered how to approach her, and for a while he couldn't decide. Xiaomei watched his shadow drawing back and forth across the floor. Then it stopped, and she felt her body tremble. But then the shadow moved away, and Xiaomei's trembling body gradually calmed down. As she watched the shadow on the ground, she suddenly saw it reach out a hand and rush toward her. What happened next was a blur; it all happened in an instant. She left the chair and ended up on the bed, where the groom laid her down on her back. She spread her arms to indicate her submission—after six years with the Shen family, she was already well accustomed to submission, and her wedding night was no different. She closed her eyes and gritted her teeth, never uttering a sound, allowing her panting, sweating husband to clumsily do with her as he pleased.

The first morning after their wedding, Xiaomei rose early as usual. By the time her mother-in-law had gotten up, Xiaomei had already made breakfast and was busy diligently sweeping the floor. Her mother-in-law hadn't expected this—the tradition in Xizhen was for the new bride not to do any cooking for three days after the wedding. Seeing Xiaomei hard at work as usual the very next day pleased her mother-in-law immensely. Then she noticed Xiaomei wasn't wearing her red jacket, red pants, or embroidered shoes, but was instead dressed in an old cotton *mian'ao,* with her hair pulled back into a bun. Her mother-in-law didn't know when she had secretly learned how to put her hair in a bun, although it was clear she'd not yet mastered it, as a few strands were already falling loose. When Xiaomei looked up from her sweeping and saw her mother-in-law standing in front of her, she assumed she was in her way, so she immediately stood off to the side with her broom.

Her mother-in-law looked at her and smiled. She vaguely began to recall Xiaomei's first morning in the Shen household six years ago, when she had burst into tears because she couldn't find that set of blue calico clothes. Now, the morning after her wedding, she had already taken off her bridal clothing. A tender warmth welled up in her mother-in-law's heart. She took Xiaomei by the hand, pressed her down by the shoulders into a chair, and proceeded to fix her hair. When she was done, she took the silver hairclip from her own hair and put it in Xiaomei's bun.

Xiaomei kept her head lowered in silence. Her mother-in-law had given her something of her own—it was the first time in six years she had felt any sort of affection from this stern woman. Without making a sound, Xiaomei began to weep, her tear drops falling one after the other onto the front of her jacket.

8.

Xiaomei rose early and went to bed late. In addition to the mending, she also had to manage the housework—she seemed not to have a moment to spare, yet her hair was always brushed back and shiny, with her bun in the back clasped by the silver hairclip.

One winter day three years after the wedding, a shabbily dressed man showed up in front of the Shen family's mending shop. Xiaomei's father-in-law, mother-in-law, and husband happened to be away in Shendian that day, where a relative had invited them to a feast in celebration of completing their new house. Xiaomei remained alone in the shop, sitting with her head bent over as she nimbly worked on some mending. The man stood outside for a long time. Although she was busy, she sensed that someone was lingering outside the shop. She raised her head and looked indifferently at the person outside, then looked back down and continued her mending, thinking it was just a beggar.

Finally, this beggar-like man opened his mouth and called out: "Sister."

Taken by surprise, Xiaomei raised her head and stared at the man, who said, "Sister, it's your little brother."

As if clearing years of accumulated dust from her eyes, an image from her memory came into focus, and she recognized the youthful but exhausted face of her youngest brother. In a soft voice, she exclaimed,

"Ah, it's my little brother."

Xiaomei stood up. She looked rather uneasily around her in the shop, then remembered that everyone had gone to Shendian, and she was the only one there. She calmed down and said to her brother outside,

"Brother—come in."

At that moment, the eyes of Xiaomei's little brother filled with tears. He shook his head and remained outside as he launched into a long, drawn-out story, which began with the approaching marriage of his second oldest brother and a woman named Caifeng, who was clearly the bride-to-be. Seeing the look of confusion of Xiaomei's face, her brother stopped and mentioned the name of another village in the Wanmudang, which was where Caifeng was from. Xiaomei scoured the depths of her memory, then gave a slight nod. With this, her brother continued on to another family in his own village, but this time Xiaomei was unable to locate their name in her memory. But her brother prattled on, no longer paying attention to the expression on Xiaomei's face. He said that Caifeng was a relative of that family, as was the person who had acted as the matchmaker for his brother. Xiaomei nodded, seeming to understand. Her brother continued to ramble, eventually getting to something about a pig named "Little Fatso," which he kept mentioning over and over. He told all about Little Fatso growing up, and how he took Little Fatso on the boat to Xizhen. Xiaomei stared at him in bewilderment, unsure at first at who this Little Fatso was—only when he mentioned selling Little Fatso to the butcher in Xizhen did she realize it was a pig. Babbling on, her brother said that the money from selling Little Fatso was supposed to be for his brother's wedding, but the string of copper coins he'd gotten in return for the pig was now gone. At this point he began sobbing. Then he opened up his ragged *mian'ao* jacket and reached into his breast pocket to show Xiaomei there was nothing there.

Xiaomei understood what her brother was getting at. He'd lost the string of coppers he'd gotten from selling the pig; perhaps they'd been stolen by one of Xizhen's petty thieves. He didn't dare go home, so he'd come here to stand outside the shop and tell his tale of woe. Xiaomei felt uncomfortable as she looked at him. The drawer beside her was filled with copper coins, but they belonged to the Shen family, not her. She had lived with the Shen family for eight years, and had never had even a single coin for her own use. As she listened in a daze to her brother's rambling lament, he seemed so unfamiliar—even when she thought of her parents and her other brothers back in the Wanmudang village of Xilicun, they all seemed just as distant as this brother standing before her. She'd had no contact with them for eight years, other than the day of her wedding.

Then the contents of her little brother's soliloquy changed. He said that his father and two older brothers had come to Xizhen, walked up to the Shen family's mending shop, and caught a glimpse of Xiaomei inside. Because her husband's parents had both been there, they hadn't dared go in. It hurt Xiaomei to hear this—this was the pain of a child bride. Her brother continued, saying that today he had also stood outside for a long time, only daring to walk closer once he saw she was alone in the shop.

This moved Xiaomei deeply. She unconsciously took a step forward and opened the drawer with her right hand. Then she picked up some copper coins tied together with a string and, holding them in both hands, quickly delivered them over to her brother standing just outside on the other side of the counter. Her brother hastened to accept them. Then he noisily placed them on the counter, undid the string, and began counting them out loud one by one. When he reached the number he'd gotten in exchange for the pig, he took the remaining coins off the string and returned them to Xiaomei.

"Sister," he said, "this is extra."

Xiaomei woodenly took the extra coins and returned them to the drawer. Her brother slowly re-tied the string on the coins Xiaomei had given him and carefully placed them in his breast pocket. Then he dried his eyes and gave Xiaomei a simple, honest smile.

"Sister," he said, "I should be on my way."

Xiaomei nodded. As he left, she saw that he had both arms crossed in front of his chest, protecting the coins. After he'd gone, Xiaomei sat down on a stool and continued her mending, but her hands seemed to have lost their dexterity, and she could only slowly fumble through.

Xiaomei grew uneasy. Her anxiety seemed to expand like vast fields stretching out before her. Her mother-in-law's stern face appeared now and again before her eyes, and Xiaomei trembled with fear—she realized she had made a horrible mistake. She knew she shouldn't have given her brother any money while her mother-in-law was away; she should have sent him back home to Xilicun, waited for her mother-in-law to return, requested the money from her then, and only then sent for her brother to come back to get it. Thinking of this, Xiaomei smiled bitterly. She knew she'd never dare make such a request to her mother-in-law's face, and that it was only in her absence that she had the courage to act so boldly.

9.

It was a stifling afternoon. Xiaomei was afraid, but afraid of what? She didn't know. She just sat there with her head down, lost in thought. When she heard the neighbors calling their children in for supper, she looked up and saw that the sky had already begun to darken. She realized that her father-in-law, mother-in-law, and husband would soon be returning, but she hadn't even started making dinner. She jumped up and went into the kitchen.

By the time it was dark out, the three of them had returned from their relative's housewarming feast in Shendian. Xiaomei's father-in-law and husband saw that the door to the shop was wide open, so they closed it up for the night. Her mother-in-law marched straight into the kitchen with an angry look on her face and reproached Xiaomei, who was busy preparing the meal:

"It's dark out and you haven't even closed up the shop?"

Xiaomei trembled with fear and considered saying she just had forgotten to lock up, but she didn't dare say anything like that. Her mother-in-law continued to upbraid her:

"It's this late, and you're still making dinner?"

Xiaomei trembled again, and her mother-in-law left the kitchen without saying anything else. She went out through the courtyard and over to the shop where, by the light of an oil lamp, she opened the drawer and took out the account book.

She counted the copper coins and figured up the income from the two days she had been gone. When she discovered that a significant amount was missing, she remained silent for a moment, then shut the ledger, closed the drawer, and went back into the kitchen. Xiaomei was just in the process of bringing the dishes over to the table, where the other two family members were seated and waiting for their meal. In an icy tone, her mother-in-law said,

"Come here."

Xiaomei wiped her hands on her apron and followed her mother-in-law out to the shop. When her mother-in-law put the account book and the copper coins from the drawer up on the counter, Xiaomei began rambling incoherently, just as her brother had done that afternoon. When her mother-in-law had gotten the gist, she expressionlessly returned the ledger and remaining coins to the drawer and walked past Xiaomei out through the courtyard and back to the kitchen.

The steaming hot food was already on the table, where Xiaomei's father-in-law and husband were seated and waiting, yet to touch their chopsticks. By the dim, flickering light of the oil lamp, Xiaomei's mother-in-law walked over and sat down. The two men noticed her somber expression as she picked up her chopsticks, although she didn't move them toward the rice or other dishes—she seemed to be thinking of something. Xiaomei's father-in-law didn't eat anything, either, but merely held his chopsticks and gazed at this woman in charge of the household. Aqiang kept to himself and slowly began eating. Xiaomei walked in with her head bowed, shivering as if she were freezing, and cautiously sat down at the table.

To Xiaomei's mother-in-law—the family's unilateral decision-maker, with her rigid, dogmatic ideas—the fact that Xiaomei took the coppers and gave them to her brother before getting permission made it theft. Xiaomei had first entered the Shen family eight years ago, when she was young and didn't know yet how to act—she had secretly tried on the calico clothes, which had prompted her mother-in-law to consider sending her back, although ultimately they kept her. Now she would have to think once more about how to punish Xiaomei.

When the seemingly endless dinner was over, Xiaomei washed up the dishes and cleaned the kitchen. Then she walked uneasily into the main hall, and back into the scene that had transpired eight years before.

Her mother-in-law was sitting there stern and erect, while her father-in-law was drafting a letter by the light of the oil lamp. When he heard Xiaomei's footsteps, he raised his head and let out a slight sigh when he saw her; then he lowered his head and continued writing. Xiaomei's husband Aqiang wore a confused expression—he opened his mouth when he saw her enter the room, but no sound came out. Xiaomei's mother-in-law gave her a slight nod, indicating she should sit. Xiaomei sat down on a stool some distance away, her hands shaking as she placed them on her lap. She saw the seal and the ink setting beside the letter her father-in-law was writing, and she knew what was about to happen—a bill of divorce would send her back to the Wanmudang village of Xilicun she had left eight years before. Xiaomei felt tears welling in the corners of her eyes, but she bit her lip and refused to let them fall.

Xiaomei's father-in-law would shake his head slightly, write for a bit, and then stop, proceeding indecisively. He raised his head several times and looked at the female head of the household as if he wanted to say something, but her stern expression stopped the words in his throat, and he could only lower his head and continue writing. When he had finished, he passed it over to her. After carefully reading it over, she was completely dissatisfied.

"Why didn't you mention theft?" she asked.

Xiaomei's father-in-law looked nervously at her mother-in-law and explained,

"Giving some assistance to her own brother shouldn't be considered theft, should it?"

Xiaomei's mother-in-law was stunned. For over twenty years

this man had done whatever she asked, and this was the first time he had ever shown any resistance. She shook her head and turned to her son, forcing him to weigh in:

"What do you think?"

A look of clarity appeared on Aqiang's worried, hesitant face as he echoed his father:

"Giving some assistance to her own brother shouldn't be considered theft."

Tears escaped from Xiaomei's eyes, while her stern mother-in-law remained unfazed. Her supreme authority in the family was being challenged, and for the longest while she didn't react, as if her mind had wandered. Then she turned toward Xiaomei and stiffly recited the same thing she had said to her eight years before:

"There are seven reasons a wife should be dismissed: if she's unfilial, she goes; if she's barren, she goes; if she's licentious, she goes; if she's jealous, she goes; if she's diseased, she goes; if she gossips, she goes; if she steals, she goes."

She saw Xiaomei's whole body tremble as tears began streaming down her face. Then she asked her the same question she posed eight years ago:

"Which rule did you violate?"

Xiaomei covered her face with both hands, tears streaming through her fingers. In a quivering voice, she answered,

"Stealing."

Xiaomei's mother-in-law nodded and turned to look at her husband. This man who had married into the family over twenty years earlier lowered his head and said nothing. Then she turned toward her son, who didn't look at her; his brows were knitted over the silently crying Xiaomei. Then she raised her voice and said:

"It's theft."

As she spoke, she held up the letter which had so dissatisfied her and handed it back to her husband. With absolute certainty, she said:

"Write, 'theft.'"

Xiaomei's father-in-law picked up his writing brush. After hesitating for a moment, he put it down again and said in a low voice,

"For the past eight years, Xiaomei has been considerate and obedient, hardworking and filial. Why must it be like this?"

Xiaomei's mother-in-law stared at her husband as if she didn't recognize him—he had now defied her twice in a row. Then she looked at her son. Aqiang lowered his head and avoided her eyes. Then, unyieldingly, he said,

"She's my wife; it should be my decision."

Xiaomei's mother-in-law stared at her son in shock. Then she ripped up the unfinished letter into four pieces and laid them beside the lamp. She looked over at her husband, sitting silently with his head bowed, and her son, whose face had turned pale with anger. She then turned her gaze to Xiaomei, who had accepted her fate and stopped crying. In a small voice, she begged her mother-in-law,

"You needn't write a bill of divorce—I'll leave on my own."

Xiaomei's mother-in-law shook her head. Picking up one of the ripped pieces of paper, she said to Xiaomei,

"This is a letter of disciplinary action, not a bill of divorce. As punishment you'll return to Xilicun for two months."

Xiaomei hadn't thought that her punishment would just be returning to Xilicun in the Wanmudang for a couple months, after which time she would return to the Shen family in Xizhen. Once again Xiaomei's tears burst forth, and she said through sobs,

"It won't happen again."

Xiaomei's father-in-law and husband, however, didn't feel there should be any punishment at all—Xiaomei had done nothing wrong by helping out her own family; moreover, it wasn't even a large sum of money. Her father-in-law once more said to her mother-in-law,

"Why must it be like this?"

Aqiang followed his father with a firm statement to his mother:

"It shouldn't be like this."

Aggrieved, Xiaomei's mother-in-law looked at her husband and son. Her intention had been to use a lot of lightning and thunder to deliver only a light punishment for Xiaomei, but her husband and son were opposed even to this. Pushed to exasperation, she wearily said to Aqiang and Xiaomei,

"Tomorrow morning, we'll go out through the west gate and onto the main road, and solve this according to the old Xizhen custom."

With that, she got up and went upstairs. Xiaomei's father-in-law and husband remained seated—they were both in shock. Never had they imagined that she would come to such a decision—they had only intended to speak up on Xiaomei's behalf, but they had ended up doing more harm than good. They knew that once water had spilled, it was spilled, and there was no way to gather it back up. At a loss, they looked at Xiaomei, who offered them an unconvincing smile through her tears.

Xiaomei saw the direction her fate was headed. After spending eight years in Xizhen, she had become familiar with all the local customs, so she knew what her mother-in-law was referring to—the three of them would walk out to the main road, and then she and her mother-in-law would head in opposite directions, forcing her husband to make the choice to follow either her or his mother. Xiaomei had heard of two examples of this method of divorce being carried out—in both cases, the husbands had been reluctant to part with their wives and hadn't been able to bring themselves to draw up a bill of divorce. So their mothers brought them out to the main road and walked in the opposite direction from their wives. In both cases the men eventually followed their mothers, deciding that filial piety came first. Her own husband was a filial son, Xiaomei thought, and would most likely do the same. She stopped crying and dried her eyes with the front of her garment. Her tears had come from her hope to remain, but a sense of hopelessness now calmed her down. She got up and left the table and, as usual, went to fetch warm water for her father-in-law and mother-in-law to wash their feet, even though her mother-in-law had already gone upstairs.

10.

That evening for Xiaomei was both endless and fleeting. She took this as her last night with this man she had known for eight years and shared a bed with for two.

For the two years they had shared a bed, only one scenario ever played out. Once Aqiang got under the covers, he moved his hands and not his mouth. He would hastily remove her undergarments, then brusquely crawl on top of her and insert himself. For the past two years, except for his panting and a few moans before climax, he never uttered any other sounds in the bed. For the past six months, after pulling off her underpants, he became too lazy to bother with her other clothing. Her breasts seemed to have been almost completely forgotten, except for the few times he would remember and stick his hand up under her shirt to give them a little squeeze.

This evening was different. After he took off her underpants, he removed the rest of her undergarments; then he wrapped his arms and legs around her and held her in a full embrace—she felt her body become bound to his. Then he started nibbling her. He began with her lips, kissing them forcefully—when Xiaomei tasted salt, she knew he had broken the skin. Then he moved down to her chin, with long, deep bites that nearly caused her to cry out in pain. But then his mouth relaxed and he began nibbling her shoulders, moving from left to right, nipping here and there. Then his mouth made its way to her breasts, where he lingered for a long time. She was able to bear the pain until he began biting her nipples, at which point she let out a few soft moans. He followed the contours of her naked body as he nibbled his way downward, until his whole body was under the blankets.

When he made it down to her thigh, his butt stuck up so high that it raised the blankets and let in some cold air. Afraid he would catch a chill, Xiaomei stuck her feet out of the blanket and used her toes to pull it tightly together. Finally his mouth reached her nether region, which was sensitive and painful. It was at that point that she began to shed tears, knowing that this man did not want her to go. He climbed on top of her naked body, felt around for a bit, and then pushed into her, filling her with that familiar sensation. It was all a great departure from his usual hasty approach; tonight he lingered, enjoying himself for a long time. He kissed her as his body twitched and jerked. When he reached her nipples, she moaned in pain. As if in response, he began moaning himself. When it was finished, he didn't turn over and begin snoring like usual, but instead continued pressing down on top of her without moving. After a long while he slid off of her, and she heard him sigh. It seemed like he wanted to say something, but she soon heard the even sound of his breathing and knew he had fallen asleep.

Xiaomei had been bruised by Aqiang that evening, yet she didn't feel any pain. Her eyes remained open in the pitch black night as scenes from the past appeared before them. The even snoring of the man beside her accented the tranquility of night—the eight years she had spent with the Shen family had been just as tranquil. The sounds of the night watchman beating the *geng* traveled over the street, breaking through the silence each time and awakening in Xiaomei the events of her past. She thought of that wonderful first time she wore the blue calico clothing, and she thought of the day after her wedding, when her mother-in-law placed her own silver hairclip in her bun . . .

A rooster started crowing in the distance, and then the neighbor's rooster started up. She knew she should make breakfast, so she got out of bed, got dressed, and tiptoed out of the room. The door creaked as she opened it, and Aqiang's snoring abruptly stopped. She stood there for a few moments without moving until she heard him flip over and start snoring again, at which point she went out of the room and shut the door with a long, slow creak. Again she stood still for a few moments before finally entering the kitchen—by then, their own rooster had joined in the crowing.

11.

Xiaomei's mother-in-law was up earlier than usual that morning. After washing her face and rinsing her mouth, she sat in front of her dresser and began carefully combing her hair, which was beginning to thin, and then put in some hair cream. Then she wound her hair up into a bun in the back. She raised her head and looked out the window at the gray, overcast sky, then got up and went to the wardrobe to select some appropriate clothing for going out. When Xiaomei's father-in-law woke up and got out of bed to get dressed, he saw that his wife was dressed for an outing. At first this surprised him, but then he remembered the events that had transpired the night before. This man, the hair graying at his temples, shook his head slightly and let out a sigh. His wife heard but didn't look at him. Instead she opened the drawer, took out a handful of copper coins, and dropped them into a sack. After assessing their weight, she decided there were enough, so she left the room with the sack of coins.

She took the sack to Xiaomei and Aqiang's room and was just about to knock on the door when it swung open. Aqiang was standing in front of her wearing a pained expression; upon seeing her there, he lowered his head and walked on past. Registering no reaction, she entered the room and placed the sack on Xiaomei's dresser. As she left, she saw Xiaomei walking toward the kitchen with some bowls and chopsticks and fell in behind her. Sensing there was someone following her, Xiaomei turned her head. Immediately she stood to the side to let her mother-in-law pass. As she walked by, her mother-in-law was startled by the broken skin she noticed on Xiaomei's lips and the marks on her chin.

The four of them sat around the table and ate breakfast. Xiaomei lowered her head and brought her bowl up to her mouth, finding each bite difficult to swallow. Her father-in-law ate slowly, clearly showing that something was weighing heavily on his mind, while Aqiang knitted his brow in a bitter expression and paused after every bite he took. Only Xiaomei's mother-in-law remained completely calm and composed as she ate, appearing no different from usual. When she saw that her son was in one of his wrinkled old work outfits he wore for doing mending, she said to him,

"Go change into something for going out."

Xiaomei was the last one to finish her breakfast. She picked up the bowl and poured the last bit of rice porridge into her mouth, swallowing it without chewing. Then she cleared the table, washed up the bowls and chopsticks they'd used, and tidied up the kitchen. She returned to her room and sat down at her dresser, where she began combing her hair once more. After she put in some hair cream and wound her hair into a bun in the back, she raised the silver hairclip in her right hand and paused. She didn't put it in her bun, but instead placed it back on the dressing table. At this point she noticed the sack laying there; she opened it to discover a large quantity of copper coins. She knew this was the money her mother-in-law was giving her for traveling expenses. She felt a pain in her heart, and her eyes grew moist.

Xiaomei got up and opened the wardrobe. She took out her clothing and packed it all up, including the three blue calico headscarves her frugal mother-in-law had given her as a betrothal gift, which she folded carefully and put in her bundle. As she shut the door to the wardrobe, she saw the blue calico clothes she had worn as a ten-year-old girl when she first came to the Shen home. She reached out, intending to take them with her, when she realized they made her feel sad. So she put them back in the wardrobe and shut the door, then walked over to the dresser and picked up the sack of coins, which she placed in her bundle.

Wearing a clean, grayish blue padded jacket, Xiaomei lugged her bundle out of the room. She saw that Aqiang had changed into a *changshan,* and her mother-in-law was wearing a cotton qipao. They appeared to be waiting for her. As soon as her mother-in-law saw her emerge, she turned around and headed outside; Aqiang followed her, and Xiaomei brought up the rear. Once they were outside, Xiaomei turned around and saw her father-in-law standing in front of the shop, wiping a tear from the corner of his eye with his finger.

12.

On this overcast morning, Xiaomei carried her bundle as she walked behind her mother-in-law and Aqiang. Unlike her first arrival in Xizhen, when she had looked all around in wonder, this time she lowered her head and stared at her feet, each footstep sounding a farewell on the streets of Xizhen. Some people they knew greeted them as they walked by, but her mother-in-law didn't respond, and neither did Aqiang, so Xiaomei just kept her head down.

The three of them proceeded gloomily out through the west gate of Xizhen. On the main road they came to an intersection, where Xiaomei's mother-in-law stopped. Aqiang stopped as well, and Xiaomei raised her head and carefully examined his face, as if to engrave its image onto her heart. Her mother-in-law stood off to the side without a word, thinking she might as well let Xiaomei get a good look. When Xiaomei turned her eyes to her mother-in-law with the same sort of stare, her mother-in-law couldn't help but avert her eyes.

Her mother-in-law looked at the main road, heading off in opposite directions to the north and south. That early in the morning, it was devoid of people.

"We'll do it here," she said.

She said she would head to the south, so Xiaomei nodded and began walking north. After about a hundred steps to the north with her head lowered, Xiaomei realized that, just as she had expected, there were no footsteps following her—she knew that Aqiang would head south after his mother. She raised her head and saw dark clouds rolling along in the distance, as if the road eventually disappeared into a dark night. Continuing forward without looking back, the cold winter wind rushed at her face, bringing with it a few drops of rain. She wasn't cold, but her whole body ached, and she felt completely at a loss. She didn't know why she felt this ache, yet it grew stronger and stronger. Her head began to droop as she walked along, trying to determine the origin of the pain in her body. After walking for a long while, she finally realized what it was, recalling how Aqiang had bitten her all over in bed the night before. When she thought of this, tears began pouring down from her eyes.

Xiaomei knew her fate—she would return to the village of Xilicun, which she had left eight years before. She stood in the cold wind as raindrops splattered on the road, thinking of how she should make her way to the Xizhen wharf. The wharf was near the east gate, but she didn't want to go back the way she'd come—that would take her back in through the west gate, where the street would be buzzing with people and activity. She wanted to be by herself, so she decided to take a circuitous route to the wharf through the east gate. She raised her hand to wipe the raindrops from her eyes. After getting her bearings, she continued on ahead for a ways, then turned on a small, winding path that led her to Xizhen's east gate, and finally the wharf.

As Xiaomei stood on the docks, several boatmen waved

and called out to her. Unsteadily she stepped on the nearest little boat, and the boatmen helped her get seated on the straw mat under the bamboo awning. As the raindrops began to increase, the boatman, outfitted in a bamboo hat and woven-grass poncho, pushed them off with both hands. He asked Xiaomei where she was headed, then sat down in the stern and leaned against a wooden plank. An oar was tucked under his left arm to guide their direction while he peddled the boat with his bare feet. The little boat made a swishing sound as it moved quickly over the surface of the water, dotted with splashing raindrops.

The middle-aged boatman looked at Xiaomei still clutching her bundle under the bamboo awning and said,

"It'll be more comfortable if you put your bundle behind you and lean back on it."

Xiaomei nodded but kept the bundle over her arm. The boatman repeated himself a couple times, and again Xiaomei nodded, but the bundle stayed put. The boatman smiled and changed the subject:

"I know you—you're the daughter-in-law of the Shen family with the mending shop."

Xiaomei nodded, and the boatman asked, "Are you returning to your parents' home in the Wanmudang?"

Xiaomei nodded once more, and the little boat with the bamboo awning sped toward the village of Xilicun in the Wanmudang. The boatman continued talking, but Xiaomei didn't listen to anything else he said.

After being away for eight years, Xiaomei could no longer remember the faces of her parents or brothers—she couldn't even picture the face of her youngest brother, who she had seen just the day before yesterday. Anxiously she tried to recall, but even in the depths of her memory she was unable to locate her father or mother. Then she remembered one of her mother's movements—she could see her raising her hand to wipe her tears, but when and where had she seen this? She finally recalled that it had been on the day of her wedding, when her mother was sitting across from her with tears gathering in the corners of her eyes. Then she thought of the five of them, her parents and brothers, and how they had all arrived with their hands tucked up in their sleeves and left the same way. Her marriage into the Shen family, with their mending shop in Xizhen, had made them all so happy and proud. Now she was being expelled from the Shen family and returning to her Wanmudang village of Xilicun. How would they react? She didn't dare think about it.

Having left her parents and brothers at the age of ten and lived with the Shen family for the past eight years, she felt in her heart that the Shens were her real family. Aqiang never spoke harshly to her, and her father-in-law was friendly and gentle; her mother-in-law, while serious and strict, had never mistreated her over the past eight years. In Xizhen, the abuse of child brides was commonplace—they were always being scolded and beaten, and would often end up hanging themselves or jumping down a well. Xiaomei herself had heard of this happening several times over the past eight years.

Sitting under the awning of the boat, she cried. The boatman was caught off guard and wasn't sure how to react. From the stern of the boat he shouted through the rain, which jolted Xiaomei from her thoughts and brought her back to reality—she knew she was on a little boat and that it was pouring rain outside of the bamboo awning under which she was sitting; she couldn't see the boatman's face clearly, but she could hear him shouting. She raised a hand to wipe the tears from her eyes, allowing her to get a clearer look at his face through the rain. His mouth was moving, but she couldn't make out what it was. When she realized he was asking if she was all right, she waved her hand to indicate she was fine. She continued to sit peacefully, and the boatman's mouth remained closed amidst the rain.

Having calmed down, Xiaomei took a look at her future. As

a woman being sent back to her village by her husband's family, her parents and brothers would all feel taken down a peg, and she would be forbidden from calling on any neighbors. She would still get up early in the morning to start the housework and then go work in the fields, but she would never be able to hold her head up as she did these things. Although she would have her parents and brothers by her side, and she would be surrounded by friends and relatives in the village, she would always feel alone. At night she would hear her father's sighs and see her mother under the moonlight wiping tears from her eyes.

13.

After Xiaomei's departure, Aqiang's mother took charge of the housework. In addition to taking on the mending work she washed the clothes and cooked the meals, which required her to rise early and go to bed late—it was all quite taxing. Truth be told, she could have easily hired a maid, but because of her frugal nature she decided to do it all herself. In the shop, she had her husband deal with all the customers, but she still managed the accounts. Aqiang's father became quite busy, receiving customers and seeing them off, nodding and smiling attentively. When it came to handling customers' unpaid accounts, he would go out to collect the money when the due dates rolled around. He barely had any time to sit down and do any mending, and when he did, he had become so farsighted that he had to hold both arms straight out in front of him in order to see the needle and thread well enough to do any work.

Aqiang seemed to have lost his wits—he would hold an item of clothing that needed mending and sit with it from morning till evening without moving a muscle. He just sat there like a piece of furniture, doing nothing at all.

Aqiang's mother knew what was going through his mind, and she didn't utter a word of reproach. But what she didn't know was that every time Aqiang changed his clothes, he would open the wardrobe and see Xiaomei's set of calico clothing she had left behind. Aqiang would stare at it in a trance, and his mind would go blank.

During this time, a matchmaker would periodically show up at their door with girls from the countryside in tow. After an initial glance, Aqiang never gave them a second look. Compared to the delicate and pretty, neat and tidy, clever and nimble Xiaomei, not even Aqiang's mother took an interest in any of them. The matchmaker also introduced them to two city girls—one from Xizhen, the other from Shendian. They were both from poor families, and the bride price suggested by the family of the girl from Xizhen so completely horrified Aqiang's mother that she naturally refused it. The family of the girl from Shendian didn't mention a bride price for the time being, inviting them to first have a look at the girl; if they took a liking to her they could then discuss it. So one morning at dawn, Aqiang's parents got dressed up and headed to Shendian to meet her.

By this time the spring flowers were in bloom, and it had already been three months since Xiaomei had been sent back to her Wanmudang village of Xilicun. Aqiang, who generally appeared cowardly and absent-minded, decided to do something on the spur of the moment that he would never be able to undo.

After his parents left, he sat alone in the shop feeling drowsy. The image of the ten-year-old Xiaomei standing in front of the wardrobe wearing the calico outfit kept appearing before his eyes. Aqiang awoke from his sleeplike daze, and an idea came to him. He leapt to his feet and ran upstairs to his room, where he opened the wardrobe and took out the calico clothing Xiaomei had left behind. He tidied up his own clothing and wrote a note for his parents. Then he went downstairs to the pantry, where he moved an old wooden chest and pried up one of the bricks from the floor, under which was a porcelain jar containing two hundred silver yuan. He opened the lid, counted out a hundred taels, then closed it again. Then he went to the drawer under the counter in the shop and took all the copper coins that were in it. He shut the door to the shop, put his bundle on his back, and walked out onto the sunny street, which he followed down to the wharf at the east gate.

In the mornings, the water around the wharf was filled with little boats with bamboo awnings, their boatmen sitting in the sterns and talking with one another. When they saw Aqiang approach with his bundle, they all waved at him and invited him on their boats. Faced with a dozen boatmen all calling him to their boats, Aqiang was a bit caught off guard and wasn't sure whose boat to take.

"Are you headed to Xilicun to get your woman?" one of them ventured.

Surprised, Aqiang nodded his head and got on his boat. As soon as he seated himself on the straw mat under the awning, the boat left the docks and headed out.

The boatman told Aqiang he would be more comfortable if he put his bundle behind him, so Aqiang did. Then he told Aqiang that he had taken his woman back to Xilicun, and she had cried the entire time—he didn't know why. He'd seen women cry when they returned to their parents' homes before, but he'd never seen one weep so brokenheartedly. It was only later that he heard she'd been dismissed from her husband's family. Then he mentioned a couple of other families in Xizhen who had dismissed their daughters-in-law; both had regretted it after a few months and gone to bring them back.

"It's been about three months now?" he said to Aqiang.

Aqiang nodded. Then the boatmen eyed the large bundle sticking out from behind his back and asked why he was bringing so much with him. Aqiang didn't reply. Xilicun was a good distance away, said the boatman, but one day was still enough for a round trip—why bring such a large bundle?

14.

By the afternoon, the little boat had arrived at Xiaomei's village. Aqiang left his bundle on the boat, gathered up is *changshan* and jumped onshore. Then he turned back to the boatman and said,

"Please wait here for a while."

Aqiang looked all around and saw that fields stretched in every direction. Only one small path extended before him, so he started down it. He saw some villagers working in the fields as he walked, and he asked them where he could find the home of Xiaomei's parents. They didn't answer him directly but instead began talking amongst themselves; then they called out to another villager in the distance and pointed at Aqiang standing on the path. He saw the villager hop over the small ridges dividing the fields and run over to him barefoot—he was a boy of about fifteen or sixteen with a face that resembled Xiaomei's. When he'd made it over to Aqiang, he looked him over and asked,

"Are you our esteemed brother-in-law?"

When Aqiang heard "brother-in-law" preceded by "esteemed," he was unsure how to react. He had a feeling this villager was one of Xiaomei's younger brothers. By this point Xiaomei's brother had fully recognized Aqiang and happily said to him,

"You *are* our esteemed brother-in-law! You don't remember me? I'm Xiaomei's youngest brother!"

This threw Aqiang a little off kilter—it was this very brother who had lost the money from selling the pig, which had ultimately resulted in Xiaomei being sent back to the Wanmudang. He looked Xiaomei's brother over from head to toe and saw that his pants legs were rolled up high and his feet were covered with mud. When Xiaomei's brother noticed that his brother-in-law was looking at his bare feet, he flashed an embarrassed smile and bent over to roll down his cuffs. Standing back up, he asked cautiously,

"Have you come to fetch my sister?"

Aqiang nodded, and Xiaomei's brother darted over to the side and extended his left hand out in front of him, gesturing for Aqiang to proceed before him:

"After you, esteemed brother-in-law."

The villagers working in the fields all straightened their backs and looked curiously at this man from Xizhen, holding up the ends of his *changshan* as he walked along the path between the fields. Xiaomei's brother followed behind him beaming with happiness, calling out to his fellow villagers in the fields,

"My esteemed brother-in-law has come to get my sister!"

The villagers in the fields understood—Xiaomei, who had been expelled back to their village, was once more a member of the Shen family with the mending shop in Xizhen. They said it looked like the Shen family had come to regret their actions— it looked like spilled water could be gathered up again, and words could be recalled.

After walking for a while, Xiaomei's brother, who was following behind Aqiang, called out to a man in the fields:

"Brother! Our esteemed brother-in-law has come for our sister!"

The man who had been bent over working immediately stood up, hopped over the ridges dividing the fields, and came running over barefoot. His face red from excitement, he called out,

"Esteemed brother-in-law!"

Aqiang gave a slight smile and nodded, realizing that this must be Xiaomei's other little brother. He continued on down the path with Xiaomei's two younger brothers following behind him. The youngest brother tugged on the older one's clothing and pointed to the rolled-up cuffs of his pants; the older brother understood and bent over at once to unroll them. Along the way they passed about seven or eight thatched cottages—men and women, young and old all looked out to see, as if they were watching an opera performance. Xiaomei's younger brothers proudly announced that their esteemed brother-in-law had come to collect their sister and take her back to the Shen family in Xizhen.

When they came to a cottage that looked relatively new, the youngest brother shouted:

"Brother! Our esteemed brother-in-law has come for our sister!"

A man came out of the cottage, took a look at Aqiang, and ran right up to him. This one wasn't barefoot, but wearing straw sandals. Bending forward, he called out:

"Esteemed brother-in-law!"

Aqiang nodded and realized this must be Xiaomei's older brother. He was now surrounded by Xiaomei's three brothers, while a few villagers began following behind them. Even more people stood up in the fields or in front of their doors to watch this smiling man in a *changshan* pass by.

Xiaomei's parents were also out working in the fields. When they heard that the young master from the Shen family had come to take their daughter back, they hurried over to the irrigation ditch to wash the mud from their feet and roll down their pantlegs. Then they put on their straw sandals, which they had placed on one of the ridges between the fields, and ran home. Xiaomei's father, who was running in front, would periodically turn his head and scold his wife for being too slow.

Xiaomei, dressed in some old, patched-up clothing, was at home making lunch at the time. When she heard the commotion of the villagers outside, she didn't know what was going on, nor did she bother to give it much thought—she just continued putting kindling in the stove and adjusting its placement with the tongs until she got the fire burning evenly. Then her parents rushed in. As her father changed out of his straw sandals into cloth shoes, he began barking directions at her mother:

"Don't let her keep cooking! Quick, get her cleaned up!"

Xiaomei's mother, tears streaming down her face, grabbed her and said, "Your husband's come for you! You're back in the Shen family."

The sudden news shocked Xiaomei. Still crying, her mother led her out to the water's edge behind the house and had her squat down to wash her face and hands. Then she ran back into the house to pack up Xiaomei's clothes. After putting them in a bundle, she came back outside with a grayish blue set that didn't have any patches and had Xiaomei go into the nearby stand of bamboo and change into them. Then she ran back into the house once more to take off her straw sandals and change into her cloth shoes.

When Aqiang arrived in front of the cottage, Xiaomei's father was already standing there to greet him, and her mother quickly ran up and stood by his side. The two of them respectfully called out:

"Esteemed son-in-law!"

Aqiang respectfully greeted them back: "Esteemed father-in-law, esteemed mother-in-law!"

No one was quite sure what to say after that, so they just stood there smiling. A number of villagers had gathered in front of the Ji family's cottage—one of them said they smelled something burning, and another asked if there was some food burning on the stove, but Xiaomei's parents didn't respond.

Two of Xiaomei's three brothers ran and got their wives. One of the women called out, "Esteemed younger brother-in-law!" while other greeted him with, "Esteemed older brother-in-law!"

Aqiang nodded to these two women he had never seen before. Then Xiaomei's youngest brother said, "Esteemed brother-in-law, please come inside and have a seat."

Xiaomei's parents, knowing what they were supposed to say, echoed, "Please come in and have a seat."

Aqiang saw Xiaomei coming out of the cottage with a bundle. Xiaomei looked over at Aqiang and then lowered her head. From her eyes, Aqiang could feel the three months worth of humiliation she had endured. His eyes turned red, and his voice broke as he said to Xiaomei's parents,

"Esteemed father-in-law, esteemed mother-in-law, I've come to take Xiaomei back."

Xiaomei's parents nodded and said good, good, good. Xiaomei lowered her head and walked up to Aqiang, her body trembling slightly as tears gathered in her eyes.

Aqiang bowed to Xiaomei's parents and said, "Esteemed father-in-law, esteemed mother-in-law, we'll take our leave now."

Xiaomei's youngest brother said, "Esteemed brother-in-law, stay for lunch before you go."

"No, we should be on our way," said Aqiang.

"Have some lunch before you go," said Xiaomei's father.

Then he said to Xiaomei's mother: "Go and put some rice in some bowls!"

Xiaomei's mother hurried into the house while Xiaomei's father gestured for Aqiang to go in and eat. Aqiang looked over at Xiaomei, who was standing beside him with her head bowed, then nudged her arm to indicate she should go in with him. Just then Xiaomei's mother emerged with two bowls of rice that had been completely scorched black—in her excitement, she hadn't even noticed that the rice was burned. She handed the bowls over to Aqiang and Xiaomei and said,

"Have something to eat before you go."

"Why are you in such a hurry?" Xiaomei's father scolded his wife, "our esteemed son-in-law hasn't even gone in the house yet!"

Only when they heard some laughter from the assembled crowd did they realize that the rice was so badly burned it was inedible. A look of embarrassment spread over Xiaomei's father's face as he said to Xiaomei's mother, who looked equally embarrassed,

"Quick, go inside and make some rice!"

Aqiang bowed once more to Xiaomei's parents and said, "I'll take Xiaomei back now."

15.

The fact that the young master of the Shen family, who ran the mending shop in Xizhen, had appeared in Xilicun, a village without a single structure made of brick and tile, to fetch Xiaomei caused quite a stir. The villagers followed Aqiang and Xiaomei as they made their way to the little boat with the bamboo awning.

Xiaomei's three brothers joyfully followed right behind the couple, while Xiaomei's two sisters-in-law became absorbed into the rest of the crowd, and Xiaomei's parents were squeezed all the way to the back. Her parents smiled as they looked out over the long line of people that stretched out before them. Because the road was so narrow, a number of people rolled up their pants and walked in the ditches along either side of the road.

As Xiaomei pressed on with her head lowered, her field of vision was entirely filled with moving feet. She kept her eyes fixed on the pair of feet that appeared below that long *changshan*—those were her husband's feet, and she wanted to stay as close to them as possible.

Three months earlier, Xiaomei had arrived in Xilicun on that little boat. She had climbed onshore and hesitantly made her way, head bowed, to her parents' house. She hadn't been able to hold her head up since, even when she was at home. She never told her parents that the reason she'd been sent back was because she'd given some coppers to her little brother—instead, she said it was because she hadn't become pregnant in the two years since the wedding, and the Shens suspected she was barren.

Her father never reproached her—he just sat there in shock without moving a muscle, while her mother quietly dabbed at her eyes. Two of her three brothers felt they had lost face, and for the next few days they barely spoke to her; only her youngest brother kept calling her "sister." After Xiaomei was sent back home, her father said that it wasn't the busy season, and there wasn't that much work to be done in the fields—it would be fine if she just stayed home and managed the house-work. Xiaomei knew her father didn't want her to go out of the house for the time being in order to save face and avoid mak-ing a spectacle of herself. Other than going out to the water's edge behind the house to clean the rice and wash the clothes, Xiaomei never set foot through the main door of the cottage. Although she always kept her head down, Xiaomei could still sense that people in the village were pointing at their house as they walked by; sometimes they would even go around back to find her squatting by the river washing clothes, at which point they would start whispering.

Now that Xiaomei was being taken back to Xizhen, her parents and brothers had a new spring in their step. Xiaomei, though, kept her head down the whole way to the boat. Only after the boatman pushed off from the shore and they began rowing out on the open water did Xiaomei finally raise her head and search for her parents on the shore. Finally she located her mother in the long, crowded line of people—she was wiping the tears from her eyes with both hands. Then she spotted her father, who was also crying and wiping his eyes with the backs of his hands.

Aqiang, seated beside Xiaomei, took the bundle she was holding at her chest and placed it behind her so she could lean back on it. His attentiveness brought tears to her eyes. This good turn her fate had taken made her want to cry, but she held it in. The little boat made its way over the waves. After about two *shichen*, thought Xiaomei, they would arrive in Xizhen, where she would walk back into the Shen family's mending shop. The thought of seeing her mother-in-law suddenly filled her with anxiety.

Just then, Aqiang said to the boatman: "To Shendian."

The boatman was confused. "You're not going back to Xizhen?" he asked.

"We're not going back to Xizhen," replied Aqiang. "We're going to Shendian."

Puzzled, Xiaomei looked over at Aqiang—it was as if she hadn't understood what he'd just said.

"Although Shendian's a little closer than Xizhen," said the boatman, "I'd still have to return to Xizhen, and it's not really safe to sail after dark."

"I'll pay double," said Aqiang.

Xiaomei looked at Aqiang in bewilderment. With a self-satisfied look, Aqiang opened up his bundle and showed Xiaomei her calico clothing placed on top. Tears gushed from her eyes—she understood. Aqiang hadn't come to take her back to the Shen home in Xizhen; he was taking her somewhere else.

Her vision blurred from her tears, Xiaomei gazed at the afternoon sunlight reflecting off the surface of the water, golden and sparkling. The little boat with the bamboo awning sailed ahead through this glimmering gold.

Xiaomei had never seen Aqiang glowing with such happiness. His eyes glistened as he looked out over the wide expanse of the water, and his voice rang out as he talked with the boatman. Their banter hopped all over the place—one minute they were talking about the small lanes in Xizhen, the next they were discussing the shops in Shendian. The clear excitement in Aqiang's voice made Xiaomei feel like the distracted, absentminded Aqiang was nowhere to be found.

Xiaomei became immersed in the sound of Aqiang's voice. She was unable to distinguish between his words and his laughter; she simply felt enveloped by his sound, which wrapped around her body like a big red cloak. When Xiaomei left Xilicun for the first time at the age of ten and walked through the streets of Xizhen latched on to a corner of her father's clothing, her eyes had sparkled with a golden light as she looked all around. Now, following Aqiang to some unknown, faraway place, that golden light returned to her eyes once more.

16.

The two of them passed a carefree afternoon and evening in Shendian. They were like a pair of caged birds now flying out into the open sky, happily beating their wings. They enjoyed themselves so much on the streets of Shendian, which were wider and more bustling than those of Xizhen, that they didn't even notice when when their stomachs began rumbling with hunger.

On a whim, Aqiang walked into a tailor shop to have a new set of clothes made for Xiaomei. The tailor took Xiaomei's measurements and said they could come back in three days to pick up the finished product. Just as Aqiang was preparing to put down the deposit, he suddenly turned around and bolted from the shop faster than a rabbit. Xiaomei and the tailor just looked at each other, unsure how to react. Blushing with embarrassment, Xiaomei left the shop. She saw Aqiang motioning to her from across the street, so she walked over to him. He told her they couldn't wait three days—tomorrow they were going to Shanghai. Once they got to Shanghai, they would find a tailor and have some new clothes made for her there—and tailors in Shanghai would be better than tailors in Shendian, anyway.

Ah, said Xiaomei—so they were going to Shanghai. The Shen family's mending shop had a customer who had visited Shanghai, and one time he'd stood in front of the door to the shop spouting off about it. From that, Xiaomei had gotten an impression of Shanghai as a place so big you could never find where it ended; it had lots of tall buildings, lots of people, and lots of foreigners.

This visit to Shendian was the first time Xiaomei had ever entered a restaurant or a hotel. Although she had seen restaurants and hotels in Xizhen, she'd never gone in, and had merely peered inside as she walked past.

Upon entering the restaurant, Xiaomei cautiously followed behind Aqiang. It was a noodle restaurant with ten "eight immortals" tables. Xiaomei followed Aqiang up to the counter, where she looked up to see two rows of bamboo strips hanging on the wall, carved with the names of various noodle dishes and their prices. Xiaomei had never realized there were so many different kinds of noodles in the world. While she was still marveling at all the choices, Aqiang went ahead and placed a decadent order of pig liver noodles and noodles with stir-fried kidneys. Xiaomei heard the copper coins jingle in his hand.

The next time she heard this jingling sound was that evening, as they stood at the front desk of a hotel. Once Aqiang had paid for the room, Xiaomei followed him up the dimly lit stairs, which creaked so loudly she felt they were about to collapse; she reached out and grabbed onto Aqiang's clothing and didn't let go until they had made it into the room. She asked Aqiang why they made so much more noise than their stairs back home in Xizhen. He said that at home only four people used them, and they all tread on them lightly. Here, though, lots of people used the stairs, and they stomped and tramped up and down them any old way.

The room wasn't large, but it had a bed, a table, and a stool, and it seemed quite clean. The evening rays of the setting sun were coming through the window and shining on a corner of the bed. Xiaomei was curiously examining the room, illuminated by the day's final sunlight, when she heard Aqiang cry out. Xiaomei jumped, and Aqiang, not yet recovered from his fright, told her that his parents were in Shendian—he had completely forgotten. Xiaomei shuddered and went pale. Then Aqiang's face relaxed and he gazed at the sunset out the window—by now, he told Xiaomei, his parents should already be back in Xizhen. Xiaomei still felt a little uneasy, and Aqiang said to her:

"We're already in the hotel—even if my parents hadn't gone back to Xizhen yet, they still wouldn't run into us here."

As soon as Aqiang had finished speaking, he embraced Xiaomei and swept her onto the bed as if they were fleeing from some calamity. The bed creaked and groaned, and Xiaomei asked if it was going to collapse; Aqiang said it wouldn't. Xiaomei asked why this bed was so much noisier than their bed at home; Aqiang said at home they were the only two people who slept on their bed, while lots of people had slept on this one.

Aqiang undressed Xiaomei with drama and flourish, then removed his own clothing without any fanfare. The two of them crawled in naked under the covers, and Xiaomei experienced another night she would never forget—the first being her final night with the Shen family.

17.

Xiaomei was in the bloom of her life, and though it was fleeting, she was still in it. She followed Aqiang to Shanghai, where they saw a two-wheeled rickshaw go by. In Xizhen Xiaomei had seen sedan chairs, but never a rickshaw. She pointed at it and asked Aqiang in a whisper,

"What kind of vehicle is that?"

Aqiang thought for a minute and then recalled seeing its name in an old newspaper. "It's called a rickshaw," he said.

Then they saw a tall man sitting in one of the rickshaws—he had blond hair, blue eyes, and a prominent nose, and was wearing a Western-style suit and shoes. Before Xiaomei could ask, Aqiang said,

"That's a foreigner."

Then he added: "He's wearing a suit."

This was the first time Aqiang had seen a foreigner or a suit outside of a newspaper. He and Xiaomei both eyed him curiously as he rode away in the rickshaw.

A man carrying a leather briefcase and dressed in a *changshan* appeared in front of them and waved to hail a rickshaw. A rickshaw puller quickly came over to him, and after he'd been seated he directed the puller:

"The Hujiang Hotel."

Aqiang imitated the man and waved at another rickshaw, which came over and stopped in front of him. He helped Xiaomei get in first, and then he got in and said to the puller,

"The Hujiang Hotel."

The puller uttered a crisp affirmation and began running. When they left Xilicun for Shendian in that little boat with the bamboo awning, their lives, which up until that point had been like stagnant pools of water, started to seem like they were heading somewhere, like the rickshaws speeding through the streets of Shanghai.

At the Hujiang Hotel they had their fist encounter with an electric lightbulb. As Aqiang was looking for the kerosene lamp that evening, Xiaomei looked up and saw a light fixture hanging from the ceiling and asked Aqiang what it was. Aqiang raised his head to look and felt like he had seen something like it somewhere before. Once again he thought back to the old newspapers he had read, and after a few moments he located it in his memory. With a note of pleasant surprise in his voice, he announced,

"It's an electric light."

Xiaomei thought back to the customer who had visited Shanghai—he had spoken of something called "electric lights" that were much brighter than kerosene lamps. "Ah," she said,

"So this is an electric light."

Then she asked, "But how do you light this electric light?"

Aqiang saw a cord hanging down next to the lightbulb, so he reached out his hand and pulled it. The light turned on, and the two of them cried out in surprise.

"You don't use a match to light an electric light," Aqiang said, "you just pull the cord and it comes on."

"What happens if you pull it again?" asked Xiaomei.

Aqiang pulled the cord again and the light went out. "When you pull it again, it goes dark," he said.

Then Aqiang let Xiaomei try it out. She pulled it three times, and the light went on, off, and on again.

Thinking back to the newspapers he had read, Aqiang thought of the word "electrocute." He pointed to the lightbulb and said to Xiaomei,

"You can't touch an electric light. If you touch it, you'll get 'electrocuted.'"

Xiaomei asked what it meant to get "electrocuted," and Aqiang said if you touched electricity, it would kill you. Xiaomei gasped, and for the next few days every time Aqiang went to pull the cord on the light, Xiaomei would warn him,

"Be careful!"

By the Jing'an temple, they saw a trolley car. It rumbled toward them, then sounded its bell and slowly came to a stop. Some people got off and others got on; then the bell sounded and the trolley car continued rumbling forward.

"What kind of vehicle is that?" asked Xiaomei "It's so big, with those two long cars connected together."

Aqiang had just heard some people walking by say in Shanghainese that they were going to take the electric trolley.

"It's an 'electric trolley,'" he said.

When Xiaomei heard that this also used electricity, she asked Aqiang, "If you sit on it, will you get electrocuted?"

Without a second thought, Aqiang said, "Yes, electrocuted."

As she watched the trolley car drive away, Xiaomei asked, "So why didn't the people inside get electrocuted?"

Aqiang immediately corrected himself and said, "You won't get electrocuted from riding a trolley car."

As the days continued to pass in Shanghai, they would sometimes ride trolley cars, sometimes take rickshaws, and sometimes ride in wheelbarrows. But most of the time they would walk, stopping in front of the shops' display windows or peering in their doors. Though their eyes sparkled with wonderment, they never once set foot inside—the customers inside all had a wealthy, extravagant appearance, wearing either suits and leather shoes, or *changshans* and qipaos. Aqiang was too timid to enter, while Xiaomei would naturally never dare to go in.

But they would go in restaurants, even big ones with lavish offerings. Aqiang would always lead Xiaomei inside, where they would sit down and he would order a few dishes. Hunger always had a way of conquering Aqiang's cowardice.

One of the restaurants they visited had a smoking room, where guests could go after their meals to smoke opium. After gorging themselves on sumptuous dishes, Aqiang sighed and exclaimed at the size and thickness of their serving of meat. Just then he heard another guest ask a server what kinds of domestic opium they had, and the server said they'd just received a shipment from Yunnan. The guest asked the server to prepare a ball of opium for him and said he would go into the smoking room later to try it out. Shortly afterwards the manager came over to the guest and began discussing opium with him. He said that last month several of Shanghai's prominent figures had brought some of the "horse hoof" variety from India, and they had taken it into the smoking room after their meal. The guest said that "horse hoof" was the best kind of foreign opium there was, and that one *liang* cost four taels of silver. The manager said this was the first time he had seen it, and that it really did look like horse's hooves—it had really expanded his horizons.

Aqiang was thinking that he would also like to try some opium, but when he heard that one *liang* of the "horse hoof" variety cost four taels, he nearly fell off his chair. He was thrilled that he'd only thought it, and not actually opened his mouth.

After they left the restaurant, Aqiang spent three coppers on a pack of "Pirate" brand cigarettes. He lit one with a match and then began smoking as they walked. He felt that from the "Pirate" brand cigarettes, he could sense the flavor of the Indian "horse hoof" opium. Seeing his awkward movements coupled with his self-satisfied expression, Xiaomei couldn't help but laugh.

Aqiang took Xiaomei to the funhouse mirrors in the Great World amusement arcade. In one mirror they saw themselves stretch tall and thin like a bamboo pole, with a few curves as well. Xiaomei cried out in surprise, and Aqiang said to her,

"That's your ghost!"

Frightened, Xiaomei hid behind Aqiang and shut her eyes, not daring to look. Then she heard Aqiang burst into laughter and realized he was teasing her. She opened her eyes and saw that Aqiang was also tall and curvy, although he looked a little different from her—below his head was another head.

"Your ghost has two heads," said Xiaomei.

"The other head is yours," said Aqiang.

"So our ghosts are together?" she asked.

"Yes, they're together," he replied.

As Aqiang said that he stuck out his hand and foot, then had Xiaomei do the same. With its two heads, four hands, and four feet, they saw the ghost in the mirror break into a jig.

In another mirror, they saw themselves become short and squat like a wash tub. Xiaomei laughed and said, "So our ghosts can change shape?"

"They can change into any kind of shape," said Aqiang.

"Any shape but human," added Xiaomei.

Aqiang took Xiaomei to the temple of the city god, where they ate some pear candies. They watched the candy seller as he stood on a stool, holding a gong in his left hand and a stick in his right—he would bang the gong as he told vulgar, rapid-fire jokes, while the people surrounding him would burst into raucous laughter. Aqiang couldn't understand the first joke they heard, but he saw Xiaomei lower her head and smile. He asked Xiaomei quietly,

"Could you understand him?"

Xiaomei nodded and blushed. Puzzled, Aqiang said, "Why couldn't I understand?"

Then Aqiang understood the next joke, and he broke out into loud laughter that was so exaggerated others turned their heads to look.

When they were finished listening to the vulgar jokes,

Aqiang went to buy some Dutch water, which meant fizzy water—Aqiang said it was the kind of water foreigners drank. They each took a drink. First their eyes bulged out, and then they tasted the sweet flavor—it was a surprising experience. Xiaomei was the first to react.

"So that's the fizz," she said softly.

Aqiang cried out as if making a discovery: "Yes, that's the fizz!"

The two of them continued taking little sips, and gradually the fizz decreased. Aqiang asked Xiaomei,

"What happened to the fizz?"

"Did it run out?" asked Xiaomei.

As if having a sudden epiphany, Aqiang announced, "Yes! The fizz has run out."

Aqiang said he wanted to take Xiaomei to try some of the foreigners' food. Three days later, they took a trolley to the British Concession and went into a restaurant. As the two of them were quietly discussing what to order, the server brought over some bread and butter. Aqiang and Xiaomei looked at each other, then back at the server—they hadn't yet placed an order, and the food was already there? The server explained to them that the bread and butter were complimentary. Upon hearing they didn't have to pay for it, they calmed down. They looked over at the neighboring table and saw that the people there had spread the butter on top of their bread, so they followed suit and did the same. They started off with tentative nibbles, but then proceeded to gobble it down.

"It's good," said Aqiang.

Xiaomei nodded. Aqiang had heard the server refer to the bread, but he hadn't caught the word "butter," so he quietly asked Xiaomei,

"What's this oily spread called?"

Xiaomei hadn't caught the name either; she said she'd been so shocked when the server brought it over that she hadn't listened very closely. Just then she heard someone at the neighboring table exclaim that the butter was quite good. She lowered her head and smiled, then said softly,

"It's butter."

They lingered for a long time in the International Settlement. The imposing buildings appearing before their eyes would often stop them in their tracks, and Aqiang would gasp in amazement. Xiaomei heard the *da da* sound of a steamboat, then looked over to see an enormous ship sailing along the river— puffs of black smoke were rolling out of its smokestack and dispersing like a long banner unfurling in the air. When Aqiang saw it, his gasps of amazement became a cry of wonder:

"That big boat doesn't use oars—it can move along by itself!"

"Is it an electric boat?" asked Xiaomei.

Once again Aqiang thought back to the old newspapers he had read and located the word. "It's a steamship," he said.

They then strolled through the area of "twelve towers and three thousand painted faces." They had seen brothels in Xizhen, but the atmosphere of this red-light district was completely different—the doors and walls facing the street all boasted lavish ornamentation, the women were all elaborately made up, and music from the erhu and pipa mingled with the sounds of singing and laughter.

They wandered up to one of the doorways and stared inside. One of the rooms had its door and windows open, and they could see a prostitute and her customer sitting across from each other—one was plucking a stringed instrument, while the other was playing a bamboo flute. Never would such a refined scene be found in the Xizhen brothels.

"Xizhen's brothels certainly don't have anything like this," said Aqiang.

At another doorway they encountered a different scene. In another room with its door and windows wide open, they saw two men laying on their backs and chatting, while six prostitutes—three for each man—massaged their backs, legs, and feet. The sounds of their playful banter drifted out in waves.

"Xizhen's brothels do have this," Aqiang said.

As they were leaving, they saw a man carrying a young woman out of one of the brothels. The woman was leaning over slightly and sitting on the man's left shoulder, while the man held onto her calves with both hands. From the discussion of others on the street, Aqiang and Xiaomei learned that the young woman was a child prostitute, and the man was her pimp. This was the custom of the brothels—for a child prostitute's first time, she couldn't go out alone; she had to be delivered by the pimp to the door of her customer.

As they roamed about Shanghai enjoying the sights, they lost track of the days. Then one day Aqiang slapped his forehead and cried out in surprise—he had only just remembered what he'd said outside of the tailor shop in Shendian. So he took Xiaomei to a clothier—Shanghai was such a big place, he said, that tailor shops were called "clothiers."

As Aqiang became more familiar with Shanghai, he became less timid. He now swaggered as he led Xiaomei around so that he could hear the silver coins jingle in his pocket. He ordered a floral qipao to be made for Xiaomei, in the Shanghai style with a slender waist and high slit. When he handed the silver yuan over to the clothier's tailor, the tailor tossed it on the counter. He felt like it sounded heavy enough, so he accepted it.

Aqiang greatly admired the tailor's behavior, and as they left the clothier he told Xiaomei that not only were the tailors in Shanghai experts at making clothes, but they were also able to judge the purity of silver—as soon as he threw it on the counter, he knew. When tailors in Xizhen received a silver yuan, they would flick it with their fingers and bite it with their teeth.

Three days later in the afternoon, Xiaomei put on the new qipao in their hotel room. The slit was very high, she said, going up even a little bit above her knee—would people be able to see her thigh? Aqiang stood up and looked, then squatted down and looked.

"Looking down from above," he said, "you can see your

knee; looking up from down low, you can see a little bit of your thigh."

"In Xizhen you couldn't go out in this," Xiaomei said.

"This is for you to wear in Shanghai," said Aqiang. Then he added, "We're not going back to Xizhen."

This was the last beautiful thing Xiaomei ever head Aqiang say. By that evening, the happy, confident Aqiang had disappeared, and the absent, preoccupied Aqiang had returned.

Aqiang sat on a stool by the window with his head tilted to the side, looking like a withered eggplant nipped by the frost. This took Xiaomei by surprise—the sudden change in Aqiang's mood gave her a bad feeling. She sat on the edge of the bed, bathed in the evening rays of the sun, as Aqiang haltingly spoke to her. He told her they had spent a lot of money these past few days; they had no source of income, and the silver yuan he had taken from home were nearly all gone.

The golden light sparkling in Xiaomei's eyes gradually faded. Her eyes had shone with this light every day since leaving her Wanmudang village of Xilicun, but now they darkened along with the sky after sunset, until the light in her eyes was completely extinguished.

Doing no mending, cooking, or cleaning these past few days had made Xiaomei forget the past. She hadn't thought about anything, assuming her life would just continue on like this—but this evening, just before dark, this life had come to a sudden halt. Xiaomei thought of the days ahead. Though they would be wandering from place to place, not knowing what they would eat or where they would sleep, at least she and Aqiang would be together, depending on one another.

That night after Aqiang fell asleep, Xiaomei thought of many things. She had seen and experienced a lot these past few days in Shanghai, and she knew what she could do in the days ahead. She could take up mending again—she naturally wouldn't have any customers at first, but she could go door to door looking for work. If she couldn't make it with her mending, she could go work as a shop attendant—her experience dealing with customers and managing accounts in the Shen family's mending shop would surely suffice to get her a job of that sort. And if that didn't work out, she could work as a servant in the home of a wealthy family. If no wealthy family wanted to hire her, she could work as servant in the home of a regular family. If not even a regular family wanted to hire her . . .

When she thought back to what she'd seen of Shanghai's red-light district, she decided she was not above selling her body to help support Aqiang.

After that, she fell peacefully asleep.

18.

When she woke up the next morning, Xiaomei was surprised to find Aqiang standing in front of the bed, still as absent and preoccupied as he was before. But when he saw that Xiaomei was awake, he said to her excitedly,

"Today we're going to Beijing."

Aqiang told Xiaomei they would go look up his uncle, the husband of his mother's sister. He had once worked in Prince Gong's mansion, so he would know how to go about things in Beijing and should be able to find Aqiang a job—perhaps even a very good job. Xiaomei was thrilled. She thought of all the plans she had come up with the previous night—particularly the one that involved her selling her body—and blushed with shame.

Xiaomei packed up her qipao. Then she put on a grayish blue set of clothes, tied a calico scarf around her head, and followed Aqiang north to Beijing. They switched from one horse-drawn cart to another, ranging from twelve horses harnessed in three groups of four to just three horses with one in front and two behind. They even took two ox carts, which went about the same speed as plowing a field and lulled the passengers to sleep.

They stayed in one roadside inn after another, large ones and small, spartan ones, all with multiple guests per room. Xiaomei would often sleep between Aqiang and some stranger, so at one point she picked up a rock along the side of the road and hid it in her bundle. When she went to bed at night, she would take it out and place it between her and Aqiang, just in case.

Of course, the very thing she had been guarding against happened. She was awoken from her dreams one night to a hand reaching into her pants and groping between her thighs. She knew it was the hand of the man sleeping to her left, so she took her rock and smashed it against the arm attached to the hand. She heard a low, painful groan, and the hand withdrew. She wasn't able to fall asleep again after that, and she continued to grip the rock in her right hand.

She didn't tell Aqiang what had happened, but from then on whenever they went to an inn, she made sure to get the spot right next to the wall—that way she could sleep with the wall on one side of her and Aqiang on the other. If someone was already occupying the spot beside the wall, she would grip the rock in her hand and stay awake all night long.

When they set of for Beijing, Aqiang was in high spirits. But this only lasted three days, and then he was back to his former, distracted self.

One day they were on a three-wagon train pulled by twelve horses, crammed in with all sorts of people—men and women, young and old, northern and southern accents. The driver holding the reins up front was shouting the whole time: sometimes it was *jia! pa! he!;* other times it was *wu, wu!* or *oh, oh!;* still other times it was *yue, yue!* and *dai, dai!.* The wagon train continued on under the driver's shouts—to the left, to the right, up hills, over stone thresholds in the streets of villages and towns . . . Heading toward Beijing gave Xiaomei a number of daydreams—that was where the emperor lived, so the streets and houses must be even more imposing than those in Shanghai. Aqiang would find a good job there, and she could take up mending again—Xiaomei grew very excited by her desire to settle down in Beijing. But her excitement lasted only three days. As the wagon train turned right on a main road, Aqiang's mood changed; before the turn he had been happy and jovial, but afterwards he became distant. Xiaomei knew there was a reason. She lowered her head, and her mood conformed to Aqiang's, just as a person's shadow conforms to their body.

That evening, as they stood by the door of a roadside inn, Aqiang told Xiaomei that he didn't know his uncle's proper name. He had only ever heard his mother say that there was such an illustrious relative—he had gone to Beijing when he was young, and as an adult he had returned once to Shendian to marry an older cousin of Aqiang's mother. This was basically everything his mother had told him—she had never mentioned his name, only that he had at one time worked in Prince Gong's mansion. It was clear that when his mother told him this, his uncle no longer worked there.

As this worry weighed down on him, he said to Xiaomei, "Beijing's such a big place—how will we ever find my uncle?"

Xiaomei looked at her hesitant, uncertain husband. He seemed to have run out of moves, she thought—he couldn't return to Xizhen, but there was no place else he could go; the only choice was to continue on their journey. Once they got to Beijing, if they were able to locate his uncle, they would find a measure of stability.

Although Beijing was big, said Xiaomei, Prince Gong's mansion was easy to find. There would surely be someone there who knew his uncle; they would just need to go wait outside the gate and ask the people coming out if they knew a gentleman from the Jiangnan town of Shendian. Surely there would be someone who had some information about his uncle.

Aqiang was buoyed by Xiaomei's words, and his spirits seemed to lift. They continued their journey north, switching from one horse-drawn wagon to another, and they continued spending the nights at roadside inns. Fewer and fewer words passed between them, but it wasn't because something had come between them; rather, it was because the further they traveled, the more illusory the uncle in Beijing became. Without saying anything, they both knew they were worried about where they were headed.

19.

By autumn they crossed the Yellow River and came to a town called Dingchuan, where they spent the night. Aqiang didn't know that Beijing was still quite far away; he thought that once they crossed the Yellow River, it would be right there. He told Xiaomei that the next day she should wear her floral qipao, and he would wear his bright blue *changshan*—when they got to Beijing, they wanted to make a dignified entrance.

Early in the morning, three horses pulling a two-wagon train carried them, along with four other passengers, clip-clopping out the main gate of Dingchuan.

As they bumped along in the wagon, Aqiang sat to Xiaomei's right, and a woman sat to her left. The three men sitting across from her all eyed the slit of her qipao at the same time. Blushing, Xiaomei moved her right leg up against Aqiang's left leg and placed her bundle against the slit on her left leg. After a while she peeked over at the three men sitting across from her—they had averted their eyes, and Xiaomei felt she had successfully hidden herself.

Around noon, they stopped for a bit at a small roadside inn. The driver fed and watered the three horses, while a few of the passengers sat on some stones outside of the inn eating some dried provisions they had brought. When the wagon set off again, the woman who had been sitting to the left of Xiaomei wasn't on it. She was standing by the door of the inn holding her bundle, looking all around as if she were waiting for someone to pick her up.

As the wagon continued on, the monotonous hoofbeats of the horses and rumbling of the wheels caused Xiaomei to lean against Aqiang and fall asleep. Aqiang chatted with the three men sitting across from them, and they asked where each other was headed. Aqiang told them they were headed to Beijing, while each of the three men named a place Aqiang had never heard of; only then did Aqiang realize they weren't traveling together. They continued rambling on about all sorts of things, their voices becoming as monotonous as the hoofbeats and the rumbling wagon wheels.

The wagon traveled on. After a long time had passed, a loud creaking sound suddenly came from one of the wheels. Just as Xiaomei awoke with a start, the wheel splintered into pieces and the wagon toppled over. Xiaomei saw the three men sitting across from them tumble out of the wagon, and before she even had time to cry out, she and Aqiang had also rolled out onto the ground.

The driver, gripping the reins with all his might, managed not to fall off. His body tilted to the side, he called out a *xu, xu!* command, and the horses dragging the creaking wagon came to a halt.

The driver hopped down off the toppled wagon. First he looked at the splintered bits of wheel scattered on the ground, then over at the five passengers, who had all stood up and were dusting themselves off. With a glum look on his face, he told them that the wagon couldn't go any further, and that he would have to put a month's earnings into fixing the wheel. Pointing off into the distance, he told them there was a roadside inn about ten *li* ahead—if they walked quickly they could reach it before dark. He then pitifully requested that when they got to the inn, they ask the innkeeper to send someone back to him with a new wheel.

So they left the woeful driver, the three men walking in front,

Aqiang and Xiaomei following behind. Xiaomei intentionally slowed her pace, increasing the distance between them and the three men up ahead, who kept turning back and looking at them. Xiaomei looked all around and spotted a small stream that flowed toward them. It followed alongside their road until evening, when it curved off into the distance.

Xiaomei stopped. She was afraid to walk into the night with these three men. She tugged at Aqiang's *changshan* and pointed to a path that veered off to the side. Aqiang followed the path with his eyes to a village in the distance. Xiaomei suggested they go to the village and stay the night there in someone's home. Aqiang knew what was worrying Xiaomei—he looked up at the three men ahead of them, then turned with her onto the little path.

20.

When Aqiang and Xiaomei entered the village, they were greeted by a brick-and-tile courtyard residence by the village entrance, which was surrounded by thatched dwellings. Aqiang quietly exclaimed in surprise at this home made of bricks and tiles. He walked toward the wall and the attached buildings that surrounded the courtyard. Two of the windows were open, so he stood on his tiptoes to look inside, where he saw a bookcase with the books all neatly arranged. He called out softly to Xiaomei to have her come look in the window. Standing on her tiptoes, she was able to see the very top row of books.

They walked around to the main gate, which was closed. Standing there beside it, Aqiang said this must be the home of a wealthy family; Xiaomei said whoever lived there must be well-educated and refined. Just then the gate opened, and the tall figure of Lin Xiangfu appeared.

As Lin Xiangfu talked with Aqiang, he stole a few glances at the graceful and elegant Xiaomei and eyed her Shanghai-style qipao with curiosity. He noticed that the slit was a bit high, causing him to avert his eyes and blush. When he looked at Xiaomei again, he saw that she was blushing and smiling at him.

That evening, as Xiaomei quietly observed Aqiang and Lin Xiangfu and listened to them talk, she felt a number of emotions. Ever since Aqiang had come to get her in Xilicun, he had made several surprising, impressive maneuvers, and this evening he made yet another one. Aqiang learned that in this entire brick-and-tile residence, consisting of two rows of six rooms each, Lin Xiangfu lived all by himself. He told Lin Xiangfu that Xiaomei was his little sister and that their parents had died. When Lin Xiangfu asked where they were from, instead of saying Xizhen, Aqiang named a place Xiaomei had never heard of—Wencheng.

Once again Aqiang appeared confident and in high spirits. He talked on and on with Lin Xiangfu, who also spoke quite a bit himself. The eyes of both men gleamed with a certain light. Not infrequently, Lin Xiangfu would glance over at Xiaomei's face, illuminated by the light of the kerosene lamp, and Xiaomei would respond with a smile; flustered, he would then avert his eyes. Only when he began speaking with her did he begin to seem a bit more natural.

Seeing Aqiang talk so confidently and spiritedly gave Xiaomei a premonition. At one point she stopped listening to what they were saying and let her mind wander to her memories with Aqiang. First she saw that distracted young boy she met when she first entered the Shen family home at the age of ten. Then she saw him quickly grow up—in an instant, eight years had passed, and it was their wedding night. Then she thought for the longest time of the humiliation she had endured after returning to the Wanmudang village of Xilicun, and how Aqiang had then suddenly shown up. This man had completely defied convention and risked universal condemnation to come get her and carry her away to some far off place. Since then, through happiness and hardship, they had stuck together down the same path.

That night, as Aqiang lay on the *kang* observing the moonlight shining in through the window, he spoke quietly, haltingly, disconnectedly to Xiaomei. Xiaomei lay beside him looking at him, his face covered by the moonlight and the shadow of the window frame.

Aqiang spoke of his worries regarding their continued journey to Beijing. He couldn't be certain he even had an uncle who had worked in Prince Gong's mansion. His mother had never seen him—not only had she never seen him, but she'd never even seen her cousin whom he'd married. Aqiang paused when he got to this point and waited for Xiaomei's reaction. Xiaomei said that when they got to Beijing and went to Prince Gong's mansion, they would find out whether or not his uncle had worked there. Aqiang had already given up the idea of continuing on to Beijing, but Xiaomei still wanted to go. Aqiang stressed that if his uncle hadn't actually worked at Prince Gong's mansion, going there and asking around wouldn't do them any good. Xiaomei remained unswayed. Even if they didn't find his uncle, she said, as long as they worked hard and were willing to suffer a little hardship, they should be able to get themselves set up in Beijing. Aqiang asked her how. Xiaomei said they could always rely on their mending skills, and maybe someday they would be able to open a mending shop.

Aqiang remained silent for a while, and when he opened his mouth again it was a different topic. This time he talked about how they were short on money. No matter how much they scrimped and saved, what they had would only last them so long. Xiaomei immediately suggested pawning her qipao, which would fetch a good price. Aqiang sighed and said that pawning their clothing could only provide temporary relief; it wasn't a long-term solution. But Xiaomei remained stubbornly optimistic. They would eventually find a way of making a living, she said—as the saying goes, Heaven never blocks all the exits. If they had to beg, they could beg their way to Beijing.

Aqiang didn't say anything more. Then, after a while, he

began talking about Lin Xiangfu. He said he was a good person from a wealthy family. Xiaomei gave a slight nod—she also felt Lin Xiangfu was a good person. After that, Aqiang began stammering as he spoke. He said that the next morning he would go off on his own, and that Xiaomei should stay behind. There was a lot he wanted to say after that, but he was unable to get any of it out—his mouth opened and closed a few times, but no sound ever came out.

Xiaomei quietly gazed at the moonlight on Aqiang's face. She knew what he was trying to get out. She waited for a bit, but he remained silent; she knew then that he was unable to tell her what he wanted to say, so she calmly asked him,

"Where will you wait for me?"

This took Aqiang by surprise. He stared at Xiaomei, then said, "the roadside inn in Dingchuan."

"You'll wait for me there the whole time?" she pressed.

Aqiang hugged Xiaomei and removed her clothing as he caressed her. Then he took off his own clothing and moved on top of Xiaomei, where he lingered in enjoyment. Xiaomei had never before experienced such warmth and tenderness—she knew this was Aqiang's answer, and she caressed him with the same tender affection. The moonlight shone on the two bodies entwined on the kang. They explored one another as they embraced, as if their each and every part had to touch the other's body.

21.

Xiaomei passed the rest of that autumn and the following winter with Lin Xiangfu. In the early spring, during the second lunar month, she quietly left. Lin Xiangfu was as strong and sturdy as the northern land itself; he was kind-hearted, full of life, and adaptable. Xiaomei felt he was the complete opposite of Aqiang, and that life here was entirely different from life in

Xizhen. Here, she watched as the leaves of the trees floated through the air and fell to the ground, and the earth gradually withered. She experienced the gentle autumn breezes turn to the bitterly cold winds of winter.

Xiaomei worried about Aqiang. She didn't know how he was passing each day, or if he had met with any trouble at the inn in Dingchuan. But whenever Lin Xiangfu returned from inspecting the fields and stood in front of her, her thoughts would always jump from Aqiang back to Lin Xiangfu, who made her feel at ease. When she heard him pounding and scraping away in his workshop, she would start up the loom, and the sounds would echo one another. Like trying to stop water by cutting it with a knife, Xiaomei's feelings just kept flowing and developing—the more she held onto her concern for Aqiang, the more accustomed she became to life here. As time passed, Xiaomei's heart underwent a slight change, and a different look appeared in her eyes. She worried about Aqiang, but she also found herself waiting eagerly for Lin Xiangfu to return from the fields.

She barely noticed as the days passed by like this, right up to that hastily orchestrated wedding, which brought them to an end. When Xiaomei saw that villager in the bright blue *changshan* come to offer his congratulations at the wedding, she felt a pain in her chest—she had a feeling it was Aqiang's *changshan*. Only when she heard the villager say he had traded half a sack of corn for it from a fifty-year-old man did her anxiety ease. Late that night after the wedding, Lin Xiangfu took the wooden box out of the interior wall and showed her the bars of gold. As if suddenly waking up, Xiaomei felt that she was about to leave. But this feeling soon morphed into confusion, as if she had suddenly found herself standing in the midst of a vast expanse of land without a single road.

That night after Lin Xiangfu fell asleep, Xiaomei tossed and turned. She couldn't get that bright blue *changshan* out of her mind. Again she had the feeling that it was Aqiang's *changshan;* the size and length were exactly the same as his, and there were just a few stains on it that couldn't be washed out. Thinking carefully back to those stains, she decided that they weren't blood, which helped calm her down slightly. She remembered that when Aqiang had left, he had only two silver yuan and thirteen coppers, which would not have been enough to live on for this long. Her guess was that Aqiang had taken his bright blue *changshan* to the pawnshop in Dingchuan; after changing hands a few times, it had acquired some stains by the time that villager got hold of it. She felt it was possible that he had pawned all of his clothing that was worth anything. She shivered when she thought back to the villager's mention of the scar on the man's forehead, fearing that Aqiang had been slashed by a knife. But the villager had said the man was in his fifties, so it was unlikely that it was Aqiang.

The bright blue *changshan* left her mind and Aqiang appeared. He looked haggard and destitute, and wore an expression like he was reluctant to part ways again. This image of him, now without his bright blue *changshan,* made Xiaomei's thoughts jump to the box of gold bars. She decided she must leave. An unusual sensation had already crept over her body, which alarmed her, though she didn't think about it any further.

For the past few days, Lin Xiangfu had been going out to the fields every day to inspect the growth of the wheat. Xiaomei stayed home and made him a new set of clothes and two new pairs of cloth shoes. Then she went to the kitchen and prepared enough food to last him about two weeks.

Xiaomei didn't use a measuring tape; she simply measured Lin Xiangfu's body and feet with the palms of her hands, putting one palm next to other as if they were walking over his body. It tickled so much that he couldn't stop laughing and his whole body shook. When Xiaomei measured the soles of his feet with her palms, it tickled so much he howled with laughter as he lay on the kang. Twice he jerked his feet away from her, but she pulled them back and held them tight against her chest to get their measurements.

When she had finished making the clothes and shoes, Xiaomei had Lin Xiangfu try them on. Everything fit, and Lin Xiangfu praised Xiaomei's skill, saying there wasn't a single other woman in the world who could compare. But his sincere, heartfelt joy didn't transfer to Xiaomei. A worried look came to her eyes, though he didn't notice. He didn't even think anything of it when he saw the kitchen piled high with food; he simply assumed it was for the lunar new year. With a smile, he said to Xiaomei that New Year's had just passed—were they going to celebrate again?

The day before she left, while Lin Xiangfu was out in the fields checking the wheat, Xiaomei took that wooden box out from the interior wall. When she opened it, she found seventeen large gold bars and three small ones. After hesitating for a moment, she took out seven of the large ones and one of the small ones, then wrapped them in a white cloth and put them in a small bundle. Then she returned the wooden box to its place in the interior wall. She organized her clothing in the wardrobe so that it was all neatly together, but she didn't yet put it in the large bundle she had prepared.

Nor did Xiaomei hide the satchel of gold bars. Instead, she placed it on a part of the kang by the wall. She didn't know why she did this. It was as if she were waiting for fate to render its verdict—would Lin Xiangfu discover it, or not?

Lin Xiangfu did see the small satchel before getting on the kang that night, but he assumed it was what Xiaomei was taking with her the next day when she went to burn incense at the Guan Yu temple. He saw that it wasn't closed very tightly, so he walked over a couple steps and tied it up. Xiaomei watched him walk over to the satchel—he only needed to pick it up to feel the weight of the gold bars. But he didn't; instead, he attentively tied it shut. She felt extraordinarily calm as she watched him walk over—it was all in the hands of fate.

Just before dawn, Xiaomei got up and opened the wardrobe. Unhurriedly she took out her clothes and spread them on the kang; then she packed them in her bundle and cinched it closed. She took her two headscarves—the one with magpies and plum blossoms, and the one with lions playing with satin pom-poms—and placed them in the wardrobe on top of Lin Xiangfu's clothes. She left them there perhaps as a way to leave behind a trace of herself, or perhaps as an attempt to leave behind her shame. The sound of her rustling caused Lin Xiangfu to stir. He stopped snoring and mumbled something indistinctly, then rolled over and continued sleeping.

Xiaomei stood in front of the kang and gazed at Lin Xiangfu sleeping under the moonlight. A feeling welled up inside her that made her reluctant to go, accompanied by a pang of guilt. She was leaving this man, but she would never forget him. She cried softly, tears streaming down her face. Once again Lin Xiangfu's snoring stopped; then he rolled over and continued sleeping.

Xiaomei carried the small satchel in her right hand and the bundle on her back. As the moonlight gradually receded, she walked out through the courtyard gate of Lin Xiangfu's home and down the small path to the village. The morning breeze blew the tears from her cheeks, and by the time she'd made it onto the main road that led to Dingchuan, her face was dry. By this point, her heart was filled with thoughts of Aqiang. When she remembered she'd been away from him for five months, she quickened her pace, as if wanting to walk out of this five months as quickly as possible. She heard the sound of horse's hooves behind her and the shouts of a driver, so she stopped and waited for the wagon. Once she was on it, she could end this period of separation from Aqiang even more quickly.

Xiaomei didn't see Aqiang at the roadside inn in Dingchuan. She had only spent one night there, and the innkeeper didn't remember her. She inquired after Aqiang and gave his description, and the innkeeper remembered him. He told her that Aqiang had stayed there for a few days and then left.

Xiaomei stood at the side of the road, unsure what to do.

There was only one thought in her head—where was Aqiang? She never considered the possibility that he had left her—she felt he would continue waiting for her, but he wasn't at the inn . . . so where was he? A wagon beside of her set off down the road, and another one pulled up in its place. The roadside inn behind her must have a constant flow of people coming and going, she thought. Without even realizing it she stood there throughout the afternoon and into the evening. Then, off in the distance, she saw a beggar dressed in rags running toward her and waving. She heard him shouting:

"Xiaomei!"

As soon as Xiaomei heard Aqiang's voice, she ran to him. She recognized his face, though he was thinner and darker, and his hair was filthy. Just before Aqiang reached Xiaomei, he stopped running and looked all around, as if he were afraid of something. Then he walked up to Xiaomei and said in a quivering voice:

"Xiaomei, you've come."

Xiaomei looked closely at Aqiang's forehead—there was no scar. Xiaomei nodded and said, "I've come."

"I was afraid you wouldn't," he said.

Xiaomei looked him over and asked him sorrowfully, "How did you end up like this?"

Aqiang told her that after he had spent all his money and pawned his clothing, he had no other choice but to beg. He then added that he hadn't pawned Xiaomei's calico clothes—he couldn't bring himself to do it. At that point Xiaomei noticed that he had an old ragged bundle on his back which seemed very light; probably the only thing in it was that set of calico clothes. As Aqiang spoke, he pointed off into the distance, to the place from where he'd just come running over. He said that a few times each day, he would walk over there and watch the inn; even after he thought she would never come, he still went every day to look. After saying this, Aqiang broke down in tears. Then he said to Xiaomei:

"You've finally come."

Xiaomei couldn't see Aqiang's face clearly; her eyes were blurred with tears. There was so much she wanted to say to him, but all she could get out were some low sobs.

22.

Upon their reunion, the five months of separation evaporated into thin air—it was as if they had never been apart. Once again they were on the go, switching from wagon to wagon. Only this time instead of heading north, they were going south. They didn't have a particular destination in mind, they simply headed south because they missed it. The south was their home. As to where their home was in a more concrete sense, at the moment they had no idea. Once they crossed the Yangtze, they would look for someplace and decide.

They no longer stayed at the noisy, bustling roadside inns, but instead spent the nights at more dignified hotels. Aqiang had never imagined that Xiaomei would show up with so many of Lin Xiangfu's gold bars; now, neither of them would have to worry about food or clothing for the rest of their days. Aqiang was in high spirits as they headed south on the wagon, striking up conversation with all sorts of people about all sorts of things. His voice never fell silent; it was a constant presence, just like the sound of hoofbeats on the road as they traveled on.

There was no joyful expression on Xiaomei's face, however, and a troubled look showed in her eyes. The smile that had appeared on her face when she and Aqiang were reunited gradually faded away as they continued their journey on those jostling wagons. Xiaomei felt that the further she got from Lin Xiangfu, the more of herself she had left behind with him. It was something that would be impossible to take with her, like the two headscarves with magpies and lions, which now belonged to him.

When she was still with Lin Xiangfu, an unusual change had occurred in her body. By the time she crossed the Yellow River on a wagon heading south, it became clearer. Several times she had to beg the driver to stop the horses so she could stand along the side of the road and vomit.

She knew she was pregnant. In a hotel one evening, she broke the news to Aqiang, whose face registered only a look of slight surprise before returning to normal. After they crossed the Yangtze, he said, they would look for a more permanent place to stay and have the baby there. Xiaomei informed him that it was Lin Xiangfu's child. Aqiang nodded as if to say of course he knew it was Lin Xiangfu's child.

Xiaomei fell into an uneasy silence; her mind was scattered. Aqiang said he would look after the child as if it were his own, and Xiaomei nodded—she believed he would. He said he would teach the child how to mend, and Xiaomei laughed. Aqiang realized his mending skills were nothing to brag about, so he quickly changed his tune and said he would make sure the child studied hard. He would be a successful scholar, like a magpie that climbs to the tip of a branch and becomes a phoenix.

This helped put Xiaomei's mind at ease. As she began to calm down, she asked Aqiang somewhat mischievously: if she had a girl, would he pass on his mending skills to her, or would he have her devote herself to her studies? Aqiang scratched his head, unsure of how to respond. In those days girls didn't have many educational opportunities, so Aqiang changed the subject: even though these gold bars were enough to support them for the rest of their lives, he said, they should still economize so they could save up and provide for the child. If it were a boy, they would need money for his wedding; if it were a girl, they would need it for her dowry. Xiaomei gazed faithfully at Aqiang and placed her hands on her belly as if protecting the fetus. In a soft voice, she said that after they'd crossed the Yangtze and found someplace to settle down, they couldn't just sit on their hands and let their money slowly slip away; they should open a mending shop. Aqiang nodded and said: if the baby is a girl, you should teach her your mending skills. Xiaomei laughed once again—she knew that Aqiang was saying this because he knew his own skills were lacking. If it's a boy, she said to him, you'll be responsible for getting him to study hard and succeed in the examinations. Aqiang thought of the calico clothing that was still in the bundle—if the child was a girl, he said, he would always have her dressed in calico clothes, and he would have a new set made for her every year until she got married. Xiaomei smiled upon hearing this, and her eyes filled with tears.

For the rest of their journey, many things weighed on Xiaomei's mind. Her mood transferred to Aqiang, who no longer seemed so excited and now only rarely spoke to the other passengers on the wagons. He assumed that Xiaomei was preoccupied thinking about the baby. He wanted to find the right words to say to her, but he couldn't come up with anything appropriate and was only able to make a few trivial comments before falling silent. Both he and Xiaomei grew more and more reticent.

When they made it to the shore of the Yangtze, Xiaomei's belly had already begun to protrude slightly, and her feet had begun to swell. Aqiang said they would stay there for the night and cross the river the next day.

The hotel was located in view of the water, but not close enough to hear the waves against the shore. All of a sudden, Xiaomei began silently shedding tears. Lin Xiangfu had given her everything, but she had stolen his gold and was running away with his child. She felt upset and guilty; it was like the Yangtze was a clear boundary—once she crossed it, she would never look back. Lin Xiangfu would never know, and he would never see his own child.

Xiaomei dried her tears and told Aqiang what she had been thinking over the past few days. She said she wanted to go back to Lin Xiangfu and have the baby there.

Holding her hands protectively over her belly, she said, "This is his own flesh and blood."

Aqiang looked at her in shock. For a moment he didn't react, and Xiaomei repeated,

"This is his own flesh and blood."

When Xiaomei uttered this phrase for the second time, her voice sounded more resolute. Aqiang's expression changed from shocked to nervous, and then from nervous to worried. After a while, he stuttered,

"You stole his gold, but now you're going to give it back . . . "

Confused, Xiaomei asked, "Why would I give it back?"

"You mean you wouldn't give it back?" asked Aqiang, puzzled.

"No," she said, "I'm giving him the child."

After a comprehending "oh," Aqiang immediately grew afraid and asked Xiaomei, "If you don't give back his gold, would he kill you?"

Xiaomei stared contemplatively at Aqiang. "I don't know," she said.

Then after a little while she shook her head and said, "He's a good person—he wouldn't kill me."

After another while, she gave a laugh and said, "Even if he did kill me, he would at least wait until I had the baby."

Xiaomei had already made up her mind: she would return to Lin Xiangfu and have the baby there. As frightened and worried as Aqiang was, he had no choice but to agree. That evening on the banks of the Yangtze, Xiaomei and Aqiang switched roles: from that point on, it would no longer be Xiaomei following Aqiang, but rather, Aqiang following Xiaomei.

After some discussion, they decided to return to Dingchuan, where Aqiang would once again wait.

"This time, you'll have to wait for a long time," said Xiaomei.

"It doesn't matter how long—I'll still wait for you," said Aqiang.

"There's a chance something could happen, and I could die," said Xiaomei.

"Then I'll wait in Dingchuan until death," said Aqiang.

The two of them looked at each other through their tears, and then smiled.

Aqiang asked Xiaomei: "After you give birth, you'll come find me in Dingchuan?"

Xiaomei thought for a minute and then said, "After the child is one month old, I'll come find you in Dingchuan."

They talked in whispers after that. Xiaomei said that carrying the gold bars was both heavy and dangerous—the next day they should go find a large private bank and exchange them for silver draft. Xiaomei took out a needle and thread and sewed an interior pocket into Aqiang's underwear, saying he should fold up the banknotes and tuck them inside—it would be safer and more convenient that way. Aqiang said he wouldn't stay in any of the inns or hotels in Dingchuan—there were too many people coming and going, and there were bound to be some thieves. During his previous five months in Dingchuan he had noticed a house for rent; he could rent out a side room all to himself, which would keep his money from getting stolen. He also said the house was close to the temple, which was just a short walk down the street. He would go to the temple every day to burn incense and pray for Xiaomei's safety.

23.

After traveling for a long time, they arrived in Dingchuan. As Xiaomei neared Lin Xiangfu, she felt her heart grow as calm as still water. The journey had been rough. She had thought of every sort of punishment she might face, and decided she would accept whatever might come as long as she was able to give birth to the child. She believed Lin Xiangfu would let her have the baby.

Xiaomei and Aqiang passed a quiet evening in Dingchuan, in the rented side room of that house. Occasionally they would hear a dog bark in the courtyard. As the night watchman beat the *geng* with his bamboo stick and the flame of the kerosene lamp flickered, Aqiang stared at Xiaomei with a heavy heart. Early the next morning, when he took Xiaomei to the roadside inn and saw her off on a wagon, he still looked at her with the same expression. As the wagon drove away, Xiaomei couldn't see his sad, worried expression, because he had lowered his head.

Xiaomei rode the wagon out of Dingchuan on a road that headed north. The dust kicked up by the wind swirled in front of her eyes, but through it she could still make out the rippling waves of wheat in the fields. Lin Xiangfu must be preparing for the harvest, she thought. Around noon, the wagon came to that tiny roadside inn; this time they only stopped for a short while, around half a *shichen*. After the driver had fed and watered the horses and they got back on the road, Xiaomei began to pay close attention to their surroundings: she remembered that little stream, and when she looked out from the wagon and saw it curving towards them from off in the distance, her heart began to pound—she would soon see Lin Xiangfu. She knew the wagon had already passed the spot where the wheel had broken the time before. She watched as the road and stream ran alongside each other, and when she saw the stream curve off again into the distance, she got off the wagon. Standing along the side of the road, she gazed out at the fields and the people working in them. There was one figure that looked like Lin Xiangfu, and then another that looked like it could also be him. As she walked down that familiar little path, she began to feel nervous.

Lin Xiangfu received Xiaomei with arms open as wide as the fields. None of the various sorts of punishments Xiaomei had been imagining came to pass. Xiaomei once again got married to Lin Xiangfu, but this time it was more formal. They wrote out a horoscope card and placed it on the shelf by the stove for a month, so the kitchen god could watch over them. Lin Xiangfu hired two painters and a tailor—he had the painters give all the furniture in the house a shiny fresh coat of paint, and had the tailor make Xiaomei a large red robe. Then Lin Xiangfu had a four-sided table made into a bridal sedan, in which Xiaomei rode wearing her red robe. The baby girl was born without incident.

Life after this seemed peaceful and quiet. Lin Xiangfu was completely immersed in it, while Xiaomei did her best to put on a smile. The birth of the baby was like a call hastening her to leave once more.

Xiaomei was constantly with her baby daughter on the kang. During the day, she would hold her close to her chest, hardly ever willing to separate. At night, she would wake from sleep and reach out to lightly stroke the face of the swaddled baby, moving her hand so slowly and gently it seemed as if she wanted to absorb the baby's scent. Only when Lin Xiangfu appeared in the room would Xiaomei momentarily move her eyes away from her daughter and look over at him.

Xiaomei hoped her daughter's first month would pass slowly, but each day the time between sunrise and sunset seemed like the blink of an eye. Then the midwife came with the barber, along with a number of other villagers—the courtyard was so packed that some people had to stand outside, while children wanting to get a glimpse of the action climbed trees and sat on the courtyard wall. The barber took a razor and carefully shaved off the baby girl's hair and eyebrows. Xiaomei's hands trembled as she gathered the shorn hair into a red cloth.

When the midwife saw that Xiaomei had gathered up the hair, she said that according to custom, after the hair had been shaved from the newborn baby, it should go stay with either its maternal grandmother or uncle for a bit. Lin Xiangfu said the baby's maternal grandmother was no longer in this world, and that its uncle was far away, south of the Yangtze, and it would be very difficult for the baby to travel there.

The midwife thought it over and said that the baby wouldn't have to go stay somewhere else, but the "one-month trip" would still have to be taken. Lin Xiangfu asked the midwife how they should take this "one-month trip," and the midwife said they would just have to do the best they could: some friends and relatives of the baby's mother should come with some clothing, bonnets, shoes, and socks for the baby, and then carry the baby south with them for a bit—since the baby's uncles live in the south, that should suffice. Lin Xiangfu pointed at Tian Da and said his family would represent the mother's family and friends, but they would need three days to prepare the clothing, bonnets, shoes, and socks. The midwife said they'd wait three days then; in three days, the baby would be taken on her "one-month trip." Before she left, the midwife instructed Xiaomei to break off a bundle of peach branches and use a red string to tie on five dyed-red peanuts and seven copper coins—the peach branches would ward off evil, the peanuts would bring longevity, and the coins represented the seven lucky stars of the big dipper.

Three days later, Xiaomei held some peach branches with peanuts and coins tied onto them as Tian Da's daughter walked out of Lin Xiangfu's courtyard carrying the swaddled baby on her back. As the villagers all crowded around to watch, Lin Xiangfu followed behind Xiaomei and Tian Da's daughter, but the midwife, who was standing off to the side, stopped him— the "one-month trip" was for the women; the men shouldn't follow. Lin Xiangfu stopped and shouted out to Tian Da's daughter above the din of the crowd:

"First take a turn around the village, and then head south on the main road for a bit."

Tian Da's daughter turned around to voice her agreement, but the midwife told her, "You can't look back when you're on the 'one-month trip'—you have to start all over if you do."

So Xiaomei, with peach boughs in hand, and Tian Da's daughter with the baby on her back both walked backwards to the gate of Lin Xiangfu's courtyard, not daring to turn their heads again. Just then the midwife thought of something and asked Lin Xiangfu,

"Was some paper with writing on it placed near the baby's chest?"

Lin Xiangfu shook his head and said there wasn't. The midwife said, "If you put some paper there, the child will be studious and well-mannered."

Lin Xiangfu quickly went inside and found a paper he'd written something on. Then he ran back out with it and gave it to the midwife, who folded it carefully and tucked it into the baby's swaddle.

"Is anything else needed?" Lin Xiangfu asked the midwife.

"Go get two green onions," she said.

Lin Xiangfu ran into another room and came back out with two green onions. The midwife tucked them into the swaddle, which looked like it was growing onions alongside the head of the sleeping baby. The villagers all laughed when they saw this, and so did Lin Xiangfu and Xiaomei; Tian Da's daughter couldn't see how funny the baby looked on her back, but when she saw the villagers all break out in laughter, she began to laugh as well. Only the midwife kept from laughing, as she said to Lin Xiangfu,

"The onion means the child will be intelligent and capable."

And so the "one-month trip" began. Tian Da's daughter took a turn around the village with the baby on her back, while the midwife and Xiaomei, carrying the peach boughs, walked along on either side. The villagers crowded in front and behind; when the street narrowed the crowd did the same, and when it widened, they would spread out. When they left the village and headed south on the main road, the baby woke up. Her head still resting against the onions, she looked around wide-eyed at all the people and listened to the commotion.

Seeing that the baby had woken up, the midwife pointed at a nearby villager and asked the baby,

"Have you seen them before?"

The baby gave no reaction, but stared around at this and

that with her black, shining eyes. The midwife pointed at another villager and continued her questioning,

"Have you seen them before?"

The baby still had no reaction, but now villagers began coming up to her and imitating the midwife, pointing at other villagers and asking,

"Have you seen them before?"

Hearing all sorts of different noises around her, the baby opened her toothless mouth and grinned. When they saw the baby was smiling, the villagers rushed forward to repeat the phrase to her. One of them used a funny voice, and the baby laughed, *ge ge ge*. Other villagers began changing their voices and the baby kept laughing, causing the two onion stalks to shake.

24.

The baby had taken her "one-month trip," but Xiaomei didn't leave just yet. Every morning when she woke up, she could feel that the time for her to part with her daughter and Lin Xiangfu was drawing nearer, yet she kept putting it off, day after day. Whenever she nursed her daughter, the baby would rest her head in the crook of her arm and move her tiny hand over Xiaomei's chest as if begging her to stay.

One day when Lin Xiangfu finally had some spare time, he stuffed thirty silver yuan in the front of his shirt and led his donkey into town. This was his profit from the harvest that year, which he intended to change at the *qianzhuang* bank for one little croaker.

That afternoon, Xiaomei, dressed in a grayish blue outfit, sat in the entrance to the courtyard holding her daughter. Her eyes misted over as she stared at the main road that led out of the village, while the baby looked up at her mother and examined her with her big eyes. Lin Xiangfu had departed that morning and hadn't returned for a long while. Only when the sun was setting in the west did Xiaomei hear the tinkling of the donkey's bell floating on the breeze. Focusing her gaze, she saw that Lin Xiangfu had already led his donkey to the village entrance.

Lin Xiangfu led the donkey with one hand while holding a stick of candied haw berries in the other. Grinning from ear to ear, he handed Xiaomei the stick of haw berries and bent down to gaze at his baby daughter. Then he and Xiaomei entered the courtyard, and he slowly led the donkey around a few times. As Xiaomei sat in the doorway holding the baby, he told her that once an animal was untethered from its load, it was best to give it a little stroll.

The sunset blazed red in the sky that evening. Xiaomei sat in the doorway, bringing the candied haw berries to the baby's mouth and letting her lick their sweet coating. In the evening rays, her grayish blue clothing looked as red as a maple leaf in autumn.

Lin Xiangfu and Xiaomei stayed up late that evening. Lin Xiangfu took that wooden box out from the interior wall and put the little croaker in it. Then they lay down on the kang, their baby daughter asleep in between them. Lin Xiangfu said that the little croaker weighed down his shirt as he made his way home that day. Each year there would be another little croaker, and after ten years he could exchange them for a big croaker—then they would have eleven big croakers. When their daughter turned sixteen and was ready to marry, they would have eleven big croakers and eight little croakers—that meant they would be able to provide her with a decent dowry so she could enter her husband's family with her head held high.

Lin Xiangfu's words moved Xiaomei to tears. Lin Xiangfu didn't know why she was crying and guessed it was from a feeling of guilt. He said that sometimes when he thought of those gold bars he would become angry, but then he would soon calm down—the past was the past.

After saying this, Lin Xiangfu fell fast asleep. Xiaomei had only been asleep for a short time when she was awoken by the baby's hungry cries. She got up from the kang, lit the kerosene lamp, and sat back down on the edge of the kang to nurse the baby. When she'd had her fill, Xiaomei opened her swaddle and laid her across her legs to change her diaper. Much to her surprise, Xiaomei saw the baby raise her head—until then, her head had always needed to be supported. Now, all of a sudden, her neck had strengthened so much that she could raise her head and look around.

Xiaomei called for Lin Xiangfu—she felt they should experience this moment together. Lin Xiangfu propped himself up and looked at Xiaomei with his sleepy eyes, and Xiaomei told him to look at the baby. As soon as he saw her he exclaimed in surprise—now he was fully awake.

The baby held her head to the right, then to the left, and then looked up; her black, shining eyes looked to the left, to the right, and then straight ahead. Lin Xiangfu laughed and said the baby moving her head around like that made her look like a turtle.

"That's just what a turtle looks like when it sticks its head out," he said.

Xiaomei's face was awash in tears. Lin Xiangfu smiled at her and said, "When our daughter gets married, you're going to be a puddle of tears."

What Lin Xiangfu didn't know was that Xiaomei was shedding tears of parting. When her daughter lifted her head, it was the first step in the long process of growing up. Having witnessed this first milestone, Xiaomei told herself it was time for her to leave.

25.

Before the stars had receded into the dawn, Xiaomei was already on the main road to Dingchuan. Her eyes were filled with tears, which glistened in the lingering moonlight.

As the sun began to rise, a horse-drawn wagon approached her. Hugging her bundle, she lowered her head and climbed on. Once she'd sat down, she dried her tears with her sleeves; when she looked up again, there was no expression on her face. She looked at the other passengers on the wagon—two women and one man—then looked out over the boundless fields. They were vast and empty, just like her heart.

The first time Xiaomei had left, she had been filled with reluctance and guilt. This time, it was heartbreaking—not only was she leaving Lin Xiangfu, but also her baby girl, who had only just come into the world.

That afternoon, she got off the wagon at the roadside inn in Dingchuan. She walked to an intersection and looked around, then remembered she should walk down the road to the left. Once the temple came into view, she would soon come to the room Aqiang had been renting. She had spent one uneasy night there and returned to Lin Xiangfu the next day, not knowing what fate had in store for her.

As she walked past another intersection, a thought suddenly occurred to her: what if Aqiang was no longer waiting for her? What if he had already left, gone back to Xizhen, returned to his parents? If this was the case, she would return to Lin Xiangfu and her daughter. But this was only a fleeting thought—she had a feeling that Aqiang wouldn't leave, that he would remain there waiting for her. With this thought in her mind, she walked past another intersection and then heard a voice call out behind her:

"Xiaomei! Xiaomei!"

It was Aqiang's voice. Xiaomei turned around and saw him excitedly running toward her. When he made it up to her, he grabbed her hands and began running back, pulling her with him as he ran—she wasn't sure what was going on. As they ran, he said to her,

"Hurry—you've got to come see this horse-drawn sedan!"

Aqiang pulled Xiaomei along to an intersection, where they

turned right and continued running. When they came up to a sedan chair and some horses, Aqiang stopped. Pointing with his right hand, he said with breathless excitement:

"Look, look!"

Xiaomei saw a sedan chair and two horses, one in front and one in back. Two sedan chair carriers were also there, each leading one of the horses. Several people were seated in the sedan. Aqiang told Xiaomei to pay attention to the horses' gait—they were perfectly in step with one another, like a couple of well-trained soldiers.

"If these two horses aren't perfectly in step with each other," said Aqiang, "the people would fall out of the sedan!"

He then added: "This is the first time I've ever seen horses carry a sedan."

Then Aqiang took a good look at his wife. He saw that her once-bulging belly had now flattened out, and her face had become round and dewy. Seeing Xiaomei perfectly intact made Aqiang smile. Not wanting his efforts to go unnoticed, he said to her,

"I burned incense at the temple every day." Then his eyes turned red and he choked up. "You've finally returned."

Xiaomei also inspected Aqiang. She felt he'd put on weight, and she noticed he was wearing a *changshan* she'd never seen before—he must have had it made at a tailor's in Dingchuan. For the first time that day after being constantly on the go, a smile spread over Xiaomei's face.

After spending the night in Dingchuan, Xiaomei and Aqiang once again set out on a long journey. By day they rode in wagons and by night they slept in inns as they continued traveling south. Xiaomei remained quiet and reserved, so Aqiang didn't say much, either. Once they crossed the Yangtze, the land of the south spread out before them—the trees and grasses grew in a lush profusion, the crops were a luxuriant green, streams and rivers crisscrossed the fields, and smoke curled up from the chimneys of the peasants' homes. When they left Dingchuan, their goal had simply been to go south, intending to come up with a more specific destination once they'd crossed the Yangtze.

Xiaomei kept on hitching rides on wagons and traveling south; Aqiang didn't know where exactly she was headed, but he followed her anyway. When they neared Shanghai, Aqiang thought she wanted to go there, where they'd spent their happiest days together. He asked Xiaomei if she intended to go to Shanghai, but she shook her head and said that everything in Shanghai was too expensive. Aqiang was confused. After a while, he asked Xiaomei,

"Where are we going?"

Xiaomei's answer shocked him:

"Back to Xizhen."

26.

After Aqiang had gone to fetch Xiaomei away from the Wanmudang village of Xilicun, the stern and severe look on the face of Mrs. Shen was replaced with one of depression. Mr. Shen had never dreamed his son would do something like this—stealing a hundred silver yuan along with every last copper in the drawer under the shop counter. Every time he read over the letter his son had left behind, he would let out a sigh and lament,

"What an unfilial son!"

About two weeks later, a familiar customer came to pick up some clothing and, out of concern, asked if there had been any news from Aqiang and Xiaomei. Mrs. Shen shook her head expressionlessly, while Mr. Shen seemed stunned. After the customer left, a look of worry and dismay spread over Mr. Shen's face—how did that man know about Aqiang and Xiaomei? Mrs. Shen said,

"You can't wrap a fire in paper."

A year later, there was still no word from Aqiang and Xiaomei. Business at the Shen family's mending shop was dropping off as well—at first the shop was simply not as lively as it had been, but now it seemed cold and deserted, with only two old people moving slowly around. Because they were often unable to return the customers' items to them within the allotted amount of time, their business decreased by the day, until several days at a time would pass with no customers coming to the shop. The old couple would get up in the morning and take down the door plank, then sit on it in a stupor until evening, when they would put it back up again.

Mr. Shen had always liked his clever, hardworking, and thrifty daughter-in-law, and after his wife had insisted on kicking her out, the following few days had been difficult. Now he would often curse Xiaomei, saying she was a she-devil who had tricked their son into leaving them. Then he would heave a sigh of regret and say they should have sent Xiaomei back as soon as she stole that blue calico clothing right after she'd first arrived. He had been too lenient from the start.

Mrs. Shen would listen sullenly to her husband's ranting without saying a word. After their son had run off with Xiaomei, she didn't say anything about it, and she spoke less and less in general. Every day she would rise early and stay up late doing the housework, until one day she fell ill.

Mrs. Shen lay in bed coughing incessantly. A maid came to take over the housework; she was so clumsy that plates and dishes could often be heard shattering on the floor. A gray-haired doctor of Chinese medicine became a frequent visitor to the Shen home. Every two weeks he would cross their threshold and enter the patient's room, followed by a thin, gaunt apprentice. The gray-haired doctor would sit on a stool by the bed and take Mrs. Shen's pulse, while the apprentice sat at the desk. Once he had taken the pulse, the doctor would call out the prescription as if he were singing opera, and the apprentice would begin writing furiously, marking it all down in tiny characters on a sheet of white paper. After waiting for the ink to dry, he would then hand it over with both hands to Mr. Shen, who would thank the apprentice and hand him some copper coins. The gray-haired doctor would then issue a few instructions to Mr. Shen and be off, the skinny apprentice following closely at his heels in the very same manner in which he'd come, as if he were afraid of getting lost.

Mr. Shen would usually then leave in a hurry to go fill the prescription at the pharmacy. When he returned home he would go straight to the kitchen and begin cooking the medicine for his wife himself, since the clumsy maid had broken one of the medicine bowls.

The gray-haired doctor called out prescription after prescription—they were really all the same mix of things, only with different dosages. But despite all these prescriptions the doctor sang out, Mrs. Shen's condition only worsened. Her coughing now produced streaks of blood that were nearly black, so a wooden basin was placed at her bedside, in which fresh water was poured each morning. By evening, the contents would be dark and thick.

After Mrs. Shen fell ill, the mending shop's account book was placed by her pillow. Tucked inside the book was the silver hairclip Xiaomei had left behind, which Mrs. Shen used as a bookmark, placing it wherever she left off before closing the book. At first she was able to prop herself up and look over the accounts as she coughed, although by that point there were no longer that many accounts to look over. As her illness worsened, she was no longer able to flip through the book, but was unwilling to part with it. When she was awake, she would shakily place her left hand on those accounts, as if they were her life.

The eyes of this once dignified woman now appeared vacant, sometimes even comatose. One evening, as she was breathing her final breaths, she suddenly called out for Xiaomei. She called her again and again, with increasing urgency. Mr. Shen, asleep in the next room, quickly grabbed the oil lamp and came over.

"Xiaomei's not here," he told her.

"Call her over then," said Mrs. Shen in a weak voice. "I want to turn the accounts over to her."

Mr. Shen held out his hand and said, "Give the accounts to me."

Weakly yet stubbornly, Mrs. Shen continued to call out, "Xiaomei, Xiaomei."

Mr. Shen could only stand there as Mrs. Shen tired herself out and began gasping for breath. Then after a while, she said to Mr. Shen,

"Call Xiaomei over."

"Xiaomei's not here," Mr. Shen answered.

Seeming not to have heard, Mrs. Shen persisted: "Go get Xiaomei."

"She's not here," said Mr. Shen, "she left with that unfilial son of ours."

"She left . . . "

Mrs. Shen calmed and slowly shut her eyes. Then her breathing ceased. This stern woman, who had always kept her feelings hidden and never revealed them to anyone, had made it clear that as she left this world, she was longing to see Xiaomei.

Mrs. Shen was placed in her coffin wearing undergarments made of bright red muslin, and a jacket and pants made of green silk. A hat with a single pearl adorned her head, which rested on a pillow with an embroidered sun and rooster.

Seven relatives, all dressed in white, came to Shendian for the funeral procession. Mr. Shen walked in front, sobbing with his head lowered as he accompanied Mrs. Shen's casket to its final resting place in the western hills. Before her death, while she was still conscious, Mrs. Shen had insisted on a simple funeral, so Mr. Shen didn't call on the Daoist priests from the temple of the city god. So there were no Daoists following along in two solemn lines, nor were there any sounds of *di* flutes, *xiao* flutes, *suona* horns, or wooden fish to fill the air as they went along. Mr. Shen had hired a cheap band of *suona* players from the countryside, and while the music they honked out was far from elegant, it was much louder than the music the Daoists would have produced. With their cheeks puffed out as they blew, they noisily made their way to the western hills.

27.

The characters on the wooden oblong sign hanging by the door of the mending shop became stained and dirty, so much so that the *zhi* 織 character in the middle became indecipherable. The door to the shop was still opened at sunup and closed at sundown, but no customers ever came. Mr. Shen sat in the shop every day, but it was as if his spirit had followed Mrs. Shen out of this world—sitting there woodenly by the counter, he was just like a piece of furniture. The maid still busied herself around the house, still breaking dishes; the sound, at least, lent the house a little bit of life.

A year passed, and then Mr. Shen fell ill. It seemed to be the same illness as Mrs. Shen—a persistent cough that produced streaks of blood. That same gray-haired doctor and his skinny apprentice once again became frequent visitors to the Shen home. Instead of lying in bed, Mr. Shen would sit up in the shop for his exam. Whenever the doctor came, several figures would appear outside the shop door to listen to him call out the prescription—the cadence of his voice was truly like an actor playing the *laosheng* role in traditional opera. The skinny apprentice would stand off to the side, leaning over on the counter and writing furiously. It was still that same old mix of ingredients.

One afternoon that winter, two sedan chairs stopped in front of the Shen family's mending shop. Out of the first sedan stepped Aqiang. He walked hesitantly toward the shop, where he found his father sitting in a stupor. Two years had passed, during which time his father had aged like a melting candle. Tentatively he called out to him:

"Father."

His father eyed him motionlessly. Again he called out to him. This time his father let out a long sigh and said in a quavering voice,

"So you've come back."

"Yes," Aqiang nodded, "your unfilial son has returned."

"Has Xiaomei come, too?" his father asked.

"She has," answered Aqiang.

Shakily his father stood up and looked outside the shop. "Where is she?" he asked his son.

Aqiang hesitated. "In the sedan chair," he said.

His father looked at the two sedan chairs and called out twice: "Xiaomei! Xiaomei!"

Xiaomei emerged from the second sedan chair and stood with her head bowed. "Come in," she heard her father-in-law say.

Keeping her head lowered, Xiaomei followed Aqiang into the shop. Only then did she look up to see her father-in-law, who had aged so much he looked like a completely different person.

"So the two of you have finally come back," he said.

The words of Xiaomei's father-in-law made her feel that the Shen family had accepted her. Aqiang saw there was a maid in the house, but he didn't see his mother.

"Where's Mother?" he asked.

His father started coughing, and it was a while before he stopped. "Gone—she went to the western hills," he said.

Aqiang didn't understand at first. "Went to the western hills?," he asked.

"She's dead. It's been a year," his father said.

Aqiang was stunned for a moment, and then the tears started flowing. "I'm an unfilial son," he said, wiping his eyes, "I've wronged my mother."

Xiaomei was crying as well. "It's all because of me," she said to her father-in-law.

With unsteady steps, her father-in-law led them upstairs to the bedroom, where he took the account book out of the wardrobe and handed it to Xiaomei.

"Right before she died," he said, "she kept calling your name. She wanted to turn the account book over to you. I said you weren't here, but she wouldn't listen—she just kept calling."

When Xiaomei received the account book, the silver hairpin that had been stuck inside fell to the floor. Shocked, she bent over and picked it up.

"It's all my fault," she said through her tears.

Her father-in-law sighed. "It's fate," he said.

The news that Aqiang and Xiaomei had returned spread quickly through Xizhen, and the Shen family's mending shop became a lively place once more. Aqiang and Xiaomei cleaned up the sign hanging by the door and once again took up their mending work. Most of the people came to the shop to hear what they had been up to over the past two years; only occasionally would someone also bring along some damaged clothing. The couple mended as they provided a vague sketch of their experiences, saying they had gone to Beijing—they had done mending work there as well, they said. There were a lot of people in Beijing, and business was booming—but the winters were too cold and dry, and they just couldn't bear them.

As they talked, their hands worked just as quickly as ever—it was clear they had been doing it since childhood. The lively scene lasted several days, and then the sparrows settled in once more over the doorway, so to speak. Aqiang and Xiaomei had already unintentionally recommenced their mending business, and because of Mr. Shen's hopes, they kept at it.

Mr. Shen felt more at ease since Aqiang and Xiaomei's return, and from then on he stayed in bed. His illness grew worse by the day—his cough became more severe, and bloody phlegm would hang from the corners of his mouth. A wooden basin was again placed by the bed, filled with clean water in morning that was stained red by evening. When he knew he was finished, he called his son and daughter-in-law to his bedside to relay his wishes for his funeral. After he died, there was no need to bathe him in water from the well by the temple of the city god; water from the well out back would be just fine. For his burial garb, they shouldn't use satin, which sounded just like the word for "break" (*duan*) and would inauspiciously imply that the family line would be broken. It was very dark in the underworld, so they also shouldn't use black—the clothing next to his skin should be red and made of muslin. He said that after he died and went to the underworld, his first stop would be the disrobing pavilion, where the demon servants would try to take off the clothing he had been wearing in the mortal realm. If they started to take off something red, they would be fooled into thinking it was blood and stop. He also discussed the coffin—it should be made from the wood of a perfectly straight and mature fir tree, which would not rot. There was no need to get the Daoist priests from the temple of the city god—that cheap band of *suona* players from the countryside would spare no effort.

Seeing that his son barely seemed to be functioning and his daughter-in-law was sobbing, he added just one more word of caution: "Our family's savings have become quite low, so from now on, do your best to economize with everything."

Three days later, Mr. Shen quietly passed away. Aqiang and Xiaomei carried out the funeral according to his specifications—it was nothing fancy, but still dignified. Then they took down the sign from beside the door, and the mending shop ceased operation. In the days that followed, few people saw the couple, but they would often see the maid. She would go out early in the morning with a bamboo basket to buy produce, and when she'd completed this task she would push open the door and go back inside.

Aqiang and Xiaomei lived a quiet life. Sometimes on a still night, the sound of mournful sobbing could be heard. People said it sounded like Xiaomei, and began speculating about what sorts of things they might have gotten up to during their two years away. After three months, though, the rumors had abated. They remained in Xizhen, and Xizhen forgot about them.

28.

After their return, Aqiang and Xiaomei became immersed in the past. When morning came it wasn't their morning, and when evening set in it wasn't their evening. It was as if their lives, like the mending shop, had simply stopped.

Every day when the maid saw Xiaomei, she had her hair up in a perfect bun cinched with the silver hairclip. Xiaomei was kindhearted and wouldn't let the maid do any of the heavy work around the house; she managed the work along with her. Xiaomei was steady and nimble, and under her tutelage the once-clumsy maid became much more careful—the crash of a dish shattering on the floor was now a rare occurrence.

The maid felt Aqiang was always seemed distracted, not knowing he had always been that way. Aqiang would often sit out in the courtyard for long periods of time without moving; only when Xiaomei called for him would he get up and go inside. Sometimes Xiaomei would enter the courtyard and sit down beside Aqiang, a smile appearing on her face as she thought back to how he'd come for her in Xilicun, and how a completely new Aqiang had experienced a fleeting joy in Shanghai.

Aqiang and Xiaomei didn't say much when they were together, but they got along well. The maid could sense their closeness—when they sat facing one another, each holding the same *changshan,* which was most likely Aqiang's, they kept their heads down and focused as they mended the little rips and tears in the fabric. Both of them had nimble hands, but Xiaomei's work was clearly better—when she had finished mending something, there was hardly any trace of it, while Aqiang's work was always quite obvious. Then he would look over at Xiaomei and smile, as if to admit his inferiority. Xiaomei would smile back and say that she had been working on little rips, while he had been mending holes.

"Rips are easy to mend; holes are hard," she would say.

The maid knew that Xiaomei had entered the Shen family as a child bride. The status of child brides was often quite low, but this was different—in this house, Xiaomei was the authority. Aqiang may have looked distracted, but as soon as something needed done requiring the strength of a man, Xiaomei needed only to softly call out his name and he would be right there.

One time when the rice was getting low, Xiaomei took the rice sack up to Aqiang and said,

"We're scraping the bottom of the rice vat."

Aqiang immediately jumped up and took the sack from Xiaomei, then went to get a smaller one as well. Although he didn't normally leave the house, Aqiang was out the door at once to go buy rice. When he returned, he was carrying the big sack on his left shoulder and the little one in his right hand. From then on, after seeing how exhausted he looked after returning home, Xiaomei would accompany him every time he went to buy rice.

When these two hermits walked down the streets of Xizhen together, Aqiang would keep his head down, while Xiaomei would nod and greet others. People who knew them would call out,

"Long time no see!"

Aqiang would remain blank, while Xiaomei would respond,

"We're going to buy rice!"

The clerk at the rice store told them that when other people come to buy rice, they consider a large amount to be half a bag, but you two want a full bag. One time the clerk mentioned that he had been careless and accidentally torn his *changshan,* but since the mending shop was closed he'd had no choice but to take a needle and thread to it himself—the result looked like a knife scar. Aqiang had no reaction to the clerk's story, but

Xiaomei caught the gist and said that although the mending shop had closed, old customers could still send their clothing over—whether a hole had been burned or torn, they would do their best to fix it.

When the couple emerged from the rice store, the people of Xizhen were presented with a scene of marital harmony: Aqiang walked in front carrying the giant sack of rice on his shoulders, while Xiaomei followed behind with the smaller sack. Aqiang walked quickly, while Xiaomei moved slowly; several times he had to stop and wait for her to catch up. When they made it to the stone bridge, they both stopped for a rest. Xiaomei set her sack of rice down on the stone steps, while Aqiang rested his against the stone railing, supporting it with both hands—if he placed it down on the steps, it would be more difficult to hoist back up onto his shoulders. As they stood there panting, Xiaomei dabbed her sweat with a handkerchief, while Aqiang used his sleeve. Everyone on the street who saw them wondered why they had bought so much rice at one time, commenting that they must have purchased two or three times a normal amount.

In her spare time, Xiaomei would sit in front of the window in the upstairs bedroom. She didn't spend much time looking out the window, though—she instead kept her head down and focused on her sewing, which she did by the light from the window. When the maid came in to clean the room, she noticed that Xiaomei was making clothing, shoes, and a hat for a baby. At first the maid thought Xiaomei was pregnant, but she later discovered she wasn't. Then she thought she must be doing this as a way of praying for a child—after all, she'd been married for many years now without giving birth. What the maid didn't know was that Xiaomei was making this clothing, shoes, and hat out of longing for her own baby daughter. Every stitch she sewed was steeped in it.

Shortly after returning to Xizhen, Xiaomei would sometimes be unable to keep from going to the wardrobe and taking out the red sachet containing her baby's hair. She would gaze at it and weep. At one point her sorrow even caused her to faint. She laid alone on the bedroom floor for a while before regaining consciousness, at which point she discovered that everything was just as it had been before: the maid was busy in the kitchen, and Aqiang was sitting in a stupor out in the courtyard. After that, Xiaomei didn't take the sachet out of the wardrobe anymore, and did her best to remain calm. During the day she was fine, but at night, in her dreams, she would see her daughter, who was always moving away from her—she would wake up crying. Late at night, the residents of Xizhen would hear those desolate sobs—the sound of Xiaomei losing her daughter in her dreams.

Every wound heals, and every heartbreak will pass. When Xiaomei had finished making the clothing, shoes, and hat for her daughter, she buried them in the bottom of the wardrobe, completely covered over by layer after layer of her and Aqiang's clothing. When she closed the door of the wardrobe it felt like a farewell. She had once had two separate lives with Lin Xiangfu, and she had once had a daughter. But this was all in the past.

29.

After the tornado, a tall northern man showed up on the devastated streets of Xizhen, walking along with a huge bundle on his back and carrying a baby girl at his chest. A headscarf with a phoenix and peony pattern was wrapped around the baby's head. In a thick northern accent, the man asked the residents of Xizhen about a place called Wencheng.

The tiles on the roof of the two-story Shen home had blown off in the tornado. Although smoke had begun puffing out of the tile kilns located outside the south gate, it would still be some time before the roof could be retiled. Xiaomei and Aqiang had temporarily moved down to the first floor, and the floor of the second floor had temporarily become their roof.

The news of Lin Xiangfu's arrival in Xizhen was relayed by the maid. She always had some gossip to bring back from her daily shopping trips, which she would recount as she did her chores. Usually, Xiaomei barely registered a reaction—it was like she was listening to the maid, but also not; when the maid finished talking, the only thing Xiaomei perceived was that she no longer heard her voice. But this time was different—this time, the maid's recounting involved a tall northern man with a huge bundle on his back, a baby girl, a phoenix-and-peony headscarf, and Wencheng. Xiaomei's expression immediately changed, which shocked the maid. Xiaomei noticed the maid was looking at her strangely, which told her she'd let her face reveal too much. She let the plate she was holding crash to the floor. The maid jumped and shifted her attention to the broken plate. Xiaomei said it had slipped out of her hand, and asked the maid to pick up the pieces—that afternoon she would take it to the porcelain shop and have it repaired.

Xiaomei left the kitchen and went into the courtyard, which was Aqiang's realm of distraction. She didn't sit down beside him like she normally did, but sat facing him. Aqiang acknowledged her with a smile. Then he was caught off guard, noticing her eyes were glistening with tears. He stared at her in anxious confusion and waited for her to speak.

At that moment, Xiaomei heard Lin Xiangfu's voice in her memory. That night in the faraway north, Lin Xiangfu had resolutely told her that if she left again, he would take their daughter and come looking for her—even if he had to walk to the ends of the earth, he would find her.

Xiaomei raised her left hand and wiped the corners of her eyes. "He's come looking for me," she said to Aqiang.

"He's come looking for you?" Aqiang repeated, not quite understanding.

"Lin Xiangfu," said Xiaomei.

Aqiang sprung up off his stool, looking as if he were about to
flee. When he saw Xiaomei sitting there motionlessly, he looked
around and realized he was in his own home. He composed
himself, placed both hands on the stool, and sat back down.
Then the courtyard fell silent, with only the sound of a light
breeze, just the same as when it had swished over the roof tiles.
Occasionally, they would hear the maid working in the kitchen.

Aqiang and Xiaomei stared at each other, but it was as if
they didn't see anything at all. Aqiang's eyes were filled with
panic, while Xiaomei's eyes were wet with tears, and neither
pair could see the other.

Like a well and a river, it was as if they both occupied entirely
different positions—one was thinking about well water con-
cerns, the other was preoccupied with river water conditions.
Lin Xiangfu's sudden appearance struck fear into Aqiang. He
had never imagined Lin Xiangfu would journey over a thousand *li* in search of them; even more surprising was the fact that
he had found Xizhen. For Xiaomei, whenever she thought of
Lin Xiangfu, her thoughts naturally turned toward her daughter. Her daughter had come, she thought—Lin Xiangfu had
brought her with him.

After a period of silence, Xiaomei and Aqiang began to
speak. One talked about well water, while the other talked
about river water. Aqiang felt like they were caught. His voice
quivered as he noted they had already changed the gold bars
into banknotes and spent some of them—what should they do?
He felt they were doomed. Xiaomei, however, showed not a
ripple on the surface, though her heart was roiling. In a gentle
voice she said that Lin Xiangfu didn't want his gold; he just
wanted her to go home with him.

Just then Aqiang heard a knock at the door. Once again
Aqiang jumped up from the stool. His face ashen, he said
that Lin Xiangfu had come—he was knocking on the door.
Xiaomei listened carefully and said it wasn't the sound of
knocking; it was the maid in the kitchen chopping vegetables

on the cutting board. Aqiang listened with a doubtful look on his face, but then confirmed that it was indeed the sound of vegetables being chopped. Still badly shaken, he sat back down on the stool.

Xiaomei felt like she was caught in a trance. She watched as Aqiang, clearly at a loss, stood up and sat down. She felt like he was no more than a shadow. Lin Xiangfu and her daughter, however, seemed crystal clear even though they were not present. It was as if she could see Lin Xiangfu holding her baby, enduring untold hardships over a thousand *li* to come find her. Her newborn daughter had come to her, wandering through wind, rain, and blistering sun.

"Why didn't he go to Wencheng?" Aqiang suddenly asked Xiaomei.

Xiaomei composed herself and looked at Aqiang. She didn't know why he was talking about Wencheng.

Aqiang had never mentioned Xizhen to Lin Xiangfu. He had only ever spoken of Wencheng, so he assumed Lin Xiangfu would be out searching for Wencheng. But here he was in Xizhen.

"Why didn't he go to Wencheng?" Aqiang asked again.

"Where's Wencheng?" asked Xiaomei.

Aqiang didn't know where Wencheng was. He just shook his head.

"Did you ever mention Xizhen to him?" Aqiang asked Xiaomei.

She thought for a moment, then said, "He doesn't know about Xizhen."

"If he doesn't know about Xizhen," said Aqiang, "Why didn't he go to Wencheng?"

Xiaomei once again asked: "Where's Wencheng?"

Aqiang once again shook his head. Xiaomei thought of what the maid had just said: that Lin Xiangfu had been asking people on the street about a place called Wencheng. She relayed this to Aqiang, which caused the panic on his face to subside. He now felt that Lin Xiangfu hadn't come looking for Xizhen, but was merely passing through on his way to Wencheng.

Breathing a sigh of relief, Aqiang said,

"No one knows where Wencheng is."

Just then Aqiang thought of something and went over toward the kitchen, where the maid was preparing lunch. From the kitchen doorway he abruptly asked the maid: how long had that northern man looking for Wencheng been in Xizhen? The maid stopped working, wiped her hands on her apron, and said that she had seen him for the past three days. Aqiang nodded, then turned and left. A bit stunned, the maid stood there a few moments before getting back to her work.

The maid's state of surprise continued for about three days. Every time she returned from shopping, Aqiang would ask her: had she seen that northern man? The maid would reply that she had seen him, walking down the street holding his baby daughter, looking as if he were searching for someone.

Xiaomei would also question the maid, although she did it in a roundabout way. Whenever she was working alongside the maid, she would almost unconsciously bring the topic of conversation around to that northern man and his baby. Xiaomei would listen patiently as the maid recounted all the trivial gossip in Xizhen, and sometimes she would ask a few questions. But when the subject of Lin Xiangfu came up, her questioning subtly increased.

"How big was the bundle he was carrying on his back?" Xiaomei asked.

The maid spread her arms wide to indicate the size. "Everyone says he's got everything he owns in there."

Xiaomei shook her head sadly and asked the maid where he slept at night. Why didn't he just leave his bundle where he was staying? The maid shook her head; she didn't know where he was staying. Then she said that when she first saw him he was carrying that enormous bundle, but that the past few times it hadn't been with him.

"And the baby?" Xiaomei asked.

"She'll definitely be a beauty when she grows up," said the maid.

A slight smile formed at the corners of Xiaomei's mouth. "Has she had any teeth come in yet?" she asked.

The maid thought for a minute. "She will soon," she said.

The maid told Xiaomei that she always saw the baby sleeping in a sack hanging in front of her father. Only once had she seen the baby awake—her shining black eyes had stared out from her father's chest, and she'd opened her mouth and smiled at the people passing by on the street. The maid had seen two white spots in her mouth, which she assumed were two front teeth about to poke through.

30.

When Lin Xiangfu appeared in Xizhen with his daughter, Aqiang had panicked at first, but calmed down. He told Xiaomei that if the maid saw Lin Xiangfu on the street every time she left the house, then he was definitely looking for them, waiting for them to appear. So all they needed to do was stay inside—Lin Xiangfu wouldn't see them, and he would eventually leave.

They passed four days in caution. On the morning of the fifth day, Aqiang suddenly cried out in surprise; Xiaomei, however, remained undisturbed, having become used to Aqiang's sudden changes in behavior. Aqiang said that Lin Xiangfu might not know Xizhen, but he did know their names—they had told them to him.

Xiaomei was stunned—she had forgotten about that. For the past four days her thoughts had been completely occupied by Lin Xiangfu and the baby. An image of Lin Xiangfu with his giant bundle, her daughter smiling at people with a big open mouth and little teeth about to come in—this was the scene that had constantly occupied her mind, either in the forefront or the background, but always there.

"If he asks anyone about us using our names, he'll definitely end up coming here."

Xiaomei nodded. She also felt that if Lin Xiangfu mentioned their names, he would find them.

Aqiang trembled with fear. He felt they were on the verge of disaster—once their theft of the gold was exposed, they would go to jail. Xiaomei had already come to terms with her fate: if prison was unavoidable, she would peacefully accept it.

"We should accept the consequences of our actions," she said.

Aqiang stared at Xiaomei; he hadn't expected her to say something like that. "We shouldn't have gone with your idea to come back to Xizhen," he reproached her.

"You shouldn't have come to get me in Xilicun," Xiaomei replied.

Xiaomei's response caused Aqiang to lower his head in silence. Feeling that she had hurt him, she said gently, "If you hadn't come for me, we wouldn't be in this mess right now."

Aqiang said nothing and went out to sit in the courtyard. Xiaomei stayed put and didn't follow; she just stared at him through the open door, sitting with his head down.

After sitting for a while Aqiang suddenly stood up and went back inside, where he said to Xiaomei: "Let's leave this place."

"And go where?" Xiaomei asked.

"It doesn't matter," said Aqiang, "we just need to get out of here."

"We have to decide where we're going before we go," said Xiaomei.

"We'll go to Shendian first," said Aqiang. "Let's go right now."

After saying this, Aqiang began panicking again. He said as soon as they left the house and went out on the street, they would run into Lin Xiangfu, who was actively searching for them. Xiaomei remained calm. She said they should wait for the maid to come back from her shopping, then have her go over to the gate in front of the chamber of commerce and hire two sedan chairs. They would simply sit in the sedans and pull the curtains shut, and then no one would be able to see them. Aqiang nodded—if they left in sedan chairs, Lin Xiangfu wouldn't see them.

Xiaomei felt they wouldn't be staying long in Shendian; as soon as Lin Xiangfu left, they would come back. They would retain the maid and have her look after the house while they were gone. Aqiang kept nodding along and repeating Xiaomei's words:

"Have her look after the house," he said.

Xiaomei asked Aqiang to show her the money that was in the pocket of his undergarments. When they had first returned to Xizhen, they had kept these banknotes in a porcelain jar under the floor of a small storage room, where they had placed them on top of the silver yuan. But then they became worried they would become too damp, so they removed them. With no other place to hide the banknotes, they put them in a pocket Xiaomei sewed into in Aqiang's undergarments. Every time Xiaomei washed Aqiang's clothes, she would take the banknotes out herself and put them in the pocket of a fresh set of undergarments for Aqiang to wear.

Aqiang stuck his hand in the front of his shirt, undid the button on the pocket, and took out the banknotes, which were wrapped in a silk cloth. He handed them to Xiaomei, who undid the silk wrapping and looked at them. Then she wrapped them up and passed them back to Aqiang, watching as he placed them back in the pocket and refastened the button.

Xiaomei began moving around the room. She took out a silver yuan and a small bag of copper coins to leave behind for the maid and put them in the drawer under what had been the counter of the mending shop. Then she hesitated. She felt there was a possibility they could be away for longer than she anticipated, so she took out another silver yuan and added it to the drawer. Xiaomei then went over to the wardrobe, which had been moved downstairs after the tornado had blown off the roof tiles. She took out clothes for the both of them and placed them on two pieces of blue calico cloth; it was summertime, so she took out clothes for summer and fall. She eyed the winter coats, but left them—she didn't feel they would be away for that long, so she tied up the two pieces of calico cloth to make two bundles. As she closed the door to the wardrobe, she spotted the baby clothes, shoes, and hat she had made, poking out from the bottom.

Sadness coursed through her heart like a bubbling stream; she could almost hear its faint sound, like crying. The clothes, shoes, and hat she had made weren't for the baby so much as for herself—she had concentrated all of her longing on them; every stitch was steeped in it. As she made them, she never gave a thought to whether or not her daughter would actually wear them.

After staring at the clothes, shoes, and hat for a while, she closed the wardrobe. But after she turned around, she found herself unable to leave, as if her feet wouldn't respond. She opened the wardrobe again. But then she heard the maid returning from her shopping trip—she heard the door open and close, and then heard her go into the kitchen. Xiaomei resolutely took out the baby clothes, shoes, and hat and headed for the maid in the kitchen.

When Xiaomei made it to the door of the kitchen, she told the maid they were going away for a few days—she didn't say where or for how long, just that the maid would be in charge of the house for a while. The maid was quite taken by surprise—there had been no inkling of this, and now all of a sudden they were going away. She didn't even have time to nod before Xiaomei instructed her to go to the gate in front of the chamber of commerce and call two sedan chairs. The maid hadn't realized they were leaving immediately.

"Should I go now?" she asked Xiaomei.

Xiaomei nodded. "Yes, go now," she said.

The maid took off her apron and was ready to leave the kitchen, but Xiaomei was still standing in the doorway, blocking her way. The maid stopped and perceived a change in Xiaomei's expression. Xiaomei passed the baby clothes, shoes, and hat to the maid—she said they had no use for them, so they might as well give them to that man from the north; maybe they would fit his daughter. She made it very clear to the maid that she was not to tell the man who they were from. Once the maid took them, Xiaomei turned around and left, but then stopped after a few steps. She instructed the maid to the give clothes, shoes and hat to the northern man first, and then go to the chamber of commerce for the sedan chairs.

31.

The maid put the baby clothes, shoes, and hat in a clean basket, went out on the streets of Xizhen, and started asking people where she could find the northern man. Someone said they had just seen him heading south, so the maid went south, continuing to ask about him as she went. She learned that he'd already left through the south gate, so she held onto the basket and broke into a trot. She spotted him after she ran through the gate—the first thing she saw was that giant bundle of his swaying back and forth on the road up ahead. She ran up in front of that bundle and blocked the northern man's path, then took the baby clothes, shoes, and hat out of the basket and pressed them into his hands. Pointing at the baby fast asleep in front of his chest, she blurted out:

"They're for the little one."

The maid remembered Xiaomei's instructions and didn't say who the items were from. After she'd pressed them into the man's hands, she spun around and quickly left. She heard the northern man call after her, but she didn't look back; she just hurried back into town through the south gate.

The maid then hired two two-carrier sedan chairs that were waiting in front of the chamber of commerce and led them back to the Shen home. She had the four sedan carriers put down their chairs and wait outside, while she went in and informed Aqiang and Xiaomei:

"The sedans are waiting outside."

Aqiang and Xiaomei were sitting at what was formerly the counter of the mending shop. When they saw the maid return, their period of waiting ended, and they each rose and gathered up their bundles. As Xiaomei hung hers over her arm, she asked the maid—had she given the baby clothes, shoes, and hat to the northern man?

The maid said she had, and that the northern man had already left Xizhen through the south gate. She was only able to catch him by running out through the gate herself.

This information took Xiaomei by surprise. She looked over at Aqiang, who also looked stunned. They stopped where they were, having already made it to the door, and stared at each other.

Lin Xiangfu had left Xizhen: this sudden news momentarily threw Aqiang for a loop. He saw that Xiaomei had already put her bundle up on the shop counter and, realizing she had decided not to leave, placed his there as well. Xiaomei walked over to the drawer underneath the counter and took out the two silver yuan she had left there for the maid, along with the bag of coppers. She passed the silver to Aqiang for him to put away, then took four coins out of the little bag, handed them to the maid, and told her to go give them to the four sedan chair carriers waiting outside.

"We have no need for the sedans," she said, "so please send them back."

For the third time that day, the maid was left completely flummoxed. Aqiang and Xiaomei had given no indication they'd been planning to leave Xizhen, and now, just as suddenly, they weren't going. Furthermore, Xiaomei hadn't exactly been polite when she sent her with the baby clothes, shoes, and hat to give to the northern man, and she wasn't sure what to make of it.

Lin Xiangfu's departure left Aqiang feeling incredibly relieved. For several days afterward, a smile would sometimes appear on his face as he sat in the courtyard. Xiaomei, on the other hand, felt a heavy weight on her heart. She had gone from feeling like she was drowning in sadness to now feeling completely at a loss. Lin Xiangfu and her daughter had been so close, but she never even caught a glimpse of them. She had especially wanted to see her daughter—counting on her fingers, she realized she'd already been away from her for over eight months. Her daughter had been sleeping when she left, swaddled in a big bundle on the kang—she'd looked so tiny and delicate. She must be a bit bigger by now, and a little prettier as well . . . She regretted not going out on the street and hiding in a corner to secretly catch a glimpse of them. She imagined the scene—her daughter seeing her and smiling with a big open mouth; Lin Xiangfu spotting her and giving her a forgiving smile without a hint of reproach.

Aqiang didn't realize what was weighing on Xiaomei's mind. Thinking she was still worried, he said to her,

"The further he goes the further away he'll get, searching for Wencheng."

When Aqiang mentioned Wencheng, Xiaomei couldn't help but ask: "Where is Wencheng?"

"There will always be a place called Wencheng," Aqiang said.

This imaginary Wencheng had become an ache at the bottom of Xiaomei's heart. Wencheng meant that Lin Xiangfu and her daughter would never stop wandering and searching.

32.

The further Lin Xiangfu went the further away he got. Continuing south, he no longer asked about Wencheng. He realized that the Wencheng Aqiang had mentioned was made up— no one knew where it was. Since Wencheng was fake, he geussed that Aqiang's and Xiaomei's names were probably fake, too.

It was a long journey that seemed to have no end. Lin Xiangfu would travel for a while, then stop somewhere for a bit. Continuing on in this pattern, he traveled all through the autumn and into the winter. He would often become lost in thought. As his body moved forward, his mind would move backward—the further he went from Xizhen, the clearer Xizhen appeared in his heart.

There was one person who stuck in his mind—that young woman carrying the basket over her arm who had stopped him on the main road outside of Xizhen's south gate. A smile playing at the corners of her mouth, she had taken a new set of baby clothes, shoes, and a hat out of the basket and suddenly handed them to him; then, after a few simple words, she'd turned around and left. He hadn't understood her rapid accent and had just stood there stunned, holding the clothes, shoes, and hat. By the time he was able to react and call out a *wei!,* she had already made it back through the south gate.

That evening, by the light of an oil lamp, he carefully examined the things the woman had given him—they were handsewn and made out of a bright red silk. Lin Xiangfu had to exclaim over the silk and the handiwork, which were both exquisite. He felt that young woman must really be a good person—she'd clearly seen him out wandering the streets of Xizhen with his baby daughter and given him these things out of compassion. But then what about her own children? This thought made Lin Xiangfu uneasy—could they have met with misfortune in the tornado? He thought about how his own daughter had been lost during the tornado, and then recovered. He felt his chest tighten and didn't dare think of it anymore.

As Lin Xiangfu continued heading south with his daughter at his chest, he kept thinking about the phrase the young woman with the basket over her arm had uttered so quickly. At one point he bent down at a stream to collect some water for his daughter, and after putting some into his own mouth and transferring it to her, he suddenly realized what she had said:

"For the little one to wear."

He smiled—so people in Xizhen called children "little ones." He found the Xizhen dialect very difficult to understand. But as he walked from the little stream back up to the main road and continued heading south, he suddenly found he was able to understand many things he had heard in the Xizhen dialect.

As Lin Xiangfu headed south, the accent sounded stranger, and less and less like Xiaomei and Aqiang. After mulling it over some more, he felt Xizhen seemed more and more like the Wencheng that Aqiang had mentioned. Then something popped into his head—he suddenly recalled that when Aqiang had spoken of Wencheng, he'd said that after crossing the Yangtze, you had to continue south for about six hundred *li*. Lin Xiangfu estimated that Xizhen was about six hundred *li* south of the Yangtze.

The sound of that young woman's voice saying "for the little one to wear" kept ringing in his ears. A scene appeared in his mind—he was back in his northern home, in the sundrenched courtyard with the Tian brothers, spreading the wheat out to dry for seedstock. He told Xiaomei that after the White Dew, he would spread the seed out in the fields. Sitting in front of the door sewing a set of baby clothes, Xiaomei looked up at him and said,

"By then there'll be a little one in these."

Lin Xiangfu stood on a bridge and remained there for a long while. Then he decided he would return to Xizhen. The Wencheng that Aqiang had spoken of, he felt, really was Xizhen.

Even though he had no idea where the two of them might be at the moment, he felt that at some point they were bound to return to Xizhen. He would wait there for them—for a year, two years, or maybe even longer.

Under the early winter sunlight, Lin Xiangfu turned himself around and headed back north, switching from one horse-drawn wagon to another. By the end of his slow journey, he entered Xizhen accompanied by snowflakes.

33.

When Lin Xiangfu eventually reappeared in Xizhen, cradling his daughter amidst the snow and ice, Aqiang and Xiaomei had no idea. The maid, who normally went out each day, was now trapped inside because of the snow, as was everyone else; there weren't even any shops open in town. Fortunately each time Aqiang and Xiaomei bought rice they got two full sacks, so when the blizzard hit they had over twenty *jin* of rice in their vat, along with two large containers of vegetables they had pickled that autumn. Because no one knew when then snow would stop, they tried to make their supplies last: every day, along with the maid, they would have two bowls of rice porridge accompanied by some pickled vegetables. After eating, they would lay down on the bed to conserve their energy and keep their hunger at bay.

Although Aqiang and Xiaomei already led quite secluded lives, the blizzard made them feel cut off from the outside world. Each day seemed to bring a deathly stillness without even a breath of human life. Aqiang began to grow restless. At first, like everyone else in Xizhen, he'd thought the snow would quit after a day or two—then the sun would come out and melt it all away. But as the snow kept blowing and swirling through the town, Aqiang grew uneasy and restless as he lay on the bed, and he soon began to grow hungry.

Xiaomei lay on the bed like a peaceful orchid undisturbed by Aqiang's tossing and turning, remaining so motionless it was as if she weren't even there. Her heart, though, was roiling. A scene the maid had described to her gradually took shape in her mind: Lin Xiangfu carrying their daughter on the road after the tornado, a copper coin in his hand, listening for a baby's cries so that he could go knock on the door; then a woman appearing and Lin Xiangfu passing the coin to her, begging her to nurse his baby girl.

The maid had described this scene to Xiaomei after Lin Xiangfu's departure. She hadn't witnessed it herself, but had heard it from a few women she had chatted with on the street when she went out to buy vegetables. One of them had mentioned the northern man who had left town, and another told of this scenario—then they all commented that the baby at his chest must have drank the milk from every lactating woman in town.

Xiaomei listened as the maid told her this, and when she got to the part about the baby having been nursed by every woman in town, Xiaomei couldn't take any more. Struggling to hold back her tears, she turned and left, the maid staring in bewilderment as she headed up the stairs. She sat on the edge of the bed and began crying silently, her tears running down her cheeks and all the way down to her chest, where they were absorbed by the fabric of her shirt.

Eventually, she regained her composure. But the image had taken root in her mind: Lin Xiangfu holding out a copper coin to beg women in the middle of breastfeeding, going from door to door, the baby nursing in every home. The scene caused her endless sorrow, like a painful stream trickling through her heart.

Late one night during the blizzard, Xiaomei woke up out of a deep sleep and looked around the darkened room. Aqiang was asleep beside her—he cried out a few times and kept mumbling, remaining unsettled even in his sleep. Xiaomei, however, didn't hear his murmuring or cries; she was too focused on

Lin Xiangfu and their daughter, who appeared before her in the darkness: they were standing on a street awash in summer sunlight, the child in Lin Xiangfu's arms as his eyes searched for Xiaomei. The image filled her with both pain and yearning. She imagined walking over to them, going up to Lin Xiangfu and removing a small leaf from his dusty hair, then taking their daughter from him and holding her close to her chest.

Xiaomei thought of the red sachet containing her daughter's hair buried deep in the wardrobe. Every time she'd opened it she could feel her heart breaking, and after the time she had fainted, she hadn't dared open it again.

Quietly she got out of bed and walked through the darkness with her arms stretched out in front of her. When they made contact with the wardrobe, she carefully opened the door and reached in with her right hand. She felt around inside until she located the sachet—her fingers burned as she pulled it out from under the clothes stacked inside. Then she softly shut the door and gingerly made her way back to the bed. She lay down on her back and put the sachet on her chest, covering it with both hands as if protecting it. In that moment she no longer felt any sadness; a warm feeling came over her. She could feel herself holding her daughter, and at the same time she could also feel herself being held by Lin Xiangfu; she and her daughter were both at rest in his arms.

When morning came, Xiaomei sat in a chair and did some needlework. Inside three of her undergarments she sewed a pocket, complete with a button—this was where she could keep some of her daughter's hair.

As Xiaomei calmly and carefully sewed the pockets, Aqiang lay on the bed consumed by anxiety. Instead of tossing and turning, he would get up to go stand by the paper window. Unable to see anything clearly, at one point he opened it and found the gray sky still filled with snowflakes. An icy wind blew some inside, and he shut the window.

The cold wind blew over to Xiaomei and carried some

snowflakes over to land on her fingers, which halted their movements. She looked up at Aqiang, who saw several snowflakes in her hair—he felt he'd been a bit inconsiderate to fling the window open like that, and said apologetically that he'd wanted to see if the snow had stopped. Xiaomei nodded and smiled. She watched Aqiang as he returned to the bed and lay down.

After Xiaomei had sewn the pockets into her undergarments, she wore her daughter's hair right next to her chest so she would never be apart from it. Not only did it make her feel like she always had her daughter next to her, but it also made her feel like she was with Lin Xiangfu. When her heart cried out for her child, it was also unavoidably crying out for him. Like the sound of swishing and rustling that accompanied the wind, her daughter and Lin Xiangfu came as an inseparable pair.

Late one night, she realized that her daughter still didn't have a name, and she didn't know if Lin Xiangfu had given her one or not. She began thinking of names herself—as soon as she thought of one, she would discard it in favor of another. Each name she would call out several times in her heart, followed by Lin Xiangfu's name, as if she were discussing it with him. As she went on trying out names like this in her mind, she was able to temporarily rescue herself from the pain in her heart. She was also able to momentarily forget that outside, the snow continued to fall.

34.

One day, someone came and knocked on the door. It was a breath of life from the outside world that had been absent for a long time. Aqiang and Xiaomei listened carefully from upstairs as the maid opened the door—it was someone sent from the chamber of commerce to notify them that the chamber had organized a sacrifice outside the temple of the city god, praying to heaven to stop the snow and let the sun shine over Xizhen.

Over the next two days, constant activity could be heard outside. People going to the temple of the city god and those coming back would stop to engage in loud conversations. Those who were going would ask those coming back if there were many people at the sacrifice, and the people coming back would reply that it was packed—from dawn until dusk, the temple was filled with people kneeling in prayer. The people going would ask if it was very cold, and the people coming back would say no—there were two rows of charcoal braziers set up in the temple, and even if there weren't, there were so many people it wouldn't be cold anyway. The voices drifting in from outside made Aqiang and Xiaomei, along with the maid, feel like the sun was beginning to break through the clouds.

On the third day of the sacrifice, Xiaomei suggested they go to the temple. Aqiang and the maid both nodded in agreement. For lunch, Xiaomei asked the maid to prepare some rice instead of the usual porridge—if they were going to pray at the temple, they needed to do it on a full stomach.

That afternoon, the three of them trudged with difficulty through the deep snow. When they made it to the temple, they found it was already completely filled with kneeling supplicants. Xiaomei looked over at Aqiang and the maid, who were both were beaming with happiness—the scene before them was brimming with life.

The three of them squeezed in amongst the others lined up on the steps of the temple and craned their necks to look inside. They were waiting for those inside to finish their supplications and leave so they could go in and kneel in prayer. One person waiting alongside them, who had come there every day, said there were more people today than the two days before—so many that they couldn't even get inside. Another said they'd been standing there for nearly a *shichen,* during which time only about ten people had come out—according to them, most of the people inside were praying for their own personal affairs, and when they finished with their own things, they moved on to pray for their friends and relatives. Hearing this, someone else said they had all come there to pray to heaven, and that's just what they should do, not pray for their own personal things—it was like a bunch of chickens taking up the coop but not laying any eggs. Another person said he shouldn't talk like that, or heaven might punish them—saying something like that could nullify a whole three days of praying. Hearing this, the man who had grumbled was at a loss for words and simply lowered his head in silence. Someone else piped up on his behalf, saying that chickens occupying a coop without laying eggs didn't count as profanity, and it wouldn't offend heaven—it would take something worse, like squatting over a latrine without shitting, to invite heaven's wrath. A woman's shrill voice cried out: now that someone had just said this vulgar phrase about squatting over a latrine without shitting, heaven was sure to get angry. Someone else pointed out that she herself had just now uttered the phrase—from now on, everyone should just keep their mouths shut and avoid trouble. In a measured voice, an elderly person said it didn't matter what you said; what mattered was your sincerity.

By this point, dozens of men and women were already kneeling in prayer in the plaza outside the temple of the city god. One person waiting on the steps turned and walked out into the plaza, saying they weren't going to wait anymore—kneeling out under the open sky would show a greater sincerity. Several others followed, including Xiaomei, who was then followed by Aqiang and the maid.

As the three of them walked out to the plaza, Aqiang noticed that he couldn't see anyone's lower legs, which were buried in the snow as they knelt. He stopped and hesitated for a moment, but Xiaomei continued on, as did the maid, so Aqiang kept following them. Xiaomei found an empty spot and knelt down in the deep snow, and Aqiang and the maid did the same. Amidst the swirling snowflakes and the rhythmic striking of the wooden fish; the sound of the *di* flutes, *xiao* flutes, and *suona* horns; and the burning scent of the three animal sacrifices, they placed both hands in the snow in front of them and kowtowed, their heads making contact with their hands. When they sat back up, snow clung to their faces.

More people kept coming and kneeling around them. The tracks they'd made in the snow were now completely covered over with kneeling supplicants; with the disappearance of their footprints, their path was also gone. As the elegant music floated out of the temple, everyone's bodies on the snowy plaza rose and fell, undulating like waves amidst the swirling snowflakes.

As more people continued to come and kneel down, others struggled to get to their feet. Those who were able to get up bent over to pat some life into their stiff, numb legs and feet, but they could find no path by which to exit—they could only advance when one of the supplicants next to them sat up; when the supplicants were bent forward on the ground, they had to wait. So the people trying to leave had to do so one step at a time, navigating around the kowtowing supplicants. When one of them sat up from their kowtow and bumped against the knees of a person trying to leave, harsh words would be exchanged. What are you doing standing right in front of me, the person kneeling would say, I'm praying to heaven, not you. Who's asking you to pray to me, the person trying to leave would say—I'm no god, I'm just trying to leave. Then get out of here, the person kneeling would say, and stop standing in front of me patting yourself. Who wants to stand here patting themselves, the person trying to leave would say, my legs are frozen stiff.

When Xiaomei, Aqiang, and the maid first knelt down, they felt the cold pierce through to their bones. Not long afterwards, Aqiang said it was too cold—they had knelt and offered their prayers to heaven; now perhaps it was time to go home. The maid nodded and voiced her agreement. Xiaomei seemed not to have heard either of them, her body continuing to rise and fall with the music emanating from the temple. Aqiang looked around at the undulating supplicants in every direction. After sitting up straight for a few moments he continued kowtowing along with Xiaomei, and the maid joined them as well.

When Xiaomei began chanting some incantations, Aqiang and the maid muttered some, too. Everyone around them was chanting, and the collective sound of their prayers to heaven reverberated across the snowy plaza in front of the temple. Snowflakes kept rushing down from the sky and falling in their hair, turning it white. The snow also fell on their clothing and turned it white; it fell in their eyes, too, blurring their vision.

After a long time, the feeling of cold gradually seemed to trickle out of their bodies, like blood dripping out of a finger prick. Not only did Aqiang no longer feel the cold; he couldn't feel his legs anymore, either. He turned to Xiaomei and said,

"Let's go home."

Xiaomei didn't respond. When she had finished praying to heaven, she began praying for Lin Xiangfu. He had traveled for thousands of *li* with their daughter searching for her, and her heart was filled with infinite feelings of pain and guilt. In her heart, she silently said to Lin Xiangfu:

"In my next life I'll bear you another daughter; in my next life, I'll give you five sons . . . In my next life, if I'm not able to be your wife, I'll serve you as an ox or a horse—if you farm the land, I'll plow the fields as your ox; if you drive a cart, I'll pull it for you as your horse, and you can lash me with your whip."

Aqiang wanted to stand up. He tried to brace his stiff arms against Xiaomei's back to prop himself up, but he had no feeling in his legs. Again he said to Xiaomei:

"Let's go home."

Xiaomei still didn't respond—she could only see Lin Xiangfu. Lin Xiangfu stood in front of her and said,

"Go home."

Aqiang said he was getting hot, and he took of his padded *mianpao*. Then the maid said she was hot and removed her padded *mian'ao*. All across the snowy plaza, people were removing their padded winter clothing. Xiaomei, too, felt herself growing warmer. She began breathing heavily and her heartrate quickened, so she undid the buttons of her *mianpao* and let it hang open. Still she felt hot, so she took it off and undid her clothing underneath.

At that moment, Xiaomei could see her baby daughter smiling happily at her with a big, open mouth, inside of which she could see two white spots where her front teeth were coming in. Xiaomei began to cry, and the two streams of tears flowing down from her eyes carried the final warmth from her body.

35.

On the third day of ceremonies at the temple of the city god, Lin Xiangfu passed by with his daughter. By the time they arrived on the scene, the plaza outside the temple was filled with over a hundred worshiping men and women, their bodies all rising and falling with the music floating out of the temple.

Before the ceremonies began, the Daoist priests had swept away all the snow. But after three days, the snow had piled up high once more. As Lin Xiangfu walked by, he noticed he couldn't see the lower legs of the kneeling supplicants, which were all completely buried in the snow. The warm breath escaping from their mouths converged in a cloud of steam that hovered in the gray sky before dispersing at the edges.

That afternoon was the first time Lin Xiangfu entered the home of Chen Yongliang. He stayed for a long time, marking the beginning of their lifelong friendship.

When Lin Xiangfu left Chen Yongliang's house and walked back to the temple of the city god, a scene of disaster spread out before him: many of the people kneeling in the plaza had frozen to death. Their corpses remained in a kneeling position, but there was no longer any warm breath escaping their mouths to form a cloud of steam in the air, nor was there any sound or movement. It was as if Lin Xiangfu had come upon a graveyard—their kneeling corpses were all white with snow and looked like a dense forest of tombstones.

Lin Xiangfu saw that a number of people had gathered around. Those who had been praying inside the temple had also come out and were now standing there. This was the first time Lin Xiangfu had seen so many people gathered together since the snowstorm began. He heard the women cry until their voices were hoarse, while the men's voices had become sharp and shrill.

At this scene of anguish and sorrow, everyone was shouting out different names, and every frozen corpse became surrounded by a group of people. They used their fingers to dig through the snow that had accumulated on the corpses' frozen faces to see if they recognized a loved one or relative. But as they dug through the snow, they also dug away some of the corpses' hair and eyebrows, and even some skin from their noses and other parts of their faces.

Lin Xiangfu saw a thin man standing on the temple steps—it was Gu Yimin. He was saying something in a loud, ringing voice as steam puffed out of his mouth and obscured his face. Lin Xiangfu could make out that he was telling people not to dig at the corpses—they should instead go home and heat some water, which they could pour on the snow covering the corpses' faces. Then, clasping his hands in front of him and making a bow, he said:

"Please do your best to protect the bodies."

Many people left after Gu Yimin's exhortations, then returned with basins of hot water, which they poured over the faces of the corpses. The steam rising up from the hot water formed a thick mist that slowly spread out in front of the temple. One by one, the faces were revealed in the mist. The cries started up once more, now even hoarser and shriller. As the people collected the bodies of their loved ones, even the white snow itself seemed to be in mourning as they trudged away.

After the cloud of steam had dispersed, the anguished cries

and wails had died down, and the hot water that had been poured over the heads of the corpses had turned to ice, all that was left was the cratered, icy surface of the snow.

Six corpses remained in the plaza in front of the temple. No one had recognized them, so they had been left behind in lonely desolation. As he stood there in the swirling snow, Lin Xiangfu had no idea that Xiaomei and Aqiang were among those six corpses in the distance. Swirling snowflakes obscured his vision, and he never saw that it was Xiaomei's head that was drooped down. Her eyes were still open, but the light in them had gone out.

Lin Xiangfu saw Gu Yimin standing on the temple steps discussing something with the senior Daoist priest; he could hear their voices, but he couldn't make out what they were saying. Then he saw a dozen or so Daoist priests emerge from the temple and walk out through the icy, uneven snow. They collected the six corpses and carried them into the temple.

Lin Xiangfu watched as the final corpse was carried over the treacherous surface of snow and ice. There were two monks carrying her—one held her feet while the other held her shoulders. Her head hung down as they carried her away.

A feeling of emptiness enveloped Lin Xiangfu like the snowflakes swirling around him. Then the sound of his daughter's crying caught his attention, and he felt the wind-driven snowflakes assaulting his eyes. His daughter's cries made him realize he had been standing there in the snow too long. He made to leave, but both his feet and lower legs had gone numb; as he made his way forward, he only had feeling in his thighs. Sensing his daughter was crying from hunger, he unconsciously began heading back to Chen Yongliang's home. Step by step, amidst the sound of the trees creaking and snapping in the cold and frozen birds dropping to the ground, he made his way to Chen Yongliang's door. By then, some feeling had returned to his lower legs.

Lin Xiangfu never saw this last image of Xiaomei—her head

hung down so low it nearly touched the snow's icy surface. The hot water poured over her face had now frozen into a thin layer of ice, crisscrossed by tiny rivulets, so that it looked both transparent and shattered. Her frozen hair hung down like icicles from eaves, sporadically cutting gashes through the uneven surface of the snow as she was carried along, breaking from time to time with a faint crack.

Xiaomei's delicate face, transparent and shattered, continued moving farther away, as if it were floating over the frozen snow.

36.

By the authority of the chamber of commerce, Gu Yimin had Xiaomei and Aqiang buried and the maid's remains turned over to her family. Xiaomei and Aqiang were buried at a quiet spot at the foot of the western hills, in between the stream and the road. The stream flowed year-round and cut through the road at this point at the hills' northern slope. The sun was never able to hit this spot; moss covered everything, and the grasses and leaves on the trees were all a deep green. This was the burial ground of the Shen family's ancestors. Among the seven gravestones standing here, one bore the inscription, "Here Lies Shen Zuqiang and Ji Xiaomei."

When the maids and servants of the Gu household prepared the bodies of Aqiang and Xiaomei for burial, they discovered the red sachet with the baby's hair and the red silk package containing many silver yuan's worth of banknotes. Gu Yimin was quietly shocked at the amount of money—it would be difficult to amass such a sum from a mending business. A maid opened the red sachet and showed him the baby's hair, and said that when she washed Xiaomei's body in preparation for burial, she had noticed stretchmarks on her belly.

Gu Yimin felt it was all a bit suspicious. No one knew what

the two of them had gotten up to when they left Xizhen for the north, but one thing was certain: Xiaomei had given birth at some point while they were away. The maids and servants also reported that right after the pair had returned to Xizhen, people had heard Xiaomei sobbing in the middle of the night. Gu Yimin thought of how Xiaomei had tucked the baby's hair into a pocket of her undergarments—perhaps the child hadn't lived very long after birth. Perhaps they had buried it somewhere in the faraway north, its gravemound beside a major thoroughfare, or a wide, choppy river.

Gu Yimin told the maids and servants there was surely a painful backstory here, and that they shouldn't go spreading rumors. Considering that Aqiang had no family left, but Xiaomei's parents were still alive, he removed the banknotes from the pocket in Aqiang's undergarments and had most of the money delivered to the Ji family in the Wanmudang village of Xilicun. The rest of the sum would be retained by the chamber of commerce, to use for Aqiang and Xiaomei's burial and for tending the family's plot. From then on, there would be someone designated to see to the family's graves—removing the weeds, adding dirt, and cleaning the gravestones.

Gu Yimin saw to everything himself. When he sent a servant to get a woodworker to make two coffins, he even specified the materials that should be used:

"The coffins should be made from pine or cypress, not willow. Pine and cypress symbolize longevity. The willow tree doesn't produce seeds, which is inauspicious and indicates a breakage of the family line."

After saying this, Gu Yimin realized that Aqiang and Xiaomei didn't have any descendants, so how could he worry about their family line getting broken—he couldn't help but laugh at himself. Then he added,

"At any rate, the coffins should still be made from pine or cypress."

When Aqiang and Xiaomei were each placed in their

coffins, the servants and maids asked Gu Yimin what should be done with the baby's hair that had been taken from Ji Xiaomei's pocket—should they divide it up and put some in Shen Zuqiang's coffin as well, since he was the father? After thinking it over, Gu Yimin didn't think so—he said that since it had been found in a pocket Ji Xiaomei's undergarments, it should be returned to its original place.

Xiaomei was laid to rest. In her life she had witnessed the fall of the Qing dynasty and the establishment of the new republic; through her death she would avoid the fighting among warlords and the proliferation of bandits, as well as the people's descent into suffering, misery, and poverty.

Thus began Xiaomei's eternal rest. Day in and day out, year after year, Lin Xiangfu never once set foot in this spot. He went to the western hills many times, climbing up with Chen Yongliang to look out over Xizhen; climbing up with Lin Baijia—first cradling her in his arms, then leading her by the hand, and then following behind her as she climbed on ahead. Father and daughter had climbed up many times, but they had never come upon this out-of-the-way plot. Xiaomei had been laid to rest for seventeen years before Lin Xiangfu reached her here.

That morning when the Tian brothers pulled the cart with the coffin out through Xizhen's north gate, Chen Yongliang's forces were just beginning to clash with One-Ax Zhang's bandits in Wangzhuang. Before they had traveled very far from Xizhen, the Tian brothers were met with a swarm of people fleeing for their lives. They told the Tian brothers not to go any further—there was a battle raging up ahead in Wangzhuang; hundreds of people were fighting. Although the Tian brothers were unable to understand their rapid speech, the harried expressions on their faces indicated danger. The brothers stopped pulling the coffin and began asking the people passing by for more information, until someone could tell them what was going on in a way they could understand.

"Who's fighting whom?" Tian Er asked someone.

Unable to distinguish between Chen Yongliang and One-Ax Zhang, the person responded: "The bandits are fighting the bandits!"

The Tian brothers didn't dare go another step forward. They asked the person if there was a detour they could take to avoid the fighting, and the person pointed to a small path leading to the western hills—once the brothers made it out of the hills, they would have already passed by the fighting in Wangzhuang.

Another one of the refugees looked curiously at the Tian brothers' cart, then came over and ran his hand over the coffin. In language the Tian Brothers could understand, he asked them,

"What have you got in such a big wooden chest? It's even got a bamboo awning covering it!"

Tian Si was not very pleased to hear him call the coffin a "chest," so he corrected him: "It's a coffin, not a chest."

Upon hearing that it was a coffin, the man immediately withdrew his hand and took a couple steps back. Feeling he had done something inauspicious, he said: "Who knew there could be a coffin so big?"

"There are two people in it," Tian Er explained, "one is our older brother, and the other is our young master. We're taking them back to the north."

The Tian brothers turned off the main road onto the path that led to the hills. Tian Wu pulled the cart from the front, while Tian Er and Tian Si steadied it on the sides, and Tian San pushed from behind. They made their way down the undulating path, which grew wide at times and narrow at others. The going was easy when the path was wide, but became more difficult when it narrowed. At the narrow portions, Tian Wu pulled cautiously from the front, listening carefully to the directions shouted by the other three brothers—they were bent over keeping a close eye on the wheels, yelling for him to go a little to the left, then a little to the right. The two wheels of the cart scraped the sides of the road and made it past this narrowest part. When the road widened out again, Tian Si exclaimed they had navigated that portion with more precision than a tailor wielding scissors.

Now on this wide part of the road, the four brothers began discussing the bandits. From behind the cart where he was pushing, Tian San mentioned the bandits around their home up north:

"You know the Sun family who runs the *qianzhuang* in town? Someone from their family was taken hostage by the bandits, and they had to hand over a huge amount of silver for ransom."

"Who from the Sun family was taken hostage?" asked Tian Wu, pulling the cart in front.

"The old master," answered Tian San.

"How did they capture him?" Tian Wu asked.

"The bandits entered the Sun home and knocked on the door to the old master's room. The old master was asleep, and when he got up to open the door, he'd no sooner cracked it open than the barrel of a rifle poked through."

Tian Si recalled the time they came upon two bandits on their trip south. "When the bandits saw that our older brother had died, they were afraid of his unlucky aura, so they hightailed it away."

"Bandits aren't afraid of people; they're afraid of ghosts," said Tian Wu from the front.

Tian San didn't like the sound of that. "How could our brother be a ghost?"

"Everyone's a ghost after they die," said Tian Wu.

"Our brother's not a ghost," said Tian San, "he's a dead person."

Tian Er told them to stop arguing. "On our way here, we didn't have a coffin," he said in a worried voice. "The bandits could immediately see our brother was dead. Now that we've got a coffin that looks more like a big trunk than a coffin, the bandits are sure to target us."

Tian San agreed with Tian Er: "Just now, that person asked us what was in the chest."

Tian Wu in front agreed as well. "When the bandits see it, they'll think it's a chest, too. They'll make us open it to see what's inside."

"If the bandits open it," said Tian Si, "their shadows will enter the coffin, and their souls will get trapped inside—they wouldn't dare open it."

"They wouldn't dare open a coffin," said Tian San, "but they would definitely open a chest."

The cart reached another narrow stretch of road. The four brothers once again guided the cart like a tailor wielding scissors. But once they'd made it past this narrow section, they saw that up ahead the road became even narrower. Tian Wu furrowed his brow and said,

"We can't make it through there."

Tian Er walked up ahead and examined the road. After going about ten meters, he came back and announced to his three brothers:

"The part we can't get through is about ten meters long—we'll have to lift it."

With Tian Er and Tian Wu on the left, and Tian San and Tian Si on the right, the four brothers stood in the ditches on either side of the road, squatted down, and lifted the cart and coffin onto their shoulders. One, two, three, they counted in unison, then hoisted up the cart and coffin and struggled forward, grunting as their feet maneuvered the uneven ditches. After about six meters, Tian Er, the oldest brother, felt his legs give out, and he knelt down on the ground. The cart tilted over, but Tian Wu was able to steady it with his shoulders while Tian San quickly ran over to the left side to prop it up. Then the three brothers slowly squatted down, allowing the bottom of the cart to rest directly on the surface of the road. Of the cart's four wheels, only one of them was able to rest on the bottom of the ditch—the other three were unable to touch the ground.

After setting down the cart, the brothers promptly plopped themselves down, beathing heavily and covered in sweat.

Tian Er was still kneeling and panting. When his legs gave out and he first knelt down, he heard some movement in the coffin—most likely Tian Da rolling over on Lin Xiangfu. After Tian San came over to help steady things, it sounded like Tian Da rolled back to his original position. As Tian Er panted and dabbed his sweat, he said to the coffin on the cart:

"Brother, young master—I've wronged you."

After resting for a bit, the four brothers lifted the cart and coffin once more and made it through the rest of the narrow passage with grunts and groans. The road ahead was hilly and difficult. As noon approached, they arrived at Xiaomei's grave. They saw the seven tombstones, and that the path broke off at this point.

By now they were utterly exhausted and starving. They heard the sound of water and saw a stream bubbling just ahead. Tian Er suggested they rest here for a bit, drink some water, and have something to eat before continuing on.

They parked the cart right beside Xiaomei and Aqiang's head-stone. Ji Xiaomei's name was carved on the right of the stone; Lin Xiangfu lay on the left side of the coffin. They were right beside one another—so close, separated only by a tiny distance.

The Tian brothers walked gently over the moss-covered ground to the edge of the stream, where they sat down. They took some bowls out of their satchels to scoop up some water to drink. The water from the stream was so cold it chilled their bones, and after a few gulps they couldn't help but cry out.

"The water's too cold!" cried Tian Er. "Just take little sips, and hold it in your mouth before swallowing."

So they sipped the water from the stream and ate some dried provisions. "The water here tastes sweet," Tian Wu observed.

The other three brothers agreed—unlike the water from their wells back home, which tasted slightly bitter, this water was pleasantly sweet.

Tian Er again expressed his worry they would meet up with bandits. "As soon as we get out of the hills," he said, "we should find someplace to buy some white cloth. Then we can cut it into strips to tie on the cart and hang from the awning, so that everyone who sees it will know it's a hearse. The bandits won't dare come near us."

"There's some white cloth in the coffin," said Tian Wu. "It was from Chamber President Gu. We can take it out and tear it into strips, and hang them on the cart right now."

"This cloth is laying over the bodies of our brother and young master," said Tian Si. "It can't be removed."

Tian Er and Tian San agreed that the cloth couldn't be removed. "Stop coming up with such nonsense," Tian Er reproached Tian Wu.

The Tian brothers began pulling the cart with the coffin back the way they came. After a narrow stretch, they turned onto another little path; then after about two or three *li,* they turned onto a wider road. In the distance they saw a thatched cottage with smoke rising up from the chimney. They pulled the coffin toward it, intending to ask the way out of the western hills.

The sky was clear and the air was fresh that day. The western hills were bathed in a warm, comfortable sunlight, and lush trees covered their rolling peaks. Tall, thick stands of bamboo were artfully scattered over their lower slopes, adding spots of bright emerald to the unbroken green of the forest. Fresh, green grasses grew between the irrigation ditches and the edges of the fields, and crystal clear water babbled through the streams. The chirping of the birds as they perched on branches and flew through the air bespoke the peaceful, leisurely nature of this place.

The sound of the cart's wheels grew fainter and more distant, as did the sound of the Tian brothers' voices. They estimated they should be able to deliver their brother and young master home before the first day of the New Year.

About the Author

Now one of China's most beloved novelists, Yu Hua was born in Haiyan, Zhejiang province, in 1960, and grew up in and around a hospital where his parents were both doctors. His books include the best-selling *To Live* (Knopf, 2003) and *China in Ten Words* (Anchor, 2011). He is the recipient of numerous international awards and honors, including the Italian Premio Grinzane Cavour and Giuseppe Acerbi prizes, and the French Prix Courrier International. In 2004, he was made a Chevalier de l'Ordre des Arts et des Lettres by the French government. His *Paris Review* "Art of Fiction" interview was published in 2023.